Darklight Delirium

Darklight Delirium

An Anthology Strange

K. Voi Veck

Sleeping Moon Publications
Las Vegas, Nevada
2010

Sleeping Moon Publications
sleepingmoon@rocketmail.com
copyright © K.Voi Veck, 2010
All rights reserved

The short stories and poems are published for the first time in this volume. Inquiries concerning permission to reprint any portion thereof should be directed to Sleeping Moon Publications, Rights and Permissions Dept., 701 Wheat Ridge Ln. Suite 204 Las Vegas, NV 89145

ISBN 978-0-9845674-3-0
Printed in the United States of America
First Edition
Cover art by K. Voi Veck

Many thanks to Rebecca, Tony, Laura, Veronica, Phillip, Tyg and Spooky

Don't go looking around too deeply in my tortuous-visual mind. Searching a labyrinth of delightful chaos; strange characters you will find. I fill many hours to conceive them, molding ideas from illustrious dreams. Creativity reaches out to me, quite imperfectly, or so it seems.

Imagination provides expression; but I pray that God forgives. These twisted myths within my head, the world in which I live. My words are only stories; you may do with them as you may. Beware of those occasions when my nightmares come to play.

I beg the reader's pardon, and I forewarn those who partake. A touch of sadness resides within but the pain is never fake. My mind is a reel to reel, recording every fantastic dream. I'm helpless against the monsters inside me, all the blood, guts, and screams.

Don't always search me for beautiful things, sometimes they're just not here. My mind is the darklight playground for all the frightening things you fear.

—K. Voi Veck

Contents

For The Blue Girl

VICTORIA'S DREAMLIGHT GARDEN

Bright, lavender mushrooms obscure her small, one-room farmhouse in an irrefutable likeness of speckled warts. The heads of the mushrooms, uniquely boxlike, emit simple yet beautiful music; the sound comparable to an orchestra of soft playing violins. Victoria Phyre sat at her wooden desk, a blue-feathered writing quill in hand, humming pleasantly as the day was slowly fading to night.

She dipped the tip of the quill into the inkwell. The writing parchment, slightly yellowed from age, looked up at her with uncertainty.

The paper opened its flat, wide mouth. "You thought of something to say?"

Victoria let the ink dribble from the quill and onto the concerned paper. "Last night, the garden heads gave me an idea. I'd like to try it out."

"By all means," replied the parchment. It closed its mouth to allow her to write.

The blue quill zipped across the top of the paper, leaving behind black loops and lines, documenting the thoughts flowing from Victoria's mind. Suddenly, in the second paragraph, the ink began to dry. The writing stopped.

Victoria dunked the tip into the inkwell, but when she reapplied the quill to the paper, it did not write. Instead, it hovered over the parchment as though afraid to touch. The parchment opened one of its eyes.

"I forgot what I was going to say," Victoria said in disappointment.

"Maybe you didn't strike the garden heads hard enough," the parchment replied.

"Thought I did. I whacked them as hard as I could, as usual."

The paper stuck out its long, slender, black tongue and lapped up the words the quill had jotted down. It swallowed the words in one gulp. "If we're going to write a book, Victoria, you're going to need strong ideas. Maybe you should plow-up the garden and replant new seeds."

"Plow it?" Victoria pushed her chair back from the desk. She stood up and went to the window. "I couldn't think of doing that. Let's just wait and see what the heads offer us tonight."

Through the window, Victoria could smell the spicy aroma of doodlebugs running delightfully between the labyrinths of purple mushroom stalks on the sides of the house. The sky above was mottled with dark red clouds. In the backyard, tilled in long, careful rows was her cherished garden. The heads emerged from the dirt were just beginning to illuminate with the setting sun. Soon all the blue-glowing heads would ripe and become ready to tell the writer their story ideas. Just as soon as the moon rises and the dreamlights shine—soon as Victoria Phyre struck them with a shovel.

She looked at the sky and then at the trees in the backyard. The tops were swaying. "Looks like we're in for a storm," she said to the parchment. "Hope there's time to cull a few ideas before it rains."

The parchment on the desk fumed, its flat, round eyes narrowing to slits. "Ah! It'll be as usual. Face it, Victoria, the garden heads are running out of ideas. All they've been coming up with lately is drivel."

"I wouldn't call it drivel," Victoria said in defense of her dreaming crop. "I rather liked The Harlequin's Nature."

"That stupid, ol' story?" The parchment rolled its eyes. "Hardly what I'd call a good idea. Especially the ending. So the Harlequin turned out to be Mother Nature. Big deal. She also was forced to live with rats in a New York City subway tunnel. I thought she should've stayed in the world of time with Gygus Gyger."

Victoria didn't reply. She stared out the window, watching the darkening sky and the rows of heads in her garden beginning to glow blue.

"I repeat what I said, you ought to get some new seeds and replant the garden."

Victoria turned from the window and glared at the parchment on the desk. "I'm not going to replant anything. In fact, I'm going out right now to see what new story ideas the heads have in mind. I think they're ready. They look ripe." She walked across the room to get her shovel that was leaning against the wall by the door. "And may I remind you that the Harlequin couldn't stay with Gygus Gyger. If you recall, he banished her from time because she kept sneaking into the human world. She wanted to be like them."

3

The parchment wrinkled its face. "Yes, and look what happened because of it. She fell in love with a common person and lost her rightful place in the kingdom of time. All because of selfish desire."

"Because of love," Victoria corrected. "Her nature required it as the title of the story implied. She couldn't help herself." Victoria turned quickly, her raven black bangs falling over her right eye. "Everyone knows the nature of love can overpower almost anything. I thought it was a good ending, regardless how sad it was."

"Sad for Gygus Gyger, maybe," the parchment proclaimed. "He loved the Harlequin, but she showed him no sympathy. How is it possible to love one, and break the heart of another?"

Victoria wore a long, slender, emerald-green dress that cut down both sides to her hips. The train flowed across the floor, hiding her bare white feet. "One doesn't simply choose with whom to fall in love," she informed the parchment. "Nature happens, and the Harlequin just so happened to fall in love with Anthony."

"Anthony died at the end of the story, so what good did it do her?"

"Because, if you remember, she knew she had to act on those deep feelings, as humans do. She had never known love until she went into the human world. And though Anthony died, she got to experience her true nature. She began to live fulfilled thereafter."

"Yes, but she left poor Gygus Gyger standing alone and heartbroken on the shore of time." The parchment showed its tiny-yellowed teeth. "I think she should've remained with him. He created her as his equal. She would have learned to accept him."

"She wasn't allowed," Victoria insisted; her voice was slightly tinged with annoyance. "I told you, he banished her. She had to live out her existence in that subway tunnel."

"With rats," the parchment growled, closing its eyes. "It was a foolish story."

Victoria opened the door. "I'm going now. Got to beat the storm."

She left the parchment sulking on the desk and went to harvest new ideas from the heads in the garden. With the train of her dress wrapped in one hand, she carried the shovel in the other. Victoria looked up at the ominous sky, and from around the gathering storm clouds, she could see the bleeding light of the moon. There was just enough radiance to find her way around the small house and to the backyard.

There she saw the rows of heads in the garden. They were glowing. Blue and bright. Victoria walked the rows, deciding which head she wanted to whack first.

"Sometimes I feel cursed being a writer," she mumbled to herself. She felt the soft dirt between her toes; the earthworms were quick to get out of the way. "If only I'd followed my sister's footsteps in life. I could be happily married. With a big house somewhere. Maybe children." She thought on that for a moment. But deep down she knew what she'd be giving up. Though writing could sometimes be laborious, she couldn't imagine living without it. The quill and parchment were as much her body as her own hands, and without them life wouldn't be complete. Just like the Harlequin, Victoria Phyre was forced by nature to seek-out what she was born to do. "Guess, it's not so bad," she said aloud, feeling a raindrop splash on her forehead. She looked up at the sky. The dreamlights weren't going to shine long this night. She'd better start whacking some heads soon, or else . . .

In the second to last row of the garden, she found a particularly bright glowing head. Its face was without emotion, eyes closed, and its lips slightly parted to allow it to breathe. With its chin rested firmly against the dirt, it appeared—as were all the others—to be sleeping. The blue light emitting from its skin gave the appearance of a halo around its head. Victoria reared back with the shovel, preparing to clobber it.

"Hope you got something good for me," she said as she lowered the boom on the sleeping head.

It burst to life, eyes popping wide open, and its mouth forming an oval. "Mother-jivin'-bitch. That hurt!"

Victoria planted the shovel into the dirt and leaned against the handle. "Got a good idea for me?"

The blue-glowing head looked up at her with a scowl. "Yeah. Go jump in a ditch, lady."

"Oh, come now. What's on your mind?"

The head took in a deep breath. "I was dreaming of a little boy named Alex Freep. He was eating cereal with his parents at the breakfast table, telling them how the moon hogs were coming after him."

"What are moon hogs?" Victoria asked. She felt more raindrops fall on her face. The sky was turning wicked black.

"They're prickly, little bogeys with white fur and twirly, short tails. They walk upright on two legs, swaying their arms back n' forth. Their snouts are whiskery, and four beady red eyes pierce the darkness of any child's room. And they have a lot of teeth, especially big, white tusks that stick out of their lips. They come from the moon to steal little children from their beds."

Victoria wiped her wet bangs from her eyes. "And where do they take these children?"

"Up to the moon, of course."

"And what happens once they get there?"

"They're turned into moonslaves. Trained to battle the sun," said the glowing blue head in the dirt.

"And why would the sun and moon be fighting each other?"

"For dominance of the sky, lady. Any more questions?" The garden head's eyes began to close as its pain was ceasing. It would soon drift off to sleep again to dream another dream.

Victoria had to hurry. "One more. What happens at the end? Do the moon hogs get Alex, or do his parents protect him? Does the moon or sun win?"

"That's three questions," replied the head. "And yes the moon hogs do get Alex the next night. They take him up and the next day his unaware parents are out working in the yard. Half the sky suddenly turns night, half of it day. His parents look up in amazement to see their little Alex dressed in shining white star-armor, leading the battle of darkness and light across the split sky."

"But does he win?" Victoria asked. She nudged the head with her toe. "Does Alex beat the sun? Does he come back to live with his parents, or does he stay a moonslave forever?"

The head closed its eyes. Its once bright glow began to dim. It wouldn't be ripe for another whacking for at least a week. "I'm done with you, lady," it said. "Go bother somebody else."

"But I need to know what happens," Victoria demanded. She grabbed the shovel out of the dirt and threatened to whack the head back to life. Ah, it was useless. It was already spent.

Victoria thought about whacking another head to reveal another idea. But the thought of the sky being torn in two by the sun and the moon seemed an interesting proposal. She reached down and took hold of the wet train of her dress. Suddenly thunder began rolling in on waves of lightning—the dreamlights fading out. Barefoot, and thrilled by her new idea, she ran quickly back to the house.

She was already anticipating what the parchment would say.

***

"It won't work, I tell you."

Victoria huffed. "It will work. If you give it a chance!" She tried applying the quill to the paper, but it refused.

Curling its edges, the parchment looked up with a snarl. "If Alex is a moonslave then how does he break his bond?"

"I'm not sure," said Victoria, wrestling to flatten the paper so she could write. "I'll figure that out when I get to it. Just lay still, will you?"

"I most certainly will not! You first must explain to me how you plan to make Alex the hero of the story. He is the good guy, isn't he? The protagonist?"

Victoria nodded. "Just lie still, please."

"And what about the setting? Is it in a neighborhood with other children in the sky, or is Alex alone to fend for himself?"

"There are other children," Victoria retorted. She slammed her fist against the desktop, rattling the lantern set next to the inkwell. "If you'd quit fidgeting and just let me write, you'd know all this!"

"I don't trust you anymore."

"And why not?"

"The last few stories I had to spit out because they were either so hideously flawed, or you gave up midway through. And I don't feel like consuming anymore half-written ideas. I'm full of them!"

Victoria put her head to the table. She was at a loss. "Then what do you expect me to do? If you won't allow me to write, what now?"

The parchment relaxed and its edges began to flatten. "I do want you to write, but I want a good, strong plotline with good, strong, solid characters. Make me want to consume the story. Make me hungry for it."

Victoria got up from the desk and paced the room. Her alabaster skin contrasted with her black hair as the lantern light cast bat-like patterns across her face. She was oblivious to the thunder and rattling windows. "I got it!" she declared. "What if I paint for a couple days? You know, give the writing a break for a while . . . let you think over this story idea about Alex."

The parchment pondered her suggestion. "One problem—what about the last time you painted? You were distressed because it didn't turn out the way you wanted, and you slashed the canvas. I don't want to sit through another one of your tantrums!"

Victoria had had enough. She looked around the room for her hammer. Where are the nails?

"You have a temper, you know," said the parchment, watching astutely from the desktop as Victoria searched the small house. "What're you hunting for?"

"The answer," she replied, curtly—without apology.

The parchment retracted, not liking the tone of her voice. "And what would be the question?"

"The answer to our little problem we're having." Victoria flung open drawers and turned over boxes. Throwing clothes on the floor, she rummaged around for the small, wooden box of nails in the back of her closet. "I know they're around here, somewhere. Saw them just the other day!"

"What's the hammer for?" asked the parchment, peeking over the top of its rolled-up edge.

"To settle you down!"

"You're going to smash me with that thing?"

"I have to write," Victoria said. "Since you won't cooperate, I'm going to nail you to the desktop."

The parchment shuddered as she continued to thrash about the house. Maybe the story of Alex the moonslave wasn't such a bad idea after all. "I'll be still," the parchment relented. "No need to get violent." The paper unrolled itself. "I get frustrated, too, sometimes. I just want the best for you and me. The best stories so we can make the best book ever."

Victoria ignored the parchment's pleas and kept looking for the box of nails.

"And you were probably right about the Harlequin," said the paper. "I suppose if she didn't love Gygus Gyger, why should she stay with him? I mean, that would only make him feel worse, right? To be stuck with somebody who doesn't love you? Because you made that person stay?"

Victoria dumped a burlap bag full of paints and brushes to the floor. No nails.

"You don't have to make me stay in place, Victoria. I'll do it because I want to. Look. See? I'm lying flat. You can write on me if you want. I won't fuss."

Victoria turned, with hands on her hips; she glared at the paper. "You can't go anywhere because you have no choice. Not like you can stand up and walk out."

The parchment's eyes welled with tears. "I don't want to be hammered down. I want to finish this book, please."

With hammer in one hand, Victoria put the back of her other hand to her forehead. "I wasn't really going to nail you. I'm just at wit's ends with you—your nagging at my ideas. All I want to do is sit down and write stories without you ridiculing every sentence." She dropped the hammer to the floor and returned to the desk. The parchment was wet; its closed eyes weeping.

"I'm sorry," she said to it. "Please, don't cry."

"You hated me," the parchment sobbed.

"I never hated you. I was just irritated."

"You were going to nail me down or slash me, just like the canvas."

"I was not." Victoria wiped the tears from the parchment.

"I'm just a stupid piece of paper, what do I know about good writing? You ought to toss me away. Tear me up and be done with it."

11

"Now what kind of talk is that? Look, I'm settled down now. I'm not mad."

"Do you love me?" The parchment opened one of its soggy eyes.

"Yes," Victoria said with tears of her own. "I love you very much."

"Just like the Harlequin did Anthony?"

"Yes," replied Victoria. "Just like that."

***

"I told you the story would work out."

Victoria put down the writing quill. "After a little urging, sure."

"Either way, I think Alex turned out to be quite the character, don't you?"

Victoria leaned back in her chair and smiled. "I sure do. And you turned out to be quite the helper, too. I liked how you added that fiery touch to the housetop when Alex batted down the sun's rays."

"Yes," said the parchment. "And how his parents were in decision to whether save their son first, or the house. But you know, I'm still not sure if that's an equal comparison. I mean, seems to me like a parent wouldn't have any problem with that choice."

Victoria stood to stretch her legs. "Yes, but his parents weren't just anyone. They were sent by the moon to make children for the hogs to harvest."

"I'm just glad it worked out," said the parchment. It opened its flat mouth, stuck out its long, slender tongue, and lapped up every word on its face. "Tastes good," it said, gulping down the sentences. "Think tomorrow we can write some more? A new story, perhaps?"

Victoria went to the window. She put her hand against the glass. "Sounds like a good idea to me."

The sky flashed with gentle bursts of sheet lightning, leftovers of the storm revealing glimpses of the sleeping heads in the garden. Victoria Phyre and the writing parchment listened as the square, musical mushrooms covering the house began to emit faint, tranquil melodies. Tomorrow the dreamlights would shine again. The heads would bring new ideas for the author to write about, but tonight she needed rest. Victoria turned from the window and told the parchment goodnight. After blowing out the lantern, the author noticed a soft glow coming from outside the window. She rushed to look. Near the middle rows of the garden, one of the heads had awakened. Its glistening, wet face was bright and blue.

24 KARAT (Diamond Life)

Plastic lovers rest on a white opal beach. Holding hands, they look out at a cracked glass ocean. A sawdust moon with chipped edges sways from a hook in the sky. The male lover points to it. "Curious is that hook and whomever screwed it into the wood paneled horizon. What a wonderful, 24 karat diamond life we are living!"

The female squeezes his hand. Her mouth parts slightly. She draws a deep breath as she looks to the sea, watching a pod of turquoise dolphins break the surface. The glass waves crash over their backs, filling the night air with thousands of tiny glittering splinters.

Above the reflective ocean is a sky full of rhinestone stars, fastened to burnished hinges. The two lovers listen. "Sounds like Heaven's doors all opening and closing at once," the male lover says to his companion.

She closes her eyes and nods, scraping her fingers back and forth across the opal ground. She likes the way it feels as she taps her fingernails against it. Adoring the man lying beside her, she takes pleasure in hearing the stars swing on their hinges; waves breaking against the shoreline, glass shattering on the solid, white beach.

She ponders a time not long ago when her longing heart felt as though it would never beat again; a time when she believed an eternity would pass by without her. A time when everyone had someone, but she did not—

and hope of ever finding true love seemed unlikely as nocturnal sunshine.

"Will you ever leave me?" she asks her stargazing lover.

He sits up and comforts her, caressing his plastic cheek against her smooth, white shoulder. "There is no wind strong enough to pull me away from you, no storm or calamity too great that I cannot hold onto your hand."

She turns to her companion and kisses him. They embrace, holding each other for hours as the night draws to a close. With their eyes shut and lips pressed tightly together, the lapidarian behind the wood paneled horizon takes down the sawdust moon, replacing the hook with a scorching, yellow gemstone. The white opal beach quickly dries in the daylight. The turquoise dolphins chase schools of fish, iridescent scales leaping from cascading waves. The tide brings offerings of pearls, black quartz, rubies, and deep-sea Jasper as the cracked glass ocean reflects the silhouettes of two plastic lovers melting together in the heat of a radiant sun.

PARADISE IN A SIDESHOW DREAM

It all happened on the beach, where the land and sea embrace as first time lovers. The surf rolls in frothy white onto the sandy shore. On the horizon, the blue sky splits its serenity from the sea, tampered with triangular golden fragments formed by the sun. I stood barefoot on the sand, allowing the waves to wash between my toes. The warmth felt good on my young feet, the heat radiating through the pores on my skin, but no matter how nostalgic this place was to me, it always held the scent of the bogeyman in the wind.

He was there, somewhere, hidden from sight by the shroud of my content. I lived in peace with him, a harmony each of us had grown to accept. This was our place to mingle; a secret rendezvous where the visible and the unseen could bring forth fellowship while holding back any presumptions of growing older. The bogey in the wind has been my companion for twenty-eight years, an existence never critical of my ever-changing body.

As with the bogey, there was a deep connection between the beach and I, though sometimes it felt as if it was somehow trying to devour me. Did the sand desire my flesh and bones? Did it need my blood and breath to sustain a symbiosis with life? I liked to think so, and I dreamt of becoming the elements as I watched the bogeyman in the wind kick a shell across the sand.

Mother Velasquez tried warning me about the beach. Always curling her long, coarse grey hair around her hand, she rebuked, "The bogeyman hides in the wind. He'll come out one day, snatch you up, and take you away."

At the time, I had little reservation about being "snatched up", but after I saw the bogeyman's face, I knew he was not dangerous. His persuasions, on the contrary, warmed me as did the sand snuggled between my toes. Mother Velasquez has always been a bit overprotective. God bless her.

"A young girl such as you shouldn't be spending all her time by herself, talking to ghosts," she had advised me. "You should be well on your way about life. Forget the beach, girl. Go into the world a while."

My silence was enough to challenge her. It was not my nature to argue, especially since she had done so well as a surrogate mother, rearing me after my parents' disappearance on the beach. Despite having five children to feed while working as a custodian at the local school, Mother Velasquez took me into her cramped, wooden cottage and raised me as though I was one of her very own.

Nevertheless, I could not keep away from the beach. I hated being disobedient to Mother Velasquez, but I felt an urgency to find the truth about the bogeyman, and if he was responsible for taking my parents. I went daily to where the sea met the land, and it didn't take long until my curiosities were sated, and my life was changed forever—

It was a typical hot day in July and the sun looked down at the world with all its blazing authority. With it came a wind that sifted through my long, dark hair, lifting the ends and caressing my neck and ears. Fine, salty mist from the ocean coated my skin. I licked the salt from my lips as I watched the sea shells wash up from the depths, tumbling on the surf. Scattering seagulls flew overhead, tilting their heads in search of something to eat. Palm trees leaned toward the ocean as if to get a refreshing drink. It seemed as if everything was vibrant and alive. Never had I felt as one with life.

I spent the day as usual, combing the beach for coconuts to pop the purple jellyfish that washed up in clumps by the waves. The seagulls, occasionally squawking in anticipation to lap the debris of the jellyfish, became more brazen as their numbers grew.

Within the hour, a gust of wind brought the scent of the bogeyman.

Grains of sand tattooed my face and hair. I sat down with my knees pressed to my cheeks, closed my eyes, and felt the patter of tiny shells on my back. Tranquility didn't last long, however. I heard something behind me. Standing up, I shook the sand from my face, and what I saw amazed me: Underneath the canopy of a nearby palm tree, there appeared a red and white striped tent.

Immediately, I went to investigate. Approaching the tent in short, cautious steps, I smelled the scent of something sweet—a floral-berry scent. The nearer I got to the tent, the more prevalent the scent became. At the front of the tent were two flaps of tattered cloth, flapping in the wind. The sand around the base of the tent had molded, hardened as rock. I knelt to examine the oddity, and noticed the sand had turned into sheets of glass lying delicately in layers.

"Look at yourself," said a deep voice from somewhere behind me.

In the shimmering reflection of the glassy sand, I saw a figure standing behind me. Quickly, I turned to see a thinly built man, dressed in a tight-fitting, black, shark-skin suit. The collar was dark and fluted, as were his cuffs. He wore no shoes, exposing a pair of swollen, blackened feet—seemingly more appropriate on someone dead. A slight grin warped his otherwise stoic face, revealing teeth encrusted with small, colored barnacles.

"Do not be frightened of me, Angela," he said with a gleam in his dark eyes. His hair was unruly and made me think of the seaweed strewn about the shore. Extending a long, narrow hand to help me up, I chose to stand on my own.

"Who are you?" I asked him.

He squint his eyes curiously; my dubiety obviously bothered him. "My name is hardly important." He covered his mouth and coughed. Black water trickled from the corner of his mouth; his lungs were full of the sea. Shielding his eyes from the sun with his hand, he replied, "All you need to know is that I have fond memories of you."

I dusted the sand from my knees. "How can you have memories of someone you just met?"

"On the contrary, I know you very well, Angela. I have known you for a long, long time. I've always known you. We live as object and shadow."

"I've never seen you before!" I snapped.

"Not in the flesh."

I looked him over once more.

"Not used to looking like this," he said. "Moving like this . . . It's rather new to me. Been a long time since I've walked about, stretching my arms and legs." He nodded his head toward the tent. "Care to come in with me?"

"What is in there?" I asked. Hesitantly, I followed him through the flaps. "It smells sweet."

"The fragrance of yesterdays gone by," he told me matter-of-factly. "But please don't touch anything." His hand came to rest on my shoulder as he pointed out crates stacked on top of each other. "Everything here is extremely fragile."

"Yesterdays?" I said, studying the crates. "How can you box-up the past?"

He combed his fingers through his scraggly hair. "Angela," he said, "have you ever thought about how it used to be? Back when life was easy. Simple as clockwork, they say, right?" He closed his eyes, tilted back his head, and snorted as salt water leaked from his nostrils. "When you got older, the days seemed to get longer and more convoluted. Before you knew it, everything became hurried. No more easy minutes for a little girl. Time needed more space and life required more time. A befuddlement of hours, days, and years. But do you remember how it was before that?"

"I've gotten older. I have more responsibilities," I said, staring at the stacked crates. I turned to him. "But when I come here to the beach, the hours fly by. Just like when I was younger."

He took me by the chin. "You belong here. This is where you need to be. Come with me back to yesterday."

I looked into his black, glossy eyes. They appeared sad and almost desperate. "How do you know what's best for me?" I asked him.

"Because we are object and shadow of each other. You are today. I was then."

"The bogeyman that lives in the wind," I said. "Coming to snatch me away."

The corners of his mouth twitched and more sea water dribbled from his nostrils. He wiped it away with his forearm. "Not in the sense of how you might think."

I suddenly began to feel at ease with him though I didn't understand why. His presence was beginning to feel strangely familiar.

"Angela, can you not see the similarities between us?"

I looked at him once more, perplexed how I knew this man. I couldn't make out the slightest bit of myself in him. This intruder in my life—on my beach—was nothing more than a mirage, I suspected. "Whoever you are," I said, "you're not me. You can't be. I'm a girl."

"Angela, I am a relic, here from your past. I still have life within me and cannot accept disbelief simply because you don't understand me." His black eyes glistened and the salt water leaking from his nose became red as blood.

I put every thought from my mind except the vision of his face. Lucid thoughts of him came to me, and I began to see him as he had been before. His skin color changed from blackened and gray to that of natural flesh, and the sweet smells of yesterday—yes, the relics— brought back long ago memories.

"Father? Is it you?"

"I know I'm not what you expected," he said. "But it is me, Angela."

He gave me a tight hug, and I realized my eyes were open. I was not at all in dream. I didn't want him to let go, but somehow I knew he wouldn't last forever.

"Angela, I want to take you with me. Back to the way it is supposed to be. Back to yesterday."

"But . . . But what about Mother Velasquez? She will be crushed if I left her."

"You don't belong with her," he said. "You belong to something bigger. She is a very wise woman. Listen to what she has told you. Go out and see the world."

"Can I come back?"

"I doubt you will want to," he said. "Come with me to yester-vu-skuff. I will show you . . . better life." His body twitched violently and his voice cracked. "Ng-rif we will live together. We will see . . . ynam. Angela, grif n—org—ahhh . . . and your real mother."

"Father!" I screamed, pushing away from him. "What's wrong with you?" His face began to fracture into broken puzzle pieces of flesh that fell to his feet. Bone and cartilage warped from his cheekbones as sharp angles of red light flickered over his body. His lower jaw fell open and light shined from the back of his throat, illuminating the tent walls. The blackness of my father's eyes turned to ooze as the light zigzagged across his head. He reached out to me but all I could do was stare at the intense flashes of red static.

The barnacles broke off from his teeth. Blood poured from his nose—his arms twitched. Static and flashes of red light. He grabbed my hand and I collapsed.

***

I opened my eyes. All around me were ribbons; long, metallic strips shimmering silver and blue. The ends of the ribbons draped across a black and white marble floor. The ribbons appeared to be suspended from nowhere—an endless sky of silver-blue stretching on and on in torment of my comprehension.

I reached out to grab one and realized they were wet with a clear, tear-like substance. Was there someone up above crying for me? The ribbons danced in a gentle breeze, and the sweet scent of berries—the relics—filled the air.

The tears on the ribbons soaked my skin. I looked down and saw that I was unclothed. The ribbons played on my back, around my arms and legs, across my breasts, and over my face. They curled around my neck, through my hair, and my entire body became preserved in their magnificent shine.

They took me into the air and held me tightly so I wouldn't fall—a million dancing partners, carrying me effortlessly through the sky for hours. The marble floor below became saturated with tears. Glossy ripples gave the floor an appearance of a pond. Small, frog eyes peered up at me from the slippery surface. A long blue snake slithered by, and I could see turtles with red shells perched like stones on small dunes of gold.

The ribbons passed me over the water and through the reverie. All the eyes of the pond followed as I was delicately manipulated through the air. The ribbons enveloped me and rolled me around. I was a morsel getting passed from tongue to tongue.

At last, I was carried to the end of the sky dance and the ribbons seemed to kiss me a thousand goodbyes. They put me down gently, and I stood and watched as the ribbons and the pond twinkled away into whatever new reality they had become.

***

The landscape around me was similar to my beach. The ocean and the palm trees looked the same, and the air carried the familiar smell of salt and oils. The coconuts were plentiful; however there were no jellyfish washed ashore, but I assumed the tide would soon be bringing them in, exciting the seagulls that were riding on the wind.

I looked down at my body. I was now clothed, and I looked to see if the red and white tent was still there. It wasn't. In its place was a new palm tree. It appeared to be moving, not by the breeze, but curiously by its own impetus.

The tree struggled to lift its roots from the sand, stretching as melted cheese pulling from a plate. The roots broke free from the ground with loud snapping sounds. I covered my mouth, watching in amazement as the tree split open. Limbs spread into wings, and from the trunk of the tree, a head formed into a body of a giant bird.

It was a Phoenix—its fiery feathers were radiant blue, purple, and green. "You're beautiful!" I gasped. In fear and awe, I hurriedly moved away from its brilliance. The Phoenix lifted its mighty head to the sky, spreading its wings. Each feather turned into a prism. I stared in disbelief, and fell backward onto the sand.

Gradually, I got to my feet and walked cautiously toward the massive bird. I stood beneath its colorful, pulsating breast. There was no heat from the fiery feathers. It lowered its head toward me and instantly my fear gave way to calmness and relief. Instinctively, I knew this beautiful creature meant me no harm. Reaching out to it, I touched its face, and its eye came to meet mine. It looked as though it were a shining ruby set within a multicolored, regal head.

"Such sweet doeth the good winds blow," said the Phoenix in a booming voice. It tilted its head slightly to one side, looking down at me.

Shivers raced up my spine. "My name is Angela," was all I could say.

The Phoenix replied, "From whence cometh thou, Angela?"

"I'm . . . I'm not sure, actually."

"Of what reason brought you hither?"

"My father. He must have. I've dreamt of him since I was a child."

"Aye," said the Phoenix. "You are of small stature?"

I nodded slowly. "Compared to you, but I'm not little in my world. Not anymore."

"A lady of age. Beset with many troubles?"

"Enough big ones and a few little ones, too."

"Of thou understanding, the purpose of thy dream, Angela?"

"I don't know," I answered, entranced by the firebird's red eye.

"Surely, thou art blind. Hath thy no desire to know?"

I pursed my lips and shrugged. "One reason is as good as another, isn't it?"

"Aye," the Phoenix replied. It reached up with its massive leg and scratched under its beak with a black talon. "Forthwith to escape?"

"That could be," I stammered. "The beach. It's what's real to me."

"Thy dream hath prevailed, knowest thou? Deep within, lies fear. Alas, dreams are of truth."

"The beach and Mother Velasquez are all I know. They've been my life since—"

"—Death of Mother and Father."

"Yes," I answered, looking down. "Since then."

"Dreams are truth. All else is dust. Dust, art thou?"

I shook my head.

The firebird's red eye narrowed. Its head came down close to my face. "Dreams are for the believer. Devotion with thine heart." The Phoenix scraped its large, sharp beak across the sand. "Dreams," it said in a commanding tone. "All must live for the dream."

"What about my father?" I asked. "If my dedication falters will he disappear forever?"

"His shadow will follow," spoke the firebird. "Shadows hath a seeing eye. Shadows too, have many sides; seeing many things." The Phoenix took steps around me. The ground quaked as it walked. "Thy dream is true. The mind of a fool, hath thy father. Upon his deathbed, the mind became whole. Now, he holds the unknown."

"A secret?" I asked, thinking back on our embrace and how nice it felt to have him out of my thoughts and finally in my life.

"The Sideshow Dream."

I raised my hands. "I don't know what that is."

The great bird stared out at the ocean. The air around me seemed to become heavy. The Phoenix closed its eyes and took a deep breath. "He gave of himself to thee. For trust and remembrance."

"But he disappeared," I said. "Cracked into static and disappeared."

"The Sideshow Dream is forever, as long as thou believeth. All else are thoughts of the mind."

I bit down on my lip and thought. "The Sideshow Dream . . . It's within me. Like you?"

"As me," the Phoenix replied.

I stared at the sand. "So, he was never really there." I wanted to know that I honestly saw my father, not just a dream of him.

The Phoenix looked down at me. A tear streamed from its ruby eye. "Where are we, young one? Where are we now?"

I felt a lump in my throat; I knew the answer. My fingers dug into my palms. I didn't want to believe the truth. My eyes became watery, my forehead sweaty. I knew where we were.

I inhaled deeply and thought of all the days that I spent ignoring the world around me. The beach kept me safe from the troublesome world. My father, the bogeyman, came to me from out of nowhere, but I was too scared to go with him. I am too afraid on the inside. Too afraid of my own dreams.

I looked up at the Phoenix. Its feathers burned bright. Its eyes beamed. "I just can't get out of myself," I told the bird.

"Thou goeth the other way."

I sighed, not understanding where I went so wrong in life. "What's your name?" I asked the firebird.

"What would thou have it be?"

"You don't have your own name?"

"As you say. It is of thy choosing."

I stared at the Phoenix for several seconds. Its demeanor seemed almost boastful. It stood on the beach with its breast puffed, and I noticed that no shadow lurked around it. Did its heatless fire keep all darkness away? "Lazarus," I said firmly. "Back from the dead."

"Lazarus," the Phoenix said aloud. It looked to be rolling the name around in its mind. "Lazarus it is. Come, Angela. Onto my back. We must hasten."

"Where to?"

"Across the ocean."

"Deeper," I whispered to myself. "Into my dream."

Lazarus lowered his head and spread his wings wide until they blotted out the sun.

I climbed upon Lazarus' back and nestled in a tuft of feathers below his neck. The purple-blue fire engulfed me; the swirling lights dazzled as many candle-lit chandeliers. It delighted my senses. Despite the uncertainty of what was going on in my mind, I felt secure; more so than any other time that I could remember.

We whisked from the ground, as I heard the *whump! whump! whumping!* of Lazarus' powerful wings chopping through the sky, propelling us across the ocean. The water below was not visible to me; however, the clouds above offered me a vision of beauty I never before imagined. Thousands of firebirds, of every color and size filled the sky! Clouds changed before my eyes, the sun a golden shepherd keeping watch over a flock of colorful, magical dragons.

If this was all a dream, then I never wanted to wake. My father was right; I didn't want to go back!

I felt heartbeats within Lazarus' body, low, dull thumping much like tribal drums. I reached out and touched a single fiery feather—blue flames leapt from my fingertips. It did not burn. It seemed as fondling the universe, every feather a galaxy, and I could move the stars around by a simple touch.

"This is our land," Lazarus said.

"Already? We went across the whole ocean?" I didn't want the flight to end.

Lazarus began his decent. The air felt much cooler. The sky suddenly became dark, and a terrible stench wafted into my face. Black shapes of gloom hovering over a lifeless, grey landscape had replaced the magical firebirds in the sky. This place couldn't be in my dream, I thought. Where has Lazarus taken me?

"It is good to behold the things we have hidden," he said. His wings expanded and we landed softly. "No need to fear, Angela. Heed my warning of the shadows."

I climbed down from Lazarus' back and found myself standing on a blackened beach. It was unsightly. The water was full of sludge and the surf was filthy with raggedy seaweed. I had to get away from here and back to my beach where I belonged.

I looked to Lazarus. "I don't want to see this disgusting place." Truth was, if this was the darker side of my mind, I wanted to put off seeing it for as long as possible. Out of sight, out of mind—but I knew there was no going back until I faced myself.

Lazarus spread his wings again and took to the air. "Come back!" I screamed at him. "Don't leave me here!"

"Thou art never alone, young one!" he said, disappearing into the sky.

The tide swept back into a pile of dust, as if pushed by a broom. The ground rolled up like parchment, and I was left standing on nothing more than a thread of hardened soil that stretched from one side of my mind to the other. My head began to ache as I took my first step.

Somewhere above me, I could hear Lazarus' wings. "Your fears," he said, though I could not see him, "are not all found at the bottom of a high. The balance of life is misunderstood. At one effort, thy footing will fail; with another, you will succeed."

I began to walk the thread. I put one foot in front of the other, trying not to dwell on anything but balancing. Everything became a silence so painful and empty that it seemed a speck of dust landing on a cushion could startle me. I felt tense and frightened. I didn't know where I was going. I was lost within my own mind.

Should I have gone the other way? Thoughts, damn them, became louder than screams. Dreams louder than reality.

Brighter than darklight.

Shadows of my life.

My heart beat heavily, and I started to run. The fear of falling off the thread overwhelmed me. I didn't want to fail Lazarus, but I could not get my feet to slow down. I could no longer see my legs as my body began to stretch. I fell to all fours . . . my hands becoming claw-like, gripping the thread and propelling me faster through my mind. I lost all control over my body. My ribs multiplied within me, spine elongating into segments of click-clacking bone; lips stretched to cover the lower half of my face.

The faster I ran the more my body lengthened. My ribs spilt openly and they, too, became like legs with the ends gripping the thread, forcing me faster across the tightrope; pushing me into the face of what scared me the most. Myself.

Locked onto the fear, I got tunnel vision. I ran at such speed that my mind ripped free from my body and shot up into the sky, passed Lazarus, through the clouds, and beyond the sun until it slammed against the back of my skull.

My eyes fluttered but I did not awaken.

I saw myself below, running on the thread. I was racing around a huge loop, repeatedly until my eyes finally reached the back of my head and I had nowhere to go but up or down.

My body rose from the tightrope as I pulled myself to the top of my skull where I re-attached with my mind. I hung there for a moment, suspended, and swinging back and forth. Suddenly I dropped. When I opened my eyes, I saw my beautiful beach. I landed in the warm, soft sand. I had finally faced myself.

"Do not desire to leave. Go inside." It was Lazarus. He came down from the sky to remind me.

I put my face against him. "I think I understand now," I whispered. "Shadows are my yesterdays. They are my memories trying to catch up to me, but I must keep walking forward through the darklight."

Lazarus closed his eyes and slowly nodded his head. "Indeed, memories are a tightrope."

"But what about my father?" I asked. "Will he ever come back for me?"

Lazarus looked up to the sky. "Thou must be with the sea," he said. He looked down at me with his ruby eye. "Thy father cannot please thee. Go forth, Angela. The sand and the sea are forever. Know thy father is near."

For the last time, Lazarus spread his wings. The huge firebird flew into the sky where it burst into splintered beams of blue, purple, and green light. He became a guiding star within my mind. I was no longer afraid of the darklight. Tears flowed down my face and into my mouth. I tasted the salt on my tongue. Wiping the tears away, I gazed out at the ocean. I wondered how many other dreamers had cried when their Phoenix had flown away and burst amongst clouds.

I collapsed to the sand. I had one last dream of a burning star. It is what I remember of myself.

Sand. Water. Salt. Wind.

I am the beach.

I feel the wind blowing over my own naked body. The surf comes to meet me. The breakers wash over me with the freshness of a warm, relaxing bath. Behind me, palm trees sway gently from a gust of wind. The sun provides energy. Yes, I *am* the beach.

There are footsteps on my back, tiny, little footsteps treading carefully across my body so as not to disturb the sand. I roll over and see Mother Velasquez. She has come to say goodbye.

Falling to her knees, she clutches handfuls of me in her hands. She lets me slide through her fingers as she whispers into the sand, promising me she will always love me. She wanted me to go into the world a while. Therefore, I did.

Something wet landed on me. A tear from her eye. Soaking it up, I will cherish it. I will hold the tear forever in my sand, never to open my eyes again. Never to awaken. Dreams need devotion. Believers. My father is here with me. So is my mother. They are my believers. For a brief moment in time, my family is alive and well. I rest here with them. A paradise in a Sideshow Dream.

MEMOIRS OF THE GRAVE AND TOMORROW

Days burn on, time fueling life, selfishly abandoning two lovers. In their peaceful abeyance, they know some form of life awaits them. Birds chirp in tune to the mystical silence, as the eyes of the world are elsewhere. Deep within the Earth, the lovers continue to engage themselves.

Above, fields of grass sway as the ocean tide; a tranquilizing moment in time.

The two lovers rest for eternity.

The clouds move on, as does the breeze. Everything pays homage to the darklight, yet only in a brief encounter. A rabbit leisurely chews the clover, oblivious to the preying, brown eyes of a near-by fox. Death pursues life, from there it begins.

Oblivious of the world above, the two lovers sleep in unison, holding to the love they still share.

They begin to write their memoirs of the grave and tomorrow:

Tomorrow, we will know this. Tomorrow, we will be this. Tomorrow, we will love each other, just as we do today and those decayed days of the past. Today we write a new story, using the paste of death-worms, and tethered sheets of parchment that once-was our skin.

A new life begins . . .

Feel the worms tumble over our bones, rotten vines of viscera strewn as ropes over, and under our interwoven bones. Our flesh turns to dust, sprinkling to the bottom of our wooden casket. Through the empty black galaxies that once were our eyes, we can see the life that we lived and loved.

We see our rib cages with flesh. Feel the quills of our love, piercing our hearts as we felt so many breaths ago when we first met. Delightful were those days, remembering the love we made, our bodies shared and entwined.

Late in life we followed the Reaper into the darklight. He smiled with black teeth, bending a finger to us. We went willingly, didn't we? Straight to the grave.

Look at us now. We lay slumbering side by side, fingers locked tightly, and our once pasty flesh now tanned to rot. We are now darker than life itself.

Him to Her: As I rest beside you, your hair is pretty as ever, flowing as a curtain of silk near my skull. It doesn't matter anymore whose bones are whose, whose hair is yours or mine. We are truly one now, as we were always meant to be—a union of flesh, love, spirit, and time. You are me; I am you. Together, we will find the place where neither breeze nor light can touch us. We will play forever, blissfully, my Beautiful Forever.

ED, THE SKY-CLIMBING FREAK

At the deep end of age, and with arthritis bad enough to register on the Richter scale, Ed still prided himself as being the biggest sucker born. He had sucked more color than any other had in his day—maybe that is the reason for the ever-elusive rainbow.

Are they near extinction? The old man refused to believe the rainbows were dying out, although he was all too aware of their dwindling appearances. He liked to think the sky had a vault of them, a bank tucked behind the clouds somewhere.

There was a time when the world was plentiful with arcing colors. As a child, Ed spent his days climbing the sky with friends. He sucked the sugary fat from all the rainbows that he could get. There seemed no shortage of them. The sky was an endless candy land. Today, however, the sweets were getting harder to find. Sitting in his rocking chair, Ed rubbed his grizzled face with his hand: "I woke up one day and got old," he said to himself, pondering his days of youth, "and the world's gotten old right along with me."

He got up and went to the window. Throwing back the curtain, he lifted the windowpane and stuck out his head. The wind whipped his face as he looked up at a darkening sky.

Ed had lived alone most of his life, oblivious to worldly matters. Presidents had come and gone, technology advancing and outsmarting itself, but Ed was not interested in any of that. He enjoyed the natural ways—literally, the flavor of the day. Other than a small radio by his bed (and an electric blender stuffed somewhere in the cupboards), Ed's lo-tech existence consisted primarily of longing to climb the sky. He wanted another taste of the sugar from a succulent rainbow before he died. One last bit of candy.

Ed's mouth was salivating.

He had always been a patient man. Patience, he had told his long-departed wife, Marlene, is what makes a desperate man civilized. She wasn't impressed. Nor did she approve of her husband tampering with nature. The rainbows were meant for everyone to enjoy. Ed sneered and shook his head: "You women don't understand. We are supposed to eat them! Why else would God make them taste so good?"

Marlene died three days later, but Ed wasn't surprised. She had it coming.

He observed the sky. "Rain." He walked over to his bed to turn on the radio. He kept it tuned to the weather station.

Ninety-percent chance of thundershowers tonight.

Hallelujah! . . . .

He kept a diligent watch on the sky throughout the night. Through the hours, Ed tried reading, but was unable to concentrate. Frequently, he would get up to look out the window, watching the lightning flashing across the sky. The Good Lord's storm was moving in. At 5:00 a.m., Ed was damned near hysterical as rain pelted the rooftop. Pacing the floor, he kept an eye on the clock. As soon as the storm passes, he realized morning will break. Then there will be a sky full of sweet meat to chew. By 7:30, the rain turned to drizzle. Bleary-eyed, Ed ran outside to search for rainbows.

As if painted by hand on the sky, he saw a glimmering arc of radiant colors.

"Just look at that beautiful girl," he said, wiping the saliva from his mouth. "She is truly fantastic. Those curves. Her luminous colors. A remarkable thing!"

Ed's legs began to tremble as he looked up in awe at the young, plump rainbow overhead. Mocking his dead wife, Ed felt empowered. "You never liked me going up there. Always nagging me about taking God's treasures. People don't care about rainbows anymore. I doubt they even notice them, what with all their fancy, little gadgets. They're too busy texting to notice what's going on right above their heads."

He was right about Marlene never liking him chasing the rainbows. Who are you to mess up what God has made? She had said this many times, but Ed rarely listened. His appetite over the years had grown fierce.

"Ready to be eaten, little one?" he asked the vulnerable rainbow in the sky. "You look so peaceful up there. Bright and colorful. But I'm coming up to get you."

Ed's eyebrows furrowed as he swept back his white hair and readied himself for the climb. He jabbed his hands at the air, fingers gnarled like claws. As if the sky was made of dough, Ed sank his talons deep into the air. For a moment, he twisted and fought with what looked like nothing, but if anyone were watching, they would see Ed the sky-climbing freak ascending the impossible. He dug in his toes, and hand over hand, he climbed to where the birds felt safe, and the clouds rested on the edges of the rainbow.

Clinging to the invisible, the sky-climbing freak was nearly fifty feet from the ground. He looked up at the disapproving sun.

"You old deceiver. You've always hated me, haven't you?" Ed grumbled. He bared his teeth at the gaseous fireball in the sky. "You're an ugly bastard. No matter, the little one is what I'm after." Ed squinted his eyes from the sun's blinding rays, but the intensity was searing. "Only a few more feet away . . . few more . . . and she's mine!"

Ed's breathing was sharp and painful, his worn-out lungs wheezing to keep up with his unyielding appetite. His claw-like fingers and toes dug into the sky, his gray eyes focused on his prey. The rainbow seemed to withdraw, trying to tuck itself into a pocket of clouds. "Run if you can, little one," Ed proclaimed, as he climbed higher and higher. "I'm coming for you!"

There was nowhere for the rainbow to hide. Like a lion sinking its fangs into the soft throat of its prey, Ed's teeth ripped the colors. He threw his legs around the trembling arc, pouncing upon it. There was a short struggle as the rainbow attempted to buck him off, but the old man's technique was tried and true. He clung on tightly, focused and determined. He had done this many times. With lips reeled back, he sank his teeth deeply into the colors. He forced his fingers down to the knuckles into the rainbow's soft flesh.

Yellow and red, orange, green, and blue all bled from the wounds as the rainbow thrashed to get the killer off its back. It was a hopeless struggle that intensified Ed's hunger. A spectrum of colors flashed about him in whirls of brilliant mist. He heard the rainbow cry out for the sun to somehow save it.

Ed was not moved by her useless pleading. He's heard it all before. His mouth was stained multi-colored. Purple and blue tasted best and he began feasting on the two colors, slinging his head side to side . . .

As he chewed his precious sweetness, he felt something intensely hot pierce into him from behind.

He whipped his head around to see what had hold of him. His face was pushed back down. As if long, heated screws had been driven into his spine, trickles of his blood streamed down his sides and fell like rain to the ground below. The torment was agonizing, but Ed's appetite was greater than any pain.

He wasn't going to let go.

However, what had him proved to be as fierce and tenacious. Ed finally loosened his prey and looked again to see what was behind him. "Who are you?" he asked, seeing nothing but the glaring sun in his face. He shielded his eyes.

"You know who I am," Ed heard a woman's voice scolding. "Look at me." Ed squint his eyes at the sun, and slowly it dissolved into the woman who had in the past warned him to leave the rainbows alone. "You have no right to be doing what you're doing, Edward. You know that. You've always known that."

"Marlene? Marlene?" Ed could not believe what he was seeing. There in the sky was his long dead wife with the head of the sun! Her face was white fire and her gaze singed his eyes. Clawing at his face, Ed lost his grip on the rainbow and fell to his death.

"I warned you to keep your feet on the ground," Marlene said as her head sprung back into the whorls of fiery gasses. "Goodbye, Ed. The rainbows are now free to unleash their natural beauty and full glory!"

A year later and a seedling sprouted from the ground. Germinating from the nutrients of Ed's decayed body, the budding young tree possessed what looked to be a rudimentary face. Its small, underdeveloped branches swayed in the breeze, arm-like appendages with sharp, prickled ends clawing desperately to get a grip of the sky.

Another freak was born . . .

GRAVEL AND THE LOVE OF
AN ADMIRING ACORN

Somewhere there is a road that leads to an abode,
the driveway made of loose gravel and dirt.
Acorns from trees, along with the leaves,
occasionally fall to the ground as to flirt.

A plunk was heard, one piece of gravel observed,
as it turned to face the strange sound.
"Excuse me, please, but the wind knocked me free,"
said an acorn to the gravel on the ground.

(*Gravel*)
"That's quite alright, just excuse my spite,
I was just thinking about moving from here.
This driveway is boring, so lonely and snoring,
but there's really no place for me, I fear."

(*Acorn*)
"Well, that's very sad, and quite too bad,
but why do you want to go away?
I think it's nice, this driveway's like spice,
there's flavor to enjoy here each day."

(*Gravel*)
"It's not for me, and I can never be free,
when my mind is so messed up inside.
I have so many great thoughts, but nobody stops,
so the love here within me has died.

(*Acorn*)
"You seem so unhappy, not cheerful or snappy,
so I ask, what has made you this blue?
I've no great thoughts to say, but I can get by this way,
just a little acorn that respects only you."

(*Gravel*)
"Well, I'm ugly and hard, unfit for the yard,
been stuck here forever and a day.
I look good from a distance, but I suspect my persistence,
has formed me eternally this way."

(*Acorn*)
"I think you are cute, and interesting to boot,
but you act as if no one really cares.
Are you the type, when you receive no hype,
to run and hide, and never share?"

(*Gravel*)
"No, I'm way passed that egotistical crap.
However, I cannot stay here for you.
I'm no good at love, so caring hearts I shove,
though deep down I believe that's not true."

(*Acorn*)
"Gravel, I grin, because your mind won't win,
over the heart and the love that's inside.
You may not like it; you may not accept it,
but the heart here that cares is opened wide."

(*Gravel*)
"Then how come at night, I sit here in fright,
that I'll never find a rock that can grow?
Of all the things that are me, no rock will ever see,
and I bore the ones that already know."

(*Acorn*)
"Then what do you want to get out of this slump,
and to help you feel more at ease?
Some rock to know of all the things that you grow,
inside of your mind just to please?"

(*Gravel*)
"No, not really, my problems are just silly,
like being a rock in a framed still-life.
You just don't understand, my life was all planned,
yet what I needed was the love of a wife."

(*Acorn*)
"Then I'll be your wife, your happiness in real life,
and my ability to understand is quite candid.
I know I'm no rock, just a nut that can talk,
but I loved you the moment I landed."

(*Gravel*)
"I want to be on strings, get attached to things,
but nobody will ever recognize me.
I dream to sit on a ring, become a very pretty thing,
but my desires are just wishes that flee."

(*Acorn*)
"Your wishes are nice, and your words are precise,
but you should really be proud to see.
I mean, you can see quite a lot, which I certainly cannot,
like being on a ring seems a great place to be!"

(*Gravel*)
"Brilliant diamonds, pure gold, bright rubies to behold,
it is unlikely you will find them here.
I am too worn and tired, cannot be admired.
Think I'll roll off now, my dear."

(*Acorn*)
"I love you, gravel, though my heart's been unraveled,
but I know there's a good rock for you.
Maybe it's still underground, some place not found.
Keep searching or you will be through."

(*Gravel*)
"I've got to go now, my little acorn pal.
I doubt I'll ever see you again.
I'm on a relentless quest, and for me that's best,
but I'll remember you way at the end."

(*Acorn*)
"Gravel, my love, you're now free as a dove,
and I know you'll find a rock that's true.
You will then be content, and your heart will relent,
and I'll sit here in your spot, and think of you."

DEATH RIDES UPON BUTTERFLY WINGS

My guardian angel will come take me away
A relieving escape from today's dismay
My guardian angel rides upon butterfly wings
How I have longed to see her and to hear her sing

My guardian is death, so white and pure
A beautiful light, a one final cure
She'll hold me and take me to my waiting grave
But I'm not dying, I'm only being saved

No troubles, no tears, no feelings of guilt
I'm leaving behind all those demons I've built
Tomorrow she is coming, must live only for today
Yesterday's sadness will be swept far away

No longing and no hurting; no heartache, no pain
I'll live in sweet peace of Eternity's rain
I'll bathe in the glory of all that shall be
Living a quieter life under a swaying tall tree

Farewell to age-old problems, farewell to flesh
Where I'm going, I'll need no breath
No more food and no more air
I need it not, not while I'm there

Goodbye, my sweet Mother; goodbye, loving Dad
Goodbye to all dear friends and the good times had
My soul leaves tomorrow like a free flying dove
In remembrance of me, I leave you my love

Death, she now appears upon butterfly wings
I can see her coming; I can hear her sing

THE FORBIDDEN TREE

Scales of fallacy circle the forbidden tree with ebullient eyes; eight bands of color, two fiery-red pupils, and long spindly legs that carry the supercilious serpent upright and wary. Its eyes wander up at the shiny fruit growing on the sun burnt branches. The serpent's eyes flicker wide, fully aware of the naked sinner who is spying from behind it.

The serpent darts its forked tongue in and out of its mouth, ready to devour the fruit's succulent drippings. The sweetness, however, instantly turns sour, a poisonous secretion that burns the serpent's mouth. It spits out the sickness, having never desired the sweet savor—it was a sham to fool the curious sinner into taking one auspicious bite. And if the woman watching from behind a blooming fig tree marveled, it could only be because of the magnificent serpent; each segment, each band of color gleaming in the daylight of the splendid garden. If she trembled, it could only be because she secretly coveted the serpent, which was certainly to blame, for it was indeed the most beautiful thing she had ever seen.

Therefore, if the fruit or the snake poisoned woman and man, shaping them into all things evil, it would be the fruit and the snake that would eventually kill them.

Alas, the most splendid garden would be hidden from humankind forever, only to be found in the darklight where woman and man shall search in vain for knowledge, and certainly crave its wretched horrors.

THEY LOVE YOU, BABY HALLOWEEN

"Blessed are they who love Baby Halloween!" shouted the days. They stood in rows, Sundays through Saturdays, all of them staring up at Father New Years. They were in awe of him.

"All my wonderful days," He said in a commanding voice. His eyes were the sky; one was full of sunlight, the other full of night. "Truly we gather in recognition of a new year. As you know, our last ended like all others. We were one day short."

The days all bowed their heads.

Father New Years spoke from his high white throne: "Since the beginning I've promised the coming of the most special of days, and now the time has come." He reached beside him and lifted an infant to his lap. Her little face was radiant. "I give to the world, Baby Halloween!"

All the days cheered.

Father New Years raised the infant for the days to see. "She shall be given October 31st as her permanent date, and all the children of the world will look to her."

Monday September 6th stepped forward. His scowl was hard as stone. "I ask thee why October receives this new day?" Monday gestured to his fellow Septemberists. "Ought not the fine month of September, who has been requesting a 31st since time began not receive such a blessing? Yet you offer her over to October? January, March, May, July, August, December eventually got theirs. I speak for all the days of my month that we should receive Baby Halloween lest our month be shortened."

Father New Years lowered the infant. His white brows furrowed. "What reasons have you besides jealousy that I should change my mind?"

Monday September 6th glanced back at the other days in his month. He could see in their eyes that they desperately wanted the new day, but none of them dared challenge Father New Years' authority. Monday stood alone. "I ask thee to reconsider so that the ninth month might be a day longer," he said. "Not unlike all the finer months of the year."

Father New Years turned to two holy days standing at his right side. "Lady Christmas," he said. "Do you find any fault in my decision to bestow Baby Halloween to October?"

"Father, surely, I ask thee, may I confer with Uncle Easter?" she said.

"You may."

Lady Christmas and Uncle Easter began to discuss Monday's request.

All the days of all the months stood quietly, waiting for the decision.

Father New Years cooed the infant in his lap. Baby Halloween's face was round as the moon, her skin gleaming light blue. Her eyes emitted light as she gave him a crescent smile.

An hour passed and finally a verdict came from Lady Christmas. "After debating with Uncle Easter, neither of us can find fault in your decision, Father. So shall it be that October is indeed the proper month for Baby Halloween."

Monday September 6th shook his fist at Father New Years. "Listen! You'll be sorry!" he shouted. He turned to all the days of all the months. "You'll all be sorry!" He stormed off, leaving Father New Years and the newborn infant on his lap.

***

At the beginning of every year, after celebration, Father New Years gives each day his or her new date for the upcoming three hundred and sixty-four days. This year, of course, will be different. The Great Calendar would be made even greater. A new day had been born, but it was already causing trouble.

"Everybody in the world shall come to fear the name Halloween," growled Monday September 6th. He rocked back and forth in a chair, scraping his knuckles together. He then stood up and paced his room, kicking furniture out of the way.

There was someone at his door.

"Who knocks? What is your business?"

"It is me, O brother, your sister Tuesday September 7th," said a soft, feminine voice from the other side of the door. "I come to talk to thee."

The door opened and in walked Tuesday.

"I've endured graciously for eons. Obeyed every command," Monday told her. "But it is as I've said: our month has been deserving of a 31st for how long? Since forever! Yet Father New Years gives this new day to October!"

Tuesday approached her angered brother. She put a gentle hand on his shoulder. "Father New Years knows best," she said. "I say to you, O brother of mine, trust him, and allow his righteousness to penetrate your hardened heart."

Monday pulled away. "Nay! His judgment is flawed! Last year I was given the 7th. Now I am the 6th. But this is the way it has always been. But I say to you, this new day, how quickly she is blessed. She's been given the same date every year. Surely she is not a holy day."

"Brother, I ask thee to reconsider. You are not being reasonable."

"My reasons are my own, and they are just." Monday turned to Tuesday. There was intensity in his eyes. His hands were trembling. "Why does this new day deserve better than all of us? What good works has October done to deserve a new day?"

Tuesday lowered her head. "I do not know. But my heart tells me to listen to Father New Years' better judgment."

"Better judgment . . . Bah!" Monday struck his fist against the wall. "How is his judgment any better than mine? He who declares himself the biggest day of the year. Always sitting on his high throne. Why don't the other days get a chance to sit up there? Why can't I?"

"Every day has its place, O brother. We are all special in our own way. We have our places in the Great Calendar. Should we ask for more?"

"Let your kind-heartedness keep making a beggar of you. Not me. Not anymore!"

"Monday, what are you saying?"

"Father New Years has exiled me from the Great Calendar. I say to you, surely, I will not be a part of it."

"O brother, know Father is pained by your motives. His judgment has been approved by the most sacred of days. Lady Christmas and Uncle Easter agreed that Baby Halloween receive October 31st. Is your heart in rebellion of them?"

Monday sat down in his chair, brooding and gnashing his teeth. His eyes grew dark and narrow; his face flushed red. "I stood no chance with them. They acted only to shame me."

Tuesday approached her brother. "What you say is not truth. Did you not witness their deliberation?"

Monday stood up and stomped his foot. "I say it was mockery!"

"Brother, I beg of thee to find it within yourself to repent. The Great Calendar is your rightful place."

"I will not be made a fool! I will go out to the world and call upon any other days that might come with me. With great vengeance I shall strike down the glory of Father's newborn day, and I shall make havoc with his ways."

Tuesday was aghast, and unable to calm her brother as he shook with rage. Turning to leave, she spoke softly, "I grieve for thee, brother. Please reconsider."

***

Behind the Wall of Time hangs a Great Calendar. For many centuries, all days have occupied their given dates, faithfully providing the world stability and security.

Without days, life could not keep track of itself. There would be no organization. No conformity or reason. Life without days would hold only destruction and desolation.

From the beginning of time, Father New Years maintained order. The months were carefully selected and named, and every day served its purpose. Mondays would follow Sundays, Tuesdays before Wednesdays, and so it was. The weeks melded together, segued in alignment, as one long, complex puzzle flowing from then to tomorrow.

Forever and ever.

Father New Years kept Baby Halloween close by his side. He was duly concerned about Monday's jealousy leading to murder; his newborn day would never see the light of . . .

"Bring to me the first day of every month," he commanded.

Friday, December 10th immediately went off to gather the days.

Father New Years spoke to Lady Christmas: "Assuredly, it has been told to me by Tuesday September 7th that a revolt is under way. Should Monday convince other days to abandon the Calendar there will be great trouble unlike any other the world has seen."

Lady Christmas knelt to wipe the closed eyes of Baby Halloween. "Could you not create new days should such a thing occur?"

"The days have all been accounted for," proclaimed Father New Years. "There shall be no more."

Lady Christmas dabbed a wet cloth against Baby Halloween's cheek. "I ask thee, your Grace, would not a compromise be made should other days defect?"

Father New Years appeared angered by this. "You ask me to consider Monday's evils?"

Lady Christmas retracted. Her mouth quivered. "Surely, I say, I dare not condone his waywardness, but maintain the integrity of the year." Lady Christmas bowed her head, displaying humility to the Father.

She looked up as he spoke to her, "Because Monday has struck unjustly against me, I shall wipe him off the Calendar," warned Father New Years. "I cannot find mercy, nor do I comprehend his wicked ways."

"So be it," said Lady Christmas. "The burden shall forevermore be put upon the Mondays of every week."

Friday December 10th returned. "Father," he said, approaching the high white throne. "I have done as you've requested." The eleven first days of the months stood side by side, bowing their heads.

There was sorrow on Father New Years' face. "I've called upon you in response to a threat to the Great Calendar. Monday September 6th has begun a rebellion. I am asking all of you to assemble the days in your months. Go speak unto them, convince them to remain faithful to me."

Thursday April 1st lifted her head. "Father, may I speak?"

"You may."

"Indeed, I have heard of this rebellion and regret that already I have lost Tuesday 6th and Saturday 24th. I fret more days might follow."

Father New Years looked to the other months. "Are there others amongst you?"

Sunday August 1st stepped forward. "I know of one in my month. Friday 13th."

Wednesday September 1st also stepped forward. "There are four in my month not counting Monday 6th. Tuesday 2nd, Tuesday 14th, Thursday 16th, and Sunday 26th."

All the first days of every month stepped forward, with the exception of January. After their calculations were complete, they realized a third of the days had defected.

Father New Years closed his eyes. "Lady Christmas?"

"Yes, Father."

"Because this has happened, Baby Halloween will no longer be of my blessings. Take her from me and hide her face under a mask. She will forevermore be known as the day of evil."

***

"Woe to you who love Baby Halloween!" shouted Monday September 6th. He stood before his new congregation, preaching his hatred of Father New Years. "October 31st shall be cursed eternal. The Father's once glorious day will now be one of ghouls and demons, witches and ghosts. The entire world will fear it. In recognition of her, the children shall wear masks to hide themselves from the Father's shame."

The fallen days chanted her name: "O how we love you! We love you, Baby Halloween! O how we adore you! O Baby Halloween, our curse cuts us inside!"

Monday smiled at this. He took his congregation and abandoned the Great Calendar, leaving behind all the days. Monday led his army into battle against Time. Thus was the beginning of the darklight nations.

O' DEVIL BY TWILIGHT

Morning of malevolence hailing on nigh
To the crouching lady spirits this demon denies
Pleading young women asking of me
"Have mercy, O' Devil, I'm married to thee!"

O' Devil turn 'round before you in white lace
Gasps a lady stained crimson with shame on her face
Lips twitching froth and emitting long sighs
Lay her down softly and close her still eyes

Then 'round to the shouting with screams to subdue
An attack of ferocity to these folks is due
A blade revealed then concealed within
Slashings and slashings and slashings begin!

Tables collapse but in haste they ignore
O' Devil by twilight is blocking the door!

PINK ICE IN MARMALADE

One. Bad. Amputation.

That's about how I'd describe her. Her eyes are like an empty birdhouse; no pupils, just sinewy tentacles sprawling from the sockets and across her face. Her left hand is resting in my lap. Feels like a dead fish. As I drive I can't help but wonder if it'll flop back to life.

I look over at her. The moon highlights a silvery contour of her face on the window beside her. She won't shut up. I've never met a person who talks so much and says so little. Not able to stand the sight of two of her at once, I fumble at my side for the switch to roll down her window. Mistakenly, I hit the button for my window instead, and feel the wind slap my face. I take a deep breath and the coldness hits the back of my throat. I reach into my shirt pocket for a cigarette, keeping my driving hand steady on the wheel, feeling the weight of her hand on my lap.

Shaking the half-emptied pack, I knock loose a cigarette. Catch it in my lips, and then I maneuver a silver lighter between two fingers. With a smooth, rolling action of my thumb I flip open the lid and strike a flame. The cigarette comes to life. The smoke roils warmly in my mouth before I suck it down to my lungs.

And she keeps on yammering.

I ignore whatever she's saying and think selfishly of myself.

It's 1977, and my name is Mars. I'm a struggling serial killer trying to make ends meet. There's not much money in murder these days, so I recently took a side job at a factory near Alice, Texas. The last year of my life has been diluted in acetone and glue; fixing and rearranging the little, square mirrors on defective disco balls. The job isn't worth bragging about, but it pays the bills. More than I can say for murder.

I've developed an extreme dependency on smoke breaks. It's good, you see, to have a little reward every now and again. More importantly, an escape from the acetone. Though death is a hobby of mine making for interesting conversation, acetone can be a real brain-cooker. The stuff does bad things. Sometimes I wonder if I'm already damaged goods because lately I've been questioning if murder is wrong. I need Workers' Comp.

There's a bigger problem in my life than acetone, however, and it's getting serious.

Her name is Sophie St. James—a girl with a face that could make a freight train take a side street. Everything about her is wrong. But, then, I have a tendency to see things differently.

Her skin is flaky as a dried out biscuit under a heat-lamp; her lips pale as moonlight. Her legs are too thin, and her knees pop and grind when she bends. She isn't too smart or pretty, either; and her breath reminds me of a restroom stall in a South Georgia gas station. She's a mess.

Oh yeah, and I am being haunted by her. Literally.

"Mars, I think you missed the turn back there."

I glance down at her hand in my lap, ignoring her constant nagging.

"Seriously, Mars. I think you passed it."

How the hell would you know? I think to myself; *as if you were paying any attention.*

Smoke breaks lead to some serious situations in my life. I met Sophie three years ago, she was sitting by the dumpster on a curb. She wore a white, sleeveless t-shirt, ripped blue jeans, and loose, leather sandals. Same thing she's wearing now only without the bruises and bloodstains. As soon as I saw her, I regretted it. She was too small, too immature, and far too obnoxious. I could tell by the way she cracked her gum as she chewed.

"Are you going to turn around or what?" she asks me.

I drive. Smoke. Ignore her.

The problem with love and murder these days is that they both stick like globulous fat around the ribs. The memories never fade. You can't exercise away the pounds.

I strangled Sophie to death within thirty seconds after introducing myself, and nobody ever noticed. There was nothing on the news about her disappearance that night, or the next night, or the next. Nobody knocked on my door to ask me any questions. I always keep an alibi handy in case of an impulse kill such as hers, but damn, never used it once. I can't recall if she struggled or not. All I know is that she's never left my side since—my little dead weight—and it's looking like she never will. Some people get overly possessive, but in Sophie's case, I believe it is an exaggerated obsession.

If a body of life ever required an amputation, then this girl would not qualify as a little toe. I often wonder if her parents remember her name. It strikes me odd at times how someone like her can be snipped from humankind without anyone noticing. It was as if the earth had swallowed her whole as everyone went on about their business—satisfied that the great beast in the dirt had been fed its millennial sacrifice. Little do they know, however, that the dirt beast doesn't get full on little toes. Every now and again, it needs something more substantial. Say, an arm or a leg. Perhaps a body or two.

That's where we're going now . . . to get something more.

"Wasn't it Clifton Street, Mars? You said Clifton, didn't you? Mars? You listening?"

"Do you ever shut up?" I finally ask, not bothering to look at her. Instantly, I feel the dead fish in my lap withdraw.

"Why? Am I igzas-bating you again?"

"It's exasperating, and yes you are. I can't hear myself smoke."

"Why can't you speak English to me, Mars? Why is it always some big, high-flutin' word that nobody knows?"

"Condensing speech. I've got a lot on my mind."

"Yeah. Sure. . . . Anyways—as I was sayin' before you forgot the turn—I knew this girl, Josephine, in high school, and all the boys taunted her, sayin', *we want more Phine! More Phine!* Get it, Mars? More *Phine*. Morphine. Josephine. I mean, like, what parent wouldn't figure that out! She was always tellin' everybody her—"

The biggest problem I have with murder is that I've never been very good at it. I've been practicing my trade for over a decade now, but so far I've only racked-up one kill. Her. Sophie. St. James. But she's a no count. What good is it when no one cares about the murder, especially the victim? Victims aren't really victims, if they *choose* to be.

Here I am prowling the streets, as usual, trying to find somebody out here who doesn't deserve it—someone that will put up a fuss; someone the papers might finally take notice of; someone with someone else in their life that cares.

But I don't see a soul, and slowly my thoughts slip back to a familiar bog that has been plaguing me for weeks. Nobody likes their job. It's a natural fact that no matter what you do in life, you'll wind up hating it. Sure, you can fake the optimism for a while; keep moving, or so they say. Keeping a defiant smirk of self-confidence will fool the masses, but eventually that dead weight inside will pull you under.

Don't get me wrong. It's not that I hate my profession—it's just a lonely one. Not like there's a Serial Killers' Society to join. No self-help pamphlets or mailings. No coaches. No pills. Or sympathy, if you think about it. I live a lonely world, driving about; looking for people that look like their mothers might've warned them about me. And it's not easy finding the right person, either. I mean, I hear people say things like, "if I went postal, I'd murder my boss," or "if I ever went nuts, I'd blow these idiots off the street."

Truth is I am not postal. I'm not even nuts. I'm the real deal, plain and simple. I have rules to abide by. True serial killers are an ethical bunch, not raving lunatics. There's a difference. We don't indiscriminately kill. On the contrary, we usually take great care in selecting our victims, sometimes going as far as studying them months ahead of time. A lunatic is guided by a voice; serial killers are driven by necessity.

But with Sophie St. James sitting next to me, jabbering on and on about Morphine Josephine, I'm beginning to wonder if I've mentally slipped over the edge.

Got to get my thoughts back on track.

"Are you even listening to me, Mars?"

I flick the cigarette butt out the partially opened window, turning my eyes to look at her. "Not if I can help it."

"God, Mars, why do I bother? You never pay attention to me anymore, Mars. You did once, back when you first met me. Remember?"

Oh boy, here it comes: Looks like I'm packing my bags for the inevitable guilt trip to Sophieland. I don't dare reveal that her insignificance is probably the biggest failure of my career, more so, than the fact that my career is devoid of any others. After the last time I made the mistake of hinting at my superfluous achievement of "taking" her out, she nearly bawled me to death, and I had to spend half a week coercing her back to her senses. What little she has.

"Sophie," I tell her in a gentle voice, "I still see you as my most worthy."

"Really, Mars?" Had she any eyes in her head, I don't doubt they'd be glinting. Her trembling frown instantly flips over to a smile. "Are you just saying that to make me feel better?"

"No, I mean it," I lie to her. "Out of all the people I've killed, you're the most special."

"Oh, Mars!" She reaches over and gives me a sloppy hug. I want to pull away but there's nowhere to retreat in this car. She grins at me with those dried-up lips. "I love you, Mars."

"Yeah, yeah, I know. I love you, too, Sophie." I could always open my door and jump for it. Hey, it's an option.

I have to admit, though, I do harbor some kind of strange fondness for her. Annoying as she is, there's this lost puppy likability about her, a little something that forces me to adore her. And I do. Deep down. It's not like she's all ruined, despite those bat cave eyes. If only she were mute.

"If we're not taking Clifton Street like you said then where're we going?"

I close my eyes tightly and pray I wreck. "Just around."

"If we don't find anybody, Mars, can we go home early?"

"Sure, Sophie."

She leans over and starts to play with my hair. I jerk my head away. She starts talking in that sexy, 50s movie-starlet voice. I call it the "Rita Hayworth".

She runs her forefinger down my cheek, and I feel the edges of her fingernails on the corner of my mouth. "If you want, Mars, you can take me home tonight and kill me all over again. I mean, like, if you don't find anybody else, that is."

"I'll find somebody," I tell her, trying to convince myself.

"But if you don't. You can kill me."

I hit the switch for the window to go all the way down. Gotta' get some fresh air, but all I can smell are the corpses in the ditches left by all the other killers before me. Maybe it's just my imagination. Or maybe it's the acetone eating my brain, I don't know which, but I can swear the city ditches are filled with bodies. Decayed bodies left by other killers years ago. Better killers than I am.

Lighting another cigarette, I blow a cloud of smoke, hoping to eclipse my imagination. There's nothing

I can do about the corpse odor. The whole city stinks. Serial killers should be more environmentally aware.

I drive around town for the better part of an hour before realizing that Sophie's not talking. I look over at her. She's sitting in the passenger seat, drooling like a wrung-out sponge. I wonder if the acetone has frazzled her dead neurons, as it had mine.

"What's wrong?" I ask her.

She slowly looks over at me with those deep, sinewy eyes. "Nothin'."

"Nothin'?" I say, but I know better. "You're quiet. Something's wrong."

"Just thinkin's all." She pulled her feet off the floorboard and tucked her legs underneath her. Her perch on the seat reminded me of a gargoyle staring down from the side of a building. "If I really was that special to you, Mars; I mean, the most special, then why do you need to kill anybody else? If I'm the best then shouldn't I be good enough?"

Thinking before I speak (something she has never done in her life . . . or thereafter), I choose my words carefully. Tone, too. If it comes out the wrong way I could produce another episode, and I don't have the energy for it. Nor the patience, and that is something we serial killers must always have. We tote patience like frat boys do kegs of beer. But, damn, they sometimes get tapped out quick, don't they? "Sophie, you are my most special. When I killed you, I meant it. I don't have any regrets."

"Not one even?"

"Not one."

She taps her finger against her chin. She does this only when she is feeling edgy. "I used to believe," she tells me, "back when I was a kid–that I'd be married with kids of my own . . . livin' in a really nice, big house somewhere." Her rotten breath fills the car. My cigarette's burnt down. I throw it out, light up another. "I didn't have many boyfriends in school," she continues. "They called me names, and made jokes about how I could slip through cracks in a fence."

"Lots of girls aren't comfortable with their bodies in high school," I say. "That's not so unusual."

"Yeah, maybe, but mine was a toothpick. I had twigs for arms and legs." She cups her kneecaps with her hands as if to hide them. "The worst part is that back in seventh grade, I developed boobs early. All the other girls were jealous and that made me feel good. I felt special for once in my life. But then everything suddenly stopped, like my body just said, nope, I'm not going any further. Dead end. All the other girls got curves while I got stuck in a toothpick body."

"You don't have a toothpick body, Sophie."

"Might as well. A toothpick with tits."

"You don't see yourself the way you really are is your problem. You've got a great body. And your curves have certainly caught up with you. How do you not see that?"

She pouts. "Guess I still see myself being sixteen."

"Well," I ash my cigarette, take a last draw then flick it out the window, "want me to take you back home now?" I sounded sincere. She knew I meant it.

I find an empty parking lot and turn the car around. The cool wind ruffles my hair, and I roll up the window. Sophie stays quiet most of the way home. I listen to her breathing, and I think to myself: *Wonder who I missed tonight? If I stayed out a little longer would I have gotten another kill? Upped my average?*

***

With the heat of the car's engine making popping noises under the hood, I step out and walk around the carport and open the passenger door for Sophie. She's staring at the dash, rubbing the faded, purple bruises around her throat. Ah, yes. My handiwork.

She looks up at me approvingly. Accepts my hand, and gets out of the car.

"Thank you, Mars," she tells me.

"For what?"

"For everything. For taking me home. For being nice to me. And for meaning it."

I give her a quick smile. "Come on, Sophie. Let's go inside. It's cold out here."

***

It's a damn shame when a corpse can beat the living to the sofa.

I toss the keys across the room and glare at her. She sits with one arm draped across the back of the couch, the other in her lap, legs spread like a pair of hedge trimmers, but there's no way I can do what she wants me to do. I decide to hit the floor instead.

I crawl across the carpet to turn on the TV, but it doesn't turn on. Maybe it, too, is repulsed by Sophie's disastrous appearance.

"I unplugged it earlier," she says in her best Rita voice. "Guess you'll just have to pay attention to me, instead." She undoes her jeans. Pulls them off and to the floor. Nothing underneath.

My heart beats hard. I want so badly to feel the sting. I call it the sting; that sharp, undeniable pang I get when I feel the urgency to kill. Somewhere deep it's in me, the murderous scorpion raising its tail.

"You can kill me, Mars. All over again. I'm all yours."

I shouldn't be feeling like I am. She's no good, remember? What would killing her again accomplish? What did it accomplish the first time?

"Forget it, Sophie. I just can't do it."

Her black hole eyes narrow. "Sure you can, Mars. You can do anything you set your mind to."

The scorpion within me lowers its tail. "I . . . I can't get it up."

She opens her legs wider. Throwing back her head, she exposes her black and purple throat. "Do it, Mars. I have faith in you."

Nobody cares about her. Killing her is useless business.

"Mars? You love me, don't you?"

"Yes."

"Then take me. Take me with your hands, put them around my neck. Do what you did to me that day. I want to feel it again. I want to feel special. Needed. I need you, Mars. I need you to do me again. And again. And again."

The scorpion is shivering. I feel its rage, the poison beginning to swell inside me. Maybe it's her words, or maybe Rita is finally getting to me. Her voice. I gotta' stop it. Gotta' put my hands around her throat and kill Rita.

My mind warps to Josephine. Ms Josephine Morphine. I wonder for a moment if Sophie had lied to me and she wasn't really who she said she was. I look at her black eyes, and now I see three faces looking at me from the holes. I see Sophie St. James. I see Rita Hayworth. And I see Josephine Morphine.

"Kill us, Mars. Take our breath away," they tempt me.

I stand up. My erection is as hard as the scorpion tail inside me. Stiff. Undeniably poisonous. Ready to strike.

I approach them: Sophie, Rita, and Ms Morphine. "I want *more* Phine."

"Yes, you do," they tell me. Fucking snake charmers.

"*More* Phine!" I scream.

Sophie's face changes in front of me. I see the real her. Ms Josephine sitting on my sofa, her legs open for me, breasts pushed out under that white, sleeveless t-shirt, nipples hard; and her throat . . . that soft, milky-white throat. So pure white. So untouched. I stare at the delicate creases in her skin, those soft, little creases that go round her young neck. I want to squeeze them. Crush them under my hands. Make a mess of all that beauty.

"I need to go home," she tells me. "My parents, they'll get mad."

Parents. Josephine has parents! A mom and dad who care whether she's alive or not. My heart flutters and I feel a release of endorphins wash away the acetone in my brain. Damn, it feels good.

"Please don't hurt me, mister. I got to go home."

She's scared. The way it should be.

"Let me go, mister. I got to go!"

I slide up in front of her, putting my hands on her thigh. I don't want sex with her. I'm not a filthy rapist. I'm more complicated than them. But her legs look so nice, so unlike Sophie's skinny twigs. Her skin is warm and smooth. I can almost feel her blood pumping through her veins.

"Pl-pl-please . . . don't hurt me."

She's crying. Her jaw's quivering. She wants to live. She really wants to live!

"I need *more* Phine," I tell her, moving my hand up her stomach, over her breasts, and to her pearlescent, delicious throat. I touch one of those little creases. Trace it with my fingertip, feeling the warmth of her desperate breath on the back of my hand. With my other hand, I touch her face, raking my fingers across her cheek, leaving bright red marks on her young skin.

My imagination soars, trying to decide how to kill her. Oh, the variations are endless—though I'm overcome with the urge to crack her skull with a hammer. I don't want it to be a clumsy, repetitious beating. More of a precise jarring to her senses. Wanna' see what her eyes look like when I yank up on the handle, mangling her cranium as bright, oxygenated blood splashes across the couch and wall. I don't anticipate her understanding at first. I'm thinking she'll probably sit and wonder for a moment what's happening, why her legs are involuntarily kicking, and why her arms are twitching as if her spinal cord had been plugged into an electrical socket. Eventually, reality will set in. It always does. When she feels the cool air seeping across the arc of her exposed brain matter, feels the warm trickles of blood running down her face, I reckon she will understand just fine.

What excites me the most, though, will be getting to look into the gaping hole. I imagine seeing bits and flecks of chiseled, bloody bone mixed in with her brain. It looks like ice. Pink ice in marmalade.

"Please . . ." she begs me. "Please, let me go . . ."

I wonder what it will be like to watch the news reports tomorrow. Will her parents be crying? Do they really care? Will I feel some kind of remorse? Am I really a serial killer or a fading, one-shot deal? I like to think better of myself.

Then I snap out of it, realizing Sophie is messing with my mind. I look at my hand around her throat . . . around her beaten to death, black and purple throat. The illusion of Josephine fades from my thoughts. I try to hold on to her, grasping onto the illusion, but it slips from my fingers.

"Kill me, Mars!" Sophie pleads. "Kill me, again!" Tears run out of her black eyes. Tears of joy and groans of stimulation. One crazy bitch.

I let go of her and she tilts her head, looking at me oddly, confused; not knowing—for the first time—what to say. All I can do is watch the tears roll out those dark holes, down through the sinewy tentacles hanging over her cheekbones. Down, down, down to her lips. Her dried lips. And then she parts them. Her tongue comes out, tasting her salty tears.

"I thought you loved only me," she whimpers. "I thought I was special."

And she cries some more, though these tears are different. These are tears of pain. I hurt her. Hurt her far worse than the day I killed her.

"Will I ever be enough for you, Mars?"

I shake my head, unable to answer her. I'm not sure she can ever be enough. I can't stop who I am. What I am. You win a hand at poker, you sorta' want to keep playing. Know what I mean?

"You're a knot on the inside, Mars. A big, tangled knot."

"Get out, Sophie. Stay out of my head." I stand up and go to the kitchen, wanting to be left alone. I know she won't let me. I'm beginning to hate her guts, but she's in love with mine.

"Mars,"—she rubs my back, mashing between the shoulder blades; I flinch—"how can I make you better? How can I untie that knot?"

"I'm fine. I just want to be left alone."

Her hands go up to my neck, fingers sliding around the sides to my throat. For a moment I wonder if she's going to try to kill me. Would I let her if she did? Would I let her put me out of my misery? She doesn't, but it occurs to me if she could kill me, I might be stuck forever with her in some kind of interminable, afterlife-limbo; dream come true for her, no doubt. It'd be worse than Hell for me. At least in Hell I'd be too busy screaming to hear her talk. An eternity of fire . . . probably a better alternative to Sophie St. James.

"You really wanted Josephine, didn't you?" she asks me, continuing to stroke my neck.

"I wanted the idea of her."

"Do you want me to bring her back? To pretend? I'd do it for you, Mars. I'd do anything for you."

I shake my head. "It wouldn't help."

"What is it, Mars? What is it that makes you want everybody else besides me? How can I be good enough? What can I do to change your heart?"

Fuck. I need a cigarette.

"Is it my eyes, Mars? Do they creep you out?"

"I'm fine with your eyes, Sophie."

"Then what is it?"

I turn and walk out of the kitchen. Head outside for a smoke. She follows me to the sliding glass door but I close it before she can come through. I reach into my shirt pocket and pull out my cigarettes and lighter. The night sky is clear and full of stars. I stare up at them as I fire up a smoke. Inhaling deeply, I sense Sophie standing behind me on the other side of the glass door, her sadness and desperation seeping through the threshold and around my feet. I don't look down. I keep staring up at the stars in the sky, wondering when they might burn out. Wondering if I might get another opportunity to kill someone before they do.

MAKING YOUR DAY

I stumble from excess hours, shaking off the mist of dreams. With outstretched arms I touch the heavens, tucking in the seams. The sun is bursting on the horizon, lifting its golden head. I gather warmth and rays for you as you are sleeping in your bed. Delicately, I fluff the dawning sky, and sweep the grass below—collecting leftover moonbeams, or any starlight that does not glow. I teach the birds to sing a song, a melody they have never heard. Verses with your name in them, to make your day assured. This is most important; your happiness my only wish. After all my work is done, I can sit back and think of this. The hours are neatly pressed, my beloved, I've washed out every stain. I cooked you breakfast under moonlit skies; would you like a cold glass of rain? When you wake with sleepy eyes, I hope that you can say: "Thank you, dear, for what you've done. I'll have a terrific day."

GIRL IN A BOWL

Such a pretty thing. Swimming round and round. She was my wife, and I'll love her forever. She used to ask me if I could be any kind of animal what would it be? I told her a bird, because birds fly freely through the heavens, looking down at people and all their problems. She said everybody wanted to be a bird, and if such a wish were ever granted, the sky would be full of self-centered, winged people, clogging up the atmosphere as they do the roads. She's probably right.

She loved fish. She used to tell me how beautiful it would be to swim in an ocean of tranquility. Seemed like nonsense at the time. I've always been a practical man; a *dry* man most certainly—I've never learned to swim.

Once, she tried getting me to go to the beach so she could teach me—to show me the ways of fish, but we never went. I used my job as an excuse. Can't find the time, I told her. Truth was I've never liked the water. The ocean, vast as it may be, always seemed confining to me. It is like a huge glass tank full of desperation of everything living in it. I told her fish were jealous of land dwellers; they swim around, dreaming what it would be like to drive a car, send an email, or simply walk into a store for food. Fish, I told her, were trapped in a constant determination of escaping the tank.

I couldn't make my wife understand that wasting time wishing to be something else was not healthy. At best, silly.

She said there's nothing silly about fish.

Sometimes I would take her to the local pet store and let her look at the tanks. It was always difficult getting her to leave. Her eyes would well up as she watched the small fish swim through bright pink castles, and around sunken, plastic pirate ships.

They need visitors, she told me. At first, I was confused by what she was saying. Fish? Need visitors? But after a while I relented. She was my wife, after all, and I loved her despite her odd fascination. They are lonely in there, she insisted. I told her that they couldn't be lonely, that plenty of people came by during the day to look at them. Most likely they're afraid of us. I mean, could you imagine how we look to them? Large, ugly faces pressed up to the tanks, smiling at them, and tapping the glass with fingers the size of tree trunks?

She didn't find much comfort in that.

It was her thirty-fourth birthday when I surprised her with two fish. She stood in the doorway to our bedroom and I told her to close her eyes. Taking her by the hand, I led her down the hall to the living room. Open your eyes, I said. On the coffee table, I had placed a glass bowl with the florescent-colored fish. They swam in circles through a green speckled castle. She cried because she was worried I had disrupted their families at the pet store, and that there were babies and I had taken their mommas away from them. I was astounded. Not because she didn't like my gift, but because I knew my wife had lost her mind.

I took the fish back and decided to stop at the pub for a drink. I had eight.

I knew the bartender rather well, and talked to him about women. I didn't mention that my wife was totally obsessed with fish; I probably would've been thrown out. We discussed women's strange ways in general. How they are.

The talk didn't really help, and neither did the beer. I left the pub probably more confused than when I went in. Frank, the bartender, said his girlfriend never liked the gifts he bought her. Said they were never expensive enough. I remained mum; my gift had hit too close to the heart. Like taking a cow out for a burger. That's the sort nonsense that was going through my mind that day.

I went back home, hoping my wife might be a little understanding. I wanted to do right. Wanted to please her, but when I walked through the front door, I knew I'd lost her completely.

She sat on the couch with a bloody knife in her hand. There were slits in the sides of her neck—not deep cuts, but bad enough to need stitches. They looked like gills. Fish gills.

I took her to the emergency room. She, of course, didn't want to go, but I threatened to call the police and have her sent to a psyche ward if she refused. I hated being cruel to her, but I was concerned about her mental health. If she was going to start hurting herself, this fish fascination would have to be examined.

The doctor at the hospital did a good job sewing her back up. My wife sat silently on the sterile white gurney, staring blankly as the doc looped the thread in and out of her neck. Though she was numbed by anesthetics, I couldn't help but wince at her dilemma, and felt an alarming sense of fear and confusion. Where was she? I wondered; certainly, not in her right mind.

On the way back home, she asked me to take her by the pet store. That was the only thing she had said after we left the hospital. I looked at her in the passenger seat. She stared out the window, watching the world go by, and daydreaming, no doubt, of being somewhere in the sea.

I slept alone that night—as I had been for the last couple weeks—waking in the early hours to find her curled up on the sofa in the living room. She wasn't asleep, and by the stoic look on her face, and her swollen, reddened eyes, I could tell she hadn't slept all night. I sat beside her, stroked her cheek, and asked what was bothering her. She just stared at the coffee table where the fish bowl had been.

After preparing breakfast, I left her to her thoughts. I had to get ready for work. While in the shower, I'd made up my mind to seek a professional to help with her psychiatric delusions. I didn't know what she was capable of doing. There were knives in the kitchen drawer; should I hide them? Take them to work with me? I couldn't stand the thought of coming home to find her cut up again on the sofa. If I had to hide the knives, it would be admitting to myself that she was crazy. She was my wife. I had to believe in her.

By lunchtime, I was exhausted. Not from overworking, but fretting. Worrying. Distraught over my wife's condition. Was she okay? Was she getting into the knives again? I fought off those thoughts for as long as I could, but finally broke down and called her. There was no answer.

I intended to wait one full hour before calling again. I lasted a minute and a half.

She answered on the fifth ring. I told her that I would be coming home soon, and if she wanted, I would take her to look at the fish at the pet store. I just wanted her to be happy. She told me she loved me, and that was the last time she spoke to me.

By the time I pulled in the driveway, the sun had already settled on the horizon. It was later than I had hoped, but I got caught up at work. I came in the house hungrier than I've ever been; ready to eat one of those delicious dinners my wife prepares so well. I gave her a kiss, washed my hands, and then sat down at the table. She brought out a plate of meat loaf and mash potatoes, a side dish of broccoli. I ate every bit of it, and went for seconds. She just sat across the table from me, smiling aloofly, never saying a word.

I asked her if she was going to eat. "Want me to take you out for something?" She sat there mute and a strange grin on her face. It was a long, uncomfortable moment.

After my dinner, we watched TV a while, but I was tired. I went to bed early that night, deciding not to probe her. I assumed she'd sleep on the couch again, or maybe she would crawl into bed with me later. I kissed her goodnight then went to the bedroom, falling asleep practically before I could close my eyes.

I dreamt of clowns at a carnival. They were shooting fireworks into the night sky; children were screaming with delight. A barker shouted, "Come see the dog dance on two hind legs with the pretty ballerina!" Hot dogs, roasted peanuts, and the smell of popcorn filled the air. A group of monkeys had organ grinders in their hands. They turned the ivory handles, grinding out strange melodies. Behind me, I heard loud popping sounds, then turned to see children using abnormally long needles to burst the animal balloons the clowns had given them. There were fish inside the balloons, and once freed, they swam into the night air, going up in a giant, flickering school of silver. The moon came out from behind the clouds, and I watched as the stream of fish swam up to it. The moon opened its huge mouth, swallowing the fish. The monkeys cheered and danced, cranking their noisy boxes. A parade was underway, one large float carried an oversized glass bowl. Inside the bowl were fish with frightening scowls on their faces. Their eyes bulged, rolling in wild circles. Their fat lips appeared to be sucking air, while their fins fanned out in display. There was no water in the bowl, but there were bubbles coming from the mouths of the fish. They were screaming at me, accusing me of stealing their mothers.

I bolted out of bed in a sweat. Rushing to the bathroom, I splashed cold water on my face. I leaned into the mirror, looking at my reflection. The dark circles under my eyes began to reveal the strain I was under. It seemed a long time when things were normal. I needed my wife back. I wanted to tell her all about the dream. It would amuse her that I dreamt about fish. Maybe she could explain what it all meant.

In the living room, I saw the horror. There was my wife in a huge glass bowl, like the one in my dream. A long, clear tube protruded from her neck with the other end dangling over the rim. She was wearing diving flippers on her hands and feet. The water was pale red from the blood coming from the tracheotomy she had performed. Secretly, she'd been getting tattoos on her body while I was at work. Silver scales. I couldn't deny, however, that she looked happy as she swam around and around. At the bottom of the bowl was a ring. It was the golden band I had given her seven years ago, the one I gave her on our wedding day. She wasn't smiling but I could tell she was happy. Her lips puckered. I knew she was happy. The gleam in her eyes proved it.

I also knew she would never come out. It didn't take long before her flesh couldn't stand the water any longer and would dissolve. There was no need to call an ambulance. It wasn't long before her body curled over, as it floated to the surface as fish do when they die. I've since wondered how she got the huge glass bowl, or how she managed to fit it into our living room. I guess none of it matters now. All I know is that I loved her, my pretty girl in a bowl.

WHERE THE BONES GO

Where do bones roll, oh, where do they roll?
Down to boxes is where they go
Down to earthen, subterranean delights
There to remain forever at night

Tell me names; yes, tell me their names!
Who are the dead, and are they insane
Who are they, and what am I
Better than them, I cannot deny

Where do bones roll, oh, where do they roll?
Down to boxes is where they go
Down to earthen, subterranean delights
There to remain forever at night

STARWATER

Claire held up her fingers. "Astronauts only. One, two, three, four, and five. Blast-off time: T-minus 10 seconds and counting. Fire up your engines. Buckle seat belts."

Rocket fingers. Blasting off from a child's hand to outer space. All five of them.

Claire's other fingers are to stay here on Earth. She needed those to catch the rockets when they come back home.

"Thumb rocket, your name is Widely 13. You go to Mercury. Pointer rocket, your name is Jellybean. You go to Jupiter. Middle rocket, you're Airplane Face, and you go to Saturn. Ring rocket, you'll be Ghost. You go to Neptune. And you, little pinky rocket . . ." she wiggled it. "Your name is Sleepy Purple. And you get to go all the waaaaaay to Pluto."

Three seconds, engines ignite.

"I'm Starwater. I'll be going with you guys."

Blast off!

Stretching her arm as far as she could, Claire's finger rockets shot through Earth's atmosphere and into the dark reaches of space. "We're going on a journey to find Daddy the best birthday gift ever," she informed the astronauts inside the rockets. "Square circles. That's what we're after, square circles from the square circle tree. But first we gotta' find it. So which planet is it on, astronauts? Where will we find the secret tree?" She made rocket noises with her mouth, holding her arm up in the air until she began to get tired. Lying in bed, Claire's eyes were getting as heavy as her hand. They both eventually came crashing down.

(WIDELY 13)

"What is it, Widely? What do you see out there?"

"Clusters."

"White ones or red?"

"White. So keep quiet."

Widely 13 was dressed in an astronaut jumpsuit, bubble helmet, and silver boots. Starwater sat with her feet curled under her, watching as the astronaut stared out the porthole and into space. She could see the glint of the sun reflecting off the sides of Widely's visor.

"Are they close, Widely?" She scooted to the edge of her seat.

"Close enough." The pudgy-faced astronaut came away from the porthole and manned the controls in the rocket's cockpit. "Maintaining course to Mercury. Initiating rocket's laser systems. Preparing to fire."

Starwater clutched her seat belt, expecting a sudden jolt. The lights on the control panel blinked in rapid succession. Blue, green, yellow, and red lights. *Blink, blink, blink.* Widely 13 pulled a lever and the overhead lights dimmed. Starwater looked to the porthole and saw an intense flare of blue light crackling around the outer shell of the rocket. She saw another light in the distance. No, there were two lights coming their way! "White clusters," she whispered, and closed her eyes.

The blue laser light formed a triangular formation around the tip of the rocket. Exploding into a web of zigzagging particles, the laser fizzled out. The rocket was left vulnerable to attack.

Widely 13 worked quickly to reenergize the laser system. "Unable to determine if we have enough backup power." He raised the visor on his helmet and looked to Starwater. "Any ideas what to do?"

Starwater unbuckled her seat belt and jumped from her chair. The rocket's floor was cold to her bare feet. "Shoulda' remembered my slippers," she muttered; hop-scotching across the floor to the control panel.

"You won't need them if those clusters get hold of us."

Starwater, dressed in blue and green striped pajamas, looked up to the taller astronaut. Her freckled face was mostly hidden behind her long, wavy auburn hair. Her lips, red as a lollipop, formed an oval. "Soooooo, what 'xactly will they do to us?"

Widely 13 didn't immediately reply. With the tip of his tongue stuck out between his lips, he moved his gloved hands over the many buttons and levers, and dials and switches on the console.

"Widely? What's going to happen?" she asked again. This time she tugged at one of the flexible hoses connected to his suit. "Will we be turned to space dust?" She turned and stared at the porthole. "Maybe they'll drag us into the sun, burn off our skin, and cook our bones."

"Worse than that, I'm afraid," Widely 13 said. He didn't bother looking down at her, but kept his eyes on the business at hand.

Starwater looked back at the console, watching the overabundance of blinking lights on the panel. She reached up and touched one. "Are we still on course to Mercury?"

Widely 13 quickly slapped the back of her hand. "Don't touch! And yes we are. But who knows for how long." He nodded to the porthole. "White clusters can turn this ship into butter with the slightest touch."

The little girl turned from the panel and leaned against it. "Space butter." She looked up at the astronaut. "I know! All we need is bread and we'll be toast!"

Widely 13 checked the locater modulator, tapping his knuckles against the glass. "This isn't the time for jokes. The clusters are moving in fast. Coming in on our star'brd side."

Starwater spun around, looking to her left then right. "Starboard side . . . starboard side . . . which direction do you hide . . ."

"Turn around, face the controls," Widely told her. She did as directed. "To your right . . ." He pointed toward the porthole. "That's star'brd."

"Oh, I knew that," she replied with a wily grin. She brushed back her hair from her eyes. "I was just making sure you did—was all." Lifting her right hand, her grin turned into a broad smile. "Funny thing, Widely, my starboard hand is a bit of a nub."

He glanced down at her.

"All my finger rockets are out there somewhere in space, searching for Daddy's gift."

"What's so special about this gift that a little girl like you would give up all her fingers on her hand?" asked Widely. He flipped several switches, and pulled a thick-handled lever. The high-pitched sound caused Starwater to jump.

"That's exactly why!" she said. "Because it's special. I thought and thought about what to get him. Something he didn't have. And I knew if I bought him something at the store, he could always have that. But nobody has square circles. So I decided to get them for him."

"But what if you never find the tree? What if all the rockets don't make it to their destinations?"

Starwater looked down at her toes. They were slightly blue from the cold, cabin floor. "Then I guess I'll have to buy him somethin' regular."

Widely 13 stopped what he was doing and knelt next to her. He took her right hand, the one with absent fingers. He held it up. "Any little girl willing to give so much for her daddy is worth scouring the universe."

"So you think we'll find the tree on Mercury?" she asked. There was newfound urgency in her voice, excitement in her round, green eyes that twinkled from the multicolored lights on the control panel.

"First things first," Widely 13 said. He let go of her arm and stood up. "We have to get rid of those pesky white clusters or we're not going to make it three clicks passed Venus."

"Stupid clusters," Starwater mumbled. She stood beside the astronaut with the pudgy cheeks who seemed to be randomly mashing buttons. More lights began to blink. "What if we turn off the main lights?" Starwater said. "Would that give us power for the lasers?"

Widely 13 scratched his chin. "Hmm. It's worth a shot." He pointed to a gold lever on Starwater's left. "Pull that down then push the button next to it. Turn the dial over there; four clicks right, two left, twenty-three right."

Starwater looked at him questionably.

"Out of the way, little one. We don't have time to waste." Widely 13 reached around her and pulled the lever, mashed the button, and spun the dial. The overhead lights went out and the cockpit was in the dark except for the brightly colored control panel.

Starwater ran to the porthole. Outside, she saw the intense white light of the clusters approaching.

"Get to your seat and buckle up," Widely 13 ordered; he kept his hands on the control panel, working as a telephone operator on a switchboard. "Five degrees left. Initiate firing mechanism. Power up!"

Starwater crawled into her seat and snapped the buckle around her waist. She tucked her bare feet back under her bottom. "We gotta' find the tree. Just gotta'."

Widely 13 pressed the red button that fired the laser. He held it down. "5 . . . 4 . . . 3 . . ."

Outside the rocket, long tails of hot, white light were whipping back and forth, like giant illuminated tadpoles in space. One touch to the rocket and it would slice open, melting the walls and sucking Starwater and Widely 13 out into the oxygen-less depths of space, probably to burn up in the sun's fiery rays.

Widely glanced over his shoulder at the young, long-haired girl strapped to her chair. "Laser system is up and ready!" He pressed another button and the blue laser light crackled around the outside of the rocket. This time, instead of fizzling out, the blue light shot out toward one of the clusters.

The rocket bounced, knocking Widely off his feet and to the floor.

"Widely! Are you OK?" Starwater asked, clutching her seat belt. "Widely?"

He got up slowly and re-arranged his helmet. "Yeah, just forgot to hold on." He ran to the porthole and looked outside. "We got one of 'em, but the other is still coming right at us."

"Do we have enough power to shoot it?"

The astronaut went back to the control panel. He checked the gauges. "Hardly. We'd have to power down everything."

"Will that send us off course from Mercury?"

"Probably, but it might be our only hope to survive." Widely 13 pushed more buttons and pulled levers. "We could try to outrun the cluster, I suppose, but that would burn a lot of fuel." He turned to Starwater. "I'm afraid we're going to have to turn around, little one. Head back to Earth."

"Back to Earth?" Starwater looked sadly at the porthole. The remaining cluster was burning intensely. The white light made it impossible to see anything else outside the glass. "We can't go back, Widely. We have to get to Mercury to find the square circle tree."

"We don't have enough power or fuel," Widely argued. "If we don't turn back now, we'll never get back home again."

"But what about Daddy's birthday? It's tomorrow, and I don't have anything to give him."

Widely 13 lowered the visor on his helmet. He didn't want her seeing his tears. "What kind of present would it be if he never saw you again? Don't you think he'd rather have you back home, safe and sound?"

Starwater rested her head against the back of the seat, her long, auburn hair cascading over her shoulders. She coiled the ends around the fingers of her left hand, while staring at her right. The other four finger rockets were on their way to other planets, heading out in search for her Daddy's special gift. "We can't go back, Widely," she pleaded. She unbuckled herself from the seat. "We'll just have to find another way. We got to go to Mercury no matter what."

Widely 13 stared at her for a moment then turned to the control panel. He muttered under his breath: "We're not going to make it."

The rocket began to shake violently and Starwater and Widely 13 were tossed about the cockpit. The rocket jarred as though it had struck a deep pothole. The walls rattled and all the blinking lights on the control panel flickered out. The astronaut and the little girl were left in the dark.

The only light was now coming from the porthole, a thick beam of white light that was making the rocket floor warmer. Any second and the cluster would rip through the walls, ending Starwater's dream of going to Mercury. The tree might never be found.

"Guess I should've listened to you, Widely," Starwater said. She reached for his hand. "Now look what I've done. I got us both killed."

"We're not dead yet," Widely replied. "Still got the ejection pod. We could escape in that. Aim it toward Earth, and hope it makes it."

Starwater crawled into Widely's lap. "It's no good. The ejection pod is only big enough for one of us. Somebody would have to stay behind."

The freckle-faced girl in the blue and green pajamas laid her head against the astronaut. They were both on the floor, resting against the control panel.

Widely 13 lifted her up to her feet. "Let's get you into that pod."

"Noooooo, Widely! What about you? I can't leave you here alone to die."

"I'll be OK. You just make sure you're back in time for your daddy's birthday. A regular gift is much better than something bad happening to you. Your dad will understand. I think he'll see you as being the most special gift he could ever have."

"But, but he's already got me."

Widely pulled her along to an octagon-shaped hatch on the wall. "There's still four other planets to search. And if you don't get going, he won't have you for long. Get in there, little one." Widely lifted his visor and smiled at her. He gave her a wink.

Starwater strapped herself into the small seat and lifted her fingerless hand. "Goodbye, Widely 13. You're my favorite thumb."

He closed the hatch, and with a sudden jerk of a lever, the outside hatch opened and the pod was ejected from the side of the rocket. Starwater watched from inside the cramped pod. Through a small porthole she could see the rocket spiraling away from her, round and round, farther and farther away; or maybe she was spiraling away from it. Either way, she felt sad leaving Widely. The white cluster wrapped its long tail around the rocket, slicing it open. Widely was sucked out to space and out of view. Starwater looked down at her fingerless hand, remembering how she used to suck her favorite thumb.

(JELLYBEAN)

"The mission is doomed! Doomed, I say!"

"What's wrong? Why aren't we moving?"

Jellybean turned to her. His nostrils were flaring behind his helmet. "Come look for yourself."

Starwater unbuckled her seat belt and tiptoed across the cold floor. She rubbed the sleep from her eyes then looked out the porthole. "What's all that goop?"

"A web of lies. We're stuck in it. This rocket isn't going anywhere," growled Jellybean. He threw his arms up in a tantrum. "All the work and preparation to get this far, and now we're stuck. Stuck in space! We're so close to Jupiter I can feel it! But no, no, no! We get stuck at the last minute."

"How'd we get all tangled up in it?" Starwater asked. She put her fingerless hand up to the glass as she stared out at the long, matted net of dripping tentacles around the rocket.

Jellybean cleared his throat. "It's your fault."

"My fault?" Starwater glared at him. "How's it my fault? I was asleep in my chair the whole time."

"Because you had to tell your dad last week you didn't have any homework when you really did."

"What's my homework have to do with getting stuck?"

Jellybean pounded his fist against the control panel. The lights flickered. "*It has everything* to do with why we're stuck. Stuck in space!"

Starwater walked away from the porthole and approached the control panel. "OK, we're stuck, but all we gotta' do is find a way out."

"No way out," Jellybean said. "Already tried while you were sleeping. I tried backing up, tried going forward. Tried doing both at the same time. Nothing. Face it, we're stuck. Just plain stuck!"

"OK, ok, already! We're stuck! But there must be another way. We can't just float around here forever."

"That's what's going to happen," Jellybean said. "We'll float out here forever until we run out of oxygen and turn green."

Starwater rolled her eyes. "We're not going to turn green, Jellybean. You give up too fast is your problem." She put her left hand on the console and started pressing buttons.

"Hey! What are you doing?" Jellybean asked, snatching at her hand. "I'm Captain of this ship. You're going to—"

—An alarm sounded. Starwater jumped. "What's that? I didn't do anything!"

"I don't know!" Jellybean grabbed her shoulder and pulled her back from the console. "Oh my, you've initiated the automatic self-destruct."

"Well," Starwater mumbled, "at least we won't be turning green."

Jellybean shook a finger at her. "From now on, keep your nosey little fingers where they belong."

Starwater looked at her fingerless right hand. Maybe Jellybean was right. Maybe she should have kept her fingers where they belonged, she thought. So far nothing was working. Why did the square circle tree have to grow on another planet? Why couldn't it be on Earth like regular trees?

Because it isn't regular, she reminded herself. She could find any ol' tree on Earth, but if she was to get the most special gift ever for her daddy's birthday, she'd have to go great distances to find it. It had to be on one of the planets she selected. They were her favorite planets; and favorite planets have special things.

"We have ten minutes before absolute Ka-Plooey!" Jellybean said, staring dishearteningly at the control panel. The lights were blinking erratically.

"Can't you stop it? Can't you turn it off?"

He shook his head. "Once the self-destruct initiator has been initiated, the whole rocket is doomed."

"Well, what do we do now?" asked Starwater. "Sit here and wait to be exploded?"

"That's about the size of it." Jellybean took off his helmet and laid his forehead against the console. "We were so close, too."

"Well, I'm not going to sit here and wait to die," Starwater proclaimed. She walked briskly to the compartment where the space suits were kept. Reaching for the handle, Jellybean grabbed hold of her. His big, buggy eyes looked ready to snap out of his head.

"What do you think you're doing?" he asked, shaking her by the shoulders. "You can't go out there. You'll float away. No one will likely find you. You'll drift off the radar, and who knows what is out in deep space. Black holes. Space storms, it could be anything." He pulled her back to the console. "You're just going to have to accept we're doomed. We can play cards or something until absolute Ka-Plooey. I have some cards in my luggage."

Starwater went to the porthole. "I don't want to play cards. I'm going to get us out of this stupid goopy mess. If we're stuck in a web of my lies—then I can get us out."

"It's useless, I tell you," Jellybean insisted. "Even if you could get us out, what about the self-destruct?"

"We'll worry about that later."

Jellybean scratched his head. "Shouldn't we worry about that now, and then getting unstuck?"

Starwater thought about it for a moment. "Yeah, maybe you're right." She looked to the console. "What if we drain all the power in the rocket? Would that affect the self-destruct thingy?"

Jellybean shrugged his shoulders. "Guess it wouldn't hurt to try. But how do you figure to drain all the power? And what do we do once we stop the self-destruct and get out of the web? If we have no power . . ."

"We'll worry about that later, too. Right now I just don't want to explode." She looked around at the console and all the buttons and switches. "Which ones work the laser?"

"These over here," Jellybean said, pointing to a set of red and yellow flashing buttons. "Let me do it. You might cause everything to get worse."

Starwater backed away from the controls and watched as Jellybean fired up the laser. "Just keep firing until all the power is drained out," she told him. "Hopefully that'll stop the self-destructor."

"I'm not completely counting on it. We might still be doomed."

"Doomed-shmoomed," Starwater replied, tapping her foot against the cold rocket floor. "Just hurry up. We probably have only a few minutes left."

Jellybean whizzed over the buttons, pushing this one, pushing that one; frantically pushing all of them.

Starwater waited behind him, trying to think of how she was going to get the rocket out of the web of lies and back on its way to Jupiter.

I got it, she thought: I'll just tell Dad the truth! Then the lies will disappear and we'll be on our way again! Yes! That's it!

"Jellybean, I have an idea," she told him, yanking on the back of his space suit. "I figured out how to get us unstuck!"

"Fine, fine," he grumbled. "Do whatever you have to. Let me concentrate."

Starwater went to the porthole. She got down on her knees and peered out the glass. The long, tangled tentacles were pressing hard against the rocket. Starwater closed her eyes and thought of her father's face: His mustache that tickled her when he kissed her goodnight and the stubble on his chin. She smiled. Thinking of him warmed her insides, even down to her little bare toes.

"Daddy, I know you might get mad at me for this," she whispered with her eyes tightly closed, "but I lied to you last week. I told you I didn't have any homework, but I did. I wanted to play, instead." She peeked from the corner of her eye. Nothing seemed to have changed outside the rocket; the tentacles were clutching ever tighter. She closed her eye and continued her repentance: "I know you told me God would get angry with me if I lie, but I didn't mean it. I just want to find the square circle tree so I can make you happy on your birthday. I'm sorry I lied to you, Daddy. I won't ever ever do it again, I promise."

She peeked again to see if the tentacles were releasing the rocket. And they were! Slowly, like an octopus letting go of a struggling fish, the web of lies were retracting. She closed her eyes. "And I also promise to always do my homework when I have it."

She looked out the porthole and the web of lies was gone!

"I did it, Jellybean! I did it!" She ran to the astronaut who was still trying to get the laser system working. "The web is gone! We can go to Jupiter, after all!"

He stopped and looked down at her. "I can't get the self-destruct to stop. The lasers won't work. The whole rocket is going to absolutely Ka-Plooey." He looked sad. Not sad for himself, but sad that he had failed the little girl who only wanted something special for her daddy.

She knew what had to be done, and Jellybean walked her to the ejection pod.

"Goodbye, Jellybean," she told him. "I'm sorry my lies got us in trouble. I won't ever lie again."

"I know you won't, Starwater. I forgive you." And after she buckled herself in, he closed the hatch and pulled the lever that shot her out of the side of the rocket and into space.

(AIRPLANE FACE)

She opened her eyes, slowly this time, wondering what new predicament this rocket might have. She looked around the cockpit for the astronaut but he was nowhere to be seen.

"Airplane Face?" She unbuckled her seat belt and got to the floor. The lights on the control panel were blinking steadily, no sign of immediate danger. "Airplane Face . . . you around here?" She looked behind her chair. She searched the compartment where the space suits were kept. The captain of this ship was not at his post. And then a scarier thought than white clusters and self-destructors crossed her mind. Was she alone? Had the astronaut ejected from the rocket without her?

She went to the ejection hatch and opened it. The pod was still intact.

"Airplane Face?" she yelled as loud as she could. She closed the hatch and turned to the porthole on the starboard side. Outside the little round window she saw a face peering in at her. "Now, that's just ridiculous. What are you doing out there?" She went to the porthole. "Get back in here, silly astronaut!"

Several minutes later and Airplane Face emerged from a hatch in the floor. "Did I scare you? Did I? Did I?" he asked, excitedly. He took off his helmet and laid it on the console. "I was out there in space, floating like a real astronaut. Did you see me? Did you'? Did you?"

"I saw you," Starwater replied. She folded her arms across her chest. "Now why did you go out there in the first place?"

"I told you, to float around like a real astronaut."

"You ARE a real astronaut. You don't have to pretend." She shook her head disapprovingly.

"Oh yeah." He bowed his head. "But I did get you something." He held out his gloved hand. In it was a speck. A little, grey and black speck.

Starwater leaned in close. "What is it?"

"I don't know, but I found it stuck to the side of the rocket." Airplane Face looked proud of himself, as though he had struck gold in space. "You want it? It's yours."

Starwater took a step back. "I don't know. What if it's alive or something. I don't want to get bit."

"It didn't bite me." The happy astronaut pushed his hand toward her. "It's just a space speck."

"A space speck? I never heard of that."

"Like an asteroid, only smaller."

"A lot lot smaller," Starwater said. She opened her left hand, still hesitant of her gift.

Airplane Face tilted his hand and dumped the speck into the girl's palm. "Now you can keep it as a souvenir, forever."

Starwater looked down at it in wonder. It seemed harmless enough, but what was it doing on the side of the rocket? As far as she knew, asteroids, no matter their size, didn't typically stick to rockets.

"OK, I'll keep it for now," she said, "but how far are we from Saturn?"

"I'll check! I'll check!" Airplane Face ran to the controls. "Uh-oh . . ."

Starwater followed him. She put the space speck in her pajama pocket. "What's wrong? Why are you uh-ohing?"

"We . . . We were supposed to go to Saturn?"

Starwater's mouth dropped open. "Yes, why? Where are we?"

Airplane Face walked away from the console. He pulled back his hair and sighed heavily. "Oh, boy. I did it again."

"Did what again? Where are we?" Starwater asked; her tone was sharp.

"I pointed us the wrong way. We're floating around the moon."

"The moon? Which moon?"

"Uh, the Earth moon."

Starwater smacked herself on the forehead. "All this time and we're only at the moon? Why didn't you go to Saturn like I told you?"

Airplane Face shrugged. "Guess I got confused. I messed everything up. As usual." He walked over and sat in Starwater's chair, covered his face with his hand, and began sobbing.

She approached him and pulled down his hand. "Oh, stop that. Crying like a baby isn't going to change anything. We're way off course now. We gotta' get back on track. I have to get my daddy's gift before he wakes up!"

Airplane Face snapped out of his trance and went to the controls. "I'll get us there, don't you worry! You'll see! I'll have us to Saturn in no time! Uh-oh . . ."

"What is it now?"

"I don't know which button sets the course."

Starwater threw up her arms in frustration. "You're an astronaut and don't even know how to fly this thing?"

"I know how to fly it. Just don't know how to navigate. But don't worry; I think Saturn's a pretty big place. We'll come across it, eventually."

Starwater took hold of his hand and pulled him around to face her. Her green eyes turned fierce. "We can't just fly blindly around space, looking for a single planet. You know how long that'll take?"

"It's a big planet," Airplane Face stated. "Look, I have a book here with a picture of it."

"It's not THAT big! Good grief, Airplane Face, move over."

"What are you doing?"

"Looking for the locater modulator. Got to get this stupid rocket going the right way."

The little space speck in Starwater's pocket began to move. She didn't feel it at first, but it was growing. Thriving in the dark pocket, the speck was nearly twice the size it was when she put it there. The blue and green fibers of her pajamas tasted good. Cotton candy good. They melted in the space speck's forming mouth.

"I think this is it," Starwater said, pointing to a section of the controls marked with arrows. "Try turning that dial to see what happens."

Airplane Face did as she requested, but the rocket continued its orbit around the moon. "Nothing."

"OK, try that one," Starwater said, pointing to another dial.

"Nope."

The little girl was at a loss. The last thing she wanted was to initiate the self-destruct mechanism all over again. "Well this just stinks." She put her back to the console and pouted.

"It's all my fault," said Airplane Face, pouting beside her. "I should've paid more attention in astronaut class."

Starwater shrugged. "You didn't have an astronaut class. Because you're not even a real astronaut. Just a silly, stupid middle finger."

Airplane Face looked down at his boots. He didn't look like a finger. He was wearing a space suit. Had a real bubble helmet and space suit. He was even inside a real, genuine rocket ship! Surely he was a real astronaut! Had to be!

"I'm never going to get Daddy's gift," Starwater sulked. "I may as well give up. Go to the store and buy something ordinary."

Airplane Face had a different idea. "What if we put on our helmets and stuff and go out and swim to

Saturn? It can't be that far away. I know how to doggie paddle."

Starwater groaned loudly. "Doggie paddle through outer space? Yeah, sure."

"It'll work, I tell ya!" Airplane face insisted. "I tried it when I was outside. I doggie paddled around the rocket!" He swept his arms in circles.

"Stop it. We're not going to doggie paddle to Saturn, so just get that silly idea out of your head." She began fuming and a bead of sweat rolled down her forehead. She wiped it away. "Why is it getting so hot in here all of a sudden? All the other rockets were cold."

"I'll check the thermostat," Airplane Face said, searching for it on the console. "Hmm . . . now where is it?"

Starwater felt her pocket moving. She looked down and saw that it was expanding. The space speck was crawling out!

"Air—Air-plane—Airplane Face!" she cried, pulling at the waistband of her pajamas to get away from the growing thing coming out of her pocket. "The space speck . . . it's alive! It's getting bigger!"

"But that can't be," the astronaut replied, turning around. "It's only a . . . Oh, my. You're right. It is getting bigger."

"Yeah, and look! It has teeth!"

"Quick!" Airplane Face shouted. "Take off your clothes!"

Starwater glared at him. "In front of you?"

"I'll turn around. I won't look, promise."

He turned to the console and kept his eyes closed just in case.

"OK, I got 'em off, so you better not turn around!"

"Cross my heart!"

"That thing is eating my pajama bottoms!"

"Maybe it'll get full and leave us alone!"

"It doesn't look like it's going to leave us alone! It looks hungry! Super hungry!"

"Well get away from it!"

"I am away from it, but it's still getting bigger!"

"Is it close to me? It isn't going to bite my butt, is it?"

Starwater ran to her chair and peeked around the side. "How do I know? I don't even know what it is!"

"It's a space speck," Airplane Face said, matter-of-factly.

"Not anymore! It looks more like a space blob to me! With big teeth! Stained green and blue from my pajamas!"

Airplane Face, with eyes closed tight as bank vaults, side-stepped his way across the control panel, portside. Starwater wasn't sure what that side of the rocket was called; Widely 13 never told her, but she knew where Airplane Face was going.

"Follow me," he said, opening the hatch to the ejection pod. "You have to get out of here before that thing decides to eat you!"

Starwater ran from her chair to the hatch. She crawled inside and buckled herself into the seat. "What about you, Airplane Face? What if it eats you?"

He didn't open his eyes to look at her but she could tell he wasn't crying. He just smiled assuredly, nodding as he closed the hatch.

"You really are a real astronaut, Airplane Face. Even if you do mess up a lot. I love you."

(GHOST)

The blinking control lights illuminated the darkened cockpit. Starwater opened her eyes to see Ghost fast asleep in the Captain's chair. She wondered how close they were to Neptune, and hoped there wasn't any more miscalculations, white clusters, web of lies, or hungry space specks threatening her journey to find the square circle tree. Her daddy would be waking in a couple hours, and Starwater wanted to be at his side first thing with his special gift in hand.

"Ghost?" she called out. She unbuckled herself and got down from her chair. "Ghost, you awake?"

His hand moved but he didn't say anything. His visor was pulled down on his helmet. She could not see his eyes.

"Ghost?" She slowly approached him. Putting her left hand on his arm, the astronaut jolted, startling the little girl trying to rouse him. "Sorry, Ghost! I was only trying to—"

"—We there yet?" he said, lifting his visor and looking frantically around the cockpit.

"I'm not sure. I was hoping you could tell me."

Ghost got out of his chair and went to the controls. He pressed several buttons and kept an eye on the gauges. Starwater stood at his side, watching curiously.

"Locater checks out fine," he said. "Fuel levels on par." He tapped a glass gauge with his hand. "Plenty of battery power."

Starwater leaned in close to the console. "But are we close to Neptune?"

If Ghost was purposefully ignoring her, he was doing a good job of it. She tried yanking the flexible hose attached to his space suit, but he didn't react. He continued operating the controls as though she were not there.

"Asteroid defragmentation indicator set to active. Good." He ran through his entire checklist, naming off every astronomical word in the book. Starwater was perplexed—why wouldn't he respond to her?

Thinking something ridiculous would get his attention, she began making up a tale . . . "One day, you see, I found a little pink birdie on the ground. It was flopping around like this." She lay on the cold rocket floor and kicked her legs about, swinging her arms. She sat up to see if Ghost was paying attention. He was too occupied with his list. So she stood up and went on with her story. "I put the birdie on top of my head and it started flapping its wings, and it carried me way up into the sky." She danced around the cockpit, twirling in circles as the busy astronaut paid her no mind. "But when big momma bird saw baby pink birdie, she swooped down from higher up in the sky and snatched me away. That's when I screamed really loud like this . . ." She looked to the astronaut and cupped her left hand around her mouth: "AHHHHHH!"

No luck. He kept his back turned to her while his fingers zipped over the gauges and gadgets, working out plans, and doing what Starwater believed astronauts probably enjoyed most . . . flying rockets.

"Fine, then. Ignore me if you want, just as long as we get to Neptune." She paced about the spacious cockpit for an hour, sighing deeply. Bored, she fell into her chair. Her stomach began to rumble and she became aware she was hungry. Did she remember to pack a lunch? Or was it breakfast time? What do you eat in space?

"Cheeeeeese burgers!" She jumped to her feet and ran to a separate compartment next to where the space suits were kept and opened the door. Behind it were four shelves, each filled with clear, green plastic packs of food. She sorted through them. "We gotta' have cheese burgers somewhere." She tossed the packs to the floor, scouring every shelf. "Ohhh, cheese burgers? Where arrre you?" Then finally. "Yes! One for me,"—she tucked the green pack under her right arm—"and one for Mr. Busy Bee."

She took the packs to the microwave.

"Now where's the stupid directions?" she asked herself, fumbling over the food packs to see how many minutes to cook them . . . and if the burgers should be wrapped or unwrapped first. She turned to Ghost. "Hey, Busy Bee, am I supposed to take the burgers out or cook them in these baggie thingies?"

He didn't answer. Too busy being an astronaut.

"OK. I'll take them out."

Inserting both burgers into the microwave, she pressed the 3 minute button then leaned against the wall of the cabin. *What if we never make it? What else can I get him for his birthday? I can't think of anything. Daddy will be very disappointed.*

"Last year," she said aloud, "I made him a birthday card. I found a picture of Jesus at Sunday School and traced it with crayons. Jesus was skinny. I drew steel gloves on his hands so when they put him on the cross, they weren't able to put nails in him." She checked the time on the microwave. Half a minute to go. "Daddy said it was a good idea. He told me it was the very best birthday gift he ever had and he'd keep it forever. But this year I'm going to get him something even better!"

A minute, thirty seconds.

"You think he'll like square circles, Ghost? I mean, what if I came all this way for nothing, and he still thinks my card was better? I could always draw him another card, I suppose."

The microwave dinged, and Starwater opened the door. The burgers inside were steaming.

"I better get us some plates." She went to the galley and found a stack of paper plates. She grabbed two. "I hope he likes square circles."

Ghost didn't react when Starwater placed the cheese burger next to his hand on the console. She stood beside him, blowing on her food to cool it. "You better eat that or it'll go to waste. And there's starving people in the world, you know." She moved the plate closer to him. He ignored it and continued to fidget with the controls.

"Back when Momma left us, Daddy used to take me to the lake a lot. Have you ever been to the lake, Ghost?" She looked at her right hand. "Guess you have. It's relaxing there. I liked to lie next to the water and pretend I was sleeping on a living mirror. I'd make up dreams about being a giant face in the sky looking down, and I could see myself and what I looked like when I was older." She took a bite of her cheese burger. It tasted sort of flat and stale. She chewed it anyway. "When I get old I'll have really long, solid white hair, sort of like God's beard, but I won't be grumpy. I'll sit on a porch in front of my big, huge house, and sing to the birds. Who knows, maybe one day the baby pink birdie will come back and pick me up and carry me up to Heaven."

Starwater took another bite of her burger but noticed Ghost wasn't touching his. She tapped him on the arm. No reply.

She gave up and went to her chair. Curling her legs under her, she sat and ate the rest of her food, staring at the back of Ghost's big, white bubble helmet. Surely, they were getting close to Neptune by now, she thought. And with such a dedicated astronaut like Ghost at the controls, no way could something go wrong this time, she assured herself. She tossed the greasy paper plate to the floor and leaned back in her chair. Putting her arms behind her head, she thought about drifting off to sleep, passing time until Ghost could get the rocket safely down on Neptune.

Her eyes shot wide open! "No! Not again!"

She looked over the side of her chair at the paper plate on the floor. The grease and hot cheese had burned a hole through the center of it. She then looked to the steaming cheeseburger on the control panel.

"No! No! It can't happen again!" she yelled, jumping from her chair and running to the console. "Ghost! Look what you did!" She picked up the plate and watched the gooey yellow mess dribble down into the panel. The lights quickly shorted out, and Ghost began to panic. "I told you to eat it, but you didn't listen! Now look! There's smoke coming up!"

She ran to find the fire extinguisher, but couldn't remember where it was.

Ghost backed away from the controls. He was at a loss as what to do.

The rocket started bouncing up and down, the smoking console spitting out sparks and all kinds of electronic madness. Starwater looked to the emergency hatch, knowing there was only one thing to do.

(SLEEPY PURPLE)

"This is it. You're my last hope, Sleepy," Starwater said, opening her eyes to a strangely decorated cockpit.

There were long, colorful tassels dangling from the ceiling. They made Starwater think of her own birthdays when Daddy filled the entire house with ribbons and confetti. The lights on the console were blinking as they should be, but standing next to them was a most peculiar sight. Sleepy Purple had (for reasons unknown) painted himself like a sloppy rainbow; his space suit stained every color Starwater could imagine. Where he got the paint she couldn't fathom. Above him, a large banner was attached to the far corners of the cockpit.

It read: WELCOME TO PLUTO!!!

"We made it! We made it!" Starwater shouted in glee. She came out of her chair too fast that her equilibrium hardly had time to catch up. She stumbled to the floor.

"Careful!" Sleepy Purple said, coming to her aid. He helped her up to her feet, and pushed back the hair from her face. "Calm down, crazy girl. Take a couple deep breaths."

Starwater clutched onto his arm. "We made it to Pluto, Sleepy? We finally made it?" Her sparkling green eyes were enhanced by the wide smile on her face. Her chin was quivering.

"Been here for an hour or more," Sleepy Purple informed her. "Tried waking you but you was conked out good, so I spent the time decorating. How do you like it?"

He stepped back and waved his hand as if presenting a grand prize on a game show.

"It's marvelous!" Starwater told him. She tilted back her head and looked up at all the dangling tassels.

"I hid the decorations in my luggage," he said, lifting the visor on his helmet. "Didn't want you finding out I had a surprise for you once we landed."

Starwater put her arms around the astronaut and hugged him tightly. "Thank you, Sleepy Purple. Thank you so much for getting me here." She looked at the porthole.

"Go ahead, take a look outside." Sleepy smiled as the excited little girl ran to the side of the rocket, gazing at the misty, ice-blue world of Pluto.

Her gleaming eyes suddenly dimmed, and her face fell.

"What's wrong, crazy girl?" Sleepy asked. He walked over to her and rubbed her head as she stared out the porthole.

"It's all ice out there! Stupid ice."

"Of course it is," Sleepy Purple said. "What did you expect, sandy beaches and palm trees this far from the sun?"

"No," she replied in a faint voice; almost a whisper. "Just one tree. Just one, special tree. But what kind of tree can grow in ice?"

Sleepy Purple rubbed his chin. Then he snapped his fingers. "I know! A special kind of tree!"

Starwater looked up at him with widened eyes. "Really? You think so?"

"Of course!" Sleepy went to the control panel. "All we have do is get in the rover and roam around until we find it. It shouldn't be too hard to find, seeing as how this is only an itty bitty planet, after all."

"You're wonderful, Sleepy!" Starwater swooned. She dashed to the compartment of space suits and selected one of the smallest sizes. She kept her pajamas on for added warmth. Sleepy Purple helped her buckle the buckles, snap the snaps, and zip the zippers until she was snug as a kitten in a blanket. He placed the bubble helmet over her head. "We'll find the special tree, I know it!" she said excitedly, blowing a stray hair from her face.

"You better believe we will," Sleepy assured her. "We didn't come all this way just for jiggles n' giggles." Through the hatch, he led her to a bigger room underneath. In the center of the room was an odd-looking, six-wheeled vehicle. It looked like a mechanical bug having two seats on top and a steering wheel. Several antennas and headlamps added to the insectival appearance. "Climb aboard!" Sleepy Purple instructed. He followed her up and into the driver's seat, and they buckled themselves in. "Off we go!"

He punched a button to start the strange contraption, and the engine whirred to life. Another button lowered a section of the rocket's wall—a ramp that led out and into the frozen, wind-battered ice world. Starwater could not stop laughing. She finally made it to one of the destined planets. She prayed the square circle tree didn't grow on one of the others. And what if it didn't grow at all in this galaxy?

The mountainous terrain was steep and fierce, but the insect buggy seemed to overcome most of the obstacles. Sleepy Purple was not only a good astronaut, Starwater believed; he was also a terrific driver. Not a bad whistler, either.

He kept his lips puckered the entire time, whistling tune after tune, allowing Starwater to be assured he knew what he was doing. Only an hour and a half into their search, steadily climbing hills and valleys, Sleepy Purple jerked the brakes and pointed. "What is that I see?"

Starwater followed his gaze to a shadowy figure in the distance. She squint her eyes, gradually recognizing the shape of . . . the shape of a tree!

"That's it, Sleepy! You found it! You found the square circle tree!"

He nodded self-assuredly. "Of course I did. Did you expect anything otherwise from a distinguished astronaut such as me?"

"Only you," Starwater said, again giving him a hug. She looked back at the dark shape in the distance.

"Well, what're you waiting for, Fourth of July?" Sleepy asked her. "Get out and get your Daddy's birthday gift before he's another year older. We have to rocket back home in time before he wakes!"

After unbuckling herself from her seat, she stood upright. Saluting, she exclaimed, "Yes, Sir!" Turning, she gave a quick wink, and climbed down the buggy to the icy ground.

It wasn't easy traversing the slippery slopes in her clumsy space boots, but she managed to stay on her feet with both arms held out to her sides for balance. Sleepy Purple watched from atop the buggy, smiling to himself as the little girl with a big prize in her eye made her way to claim it.

He waved good-bye, and slowly closed the cabin door.

(DADDY)

"Claire? Claire, wake up, sweetie. Open your eyes." He stood over her, shaking her gently by the shoulders, trying to ease her out of dream.

"Huh? Where am I?" she asked, wiping her eyes with both hands.

"You were having a bad dream, precious. I heard you shouting all the way from my room."

Claire sat up and yawned. She quickly looked at her hands. They both had fingers. "It wasn't a bad dream, Daddy. I was shouting because I found something that made me really happy."

"What was it?" He sat down next to her and smoothed the matted hair from her cheeks.

"A tree with special shapes growing on it. Square circles, and I was going to bring some back to you for your birthday."

Her daddy leaned over and gave his daughter a hug. "Well, I'd love to have square circles for my birthday. I bet no other dad in the world has those."

"That's why I wanted to get them for you," Claire said. She pulled away from him. "You aren't sad because I really couldn't bring them back, are you?"

Her dad smiled. "Are you sad because you couldn't?"

Claire remained quiet for a moment, pondering her feelings. Finally, she looked up. "Not really, I guess. I just wish I could have said goodbye to Sleepy Purple, though."

"Who is Sleepy Purple?"

Claire raised her right hand and wiggled her pinky. "The best astronaut in the whole world!"

She looked to the ceiling, imagining the universe. Somewhere out there on a far away planet. . . way, way, waaay beyond all the known galaxies grew another tree with a never-before seen color. She called this color gloopul, and could not wait to get her hands on it before her daddy's next birthday!

CORD U. ROY BOY

He wakes to play with things so mad
In Nightmare City lives a very strange lad
Feral senses enjoy the stench-weed of rot
A festive of creatures to be or not
Betrothed in mind, he loves what he is
Kissing on corpses and to cherish what's his
Never, oh never, does one cell betray
In the wrath of his mind, out comes the day
Squirming and worming, he slides into skin
Oh god, it's his creation; what a way to begin!
On a stool he crumbles, as his eye catches this . . .
Out comes a girl with knots on her lips
He writhes and shakes, and wiggles his toes
Yet she hides her beauty under a long, crooked nose
"Your face is odd, but your lips are divine,
I say to you, you are everything fine."
The girl with knots, murmured and quaked
To this boy not, did she want to partake
He was handsome and round, and all that is sweet
But her features were horrid, like rotten, black meat.
"I cannot, and will not, and I must insist
To leave me alone to sulk in my midst."
Cord U. Roy Boy smiled as he pondered her stuff
"To heck with that and your melancholy puff."

With hand in air, he pounded away
Was he to lose his love this way?
She lowered her head and began to pace
But his becoming voice tempted her face
On a skinny-little neck, she looked back and smiled
"Oh, Cord U. Roy Boy, you're so adorable and wild!"
She swiftly walked over with a big silver tear
"I would love to love you, but I cannot, I fear . . .
You see, how I could ever fall for your charms.
My tangled-up lips would get caught on your arms!"
Cord U. Roy Boy leaned back and released a big grin
He knew what he was, and all that's within
He imagined them together in a covey of love
He could untie her lips freely, let them sing like a dove
"Never, oh never, I'll just keep them wide!"
He said with a smirk, and newfound pride
He stretched out his arms, the proof of his span
In this exposure, it corrupted his plan
What he saw in her was very rare in a girl
Her knots became alive, and started to swirl
"I see what I see, and I like what I know."
She twitched her lips, and the knots did roll.
One side to the other, Cord U. Roy watched them slide
Backwards and forwards, as the poor girl cried
The knots were alive on her pretty, young face
But she was too embarrassed to notice his distaste
She ran and ran far away from his smile
Cord U. Roy Boy fell over in laughter awhile
The girl found a tree and sat under its leaves
Arms over her head, to God she pleads
She hid from the sun, and hid from the moon
"I'm ugly and stupid, such a laughable buffoon.
I wish I were dead, and then nobody could see
These atrocious knots that are ruining me."

124

Suddenly her body rose from slump
Her spirit resurrected from out of the dump
There Cord U. Roy Boy stood to her pleasant surprise
He touched her cheeks, and slowly wiped her eyes.
"I love you and adore you, and I shall be true.
I want to kiss you, and this I'll do."
The girl with knots quickly dropped into place
And as they kissed, he untied her face.

THE OL' HOUSE 'CROSS THE WAY

Children ain't supposed to think bad things. Least, we ain't supposed to talk about 'em if we do. We're not supposed to play in the mud neither, throw rocks at windows, or reach over the dinner table for 'nother helping of mashed taters. Children ain't supposed to do a lot of things, but as for me . . . Well, I'm mostly not supposed to go snooping round the ole house 'cross the way.

It's late summer again and my parents are taking me to my grandparents to stay the weekend, before school starts. Dad, as usual, rattles off a list of do-and-don'ts—and tells me to help out all I can. Mom reminds me to mind my manners (napkin in my lap at dinner, and 'No thank-you's' and 'Yes ma'ams'). All the kinds of things that make a young boy cringe.

Before I know it, I'm left stranded for two whole days with the wickedest, old lady that ever lived. My dad once said some people are too stubborn to die. Mom figured them to be too dumb. But Grandma Birdie . . . She's different. I 'spect, she's just plumb too mean.

Birdie might well have been alive when Moses was around. Her white hair seemed to glow even in the daylight; her skin sagging from her bones like dripping wax. Despite her frailties, she always looked big to me; bigger than a woman ought look, anyway. Her deep set, feral eyes glare out from a scowling, rat-like face. I wasn't sure if she knew how to smile, and wondered if she'd die trying.

I rarely call her Grandma on account she don't look like one. Least, not one I ever saw. All my friends got grandmas that wear aprons and keep a Bible close by— spend a lot of time in the kitchen, and tend to give out heaps of candy.

Not Birdie.

She don't give out nothing. All she does is holler at Grandpa, and all he does is lie around on an old, dingy couch, watching boring reruns of The Real McCoys. What I don't understand is why he doesn't get up and holler back. Seems if I was him, I'd holler even louder. That's the good thing about being old: You get to holler whenever you don't like something. But, us kids . . . We ain't supposed to say nothin. We just take what we get, is all, and we darn-well better like it.

Sometimes I get a notion to yell back for Grandpa, but I done tried it once and learnt real quick Birdie means business when she storms out the front, screen door, and off the porch to fetch herself a long-switch off the ol' willer tree. That day I won't ever forget. I got a swattin the likes no kid's ever had, and it hurt more than my pride and backside that Grandpa didn't even bother to stand up for me. All he done was get his fiddle out from that dusty, black box he keeps on top of the chiffarobe in the back bedroom. I don't put much count into Grandpa helping matters much. He may as well pick around on his fiddle and forget I was there.

The worst part is that Grandpa can't play a lick on the fiddle, but he still gets it out from time to time. My dad says he is trying to forget the war, but I think maybe Grandpa is doing his best to drive Birdie crazy. His way of trying to get her in the grave a little sooner so he might have a year or two of peace before his time.

I been here for less than an hour and already I'm itching to get outside and play. I supposed to be doing as mom told me and showing some manners before I go "blastin out the door." I try and pass a few minutes without inhaling too much. The house always smells musty, as though the inside has never been aired. Not to mention Grandpa's old man ointments. And then there's Yella Dog. The flee-bitten hound is always lying around somewhere on the floor, scratching and licking himself in places where it ain't decent. Birdie must've been in a generous mood the day she let Grandpa bring that old flea bag home.

The wood floor is heavily worn and covered with dog hair. My eyes are itchin'. They always itch when I'm here. Dad once joked that the only purpose Birdie had for a broom was to fly to midnight covens. Whatever that means. She sure didn't use 'em to sweep. I try passing a few more minutes by counting the gaps between the floorboards, stopping to inspect the insect legs and flecks of old beetle heads gummed up in the cracks. And then it happened: The old cuckoo clock on the wall pops its little door and the faded, yellow cuckoo with a busted red beak shoots out on its perch and starts a-rattlin' on despite it's still three minutes before the hour.

I hate that clock. The only good thing about it is that every time the bird comes out means one less hour until my parents come back for me.

It's always a long two days, and the only part of summer I dread.

"I'm going out to play now!" I yell, running passed Grandpa on the couch, and making headway for the front screen door.

"Wait a doggone minute!" I hear Birdie say from the kitchen. Slowly, I turn. She comes into the living room with a dough roller in her hand, shaking it like she's thinking about clobbering me. "Don't go over the hill, you hear?" Her faded, gray eyes remind me of dirty dish-water. "Don't go messin round that ol' house."

"I won't," I tell her.

She lowers the dough roller and walks off, mumbling to herself.

I turn back to the screen door. From here I can see the trees beckoning me to come climb them. It's as if the swaying branches were waving me to safety. Get out of there, I imagine the trees saying to me; come out here where you can breathe and play.

The grass is slightly browned from the scorching sun, and the afternoon bugs are busy hopping through the patches of dandelions. I find myself wishing I had a set of insect wings; I could fly away, climb the sky, and never come back down. But my dreams are shattered by Birdie's congested wheezing; the witch had snuck-up behind me.

"I got supper on the stove, so don't be out where I can't holler for you," she growled.

"Yes, Ma'am."

"Don't know why you young-uns can't sit still and be fit for comp'ny. Always runnin round like you're born in a doggone zoo."

With my nose still pressed against the screen door, I feel Birdie's hard fingernails dig in my shoulder. She yanks me round, and I stand firm, staring into the tar pits of her eyes.

"Back when I was a young'un," she said, slightly shaking me by the shoulder, "I didn't have time for wastin'. I had to churn butter, milk the cows, warsh the laundry, and cook supper for the entire family. Let me see them hands of yours, boy." She grabbed my wrist and pried open my fingers. "Not a callous on em. Why, a boy ought to take a notion for working instead of goofin off all day."

I thought about making a run for it, but Birdie has a way of taking hold of me no matter how far off I get. She's got a reach long enough to be sitting in a carriage and hand-feeding the horse at the same time.

"Yes, Ma'am," I said, remembering my manners.

"Go on, now," she said, releasing me. "I got supper to finish. Just keep in mind what I said 'bout not getting off too far."

I was already out the screen door and jumping off the steps of the porch, dashing round to the side of the house. I heard the screen door slam against the doorframe. I was free at last!

Time to hunt for rocks. The bigger ones are getting harder to find every year, mostly on account that I've already tossed a heap of em into the stone well. I scour the yard, looking around the trunks of trees, poking around the base of the house, but wind up resorting to digging in the dirt. I finally find a rock about the size of a potato. I pull it out of the ground then bounce it in my hand, shaking off the dirt and a squiggling earthworm.

I run to the well, barely visible through all the weeds grown around it.

"Hello down there!" I scream into the dark hole. "It's me!" I turn my head to the side and listen as a hundred voices shout back.

Hello down there . . . It's me . . . Hello, down there . . . It's me . . . Hello down . . .

I cup my hands around my mouth. "Herman, you down there? I brought you some rocks!"

Herman Olive. He's a rock eater that lives at the bottom of the well. He's only an echo, but when I visit I try to feed him best I can. I throw the rock into the depths of the well. A couple seconds and then I hear a splash. "Hold on, Herman! I'll find some more for you!"

I run to the woods near the back of the house where I dig up several good-sized rocks. Pulling up the bottom of my shirt, I put the rocks in the makeshift sling. A bee follows like a curious, little brother as I run back to the well. Circling my head, I swat it and run zigzag, trying to get it away. It won't leave me alone! I stumble and drop the rocks to the ground. The bee lands on the side of the well. Standing up, I dust myself off, and stare at the bee with its wings whizzing and its little black head looking up at me. I look around and find a stick.

"Dern ol' bee. Go back where you came from!" I watch its antenna flicker on its head and then I come down on it with the end of the stick, mashing it against the side of the well. The bee curls up, its legs twitching, and I see its stinger jabbing the air. I mash it again then flick it off the well and into the grass. "Told you to leave me alone." I pick up the rocks, and one by one, toss them down to Herman.

"That should do you for awhile!" I holler. "I'll be back later to find you some more!"

Another fun thing to do is stomp dandelions. With my arms held out to my sides, I pretend I'm a B-29 bomber on the hunt for enemy bases. The yard is always full of dandelions, and I growl like an engine, swooping down, and pretending my feet are bombs smearing villagers into the dirt. There's not enough hours in a day to get them all, but after twenty or so minutes, I've done my best. Today's air raid on Birdie's front yard was a smashing success!

She hasn't called me in for supper yet so I go back to the well to tell Herman Olive my new idea: "Guess what I'm going to do today?" I shout down to him.

What I'm going to do today . . . Going to do today . . . To do today . . .

"I'm going to check out the ol' house cross the way."

The ol' house 'cross the way . . . Ol' house 'cross the way . . . 'Cross the way . . .

"Yep, I'm finally going inside to see."

Finally going inside to see . . . Going inside to see . . . Inside to see . . .

"I bet there's something real bad in there."

Something real bad in there . . . Real bad in there . . . Bad in there . . .

"But I can't let Birdie catch me or I'll get it good."

I'll get it good . . . Get it good . . . Get it good . . .

"I hate her."

I know you do. I hate her, too.

"Why'd she put you down there, Herman?"

On account I did what you're aiming to do. I went and snooped, and now she won't let me back out. It's cold down here. Real cold.

"How long you been down there?"

For years and years. Even before you were born.

"One day, when I get big, I'll come back and get you out of there, Herman. I promise."

I'd like that.

"I better go now. I want go see what's in that house!"

Be careful. Don't let Birdie catch you or she'll put you down here just like me.

"She ain't going to catch me!"

Ain't going to catch me . . . Going to catch me . . . Catch me . . .

I check the front porch to see if the old witch is looking and then hurry into the woods, sprinting up the steep hill that she told me to never climb. I gotta move fast afore she takes a mind to look out the window and sees where I'm heading. I get about a fourth of the way up then duck behind a big tree to catch my breath. I sit down and hear something rustling round above me. I look up and see squirrels leaping from tree to tree, legs spread like longheaded monkeys in the jungle. I'm distracted by something else behind me; something that doesn't sound like it belongs in the woods—something clumsy; something ruffling the leaves on the ground. I peek around the tree and get a glimpse of a shadow taking shelter behind a large tree. Can't tell what it is . . .

Getting to my feet, I run farther up the hill in hopes of escaping whatever's following me. If it's Birdie, I can surely outrun her. Unless she uses her evil magic on me. If it's Grandpa . . . Naw, couldn't be him. But, what if it's something else entirely? Something not from this world. What if it don't want me to see the ol' house, either?

I quicken my pace. About half way up the hill, I glance over my shoulder, but I don't see the shadow. Maybe I was just seeing things.

I hear it again, something moving about in the leaves. I see a dark shape moving between the trees. It's too far downhill for me to tell if it's a man or not, but I sure wish I had Grandpa's shotgun. I turn and charge up the hill. A branch lashes out at me from nowhere, slashing my cheek and I fall to the ground.

I get up, wipe blood from my face, and race to the top of the hill. From here, I can make out the rusted, tin roof of the ol' house. I dash down the hill, careful not to trip on the roots crisscrossing the ground like veins on the back of Grandpa's hand.

When I get to the bottom of the hill, I find myself snagged in briars. I carefully wade through the thorns, arms held up and bent at the elbows, walking slowly and listening as the prickers attached to my shirt rip free. I make it to a clearing on the other side and rub the itchy spots on my skin. I turn to the house. It sits in the woods, looking at me like a monster hiding under the trees from the sun.

The paint is dark gray, peeling in places, revealing weather-damaged wood underneath. The front porch is rickety and lopsided. The chimney bricks are all busted and scattered across the front yard. The whole top floor of the house looks ready to slide off should there come a strong wind.

Scary as it is, I know there's got to be something in there worth finding out about. Why else would Birdie be so worried about me going in there? Not like she's one to fret about a kid's well-being or anything. Maybe she has bodies in there? Bodies she killed from evil magic. Whatever's in there, I aim to find it.

The boards creak as I step up on the porch— groaning almost, as if my footsteps were knocking the breath out of the house. Somewhere behind me I hear the leaves stirring in the woods. Then I remember I'm being followed!

I tug hard on a board nailed across the front door of the house. It rips free, causing me to stumble backward. The board crumbles into pieces in my hands, and hundreds of termites scatter across the floor and fall between the cracks. I toss the broken pieces to the floor and look back at the woods. All I can see are branches, but something is getting closer.

"Who's there?" I yell. "Hello?"

No answer.

I turn around and push on the front door. It swings open, but there's little sunlight inside for me to see. My eyes widen and I slowly go in, waving my hands out in front of me so as to feel my way around in the dark. I call out my name, hoping to befriend any ghosts or goblins that might be walking near me.

I hear something clawing its way onto the front porch. I turn quickly, but the sunlight outside blots out any detail of who or what is coming after me. With my eyes squinted, I see a dark shape making its way into the house. It's big . . . whatever it is . . . Breathing heavy . . . Snortin' like a hungry pig . . .

Then I see it.

"Dern it, Yella Dog! You scared the bejeezus outta me!"

I rush toward the door and the dog runs out and into the front yard. "Go away! Shoo!" I scream, waving my arms in the air. "Get on outta here!" I jump off the porch and find a small rock to throw. "Go on back home, you no good flea bag!"

The dog is older than dirt, maybe fifteen or twenty years, who knows? Grandpa says it's on its last leg, sort of like he is. The dog's nose is half-rotted off, and it stinks to high heaven. The last thing I need is a fleabag, snortin' mutt drawing attention to me, but the stupid thing won't go home. All he does is stand there in the weeds, wagging his raggedy tail.

Dumb ol' dog.

"Go home. Go on!" I reach down and pick up a chimney brick and rear it over my head. "You're going to get me in trouble. Go on home!" I hurl the block at him, but he just stands firm, and the next thing I know the block smacks him right square between the eyes. I stare in disbelief as the old dog goes down, legs buckled and eyes rolled up without so much as a yelp.

I rush over to see if he's alive. I nudge him in the rump with my shoe, but the dumb thing won't stand up. He won't even move.

"Get up," I said, giving him another nudge. "Come on, Yella Dog, get up."

I see something white in the dirt. I bend over and see it's one of his front fang teeth. I pick it up and that's when it hit me what I done.

"I didn't mean to kill you, Yella Dog. Why didn't you go back home like I said?" My eyes well with tears. "I didn't mean to kill you. It was a mistake, Yella Dog, honest. I was aiming beside you. Just trying to scare you off was all. Didn't mean for it to hit you, but you should've listened to me. Come on, dog, get back up."

I can't leave the poor dog here, but I don't know where to take him. Can't take him back home; Birdie might know I had something to do with it. What about the house? I could hide him inside the ol' house, and if anybody happened upon his bones one day, they'd think he just wandered in to die on his own.

I look back at the house. If I didn't know better, I'd say it was glad that I killed poor Yella Dog. The way the wind is whistling through the front door, it might even be laughin about it.

I pull Yella Dog across the ground and up to the porch. I peek inside, only able to see a few feet ahead of me. The air rushing out is cold—much colder than I remember it being.

There's something moving in there. I leave Yella Dog on the porch and take a step inside. What's all that racket? I can't see. The air in here smells like old people, like maybe this was some kind of hospital years back that closed down but forgot to take out the dead. Another step and everything went silent. All I hear is my heart beating. I turn around. I want out of here, but I stop . . . My heart skips beats . . . There are eyes watching me from the porch! Whimpering . . . Moaning . . . Staring at me . . .

"Yella Dog?" My voice sounds raspy and high-pitched, as if I had something stuck in my throat. "What you doing up? Ain't you dead?"

Yella Dog's head is busted-up pretty bad, and I know, even being a kid an all, that he don't stand a chance at living. He wobbles side to side, trying to get his balance.

He must be one of them that's too dumb to die.

Cold chills run down my spine; boney fingers tapping up and down my back. I turn around to get another glimpse of the inside of the house, and I see it . . . I see what's been making all that noise. See what's been stinking up the place . . . I also see why Birdie don't want me snooping round in here . . .

I run out of the house and grab Yella Dog from off the porch. "Come on, boy!" But he falls to the ground, unable to keep up. Desperately, I drag him by the neck half-way into the pricker bushes before I realize my heart's pumping so hard it feels like it could explode. I can barely see through the tears streaming from my eyes. I fall down and look at my hands. Got blood on em. Yella Dog's blood. I'm breathing so hard I can't catch a breath. Can't feel the prickers jabbing into me. Blood all over my fingers, but where's the dog? Can't find the dog!

I look at the house but it ain't smiling back. It looks angry. Like Birdie's scowlin' face when she's got a switch in her hand. I can't get up. Can't get out of the prickers. The thorns hold me like Birdie's cold, hard grip. I'm stuck. The house caught me snooping, and somehow I know Birdie's going to find out . . . She'll find out and surely throw me into the well.

"Let me go!" I scream, as if the prickers were alive and listening—or was it the house I was pleading to? "Please, let me go!"

I hear Yella Dog whimpering somewhere around me. The blood on my hands feels like dirt. Was it blood or dirt? I can't tell. My body seems to come back to life, and I quickly stand up, wiping the tears from my face. I look down to find that I was sitting on Yella Dog. He tries to moan but all that comes out of his mouth is white, foamy stuff and red bubbles. I reach down and scoop him up into my arms, carrying him through the briars and up the hill. Every step the dog seems to get heavier and more like rubber. Every step I feel like I might fall backward and roll back down the hill and into the mouth of the ol' house. It'll chew me up. Swallow me whole.

"What do I do with you, boy?" I say to Yella Dog. His head flops over my arm. He's so lifeless. It seems to take me forever to get down the other side of the hill. I almost drop him several times, but somehow manage to keep him tucked against me. At the bottom of the hill, I stop and look to the well.

Herman . . . He'll know what to do.

After making sure Birdie isn't looking out the window, I quickly carry Yella Dog to the well.

"Herman!" I yell down to him. "Herman, I got a big, big problem!"

A big, big problem . . . Big problem . . . Big problem
. . .

"I hurt Grandpa's dog, and I'm going to be in trouble!"

Give him to me. Drop him down here.

"You sure, Herman? He's hurt real bad."

I'll take care of him, don't worry. He'll be fine down here with me.

"What do I tell Grandpa and Birdie? What do I tell them 'bout Yella Dog?"

Don't tell them anything. They know he's old. And old dogs sometimes wander off to die.

"But that'd be lying."

Just give the dog to me. He'll be okay. Trust me.

"I do trust you, Herman. I'll drop him down to you."

The splash was like nothing I ever heard in my life. A sloshy-thud. I don't know if Yella Dog died when he hit the bottom or if he was already dead before I threw him in, but I was glad to be rid of him. I didn't want to have to explain to Birdie and Grandpa. Now all I got to do is get the blood and dirt off my hands before anybody sees it.

"Herman?" I ask. "I got blood on me. How do I get it off?"

Put your hands in the well. Hold them out to me.

I reach over and do what Herman says, feeling something cold and wet brush against my fingers. When I pull them out they are perfectly clean. Even under the nails. No blood. No dirt. Nothing to make Birdie think I've been up to no good.

Suddenly, I remember the scratch I got on my cheek from the branches in the woods. There's nothing I can do, but long as I'm going to be lying, I'll just tell Birdie I tripped and fell, if she even bothers to ask.

I lean back over the well. "Herman, I got to go now. I better get inside before supper's ready. Take care of Yella Dog for me, okay? I'll be back in the morning, just soon as I can, okay?"

Don't mention what you seen in that house. Don't ever say a word about it to no one.

"I won't, Herman. Promise. I don't ever want to think about it."

Want to think about it . . . Think about it . . . It . . .

Birdie was a'waitin for me, of course—sitting in her rocking chair with a newspaper rolled up in her hand and a scowl on her face just like the one on the ol' house. Her glare almost got me to tattle on myself, but I kept my mouth shut. I sat down on the worn-out couch next to Grandpa.

As always, he was watching The Real McCoys. As if his bones were fixed with glue, he slowly reached over, picked up an empty tin can off the coffee table, and spat tobacco juice into it. I wince as the brown drool dangles from the corner of his mouth, and his old, pink tongue comes out to lick the juice. There's still a flake or two plastered on his chin, but I don't make mention of it. Figure an old man like Grandpa has a right to keep his tobacco wherever he wants it.

"Cornbread and beans are on the stove," Birdie said. "Meatloaf will be done drect'ly." She slithers out of the rocking chair; eyes focused on me. She then turns and walks to the kitchen.

I look over at Grandpa but he doesn't take his eyes off the TV set.

"Grandpa, what happens when old people get ready to die? Do they run off somewhere?"

He sits and chews for several seconds, leaving me unsure if he even heard what I said.

"Reckon some might," he finally mutters, spitting out another mouthful of tobacco juice into the can.

"If you ran off, where would you go?" I ask.

He shrugs his shoulders then leans back. "Reckon I'd head off to somewhere nice. Somewhere quiet, I 'spose."

"But what if you just died on the couch and you didn't have time to get up?"

He didn't answer—just keeps chewing his tobacco.

"Grandpa? What if you never made it to where it's nice and quiet?"

"Reckon I couldn't complain much, seein' as I was dead."

"Well, I hope you get to go wherever it is you want to go to, Grandpa."

He looks over at me, doesn't smile, but I can tell by the look in his eyes he was grinning on the inside. He knows what I mean.

Without another word, we stand up together and go to the kitchen. I let Grandpa lead the way. Birdie is pruning at the far end of the table, fingers drumming against the tabletop, and her eyes looking colder and meaner than ever. Her hair is frazzled and white as cotton, and I can see her chest heaving every time she breathes.

Two plates had been laid on a red and white, gingham tablecloth. The big'un is for Grandpa, the other'n is for me. Birdie don't eat. Least, not when I'm around, she don't.

"Milk went sour," Birdie mumbles, watching as Grandpa slowly made his way down into his chair. "Yuns'll have to settle for ice water. Butter for the cornbread is in the frigidairy. I ain't no servant, so yuns get up for yourselves."

"Can I have soda?" I ask. If I had kept my wits, I wouldn't have bothered. Asking Birdie for soft drinks or sweets is like asking a grizz'ly bear for a hug.

"You know the rules, boy. No soda after five o' clock. Stuff keeps you up at night, and I ain't about to have no kid traipsin' around all hours of the night, doin' the Devil's work. You just drink your water and when next you open that mouth, stick some food in it."

"Yes, Ma'am."

Grandpa is already hard at work digging around on his plate. For some reason he always scoops up his food and puts the fork in his mouth upside down. I decide to give it a try.

"Now look what you done! Gone and made a mess all over yourself!" Birdie growled. "Don't you have any manners, boy? The table ain't for making messes, it's for eatin'. Properly."

"I was just trying to do it like Grandpa does."

"You never mind him. Eat your food the way you 'spose to. Get with it, boy, show some respect in this house."

"Yes, Ma'am."

One thing I've noticed is that Grandpa and Birdie rarely speak to each other. As for Grandpa, I understand why he keeps to himself. Who'd want to speak to an old witch, anyway? Birdie's filled with nothing other'n ornery and meanness. I don't know why she won't talk to him, though. They always act like they're soured at each other. It don't add up why they're married. Not to me, it don't; but I guess marriage ain't supposed to make sense to a kid.

"I saw a big bee today," I told them while trying not to chew with my mouth open. "It had a mind to sting me but I got the better of it. I mashed it on the well with a stick."

"I've warned you 'bout tossing rocks down that well, boy. You get that thing clogged up and I'll bust your hide, but good."

"Grandpa told me last year he don't use it no more. It's good for nothin'."

"Boy, you best mind yourself or I'll have you go fetch a switch. And he never used that well. I did."

That got me to wondering. I always trusted Herman Olive, but this was coming from Birdie herself. I wonder how much she really used that old well? Was there anybody else down there with Herman? Besides Yella Dog, I mean.

"You don't listen, do you, boy?"

"I listen, Ma'am. You told me not to ever go over to that ol' house and I don't."

If Birdie's eyes were knives, they'd have decapitated me. My throat feels stuck. All of a sudden, I'm warm all over and I wonder if Birdie can tell I'm lying. I expect any second for her to get up and head for the willer tree.

I drop my fork out of nervousness. It clatters to the floor and slides under the table.

Birdie's eyes don't leave mine. "Pick it up," she demanded. "Less, you plan on eatin' with your hands like a derned heathern."

Carefully, I reach under the table and poke around for the fork, but my arm isn't long enough. I don't dare get out of my chair. In Birdie's mind, that counts for leaving the table without askin', and I know what happens then . . . I don't get to finish dinner.

"May I be excused to get the fork?" I ask.

"Go 'head," Birdie said.

I can tell it annoyed her. Everything annoys her. I push the chair back and get under the table to find the fork. I look around everywhere but it's not . . . Wait . . . I see it, but it's under her foot! Eating like a heathern don't seem like such a bad idea, after all.

I lift my head up from the side of the table. "It went under your shoe."

Birdie looked down and snarled.

I look under the table and catch her pressing her foot down on the fork until it's flat as a squashed bug.

"Well?" Birdie said. "You planning on eatin' your food down on the floor?"

Slowly, I crawl back up to my chair and stare at Grandpa. He acts like he don't hear nothing going on around here.

Birdie's face turns grim. "Where's your fork, boy?"

"Guess I broke it."

"You broke it? Come over to my house and start a'breakin whatever you get your hands on. Can't even eat dinner without you boogerin' up the dinnerware. Go to your room, boy! You can do without tonight and see how that strikes you come mornin'. And I 'spect that bed to be made up tight as wire when I come in."

"Yes, Ma'am." If I knew more about cussing, I might give it a go about now. Fact is, I never felt like cussing nobody before now. It ain't a good feeling going to bed hungry, but I reckon it's a heap better than having to sit here any longer with Birdie.

I get up and go to the guest room but before I close the door, I hear Grandpa say something to the witch. I listen carefully . . .

"You shouldn't be so hard on the boy. He's just a sprout and you push on him like he was a criminal."

"He ain't good for nothin' but getting into trouble all the time. That boy stays in this house, he'll learn to follow the rules."

I shut the door and sit down on the bed. I hate this bed. It's stiff and the covers are scratchy, but Birdie don't like me bringing my own blankets. She says it's rude. I just wish Grandpa would take her outside, round back of the house, and put the gun to her. The fiddle playing just ain't workin fast enough.

There's a knock at the door and I quickly pull back the covers and slide into bed. Grandpa opens the door. He stands there for a couple of seconds, scratching his chin, and for the first time in years I see a faint smile appear on his face. "I'm proud of ya, boy." He puts something on the end of the bed. I sit up and look at it. It's buttered cornbread and a bit of meatloaf wrapped in a napkin. Grandpa turns round and leaves the room, closing the door behind him. I hear him traipsing back to the couch, and I'm left wondering why he came in and said that.

"Thanks, Grandpa," I whisper to myself. After eating, I pull the covers over my head and go to sleep with the light on. One more day and my parents will be back to get me, and I look forward to going back home. I'll miss Herman, though, but I'll spend all day tomorrow with him. Feeding him rocks, of course. And before I know it a whole-nother year will go by . . .

***

I didn't know it then but that was the last summer I'd spend at Birdie and Grandpa's house. It's now been thirty years since. Mom and Dad came and picked me up early the second day, and I was grateful. School started and sometime not long after I lost interest in crushing dandelions and pretending to be airplanes. I found a new fascination in girls, cars, and growing up. Grandpa died during the winter of that year, but none of us went to the funeral. We didn't know he was dead until a month later. Maybe nobody ever found him? I like to believe that on one snowy day he just calmly got up from that dingy, worn-out couch, spat a mouthful of tobacco juice into his tin can, turned off the TV, and casually went out the front door to find him a nice, quiet place to lie down. He might've even taken his fiddle with him. That's what I like to believe, anyway.

As for Birdie, I don't know what happened to her, but I imagine she stuck it out in her home to the bitter end, probably sitting in that "doggone" rocking chair and carving switches from the ol' willer tree for a bad grandchild that never returned. Maybe she liked it that way, or maybe she was just too hateful to give a damn. Somehow I think she realized that meanness couldn't save her from the grave forever.

Never did go back to get Herman out of the well like I promised. Figure it's been so long now that he probably done forgot. Besides, somebody's got to take care of Yella Dog. I sure do miss him—good ol' Herman Olive.

I did keep one promise, though. To this day I've never told a soul about what I saw in the ol' house. I can remember it clearly. I also remember Yella Dog's blood on my hands and the slash across my cheek from the tree branch. I remember the way my heart was galloping in my chest as me and the dog lay in the briar patch.

The nightmares are so intense that I frequently wake up trembling, as if it all just happened yesterday. I remember it vividly and when that day comes when it's my turn to wander off to find a nice, quiet place to die, hopefully I'll have someone around to finally tell, and I might finally be relieved of the haunting memories of what I saw that August day in the ol' house 'cross the way.

GOODBYE, JAYNE

Jayne slumped against the armrest of the sofa. Sweat dripped from her chin and down between her breasts where it pooled in the wrinkles of her stomach. Her skin drained of color, and her legs twitched. Long, dark hair matted to the fixed expression on her face. Her hand tumbled down her belly and rolled over her thigh as she watched the curtain of blood come closing down. The show was over, and the warm, gray gun fell from her fingers and clattered to the floor.

HEART OF A GHOST

Forever we cry, forever we die

Forever we'll always be wondering why

Why do our hearts go to those who shove

Pushing us away and all of our love

Though, later in life they miss their mates

Hoping to repair the damage they create

Love is tender; but most often it's hard

Constantly keeping your heart under guard

Yet in the end what matters the most

If you love at all—and not live as a ghost

THE GREAT WHITE KIND

Dennis wiped the crimson stain from his upper lip. The wine tasted bitter in his mouth, souring his stomach, but he was convinced if he maintained a guise of sophistication it might just land him the night in bed with Kiki. Keep the conversation on its toes, he reminded himself; keep myself interesting. The night was young and there was plenty of time to screw up. Dennis had to tread quick but carefully on this verbal high wire. Put one lie in front of the other, he thought, don't lose balance.

The wine had been her idea, but it helped him walk the lie.

He hated wine.

"I'm a marketing relations editor for a European video graphics company," he said with boldness. He never blinked. Truth was he had lifted that bogus title the night before from the back of a video game manual. He thought it sounded impressive. It was a ruse to keep her from asking too many in-depth questions about his real life.

Kiki sipped her wine. If she had any reservations about him, she wasn't showing it. With her hands in her lap, Kiki leaned forward, her silver necklace glittering inside the V-cut of her black silk dress. She smiled demurely, taking the bait.

The candlelight on the table reflected in her eyes, her full lips glistened.

"Most of my trips to the States involve meetings with designers," Dennis continued. "I split my time between being a manufacturing quality inspector, and helping innovate audio/video production ideas. I get wined and dined frequently . . . grand hotels, best tickets to sporting events, box seats at the theatre—the whole bit. Depending on what city I'm in at the time—the job definitely has its perks. Sounds more glamorous than it actually is." Dennis waved his hand as if to dismiss the importance. But he wasn't lying about one thing: He was a professional in the world of video. Most nights he sat on the sofa with a bag of pretzels between his hairy legs, while staring at the television with a plastic, semi-translucent blue controller in his hand. His ambitions in life were far-reaching: Get to the next level. With Kiki it was no different. The dinner date was only a sub-stage to get to the level boss. Her bed.

"Odd," she said, managing to squeeze a word in between her sips of wine and his blatant bragging. "You don't sound European."

Dennis' right leg began to twitch just as it did when he was about to lose a final life. But this game was different. Kiki had just fired a barb of doubt, and there were no floating, rotating icons in the corners of the restaurant to "up-his-health."

Keep focus, fat boy, he thought to himself. Mess up and you'll be going home alone again. "I was born and raised here in the States, actually," he said with a quick wink. He kept direct eye contact with her, but his leg was getting more active. Don't knock over the table, fat boy. Calm down. He took a sip of wine and then placed his hand on his leg. He had to force himself to keep looking into her blue eyes and not glance down at her breasts. "Las Vegas," he muttered. "After graduating from University of Nevada, I moved to Germany, then to Switzerland where I found employment with a company. After several years, I was promoted to the marketing department."

He studied her facial expressions. The corners of her mouth didn't move; her eyes were steady, nothing demonstrated any sign of doubt.

He was good.

Kiki set her wine glass down between the salad bowl and the white, porcelain butter dish. She picked up a napkin and dabbed her lips. "No one is from Vegas, Dennis. People just move there."

Another barb. Was she leading him along in his lies, or was she simply taking a stab at humor? Rich girls are all alike. Dennis played it safe by ignoring the remark. "It's too hot in the desert. Everybody calls it a dry heat, as if that makes it any better."

Kiki's teeth were white as the porcelain dishes. Her smile was infectious, and it made Dennis think he might be getting somewhere with her. She showed no sign of wanting to leave.

"I once had to duck into a casino restroom just to wring out my boxers after a three-block walk." He presented a smile of his own. "There's nothing dry about that kind of heat. I knew then that it was time to get the hell out of that place."

"You're funny, Dennis." Kiki leaned back as the black-haired waiter delivered two entrées. He set one plate in front of her and the other in front of Dennis. He filled their wine glasses, politely bowed, and asked if they needed anything else. Kiki looked up at him with her usual alluring smile. "We're fine. Thank you."

155

Dennis noted she had spoken before he had a chance to answer the waiter. He also realized he needed to change tactics. Hadn't he read somewhere that rich-bitch women prefer a man with Donald Trump self-assuredness, but appreciate it when he loosens his tie every now and then? He abruptly changed the focus to her.

"What about you?" he asked, picking up his napkin and placing it on his lap. "Tell me about yourself. What are you into?"

He instantly regretted his choice of words. They reeked of connotations. He wondered if she had mistaken his meaning. She wouldn't have been so wrong.

Kiki had lemon-sole. Cutting the fish with her fork and knife, she held the utensils elegantly. "I sometimes experiment with a girlfriend of mine on her dinghy while she tells me shark stories. I love sharks. Mostly those great white kind." She chewed her food with a devilish grin.

Now both of Dennis's legs were bouncing. He was beginning to squirm. "Really? You mean . . .?"

Kiki nodded sarcastically. "Mm-hmm. I really do love sharks."

"I mean the other part. About the girlfriend."

Kiki put down her fork and took a sip of wine. "Never tried it. I don't see much use in playing with toys that I already have."

A hot flash rushed through Dennis's head. The conversation had swerved from uppity small talk to a head-on collision with Kiki's sexuality. Even hinting at it made his heart beat faster. His palms were sweating. He couldn't have dreamt that things would have taken this turn for the wonderfully unexpected. A secret portal had just opened for him. He had leveled-up.

"I'm joking," Kiki said, cutting her fish into bite-sized portions. "My sense of humor sometimes gets a bit twisted. A character flaw, or so I've been told."

"Oh, it's fine, it's fine," Dennis said with animated eyes. He thought it might be a good time to take a visual at her breasts. He could always blame his shamelessness on a character flaw.

"My friends tell me that my mouth gets me into trouble," she told him. She wasn't looking at him as he stared at her breasts. She kept her eyes on her plate, slicing the fish. "I used to try to watch what I say, but why bother? I mean, if I offend somebody, then so be it. They are only words."

She looked up.

"Oh, yes, you're right," Dennis anxiously agreed. He quickly looked away and toward another couple at a nearby table. They were engrossed in small talk.

"I didn't embarrass you, did I?" Kiki asked.

Dennis looked back at her. Her blue eyes were almost neon in the light. Sparkling like ice. "Not at all. I don't embarrass easily," he said. "We can talk about it. I really don't mind."

Kiki's expression changed. "Talk about it?" Her eyebrows knitted. "Talk about what, exactly?"

Dennis was faced with a difficult decision. Turn left and it would drop the subject back into the lap of mundane chitchat; turn right and he might come across as desperate. But he didn't want to talk small anymore. He charged onward.

"Well, with your toys, I certainly wouldn't need any others." He gripped his thumbs under his fingers, waiting nervously for her reply.

She smiled, showing her extraordinary white teeth.

"I'm sorry," he admitted. "I didn't mean that to sound . . . creepy . . ." Had he fallen off the high wire? Would she extend a safety net?

"I've been interested in sharks since I was a kid," she said, matter-of-factly, as if fish had been the intended conversation all along. There was no hint of enticement in her voice or expressions. No deep breathing, no licking of her lips. Her eyes were still sparkling, but she spoke to him as dryly as though discussing corporate marketing.

A safety net, he supposed.

"I wanted to be an oceanographer. I called them skin divers back then."

Dennis's eyebrows lifted. "Skin divers?"

"Scuba divers," she informed him. "I have no idea where I got skin divers from. Maybe it was just something in my head. You know how kids come up with their own weird terminology about things. I call them weirdities. Instead of oddities."

"Skin divers," Dennis repeated. "I like that."

"I've always been fascinated with ocean life. But especially sharks." She took another bite of her fish then swallowed it down with a gulp of wine. It stained her white teeth for a moment, reminding Dennis of blood. She licked them dry. "I would pretend when I was eating food that I was a shark attacking a sea lion."

"Or a skin diver?" Dennis said.

She nodded. "Or a skin diver. My friends thought I was weird."

Dennis took a bite of his food and swallowed. "I don't find it weird. I guess we all have our little idiosyncrasies. Our weirdities, as you call them."

"So, what's yours?" Kiki asked. "What's your weird thing in life?"

Dennis had ordered a filet mignon. They had cooked it a bit dry for his taste, but he ate it without complaint.

He thought for a long moment, deciding whether he should make up another lie to impress her. He opted for the truth, however, figuring what's the harm in revealing a little of himself. His weirdity wasn't something he did every day, but it was humorous to say the least. Not too unlike eating fantasy skin divers.

"Oh, come on," Kiki urged. "You've got to do something. Everybody has a quirk or two. What's yours?"

"Well," Dennis said, still unsure if he should reveal his thoughts, "mine's sort of embarrassing."

"I thought you said you didn't get embarrassed easily?"

"Not easily," he said. "But this is umm . . . different."

"Try me."

Dennis opened his mouth to speak, but before he could get out the words the black-haired waiter came back to the table. He asked if everything was alright. Kiki nodded. Rich bitches liked to feel in control.

She immediately pressed Dennis again. "You going to tell me? What's your quirk?"

"It has to do with bathrooms," Dennis told her. His face went red.

"You mean the bathroom itself, or what happens in the bathroom?" she asked.

"Both."

"Explain."

Dennis swallowed. "Well . . . sometimes, but I haven't done it in a really long time, I get sort of paranoid when I have to . . . you know . . . go to the bathroom. Nature's call." He took a sip of wine. His head felt hot

159

again, but this time it wasn't from excitement. The conversation had now veered off the path of elation to that of late-night campfire talk. "When I sit down on the commode, I feel like somebody is watching me. Watching me through the light switch or an electrical outlet. So before I can do my business, I have to take a small screwdriver and take off the plastic panels to make sure nobody is looking from behind them."

Kiki kept chewing her food. She remained expressionless.

"So that's it. That's my weird thing."

She swallowed and patted her mouth with the napkin. "You're kidding, right? You really do that?"

"Not in a long, long time," Dennis said. He looked back to the couple at the table close by. Whatever they were talking about he wished he was now a part of it. He felt about as dried-out as his steak.

"Well . . ." Kiki looked down at her purse draped on the back of her chair. "When you're done, I guess we ought to pay up."

***

"Guess I sort of blew it back there, huh?" Dennis said, opening the car door for Kiki.

The night air was chilly, but not enough to cool down the heat in Dennis' head. His heart had gone from pounding to flat line. He felt as dead as the fish on Kiki's plate.

"Depends on what you mean," she replied. Kiki got comfortable in the passenger seat, strapped her seatbelt, and waited as Dennis walked around to get in the other side. He slid into the driver's seat and started the car.

"For another date." His voice was weak, as though he half expected her to laugh at the thought.

"Why do you say that? Are you ready to go home?"

He looked over at her.

"I thought we could hang at my place for a little while." She smiled again. Her white teeth seemed to glow as brightly as they did from the candlelight. "We can have a couple drinks and talk about more weirdness."

Dennis' leg began to bounce.

***

Kiki's house was located on a dead end of a ritzy neighborhood, shrouded in a thick plot of trees. Dennis drove the car up a winding, brick-driveway, following the subdued lights on either side. At the top of the slight incline, Dennis pulled onto the plaza in front of the house. He left the motor running.

"It's huge!" he almost gasped.

"Architecture is another longtime appreciation of mine," Kiki replied. She released her seatbelt, letting it slide back into place beside her seat. "My father was a well known architect. This house was his last work before he died. He knew how much I enjoyed the ocean, so he decided to design his house with an aquatic motif. He put me on the deed, as the beneficiary of his estate."

Dennis cut the engine and got out. Security lights near the ground instantly came on, further revealing the uniqueness of the house. It was much larger than Dennis first realized. The walls were brown and white stucco, multi-angled planes giving the abode no particular shape. The roof was flat and bordered by gutters. Though the house appeared to only be one story high, the windows were set high on the walls. Under a green veranda, the beveled glass front door was aglow from the showcase lighting.

Dennis walked around the car to the passenger side and opened the door for Kiki. She stepped out with her purse in hand. Her slender legs were long and curvy. Her black strappy high heels complimented her red polished toenails.

Leading Dennis to the front door, she asked, "You do know how to swim, don't you?"

He looked at her incredulously. "You have an indoor pool?"

"Something like that," Kiki said, giggling to herself as she dug in her purse for the house key.

***

Had Dennis' eyes not been attached to sockets, they may have fallen out. He stood in the foyer by Kiki's side, marveling over the inside of her house. The walls were covered with Oriental gold wallpaper. Several Chinese paintings hung in black lacquer frames. An Oriental lamp was set on the elaborate credenza near the foyer. He noticed several sets of keys on the table-top. Everything looked normal except the floor. It was all water. Floating on it was a small blue and yellow dinghy.

"So, what do you think?" Kiki asked with her hand held out. The tone of her voice was such that she had already decided he would be impressed. Her blue eyes were wide and full of anticipation. The corners of her mouth were twitching. She waited for Dennis' response.

"Well . . ." He knelt and put his hand in the water. It was surprisingly warm and smelled as though it was saltwater. "I'm not sure what to say . . . I mean, wow . . . It's . . . It's different, that's for sure."

"As I said, father chose an ocean motif." Kiki grabbed Dennis' hand and led him to the small dinghy tied to a wooden pier. In fact, that was exactly what the foyer was, a pier . . . floating on buoys.

"Is the entire house like this? All water?"

Kiki helped Dennis into the front of the dinghy. She took the rear seat. "Everything's on pontoons, designed to float. Tables, the fridge, the stove, electronics, washer and dryer, the furniture, everything. Including my bed. It all took a little while to get used to, but now that I have my sea legs, I love it." She twisted around and started a small motor on the back of the dinghy.

Dennis scratched his head. "Floor made of water. An original and unique concept, I have to admit."

Kiki untied the dinghy and pushed off from the floating foyer. "There's a built-in filter below the house. Keeps the water clean. And salted."

Dennis leaned over the side of the dinghy and let his fingers drag the water. The dinghy wasn't particularly fast, but then he guessed it didn't need to be in a house and all. It was meant to travel from room to room.

"Why is it salt water?" he asked, moving his hand across the surface of the water.

"For Barney," Kiki said as though he should know already. "Which reminds me, you probably ought not have your fingers in the water like that."

Dennis looked back at her with a half-cocked grin. He was afraid to ask why.

"Barney's my pet great white shark. He swims around the house." She wasn't smiling. "So, you see, it might be good not to have your hand moving around in the water."

Dennis looked down at his hand. The last thing he wanted was to come across as being gullible, but then the idea of having his fingers bitten off by a . . .

That's impossible.

But he withdrew his hand anyway. "You don't really have a pet shark, do you?"

Kiki giggled. She turned the handle to the motor and the dinghy entered into the next room. Everything in this room, besides the floor, appeared as a typical living room: There was a davenport, a glass coffee table, and two brown, comfortable-looking chairs. They were all balanced on a teak float. On the walls were paintings—pictures of the seaside.

The room was mostly lit by lamps attached to the walls, but on the ceiling were several large chandeliers, lit by tiny white glowing bulbs.

"So where's this pet shark, now?" Dennis asked, scanning the water as if the beast might lift its head to see who its master had brought home.

"He's probably circling about somewhere," she told him, aiming the dinghy toward the floating dock.

It dawned on Dennis that something even more sinister might be lurking. Had the bitch brought him home to become Barney's dinner? A sort of take-home sharkey bag?

"What does Barney eat?" Dennis turned to see what Kiki's expression might be. He could usually tell a lot by a person's eyes.

Her eyes revealed nothing. Kiki guided the dinghy to the floating dock in the center of the room. The bow bumped against the side of a pontoon. She stood up to tie the nylon rope to a wooden post similar to the one in the foyer.

"Tuna and horse meat," she said as her expert fingers formed a single hitch knot. "And lots of it."

Dennis stepped out of the dinghy and onto the floating dock. "Where would you possibly get horse meat for a shark?"

"I raise them 'round back of the house. I have a stable and when they get fat enough . . ."

She let the sentence dangle, but Dennis was beginning to get the picture. She had a sense of humor, alright. She called it twisted. Yes, that was it. She was kidding. About the horses. About the shark. Surely, about the shark.

But there was no denying that her house would make the cover of any home interior magazine. Dennis spotted a large screen television in the corner. It was floating on a smaller-sized pontoon.

"Hope you have a remote for it," he said, nodding toward the wide-screen television.

Kiki looked at him blankly.

"It was a joke," he said, sitting on the brown leather davenport. He looked down at the coffee table. Books on art and architecture; beside them was the TV remote.

"Care for a drink?" Kiki asked, already heading toward a teak bar on the other side of the floating dock. "Wine, bourbon, vodka, gin. Name your poison."

"Bourbon," Dennis said as he looked around the immense room. He wanted to see more of the house but refrained from asking. He wasn't in a big hurry to meet Barney. If, indeed, there was such a thing.

Kiki came back with two, monogrammed bourbon glasses. She set them on the table and went back for the whiskey. "Father never got to see how it all turned out. He died in the hospital of pneumonia the same day the workers were pumping in the water. Strange day." She came back to the davenport, sat down next to Dennis. "Getting the home of my dreams the same day my father dies . . . How is that for luck? My father had the best architectural ideas in the world. He also had a knack of making them work." She poured Dennis a drink and then herself.

"A genius," Dennis added, still observing the room. "Who would've thought somebody could put an ocean inside a home. Sort of gives a whole new meaning to beach house."

Kiki smiled broadly. "I like you, Dennis. I enjoy your company."

Dennis reached for his drink. "Well, I like you, too—Kiki."

Her face was gentle, and the soft glowing light from the chandeliers glimmering from the surface of the water reflected in her eyes. "I'll take you on a tour of the house in a bit," she said, wiping her bottom lip with her pinky finger. She then took a sip of her drink. "First I want to relax a little. Talk a while."

Sure you do, Dennis thought to himself; get me drunk so you can feed me to your shark. He changed his mind before repeating it. "Where did your father go to school to learn how to design something like this? I mean, I can't imagine all the complications it takes to create something like this."

Kiki swished her drink around her mouth then swallowed it in one swift gulp. "It's not as complex as you think. Like I said, under the house are all the pumps and filters. The salt is regulated by a built-in computer, and Barney's poo is—" She broke out in laughter, slapping her leg. "I'm sorry. I shouldn't go into such details."

Dennis responded with a smile, though not as generous as hers. "It's not like I expected a fish to have a litter box or something," he said. "And what would the neighbors think if you took it out on a walk?"

Kiki laughed louder than she had all evening.

Wiping a tear from her eye, she continued laughing. "Barney's a lot of fun."

"Fun?" Dennis said with a raised brow. He took another sip of his drink.

"Sure. Everybody has a dog or cat. Maybe a parrot. Some people even have monkeys, but how many people you know have a pet Great White?"

Dennis followed her gaze to the water. The surface was dark. There were no ripples. Other than a slight rise and fall, the water was almost placid. "You're the first," he said.

Kiki put her hand on Dennis' knee. "One day I hope to make it two."

This suggestion was almost more alarming than had Barney himself emerged from underneath and bitten off his right foot. Was she hinting that the two of them might get married one day? Or was it simply a rhetorical statement, that one day she hoped to land a self-assured but open-minded man who could stand sharing a house with *Carcharodon carcharias*?

Barney was surely a beast to live with, Dennis presumed, but he had yet to see this grand specimen of exotic house pets. The water looked dark and mysterious, sure; but could it really be home to a predatory white shark?

Absurd.

"Barney," Dennis said, still glaring at the dark muted water, "he isn't like going to jump out of the water any minute and onto my lap, is he?"

Kiki gave him an awkward glance. Her smile turned up at the corners. "Barney doesn't jump. He patrols. He might break surface every now and then—with his fins."

Dennis smirked. "Sort of his way of flipping you off?"

Kiki playfully punched his arm. "You're not making fun, are you? You do believe me, don't you?"

"About your liking me or having a shark swimming around your house? A shark that eats horses that you raise in the backyard."

Kiki slid away from Dennis. Her characteristic smile formed into a frown. "You really don't believe me. You think I'm making it up!"

"I didn't say that." Dennis finished his drink and put the glass on the coffee table in front of him. "I didn't mean to come across as doubting. It's just, well; the whole thing is so unusual, for lack of a better word. I just never knew somebody could, or would even want, a shark for a pet."

It took Kiki a few seconds and a drink before she replied. When she spoke, her voice was gruffer than normal. "I guess some years ago having a dog inside your house might be considered out of the ordinary. My grandfather was a particular man, he would have none of it. Animals were meant for the outdoors. That was how he thought, but then he was what I consider old-fashioned."

Dennis was slightly taken aback by the harsh tone of her voice. Was she now angry with him? He imagined her at any moment snapping her fingers, and whistling for Barney to come for feeding time.

Dennis decided to play it safe. If he was to level-up again, he better not piss her off. And even if there was no shark, provoking Kiki might prove just as deadly. "I believe you," he said with as much assurance as he could muster. He wasn't sure if the lie came out smoothly, but judging by the easing of her eyes, he thought he'd done alright. "I'll have to say, though," he reached to refill his glass, "I'd probably prefer the horses to the shark. I never was much into man-eating goldfish."

Kiki smiled and Dennis could breathe again. At least for the moment. He raised his glass to hers and they toasted. "To a woman's best friend, Barney the shark."

CLINK.

Both swallowed their drinks.

"So why the name Barney?" Dennis' face grimaced as the bourbon settled in his stomach. "Seems rather gentle for such a carnivore."

Kiki ran her forefinger over the rim of her glass. She appeared to Dennis to be in deep thought, as though contemplating telling him the truth. "Bernard was my father's name," she finally said. Her eyes became misty at the corners. "Sort of my tribute to him."

Dennis touched her hand. "I'm sorry. I didn't mean to—"

"—It's OK. You didn't know," she interrupted. "Hey, how about that tour now? You want to see the place? Maybe we'll run across Barn somewhere. He's probably getting hungry, anyway. You can watch him eat."

Watch him eat, Dennis thought. Up close and personal. Sounds great. "Let's do it," he said, again unsure how his voice sounded. He hoped he hadn't come across as nervous, but truth was he was getting paranoid. It wasn't likely that Kiki actually had a roaming, man-eating guard shark in her house, but maybe it wouldn't take such a thing. Maybe *she* was the true killer with those big white teeth.

She stood up and went to the dinghy. After untying the rope from the post, Kiki held out her hand to Dennis. "And I do like you," she said with sincerity. "You have a terrific sense of humor."

Dennis looked to the bourbon bottle for reassurance. Could use a last shot, he thought; but instead went to the dinghy. That's when he felt it. A slight bump.

The dock began to bob up and down. Either he was drunker than he realized, or Kiki's goldfish was rubbing up against the bottom side of the floatation. Unfortunately, he didn't feel all too intoxicated.

Another bump and he feared that the float might unhitch from what was anchoring it. Dennis looked desperately to Kiki.

"It's just Barney," she said without concern. "Coming to say hi."

Dennis looked to the dinghy. Damn. I'm supposed to get in that puny thing with a shark in the water? Sure, maybe Barney was in some kind of animalistic alliance with Kiki—she did feed him, after all—but Dennis stood no chance. Would the shark tear through the bottom of the boat to get at him?

"Maybe you should feed him first," he suggested to Kiki. "If sharks are anything like dogs, they are territorial, but in this case I don't think he'll warm up by sniffing my leg."

"Oh, he'll be fine," Kiki said, confidently. "He won't bite."

Was that supposed to be funny? Dennis began to wonder. Maybe it was something Kiki liked to say to all her vict—umm, dates—she brought home right before the big splash. Get 'em drunk and in the dinghy, and then push them overboard and who would be the wiser? A perfect eating machine lived right below the surface. Nothing left for the police to find.

"Could we go see the horses first?" Dennis asked. He wanted to be sure they existed. He could live without another date with Kiki. This was not his game, after all.

"We'll get around to that," she told him. She had the look in her eyes: I am woman, you are man . . . you are my victim.

Predatory rich-bitch.

Barney began bumping the bottom of the dinghy. Though Dennis could not see any part of the shark, he didn't doubt its power. The dinghy rocked side to side, dangerously close to capsizing.

"Come on in," Kiki said nonchalantly, not appearing the slightest bit concerned the dinghy would tip over. "He's just showing his ass."

"It's not his ass I'm worried about," Dennis retorted, carefully stepping into the dinghy. His knuckles went white.

"Barney, cut it out!" Kiki shouted at the water as though scolding a mischievous child.

Surprisingly, the monster under the dinghy obeyed. A web of silver-white foam spread across the surface then dissipated. Everything became still. Dennis felt his heart beating. It sounded as though it had moved into his head. "I don't think he likes me being here," he said, too afraid to move. He sat ridged, his eyes darting back and forth, looking for the shark.

"That's silly," Kiki argued. She pushed off from the living room dock and started the motor. "Barney's just being frisky."

Frisky? Dennis wiped a bead of sweat from his forehead. Cats are frisky, not sharks. Sharks are fucking hungry.

As Kiki steered the dinghy toward the next room, Dennis remained silent and on guard. He did not want to appear fearful. With his back turned to her, he kept looking down at the water, while stealing glances at Kiki. Was she going to sneak up on him, maybe whack him on the back of the head with an oar? He couldn't get the vision out of his mind. He imagined himself floating face down in the water, staring at the most terrible jaws through a red, bloody haze.

"Tell me another weirdity about you," Kiki insisted. The thin whine and sputter of the motor echoed around the room, sounding as if it might die any second, and leaving Dennis to the mercy of the shark or its equally intimidating master.

Dennis contemplated. Weird truth? He didn't have anything to compete with hers. Kiki was the *weirdest* thing that ever happened to him.

"Well then, I'll tell you one," she said, directing the dinghy down a corridor.

Dennis looked up at the walls. They were decorated with elegantly painted portraitures. The glass covering the portraits were flecked with salt. He did not ask about the paintings. Were they of her ancestors? Family? Or more likely, victims?

It made his heart race to think he would likely have his own portrait in alignment with the others.

"I pretend I'm a shark when I am eating," Kiki told him. She kept the dinghy steady as it glided between the two walls. There were smaller chandeliers on the ceiling, reflecting light off the water. Dennis listened as she proudly revealed another weirdity about her. "For instance, if I eat an apple, I'll hold it up and pretend it's an injured sea lion. Then I'll move in close to it with my mouth, nudge it with my nose, and then take a bite. I'll move back, swallow, then come in fast for a full attack. I call it *flirting!*"

Dennis wasn't sure who or what was terrifying him the most, the shark or the woman behind him.

"It has to be an ego thing," she admitted. "Pretending I'm something bigger and stronger than what I really am. I think a lot of women secretly desire to devour the weak. A repressed curiosity. Ever run across a woman like that, Dennis? It has to come from the subconscious. What I'm not sure about, though, is what my subconscious wants to eat. Apples, sea lions . . . or men?"

Dennis became alarmed and once again turned to see if she was sneaking up on him. He managed to keep his voice steady. "I wouldn't know. Maybe you like to be in control of the situation."

Kiki grasped the handle of the motor. The dinghy moved quickly through the still water. Dennis spotted a room off the corridor. Kiki abruptly turned the handle and steered the dinghy into the kitchen. Dennis held on tightly to his seat.

Against the far wall of the room was another large floating dock. It was the kitchen with all the ordinary appliances. Next to a stainless steel table were four

173

appliances that appeared to be freezers. They were a shiny, lemon yellow color.

"Do you think I have an ego problem?" Kiki asked Dennis. She cut the motor and let the momentum carry the dinghy close to the float. "You don't think I have a power bitch complex, do you?"

"Power bitch?" Dennis felt nauseous.

Kiki laughed. "Ah, maybe it's true." Kiki stepped out of the dinghy and onto the floating dock. She tied off the dinghy to another post. "Guess all women have it. Men say we're all crazy, but I think that's just a nicer way of putting it. Really we're all a bunch of power-fiends fighting the urge to eat men."

Dennis wasn't sure whether he should stay in the dinghy or get out and plead for his life. Getting out might be playing right into her hand. She could push him into the water. But why hadn't she done it already while in the living room? Dennis pondered the idea of waiting until her back was turned. He could jump to the back of the dinghy, crank the motor, and get the hell out of this mad woman's paradise. He looked to the rope tied to the post. Forget it, he decided. The knot appeared as tight as his situation. Besides, I've never operated a boat in my life. What if I fumbled getting the motor started? Would she command her shark to seize me?

"Stay put," she told him, walking to one of the four freezers. "Just need to grab some yum-yums for Barney then we'll be on our way with the rest of the tour."

So much for seizing the initiative.

Dennis expected Barney to lift his pointed head out of the water, tongue wagging like some desperate, begging pup. "Aren't you a little afraid that if you fell into the water he might eat you?" Dennis asked. His voice sounded on edge. He cleared his throat.

"Barney, eat me?" Kiki opened the freezer, leaned over, and reached inside with both hands. She came out with an obscenely large chunk of meat wrapped in clear plastic. She heaved it onto her shoulder, balancing it with one hand as she closed the freezer door. "He wouldn't dare."

Dennis watched, amazed at her unforeseen strength. "Have you actually tried it? I mean just to see if he would bite?"

Kiki had a puzzled expression on her face. She couldn't weigh more than a hundred and twenty, maybe a hundred twenty-five pounds, Dennis guessed. Even in high heels and a sparkly dress, she didn't look to be troubled keeping that meat balanced on her shoulder. Power bitch . . . maybe. Barbie the butcher, no doubt about it.

She turned and dropped the meat on top of the freezer. "I'd like to believe that Barney and I have a sort of understanding." She went to the cupboard and retrieved a large knife. She held it up in a homicidal position over her head, letting the light gleam off the blade. She stabbed through the plastic as she talked. "I don't go swimming with him, mind you," she said with her back turned to Dennis; "I mean, why provoke nature, right?

Barney and I live in complete mutual respect." She stopped for a moment and set the knife down. Her back remained turned to Dennis. "Funny how a woman can get along better with a shark than a man." She tentatively turned to look at Dennis. "I'm not meaning you. Just most men. Speaking of sharks."

She picked up the knife and finished cutting the plastic. After pulling back the flaps, the frozen meat was exposed, dark and thick; parts of it covered in frost. There were bones jutting out the sides.

"Sounds like you've been married before," Dennis said.

Kiki either half laughed or half groaned. "Twice," she said, scraping off the frost with the edge of the blade.

Dennis wasn't sure what to say. Did he dare aggravate matters by talking about her past? He decided to let her lead this dance.

"They were both my fault," she told him as she yanked the plastic from around the meat. "The failures, I mean. Marriages. I wasn't ready for them. At least not to those two idiots. Carl, the first one, had no respect for me, or my family. He was always griping about my father, calling him a blowhard. Of course, you could just imagine how it would rattle me." She looked over her shoulder at Dennis. He was sitting at the front of the dinghy, stealing glances at the water, expecting Barney to be making his appearance any moment. "Then there was Karl. Yeah, I know, I know, what's the chances of that?" She giggled again, that soft, girlish chuckle one might mistake for innocence had they only known better. Kiki the man-butcher, pulling the plastic from around her dead husband. "He's not even worth mentioning."

Dennis began to focus on the meat. It wasn't human. Couldn't be. The bones were too big.

"Anyway, enough of all that ex-husband nonsense." Kiki dropped the knife to the freezer and picked up the meat. "I'd rather talk about something fun. Ex-husbands are like old trash." She heaved the hunk of horse meat into the water. "Best tossed and forgotten."

Dennis watched as the meat bobbed up and down.

"You want to see the rest of the house?" Kiki asked.

Dennis cringed—as if I have a choice? "Sure," he said, unable to take his eyes off the bobbing meat.

Kiki untied the rope and stepped into the back of the dinghy. She pushed off from the floating dock, started the motor, and headed toward the corridor. Dennis heard something behind him, something in the water. He did not look back.

(OPEN WATERS)

"So, what other weirdities do you have?" Kiki asked again, nonchalantly. It was as though she expected Dennis to have an archive of strange facts about him; an endless crypt of personal quirks to keep her ghoulish mind entertained.

Dennis looked back at her. She was inscrutable.

He didn't feel like talking about idiosyncrasies. Not with a shark in the water, not with Barbie the butcher sitting behind him. "Why do you want to know all this about me?" he asked. He didn't care how is voice came across; he was all passed that now. He looked back to another corridor before him, and more portrait paintings on the walls.

Kiki kept the dinghy steady, the handle of the motor firmly in hand. "After Carl and Karl, I don't care for boring, mainstream people. Just want to be doubly sure I never have another one."

Dennis rubbed his leg fretfully and cracked his knuckles. Was she sizing him up for a husband or Barney's near-midnight snack? Were sharks as particular as women? "I don't have anymore weirdities," he told her. "Not that I can think of."

"Oh, come on," Kiki said. She jerked the handle, showing Dennis that she was in control. The dinghy careened and Dennis grabbed the sides.

"Please, don't do that! You'll capsize us!"

"Tell me, Dennis. I wanna' know another weirdity about you," she demanded. She jerked the handle the opposite way. The dinghy rocked to the other side.

"Stop!" Dennis gnashed his teeth. "There's a freaking shark in the water! Are you crazy?"

Kiki smiled and jerked the dinghy again, this time dangerously to its starboard side. "A little. But isn't every woman?"

Dennis breathed profoundly. "OK! OK! I'll tell you. Just stop messing around!"

The glimmering lights from the chandeliers revealed a slight grin on Kiki's face although Dennis wasn't looking at her. "In the shower," he said, barely audible over the humming motor. "I sometimes pretend the bar of soap is a bank vault door. I hold the soap in one hand, and have a set of tweezers in the other. On one side of the soap I'm an escaped prisoner hiding in this vault. On the other side, I scrape at the soap with the tweezers, pretending to be a police squad breaking through. After a while the wet soap starts to dissolve and crumble, and the tweezers go through the soap."

Kiki steered the dinghy steadily down the corridor and toward a closed door at the end.

"So what then?" she asked, slowing the dinghy. "What happens after the police break through the vault door?"

Dennis shook his head and sighed. "I don't know, Kiki. It's just a crazy thing I do. That's all."

Kiki let go of the handle and the dinghy coasted to the closed door. "No, Dennis," she said. "Something's got to happen. I mean, how do you feel when you see the tip of the tweezers going through the soap? What is the first thing you feel?"

Dennis thought about it. "Desperation."

"To get out of the vault?"

"No," Dennis replied. "To get out of the shower."

"What kind of soap?"

Dennis turned and looked at her quizzically. "Why does it matter?"

"It matters. Because there are all kinds of soaps. Industrial bars; tiny, travel bars; fragrance-scented or the kind of soap your mother used to wash behind your ears."

"Thin and unscented," Dennis said, deadpanned. He folded his arms across his chest. He wanted away from this woman. Wanted away from all of them. Leave these heartless carnivores alone. He wanted to go home and play his video games. He wanted his sofa and a bag of chips on his lap, and his boring, predictable life back. That most of all. Predictable.

"Like the kind of soap you find in motels?"

"Yes, Kiki. Just like that."

"Do you use those so it doesn't take too long for the police to drill through?"

Dennis rocked back and forth in his seat. He stared at the closed door before him. "Right."

"But if you didn't want to be caught, why use thin bars? Why not a big, fat one?"

"I don't know, Kiki." Dennis stared forward, arms still tightly folded across his chest. He was exhausted from all the weirdity game.

Kiki was unrelenting. "So what did you do to make the police come after you?"

Dennis turned in his seat to face her. He dropped his arms to his sides. "Kiki, this is . . . I mean, I told you the dumb story. Can we please stop all this nonsensical interrogation?"

Kiki put her hands in her lap. The dinghy's wake slapped against the walls, making the small boat slosh side to side. She didn't say anything. She didn't have to.

"Nothing," Dennis insisted. "I didn't do anything. It's only a weird thing I've done in the shower. That's all. I never did anything to anybody, I swear it."

The corners of Kiki's pretty mouth turned downward. "How old are you, Dennis?"

"Forty-two."

"OK. You're telling me that in thirty-nine years— we won't count the first three—you've never done anything to hurt somebody? Not even once?"

Dennis let out a long breath. She was counting, huh? He smiled nervously. "Nothing criminal. I mean, I never stole anything big, never raped anybody. Never murdered, or scammed anybody's identity. Never done anything significant."

"And what is significant?" Kiki asked. "Significant to you, or significant to someone else?" Kiki stood up and rubbed her hands together. "Dennis, I think you are trying to hide something from me, and more importantly, from yourself. That's the second weirdity you have in bathrooms. And in both you're hiding. Trying to get away from someone. Could it be your own conscience that you're hiding from?"

Dennis sat, dumbfounded. He didn't know what to say. He raised his hands, palms open.

Kiki sat back down and pointed to the door. A pleasant look crossed her face. Her voice eased: "I'm just picking at you. Go ahead, Dennis, open the door."

He turned and looked at the closed door in front of him. He had to stand up to reach the handle. Had to lean over the bow of the dinghy. Had to lean dangerously over the water.

(STEPPING STONES)

She'd brought him to her bedroom. Despite his anxiety, Dennis felt a slight tingle of anticipation. He hadn't been in a woman's bedroom in years. For a moment he saw himself walking across the carpet, barefoot, with her leading the way to the bed. She was wearing only a black nightgown that barely covered the soft, pink flesh of her buttocks. He watched as she climbed onto the mattress, exposing herself, as her blonde hair cascaded over her shoulders. She pulled back the silky, white cover, and motioned for him to join her.

They kissed each other's necks and then their mouths. Forcing her mouth wider with his tongue, they briefly scraped teeth, but that only agitated their play. Dennis slipped his tongue deep between her lips where it was wet and warm, and his fingers did likewise below.

He felt himself getting hard.

"If you need to use the bathroom, it's over there," Kiki said, pointing to a door on the far side of the room.

And far was a pretty good description. Kiki's bedroom was bigger than the living room. In the middle was another float on pontoons supporting her bed, two chests of drawers, a hamper for dirty clothes, and a nightstand with a green lamp; and, of course, the mandatory dinghy post. Across the water, hanging on the wall in perfect view from the bed was a large, flat screen TV. The screen was black.

Round, gray stones—slightly larger than hubcaps and merely inches above the waterline—led from the bedroom float to the bathroom. Stepping stones. Dennis hated to think of having to relieve himself on a floating commode with a shark circling his ankles.

Kiki shut off the motor and drifted to the float. "Mind holding the post?" she asked Dennis.

Reluctantly, he stood up and did as she asked; keeping one hand on the post so the dinghy wouldn't drift away. Kiki made her way passed him and onto the bedroom float. She took the rope and tied it to the post then politely offered a hand to help Dennis out of the dinghy.

He had no idea what she had in mind by bringing him here. Was she planning to make love to him? Or would she tease him, get his heart pumping only to toss him over the side and into the water so that she could watch the blood spray from the comfort of her own bed? Was that her game with men? Maybe she got off on seeing helpless men in panic, thrashing in the water as her shark toyed with them.

Dennis had to think of something fast. An emergency plan. He could punch her in the face, if it came to that. Knock her out. Not that he had a thing for hitting women, but if faced with death, all possibilities were on the table.

As was a pistol.

On the nightstand, next to the green lamp, was a shiny, chrome revolver. So that's *her* game, Dennis thought; mercy at gunpoint. It crossed his mind to snatch the gun before Kiki could get hold of it. I could point it at her; make her take me back to the car.

But then there was something else on his mind. She had brought him to her bedroom. What if? What if the gun was for protection only? Would I be giving up a chance of making love with her? Anything was possible. Life or death? Death or a night of love-making? She might crawl onto her bed and play the weirdity game with him. He had some new ideas.

Barbie the butcher wasn't paying attention. She was fumbling with a TV remote, aiming it at the large flat screen on the far wall. Dennis watched as she pushed the buttons as hard as she does men.

"Damn it," she cursed, striking the back of the controller with the palm of her hand. "Stupid batteries keep falling out. I need to tape the cover or something."

Dennis had no desire to watch TV. His hand went down to massage himself. He stared at Kiki's ass. She looked amazing in that sparkly dress. Her legs were smooth and long. Her figure reminded him of an egg timer his mother had years ago; a small hourglass-shaped utensil kept on top of the stove. Three minutes worth of sand. He used to play with it obsessively, flipping it over and over, just like he wanted to do to Kiki on the bed.

"Good grief," she said, snapping the cover back on the remote. She tried the power button again and this time the TV flicked on. "You'd think after sending a man to the moon they could make a plastic cover that can stay in place." She looked over her shoulder at Dennis. "What're you up to over there?"

He smiled. "Observing."

She went back to working on the remote.

Dennis decided to take a chance. As Kiki grumbled about the state of defective technology, Dennis moved close behind her. He sniffed the perfume on her neck, and the sweet fragrance her shampoo had left in her hair.

She turned around. "They don't pay attention to— Oh!"

He stared into her eyes. She didn't flinch, but there was a look of confusion on her face. What do I do? Dennis wondered. He couldn't back off now, not when he finally had her under his influence. He put his hands around her waist and pulled her to him.

She put a hand to his chest. Dennis let go.

"Well . . . *This* certainly is unexpected," she whispered. Her eyes were wide and her breathing fell deep. "Here I was thinking I was going to have to make the first move."

Dennis took the remote from her and dropped it to the floor. The batteries rolled out. He led her to the bed. Falling onto his back, she went willingly with him. Their arms became like tentacles, enveloping each other as they kissed passionately under the glowing chandelier.

The gun on the nightstand no longer felt like a threat, and neither did Barney the shark. Despite all, Dennis had done alright tonight. He'd leveled-up.

***

The dinghy was gone and so was she. Dennis sat up and wiped the sleep from his eyes. The TV was on. The volume was turned down. But where was Kiki? Where was that damn shark of hers?

Dennis threw back the covers, slightly startled to find himself without clothes. Sleep seemed to have put a barrier between last night and now, dividing his awareness from what had happened with what will happen. Was Kiki off feeding the shark, perhaps? Or was she getting it ready?

Dennis looked to the bathroom. He had to go. But the only way there was walking the stepping stones.

He got out of bed and searched the floor for his clothes. Where were they? He looked under the bed and the top of the bureau. What did Kiki do with them? Washing them, maybe?

Dennis approached the edge of the float and looked down at the first stepping stone. He stared at it for a long moment, deciding whether or not it was worth risking. With Kiki out of the room, could he not whiz right off the float and into the water? What would be the harm?

Fearing Kiki might come back in mid-action, Dennis decided to try for the bathroom. He took the first step. There was a good two feet of water between every stone. Not enough for a shark to squeeze between, but nevertheless threatening. One slip and Dennis would be in trouble. Pissing would be the least of his worries.

Halfway across the water and to the bathroom, he stopped and looked back at the float. He imagined himself and Kiki making love on the bed. The fog of morning hours made it seem so surreal, as though it never happened but only in dream. He was unclothed, it had to have happened. In his mind's eye, he could see the two of them together.

He smiled at that and continued across the water, walking the stones as carefully as he had his high wire act the night before at the restaurant . . . when he was lying through his teeth about being a marketing relations editor.

In reality, he felt like a cad.

The bathroom was the only normal thing about Kiki's kooky, aquatic habitat. The toilet rested upon honest-to-goodness carpet! Dennis hopped from the last stone and landed with pleasure to have his feet on something solid and not supported by pontoons. He immediately checked himself in the mirror. He found lipstick marks on his face and neck.

"She's probably in the kitchen making room for me in one of those goddamned freezers," he said to his reflection, wiping off the makeup. "Wicked bitch."

He finished his business and then stood at the threshold of the bathroom, looking out at the water. Great White sharks, he thought to himself . . . What's so fucking great about them?

The door leading to the corridor was open. He listened for the motorized dinghy but didn't hear anything. The only noise was faint voices coming from the TV on the wall.

What if she doesn't come back for me? I'll be stuck on that blasted float for who knows how long. His mind raced with all kinds of horrific thoughts: It's another game of hers! She lures men into her trap, tacitly allowing them to make a decision to die. They wait on her bed for hours . . . no, for days! They wait and wait, no food or water; do they choose to starve or take a chance swimming for the front door?

Every stepping stone seemed to possess its own nightmare. Terrified and trembling, by the fifth one, Dennis nearly lost balance. Wonder if she is filming me?

She's probably watching from some other room in the house. Laughing at me.

Dennis wanted a giant bar of soap to hide behind.

But what if there was no shark at all? She may have been lying, just as he did to her about his careers. He never saw the shark, after all. How realistic was it that her father could really design a house, no matter how large, to occupy a four thousand pound fish naturally suited for the ocean? It was ludicrous! This was all some terrible, demented game.

Dennis walked the stones with more confidence. As he approached the float, he was almost skipping them. "Alright, Kiki-girl!" he shouted to the ceiling with arms outstretched, fully exposing his nakedness. "You got me good! I admit! You can come out now, wherever you're hiding!"

He looked around the room but there was no sight of her. He listened again for the dinghy. Silence.

He sat on the bed, covered his privates with the sheet.

"I'm just going to sit here, wait you out," he said. "I know you'll come back."

He remembered the gun on the nightstand. He turned to it. It remained beside the green lamp. Was it loaded? Only one way to find out . . .

He got up and checked the chambers. Fully loaded .44 magnum. Big gun for such a small woman. Or was it meant for a man?

Could Kiki still be married? Was this some kind of twisted sex game, and her husband had been watching all along? Maybe from a camera somewhere? Dennis searched the ceiling and every corner of the room.

"The bureau," he said to himself, and went to investigate. He pulled out the drawers, rummaging through undergarments, jewelry, t-shirts, hosiery, and belts. No sign of male clothing. "Kiki!" he yelled at the top of his lungs. He pounded his fist against the top of the furniture. "Damn it, Kiki! Enough, already!"

He listened for any sound, but all he could hear was his heart beating in his chest. Combing back his hair with his hand, he sat on the bed, waiting for any sign of life besides his own. His mind was racing again. He reached for a pillow and threw it into the water. He slammed his fists repeatedly against his thighs. "Fuck! Fuck! Fuck!"

(ANGER MANAGEMENT)

An hour passed, and he got up from the bed. His stomach began to rumble. "Got to get to my car," he mumbled, standing up and pacing back and forth across the bedroom float. He looked at the flat screen TV on the far wall. A fast food commercial.

Dennis was tempted to start kicking and throwing Kiki's belongings into the water. If the power bitch wanted to play games then so would he! It occurred to him to fire the gun. He had power in his hands.

That would get her attention.

What would he aim at? The TV? The water? The ceiling?

Maybe she had left the gun in hopes he'd aim it at his own head. She enjoyed seeing men in torment.

"Not a chance," he swore. "You will not beat me."

He looked at the TV and raised the gun. The trigger was tighter than he'd expected, but the kick was right on par. The deafening boom echoed around the large room, the sound ricocheting off the walls. Dennis tried listening for the dinghy, but all he could hear was ringing in his ears. He tossed the gun to the bed and sat down next to it. The TV crackled and popped.

It took several minutes for the ringing in his ears to stop, but when it subsided he heard the distant hum of the dinghy motor. She was coming back! Dennis jumped up from the bed and stood at the edge of the float, his left hand clinging to the sheet protectively covering him.

Her eyes went from Dennis to the TV. "What in the world . . . ? You shot my TV?" As she pulled the dinghy up to the float, her eyes narrowed, her lips taut and white. "Why'd you shoot my TV set, Dennis? What the hell?"

"I—I thought you left me. I didn't think you'd come back."

Kiki sat in the dinghy, staring up at him. "I can't believe you did that. You wasted my new, wide-screen television!"

"I'll buy you another one; just take me back to my car!"

Kiki casually stepped out of the dinghy. She turned around and picked up a tray of covered dishes. "I made us breakfast. Thought you would be hungry when you woke." She looked back at the smoking television screen. "I never thought you'd do something like that."

"I was scared," Dennis said. "Is that what you want to hear? Is that the game? You like pushing men to the point of insanity; admitting that they're frightened? Well, I was fucking scared shitless! OK? Does that suit you?"

Kiki took a step back from him. "Scared of what? What did I do?"

Frustrated, he thrashed his arms in the air, and shouted, "First, you lured me into this . . . this . . . fucked-up house, then you tell me you have a shark swimming around! You bring me to your bedroom, make love to me, behaving as if it was something you wanted . . . then you leave me guessing where you are, or if you'll ever return!" His chin began to quiver. He was heaving. "And where the hell are my clothes?"

Kiki stood with mouth agape. The breakfast tray was in her hands. The dishes were shaking. "I never lured you anywhere, Dennis!" she shouted back at him. "You lured yourself. It all started when you told me all that bullshit about working for a European video company. Didn't think I knew the truth, did you? I'm not an idiot, Dennis! But you had no problem lying. I wasn't even going to say anything about it. Just let you live-out your pathetic, little fantasy. You said you haven't hurt anyone in your life. Nothing significant, you said. So my feelings aren't significant? I'm only worth a few lies to get into bed with, is that it?

Men, I swear . . . . And what else am I guilty of? Oh yeah, I'm guilty of being a good hostess, and cooking you breakfast." She hurled the tray into the water. "Fuck you, Dennis! You talk a good story, but in the end you're nothing but an egotistical, self-centered, frightened jackass hiding behind a bar of soap." She pushed him backward. "And that's for fucking me. Not in bed, but in the heart. I hope you're pleased with yourself!"

They stared at each other for what seemed to Dennis an eternity. She wasn't backing down. Not her style. Damn her.

There was the pistol.

Kiki walked over to the bed. Dennis followed her. "I need my clothes," he said anxiously. "Look, I'm not comfortable here." He watched as Kiki reached for the gun. "Please. My clothes?" He put his hand on hers. I just want to go home. I'll never bother you again, I swear it."

Kiki held the pistol in her hand. She turned it over. "When I was very young I had a little, brown submarine that ran on baking soda. You know the plastic kind you used to find in cereal boxes?" She checked the gun to see if it was loaded. "I tried it out a few times in the bathtub, but I wanted to go deeper. I found my father's tool box, took out a screwdriver, and opened the drain at the bottom of the tub. I tried pushing the submarine into the drain but it jammed in the pipe. So I put my finger down in it. Tried feeling around." Kiki walked to the edge of the float with the gun in hand. She looked down at the blue and yellow dinghy. "I felt something down there, Dennis. It was hard and round. I wasn't sure what it was at first, so I went to get a flashlight."

Dennis kept his hands over his privates. He looked at the breakfast tray floating on the water, moving alongside bits of yellow egg and soaked strips of bacon. Was Kiki going to shoot him, after all? Was she that crazy?

She raised the gun and fired.

"What—what are you doing?" Dennis yelled, running to the dinghy. "Are you nuts!"

She fired again, and again, emptying the gun. Her finger kept pulling the trigger, the hammer striking uselessly against the firing pin.

Dennis pulled at his hair. "I don't believe this! Now how are we going to get back? You shot the fucking boat!"

Kiki turned to him and smiled pleasantly. She tossed the gun to the water. "You'll have to go down and open the drain, Dennis."

"Down . . . where?" He pointed to the water. "Down there? No way! Fuck that! I'm not touching that water!"

"It's the only way for you to get back home, Dennis. The only way back to your miserable life."

Dennis clenched his jaws and stared at her for a few tense seconds. He rushed past her, pushing her aside, and ran for the dinghy, leaping over the front seat and to the back. Kiki righted herself and stood patiently on the floating dock, watching the desperate man struggle to get the motor started. It was futile. He tried several times before he noticed the dinghy began to fill with water.

"You're clumsy under pressure, Dennis," Kiki told him in a composed voice. "Clumsy hands. Clumsy lies." She watched him fight with the motor. "One big clumsy life." Kiki clasped her hands in front of her, scrutinizing Dennis. "How many women have you drowned with your lies? How many innocent dates turned into sexual chum for your predatory ego?" She smiled viciously.

Dennis continued to labor in vain. He cursed loudly, sweat dropping from his forehead. He pounded his fists against the defiant engine.

"Sharks will eat their own kind, you know," Kiki told him; her voice was annoyingly calm. Trance-like. "Sort of like men. They aren't too particular."

Dennis glared at her. His eyes widened. "You're insane, you know that!" He pounded the motor again, unrelentingly as if that would resuscitate it. "Completely whacked out of your mind!"

"Aren't you the least bit curious what I found in the drain?" she asked.

Dennis sighed heavily, lowering his head to his hands. "I wish you'd have drowned in that tub."

Kiki turned and slowly walked to the bed. She lay down to watch Dennis thrash about on the sinking dinghy. "I think we're beginning to see the real you, Dennis. Our true weirdities always come out eventually." She chuckled to herself, thinking back to her ex-husbands. "At least sharks are sincere creatures."

Dennis stopped and looked down at the water near his knees. He looked up at Kiki. Her smile was deliberate and threatening. He could see Barney in her eyes as she stood up and casually walked to him. He hadn't the nerve to stop her. He just let the dinghy drift away from the floating dock and toward the middle of the room.

"There was a little, plastic skin diver stuck in the drain, Dennis."

He shook his head in disbelief.

Something bumped against the bottom of the dinghy, causing the small craft to drift further from Kiki. Dennis shut his eyes and prayed intensely. He lowered his head and began to cry. He collapsed into the dinghy, and began striking the hull with his fists, "God, don't let me die like this . . . !" The dinghy was bumped again, presumably Barney, sizing-up his meal. The dinghy now spun counterclockwise. Dennis lifted his head and looked frantically to Kiki. Her countenance became dark, befitting a man-eating creature. The corners of her mouth twitched. Her eyes were bright and full of life.

She blew Dennis a farewell kiss, smiling, revealing those great white teeth.

SOMETIMES

Sometimes are happy
Sometimes are mad
Sometimes are better than other times had
Sometimes are fun
Sometimes are sad
Sometimes are love and that's not so bad
Sometimes are lonely
Sometimes are friends
Sometimes are arguments to see who will win
Sometimes are healthy
Sometimes are not
Sometimes are sickness all covered with rot
Sometimes are smart
Sometimes are dumb
Sometimes are finicky and drunken with rum
Sometimes are exciting
Sometimes are dull
Sometimes are patience in fixing the lull
Sometimes are hot
Sometimes are cold
Sometimes are wishes to somehow unfold
Sometimes are words
Sometimes are screams
Sometimes are hearts dancing around in our dreams

Sometimes are crazy
Sometimes are snug
Sometimes are creepy like that of a bug
Sometimes are great
Sometimes are wrong
Sometimes are sweet as a lullaby song
Sometimes are hellos
Sometimes are goodbyes
Sometimes are truths or the worry of lies
Sometimes are black
Sometimes are white
Sometimes are confusion that leads to a fight
Sometimes are smiles
Sometimes are frowns
Sometimes are funny when men wear nightgowns
Sometimes are soft
Sometimes are loud
Sometimes are things in which make us so proud
Sometimes are wants
Sometimes are needs
Sometimes are words in a soft spoken plead
Sometimes are bells
Sometimes are rings
Sometimes are you and the hope that brings

A GIRL TO DIE FOR

6:02 a.m.

Her name is Purpose. When I told my friends, they gave me a hard time about her name, but I didn't care. She has a use in my life; a function different than any other girl in the world. My baby is to die for and I'd gladly take her to my grave. She is special. For one thing, she has a flat, silver head. She may not be conventionally attractive—probably characterless and uninteresting to the average eye—but I was mesmerized the moment I saw her on the shelf.

Allow me to explain . . .

Purpose is a shovel. I bought her a week ago when I went to Harpy's Hardware to purchase a new hammer. Rarely do I admit my magnetism for tools, but Purpose instantly caught my eye as she was posed eloquently against the white pegboard on the end of the gardening aisle. Forgetting all about the hammer I'd come for, I took Purpose home with me and put her against the back wall in my garage. I closed the door, knowing I would be coming back for her later.

Later came sooner than I expected, and here we are sitting at the breakfast table together—she's propped against the chair across from me, gazing forward with her silver, sparkly face. I made us eggs and bacon, poured two glasses of freshly squeezed orange juice. I ask her what she wants to do today.

She sings to me like a dreamy poet: "I know the place where nothing ever settles, where the dirt is fertilized with the nutrients of metals. I know the spot very close to here. Carry me gently and I'll show you, dear."

Troubled by her words, I wince and tighten the drawstrings on my robe. I slowly stand up and walk around the table, picking up my store-bought sweetheart and taking her outside. Does the sun know where we are going? Through a patch of early morning clouds, it shines its light on me. I feel unprotected and exposed.

"You know and I know," Purpose sings to me, "where the spot is that we're supposed to be."

I know exactly—on top of the hill near the side of my house. I hold Purpose close to my heart as I walk, and I sing back to her: "Expressing my feelings, I'm not sure how to begin. But to tell you you're beautiful from head to stem. How do you know of my secret little spot, where I've taken my lovers to lay and rot?"

With her silver head against me she confesses to my madness: "I'm only a thing that's alive in your mind; a means to an end that you've longed to find. You've loved hammers, wrenches, and pliers for years, but buried them all to conceal your fears. You exhume them later and lick on the rust, kissing on spoons and scissors with lust. But in the darklight your conscious relays, deviant desires and the ways you've behaved. So take me yon up to this sacred place, where tools and utensils lay in disgrace. My function in life is to unearth a cave, knowing today I'm digging your grave."

HOPE

She was lonely and full of rain. She'd spend hours staring out the window at make-believe thunderstorms, hoping for a glimpse of someone brave enough to appear from the tempest to claim her dying heart.

. . . IN THE EVENT OF SKYGIRL

Grandpa's Face was the best place in the world to sit and watch the sun go down. Max and his father, Geoff, had given the hill its name due to a strange rock-outcropping on one side, resembling an old man looking up at the sky. "And the grass on top is his toupee," Geoff had told his son when they'd first come upon this magical perch several months ago. Since then, every Thursday evening they came to the hill to spend time together; father and son with a bucket of popcorn in hand, and silver thermoses filled with orange soda. It was to become tradition.

"Do you think Mom can see us from Heaven?" Max asked his father. They sat down in their usual spots in the grass. The sun was turning orange-pink on the horizon.

"If she can't it's only because God's light shines too bright."

Max looked up at his father. "Don't they have sunglasses in Heaven?"

Geoff put his arm around his son. "I'm sure they do. How else are all the moms supposed to keep their eyes on their children?"

"Why do moms die?" Max asked.

Geoff offered some popcorn to his son. "It's not just moms. Dads die, too, you know."

Max's lips quivered. "Are you going to die?"

"Some day, I will." Geoff patted his boy on the back. "But not for a long, long time. Remember, I promised I'd stay here with you until you're all grown up."

Max looked up to the sky. "I wish Mom would have made that promise, too. Then we could all sit on Grandpa's Face and watch the sun go down."

The early summer air was warm and a breeze lifted the hair on the heads of the two sky gazers. Geoff pointed to a cloud in the shape of a bear. "See that cloud there? I bet there are a hundred people somewhere looking at that very cloud."

Max took the lid off his thermos and took a sip of orange soda. He grabbed another handful of popcorn: "How do you know that, Dad?"

"Because people like to look above to the heaven. People are fascinated with what's beyond the Earth. It's always been that way. Since people were first created."

Max picked a blade of grass and began shredding it. "Why are people so interested with what's above them?"

Geoff took a handful of popcorn. He chewed for a moment then swallowed. "I guess it's because they like to see things they can identify with in the clouds. Animal shapes. Cars. Faces. Things like that."

"Cars?" Max said, incredulously. "But what about back in the cowboy days? Even they saw cars in the clouds?"

Geoff smiled. "No, son. They probably saw horses and carriages."

Max scanned the sky for other identifiable clouds. "That one—way over there," he said, pointing with his finger. "It looks like a girl in a dress!"

His father tilted his head. "I suppose it does. Or it could be a pinwheel."

Max strained his eyes. "I think it's a girl in a dress. A real pretty, fluffy white dress."

"Okay," his father agreed, "a girl it is." He pointed back at the bear cloud. "Think the bear will eat her?"

Max giggled. "Dad, clouds don't eat other clouds."

"Then what do they eat?"

Max looked confused. He thought for a moment. "They don't eat. They just float while God puffs them around the world."

"Guess I can buy that," Geoff replied, content with his son's answer. He leaned back on his elbows with legs outstretched in front of him, continuing to stare at the big pink sky. The horizon was hungry, swallowing the sun. He watched as God blew the clouds toward the East; all but two clouds, the bear and the girl in the dress. They weren't following the others. On the contrary, it looked as though the two clouds were coming in direction of the hill.

Geoff sat up straight. "Hmm. That's odd," he said, looking back and forth from the two clouds to all the others. The bear and the girl were definitely getting closer, defying God's breath.

"Dad, look!" Max said, getting to his feet. He pointed to the skygirl. "She's coming! She's coming our way!"

"I see that," Geoff agreed. He rose to his feet as the skygirl drifted overhead. She remained in place over them, her long, white-frilled dress flowing in the wind. The pink sky illuminated her. Was she extending a hand to the two sky gazers?

"Dad, I think she wants to touch us." Max's head was lolled back on his shoulders. His blue eyes were wide and full of wonder.

Geoff nudged his son. "Raise your hand. See if she'll take it."

Max did as his father said and lifted his arm. He opened his hand and as his fingers straightened, he felt something soft close around them. Skygirl was touching him!

Geoff looked to the sky behind her. The bear cloud was quickly approaching. Its wide mouth was peeled back, exposing a set of sharp teeth. Geoff instinctively reached to protect his son.

Max felt himself being pulled two different directions. As his father watched the bear cloud, Skygirl was lifting Max from the ground. Geoff lost his grip. "Dad!" Max yelled. "She's taking me away!"

Geoff jumped to reach for his son's leg but Skygirl had lifted Max out of his reach.

She turned to see the bear closing in behind her then looked down to the little boy's father. He was grasping desperately at the air; swaying his arms, trying to reach his son. "I'll return him to you," Skygirl shouted back to him.

Geoff stared up with disbelieving eyes. "Where are you taking my son?"

Skygirl looked behind her. The bear cloud was racing across the sky, its billowing-white legs thick and muscular; its rigid fur becoming a dark thunderhead. It gnashed its teeth and rain began to gush from its mouth. Skygirl looked back to Max's father. "I'm taking him to where the sun goes at night, and where the day hides the moon!" There was a strong sense of urgency in her young, feminine voice. "I'll bring him back between today and tomorrow. Meet me here. On top of the hill!" And then Skygirl lifted the hem of her dress and dashed across the sky to escape the charging bear. She kept Max nestled to her bosom.

Geoff sprinted with arms outstretched, but he couldn't keep up. The sky above him became foreboding, and threatening. The bear cloud flew by overhead, thrashing rain from the sides of its mouth. The rain stopped suddenly, as the bear passed, leaving the soaked and distraught father alone on the hill. He watched helplessly as his son was carried toward the diminishing horizon. Standing motionless, he felt a stark emptiness and began to weep.

***

Geoff wiped the rain from his hair and shoulders. With his head hung low, he began walking back to the spot where he and his son enjoyed watching the sun go down. The popcorn bucket was turned over, the grass littered with popped, white kernels. Geoff looked up to the sky. All the other clouds were herding toward a far corner on the horizon, trying to find somewhere safe from the preying bear cloud.

"Between today and tomorrow?" Geoff asked himself aloud. He looked back to see if the bear or the skygirl were still in view. He couldn't see them. Where had the cloud taken his son?

Geoff looked at the setting sun. He scratched the back of his neck, wondering what to do. He felt helpless, and so he sat and waited.

Waited eagerly . . . in the event of Skygirl.

***

Skygirl's grip was snug but not constricting. Max felt strangely comforted by her hold. He couldn't see the bear chasing them, but he knew it was there. He could hear it snorting thunder. Was it after the girl, or would it eat him, too?

Max looked down at the ground. The land was wrinkled patchwork as far as he could see. It looked to Max like a quilt had been thrown across the Earth.

"Don't be afraid," Skygirl told him. "We're almost there."

Where was there? Max wondered. All he could see was a cloudless sky and the patchwork ground below; and, of course, Skygirl's fluffy-white fingers around him.

"I hope you don't mind too much but I had to take you with me," Skygirl said. She was running but didn't sound out of breath. Could such a thing happen to a cloud? "I ran away from Barkus Snout," she informed Max. "He's the foreman of Triespion. That's where the sun goes during the night, and where the moon is kept during the day."

Max looked up to the skygirl's face. Her eyes were almost colorless, yet defined. He could see her pupils, a light shade of gray within a ring of white. Her lips were full, and her cheeks soft-looking. She was a young cloud, Max determined; possibly not much older than he. "I don't know what a four-man is," he told her.

"The boss," she said, glancing over her shoulder to see how far ahead she was from the bear. "Barkus Snout is the boss of Triespion. He lives in a trailer on top of a mud hill, looking down at all the workers. He won't let any of us out. We rarely get a break. We work night and day, fueling the sun, pushing it out. We have to haul in the moon, replenishing its dust. Night and day. Over and over. We never stop working."

"Neato!" Max said, marveling at the idea. "That's where you're taking me? To see where the sun and the moon come from?"

"Yes," she answered. "And to kill Barkus Snout."

Max was stunned. "Me? How can I kill the foreman? I'm just a kid. I've never killed a person before."

"Shh," Skygirl said, putting a finger to her mouth. She came to a sudden stop in the sky. "Voru Nuul." She turned to face the bear cloud. "He's been after me since I ran from Triespion. But maybe if you were to reason with him, he might leave us alone."

Max's eyes widened at the sight of the bear cloud. It was moving fast. Its body was almost completely black. Max could see lightning striking between its teeth.

"How—how can I stop him?" Max shrieked. He crawled down into Skygirl's hand to hide.

"You can do it," Skygirl said. "I know you can." She held Max out to the charging bear. "Talk to him. Tell Voru Nuul your name."

"But what if he eats me?"

Skygirl kept him exposed in the palm of her hand. "He can't eat you. He's a cloud."

Max wasn't sure if Skygirl was telling him the truth or not. Sure, clouds don't eat other clouds, but what about little boys? The bear had teeth and lightning in his mouth; but what choice did Max have but to try and reason with the monster? He certainly couldn't jump from this height.

He opened his mouth to speak: "My name is Max," he told the charging thunderhead. "Max Meadows. I'm nine years old."

The bear wasn't slowing. Its dark legs were charging full force.

"I live on Earth." Max pointed down as if the bear was unaware of the world below. "I know I'm not supposed to be up here, but I don't want to be eaten."

The bear's black, cavernous eyes narrowed on its prey.

Skygirl thrust her hand forward. Max looked at her with desperation then back to the bear. "Please, Mr. Bear Cloud!" he pleaded. "I don't want to be eaten! I'm only a child!"

The bear's eyes were fixed on Max and Skygirl.

Max tugged at her hand, trying to pull her fingers over him. The bear was almost upon them, its large mouth opening wide to a thunderstorm within. Max looked desperately to Skygirl: "Run toward the ground!" he instructed. "Straight down! Bears can't run straight down!"

Skygirl retracted her hand with Max rolled up in her fingers. She lowered her head and ran toward the ground below. Directly behind her, the bear snapped its jaws on the hem of her dress. Skygirl ripped it from the bear's teeth and ran as fast as she could, the wind pushing against her cheeks and whipping her long white hair.

Max closed his eyes. "We're going to crash! We're going to crash and die!" he shouted. He thought of his father on the hill. He thought of his mother in Heaven. Was she wearing her sunglasses?

Skygirl kept running. The ground was coming-up fast, but she didn't slow. Then suddenly, in midair, she slammed down her heels. Skidding through the sky, the growling bear rolled passed her. "Max, you did it!" Skygirl said, opening her hand so he could see the bear rolling head over end to the ground. The bear cloud slammed against the earth, evaporating into mist. Bolts of electricity crackled across the ground . . . then faded out.

"Bears can't run straight downhill because their claws are curved," Max exclaimed breathlessly. He watched the excitement on Skygirl's young, white face. "I read that in a book of facts my dad gave me."

"I knew you'd know what to do," she said to Max, winking at him. She climbed back higher into the sky, carrying the little boy in her hand, and heading toward the horizon where Max saw a huge, floating object.

It looked like steel, sliding doors built into the sky. Battered with rust, the doors looked big enough for the sun!

***

As Skygirl approached the massive doors, her hands began to tremble. Max feared she might drop him. "We'll have to move fast," she warned Max. She set him down in the sky and he was able to stand on his own. He couldn't see anything below his feet, not a simple house light. Everything was black. Skygirl caressed the door, wiping her misty, white fingers across the green and brown rust. "When Triespion opens, we have to make it in before the moon is pushed out. If we get caught between the moon and the door, we'll be—"

"—Squished flat?" Max said, touching the door with his finger.

"'Xactly."

Max didn't understand how such a thing as Triespion could be floating in the air. How did it remain out of sight from the world below? Skygirl kept rubbing the door with her hand as if that would somehow entice it to open. It seemed to be working. She pushed Max to the side as the enormous, steel doors began to part. Max peeked around her. He saw the silver-blue glow of the moon radiating from inside. His eyes grew wide with wonder . . . The moon was coming out!

Max clutched tightly to Skygirl's dress. "Why is it no one can see Triespion in the sky?"

"Because Triespion is always on the other side of the world," she told him.

"How can that be?"

"Well, if you were on this side of earth, looking up, then Triespion would be on the other side. If you were on that side of the world, Triespion would be on this side. It is on the other side of the world no matter where you are."

"Sort of like a reflection?" Max asked.

Skygirl looked down at him and smiled. "'Xactly."

As the moon was being pushed out, Skygirl pulled Max close behind her. Max was amazed at the sight of the moon so up close. There was a fresh coating of dust on its surface, craters deep as riverbeds, and mountains taller than skyscrapers. The moon rested on a vast cradle that was slowly and carefully moved out of Triespion on a moving track.

Max had questions—a million of them, in fact. Why wasn't the sun and moon in outer space where they belonged? Where were the stars kept? Did Triespion make clouds, too? Was he the only person in the world to know the truth about the sky? Did the astronauts know?

But as Max watched the moon move by him, he decided to keep his questions to himself.

Skygirl and Max walked carefully along a wall, sliding between it and the moon. A sudden jolt vibrated the floor. The moon tilted off its cradle and was dumped into the night sky where it floated freely, wobbling on its axis for a moment before straightening. Within seconds, it seemed to gain its equilibrium and began to drift away.

The giant, steel doors of Triespion slowly closed shut.

KA-THUM!

Sealing Max and Skygirl inside.

Max's eyes darted back and forth. The inside of the celestial warehouse looked like a giant, alien throat; everything was a sepia brown or darker shades of green, stained with splotches of black. Scorch-marks from the sun left the walls charred, and piles of excess moon dust lay on the floor. Large scoops, pushing the dust, were coming down the tracks toward Max and Skygirl. The scoops lifted the so-white-it's-almost-blue powder into large chutes set within the walls.

The ceiling of Triespion was miles above Max's head. He looked up and saw massive vents sucking in clouds of moondust.

"Mind your feet," Skygirl said, noticing Max wasn't watching where he was going. "You'll have to jump the cogwheels when they come out, or risk getting your legs cut off."

"Legs cut off?" Max mumbled. A moment later, Max saw what Skygirl meant. A huge cogwheel was sliding over the floor toward them. It had come out from a long slit at the bottom of the wall. The edges of the cog looked sharp, and like most everything else in this place, it was covered in rust. Max and Skygirl jumped onto it as it got closer to their feet. Another wheel came from the bottom of the wall, rotating counter-clockwise. Max and Skygirl jumped on top of it, riding it to the next cog.

"It's like we're inside a huge clock," Max said, watching out for the next cog to come from the base of the wall.

"Triespion is where time is manufactured," Skygirl informed him. "So in a way you're absolutely right. It is a clock. A clock in the sky."

They continued their dance over the wheels, heading toward the center of Triespion. Max saw other clouds at work. Some had human qualities about them, others were more similar to animals. He didn't see any that resembled cars or carriages, but all the clouds were hard at work either greasing the tracks, shoveling moondust, or using giant-sized wrenches to tighten giant-sized bolts on machinery that looked to serve some important purpose, but for what Max couldn't imagine. Smaller, less distinguished clouds were laboriously pushing wheelbarrows to and fro, their heads down and weary shoulders slumped.

Max heard a shriek. It sounded like a cross between a stuck pig and a screeching tire. "What was that!"

"Barkus Snout," Skygirl answered, keeping Max close to her side. "That is him shouting at the workers to work harder. There's no pleasing him. His demands are impossible."

Max covered his ears. Though he couldn't see the foreman of Triespion, killing him now seemed even more frightening. Max began to back away.

"Don't leave," Skygirl pleaded. "We need you, Max Meadows. You're the only one in the world who can end our misery. The only one who can kill the terrible foreman."

Max looked up at Skygirl. "But why me? Why not some other kid? Maybe somebody in the Army. That's what you need! The Army!"

"Because this is your father's dream, Max." She patted him on the shoulder. "And you're always a hero in your dad's eyes."

"My dad is dreaming all this?"

"Follow me, I'll show you." Skygirl led him through a circuit of strangely-shaped machines to a small porthole in the floor of Triespion. She knelt and pointed. "Take a look for yourself." She moved out of the way so he could see.

Max slowly approached the porthole. Dropping to his knees, Max looked down to the earth below. He could see a hill. "That's Grandpa's Face!" he said with excitement. He saw his father lying in the grass. The popcorn bucket was beside him, and the two silver thermos. And there was Max! He was sitting up and pointing to the clouds on the horizon, appearing to be so distracted by them that he never noticed his father had fallen asleep.

"How can I be here and there at the same time?" Max asked.

"Because Triespion doesn't follow the laws of time," Skygirl tried to explain. "We are neither in the past nor present. But on Earth, you have the sun to divide the days."

Max kept looking through the porthole at himself and his sleeping father.

"Your father's dream is making us miserable," Skygirl said to Max as he stared through the porthole. "You have to kill Barkus Snout."

Max looked up and rubbed his eyes. "But if my dad is dreaming this dream, won't it all disappear soon as he wakes up?"

"Yes," Skygirl said; she appeared saddened, "but to us in Triespion, it will seem like a million years while your father naps."

Max again looked through the porthole. He could see himself and his father on the hill. "I love you, Dad," Max whispered, running his finger across the porthole glass.

Skygirl tapped him on the shoulder. "Come. We must go."

***

A loud buzzer rang and all the clouds immediately tossed down their tools and abandoned their wheelbarrows and ran to their positions by another set of giant, steel doors. Max looked to Skygirl. She pointed to the doors as they opened.

"First the sun must be extinguished," she explained. "Once the flames are put out, the core must be scrubbed spotlessly clean. A new layer of flammable grease will be added, and after several hours of soak time . . . *ta-da*! The sun will be ready for a new day!"

Max watched as the giant core of the sun was pushed into position to be greased. Long, skinny rods came out from the walls. The brushes on the ends began to scrub the core, removing the previous day's black marks. The core was left bright and shiny as a pinball—a pinball big enough to only be in God's arcade.

Max heard the foreman's piercing orders.

"Greasers, get to work!" the foreman yelled. "Any cloud not working its hardest will be vaporized!"

Skygirl sighed heavily. "See how he treats us? He is relentless, Max. You have got to get rid of him for us before we are all overworked to death. If you can push him off the hill, the cog wheels at the bottom will finish him off."

"Like the game king of the hill. Except in that game nobody dies."

"'Xactly," Skygirl said, leading Max to where Barkus Snout resided. She pointed to a dilapidated trailer parked on top of a steep mud hill.

One side of the trailer was propped up on cinderblocks. A rickety porch appeared to be barely holding on to the front of the trailer. Three white lawn chairs were on the porch. One of them moved! Max squint his eyes . . . No, they were not lawn chairs. They were women with plastic, white strips for bodies!

Max looked to Skygirl for an answer.

"Barkus Snout's sun girls," she told him. "Good for nothing hussies."

"They look like lawn chairs," Max said, staring at them. And he began to laugh.

"Never mind them," Skygirl replied. "They won't help you. All they do is sunbathe." She pulled Max out of view of the hill. "What's important is getting you in close proximity of the foreman. And I have just the idea how to do it! Follow me."

She led him through a circuit of machinery. Behind a bronze conduit was a wheelbarrow filled with white fluff. Beside it was a bucket of grease. Skygirl scooped out a handful and offered it to Max. "Here. Smear this on."

Max took the goop and smeared it over his arms and legs. The vapors made his eyes water. Skygirl reached down to the wheelbarrow and grabbed a handful of white fluff, a cottony fabric that was used to disguise him as a cloud-worker. "I feel ridiculous," Max complained. "I don't look a thing like a real cloud."

Skygirl didn't reply, but ruffled the fluff stuck to the boy's body. She took a step back and examined him head to toe. "That should do the trick."

"So, all I have to do is push him down the hill?" Max asked. "Not shoot him or stab him or anything?"

"Just push him down the hill, the cogs will do the rest," Skygirl said. "But it might not be as easy as you think. Barkus Snout isn't easily fooled. You're going to have to find a clever way to get him off the porch and near the edge."

"What if he doesn't die? I mean, what if I push him down the hill, and he just gets up and climbs back to the top and pushes me down?"

Skygirl pointed to the floor. "The cogwheels are most numerous around the base of the hill. They'll chew him to pieces in no time."

Max looked terrified. Could he actually go through with it? Could he really sentence someone to death at his age?

Skygirl grabbed Max's hand and led him through the maze of pipes and machinery until they came upon a curious-looking cloud hunched behind a set of pistons. Skygirl jumped in front of Max to keep him out of sight. "What are you doing here?" she asked the cloud.

"Hiding," it replied.

Skygirl looked around in case other eyes were watching. "If Barkus Snout catches you, you'll be vaporized."

"I know, but I don't care," said the cowering cloud. It was in the shape of a cat. "I can't work anymore. I'm exhausted."

Skygirl glanced behind her at Max. She looked back to the cat cloud. "Can you keep a secret?"

The cat cloud barely looked up. "I'll be vaporized soon enough. I have no reason to tell your secret."

Skygirl stepped out of the way and exposed Max. The white fluff stuck all over him made him appear more like a human cotton ball than a cloud.

"What is that?" asked the cat. Its cavernous, white eyes grew large at the sight of the Earth boy.

"That," Skygirl said, "is our ticket to eternal freedom."

The cat cloud stood up and lowered its face to study the boy. "How is that piddly, little thing going to free us from the evil Barkus Snout?"

Skygirl's white dress puffed up. "I have a plan. What is your duty?"

"I operate a grease scrubber. That one—over there." The cloud pointed to a nearby console. "Arm number 883."

"Perfect." Skygirl took hold of Max's hand and led him to the console. "You're going to take over Scrubber 883," she told him. Pointing to a complex arrangement of levers and buttons, Skygirl stepped to the side so Max could get into position.

He looked in doubt after studying the console. His chin quivered. "How do I work it?"

Skygirl reached over his shoulder and tapped her finger against the faceplate of the console. "Just play with the buttons and levers. You'll get the hang of it."

"But . . . but I don't know what I'm doing." Max reached to the controls. "What if I mess up something?"

"'Xactly. We're counting on it," Skygirl said.

***

It didn't take long for Barkus Snout's ever-watchful eye to catch something going awry with grease Scrubber 883. He stood on the porch of his trailer with his arms crossed against his chest. The sun's core was moving slowly down the tracks. All the other mechanical arms were busy working as the clouds at the controls expertly maneuvered the long arms in careful sweeping arcs. Max's arm, on the other hand, was causing a major distraction.

Skygirl leaned close to his ear. "When he grabs you, don't put up a fuss. He'll take you to the top of the hill. Remember, you have to find a way to get him off the porch and push him down the hill."

Max began to tremble, his knees buckling— "He's going to grab me?" He turned from the console. Over Skygirl's head he saw a mechanical claw coming down for him, its three pincers gnarled as witch's fingers. The claw was on the end of a long, bending arm extended from the ceiling. The pincers snatched him by the back of the pants and lifted him high above the machines.

Max could see all of Triespion. There were hundreds of clouds working to grease the sun for a brand new tomorrow, but not one of them dared look up as the claw carried the Earth boy overhead. They were too afraid of getting distracted from their duties.

Other than the sun, Barkus Snout's mud hill was the tallest thing in Triespion. Max could see the run-down trailer on top. The sun girls on the porch were applying lotion to each other, eagerly waiting for the sun to be ignited so they could tan. Barkus Snout came from the trailer—his pig-like features offset by a protruding megaphone for a mouth. He immediately started shouting at the sun girls, and the cloud-workers, swinging his short, flabby arms in circles. He had a stubby, corkscrewed tail that swayed back and forth, and his skin was a discoloration of dark pink, black, and swells of blue-green.

When the claw lowered Max to the top of the hill the piggish foreman did not immediately acknowledge the young boy. "Keep the grease coming!" Barkus shouted to the workers through his megaphone snout. "I want tomorrow's sun to shine brighter than any day before!" He turned to Max with beady, black eyes. "And you . . . What is your kind doing in my domain?"

"I—I didn't mean to, Mr. Snout," Max stuttered, dangling a few feet from the porch. The claw kept a hold on the back of his pants. "It wasn't my choice. I—I was taken by a cloud. Up into the sky."

"You were, were you?" Barkus Snout snapped his fingers and the claw let go of Max. He fell to the porch. The foreman stood over him, pointing a stubby finger at the boy. "A snoop is what you are. A spying, no-good nosey snoop. I don't like snoops. Especially ones from down below."

Max sat up, rubbing his knee. "I'm not a snoop, Mr. Snout. I'm just a boy from Earth."

"We'll see about that." Barkus Snout pulled the boy's ear and dragged him into the trailer. The sun girls followed, giggling, and their curvy hips swaying as they walked. They helped the foreman sit Max in a chair made of wood—but it wasn't any kind of chair Max had seen before. The armrests came to life, turning over and grasping the boy's wrists, holding them firmly. Barkus leaned down to Max's face. "Can't have you going back running your mouth about what you've seen here. Triespion doesn't belong to your kind."

Max pleaded with the foreman. "I won't say anything, Mr. Snout. I promise. Besides that, nobody would believe me anyway."

The pig man's beady eyes seemed to sink further into his head. "What reassurance do I have? No . . . No, I'm going to have to dispose of you. Permanently."

Max squirmed in the chair, twisting his arms in hopes of getting free but the chair's crooked, wooden fingers only tightened.

"It's hurting me!" Max complained.

Barkus Snout smiled. "Good."

The foreman pointed to one of the sun girls. "Bring me some matches. We'll take him out on the porch and set him on fire." Barkus turned to Max; his megaphone mouth was inches from the boy's face. "Teach you to stick your nose where it doesn't belong." The sun girl came back with a book of matches. She handed it to the pig man. He commanded her to open the door.

Max sank against the back of the chair. He had to think of a way out, and quick. He pleaded for his father to wake up so this nightmare would end. But as he was contemplating his escape, the chair stood up, the four legs clattering across the trailer floor, toward the front door. Barkus Snout walked behind, flicking the book of matches in his hand.

The chair carried Max out to the porch where the boy could see all the clouds hard at work layering the sun with flammable grease. Max had an idea. "If I can prove

I'm smarter than you," he said, turning his head to see the foreman behind him, "will you set me free?"

Barkus Snout laughed, his plump body jiggled all over. "You? Smarter than me?" He walked around to face the boy. "I'll accept your challenge, Earth boy, but if I win I will set you on fire."

Max agreed. "But if I win, you have to sit in this chair and let me push you down the hill."

Barkus Snout turned and looked at the grinding cog wheels at the bottom of the hill. He looked back to Max, and his eyes sharpened. "You've got yourself a deal, whippersnapper."

The sun girls stood around the boy in the chair, giggling; their hollow bodies nothing more than long white strips with half-inch spaces between them.

"We get five questions each," Max said. "You ask me five, and I'll ask you five. Any question asked during the challenge—whether you mean to ask it or not—qualifies as one of the five questions."

"Fine. Suits me," Barkus snorted.

"The questions can be about anything in the world," Max said.

Barkus Snout leaned over and snarled at Max, shaking a finger in his face. "I can already smell your bones cooking, Earth boy." He stood up straight and rubbed his chin. "Who goes first?"

Max looked around at the workings of Triespion. The massive claw arms of the grease scrubbers reminded him of spiders, as though he were in a giant web with mechanical arachnids cocooning the flameless sun. The clouds working these bending appendages needed a break even if that meant the world below might go without a moon or sun. Max wondered what it would be like to not have day or night; nothing in the sky to distinguish today from tomorrow.

"I'll go first," the foreman said. "Seeing as I'm the boss." He paced back and forth across the porch, trying to think of his first question. "Ah-ha!" He walked up to Max. "The painting of the Mona Lisa . . . it is known for her gazing eyes and alluring smile. But what part of her face is missing?"

It took Max a moment to remember what the Mona Lisa looked like. He had seen it in his school art book, but never actually studied it closely. He closed his eyes tightly, trying to remember: what part of her face is missing . . . what part of her face . . . .

"You have to answer the questions within a minute," Barkus Snout said. He held the book of matches close to Max's face. "And to think that was just a simple question!"

Max continued to ponder.

"You have thirty seconds . . ."

Was it her ears, Max wondered—do ears count as part of the face? No, that's the side of the head. What about her nose . . . ? Or . . . could it be . . . ?

"Fifteen seconds," Barkus Snout said, tapping his foot excitedly.

"I know what it is!" Max shouted. "Her eyelids. It's her eyelids."

The foreman rubbed his hands together. "Absolutely, positively . . . wrong! It's her eyebrows! It was the fashion during the time that painting was made to shave your eyebrows. You have that one wrong!"

"Fine," Max said, "but now it's my turn to ask you a question." Max closed his eyes again and thought. "OK. Got it." He opened his eyes and smiled. "When glass breaks, how fast do the cracks move?"

Barkus Snout growled. "How am I suppose to know?"

"Because you're the boss, you should be smarter than me. And that's your second question, by the way," Max said with a deliberate smile.

"You think you're pretty slick, don't you? Think you can beat me with your petty trickery?"

Max shrugged. "I might not be the smartest kid in the whole world, but my dad says I'm persistent, and since it's his dream . . . So far, I *am* winning with my tricks because you only have one question left."

Barkus Snout pounded his fist against the back of the living chair. "That doesn't count! Those weren't real questions."

"The rule was *any* question counts."

The foreman stomped across the porch. "It doesn't matter. My last question will be impossible to figure out!"

"First, you have to answer my question," Max said. "Because you said we only have a minute to answer; now you have about twenty seconds left." Max smiled victoriously. "When glass breaks, how fast do the cracks move?"

Barkus Snout scratched his jowls.

Max rested more comfortably in the chair. "What food in the world never spoils? Do forest fires move faster uphill or down? True or false, a lightning bolt is five times hotter than the temperature of the surface of the sun? What is the longest word in the English language with all the letters in alphabetical order?"

"Hey! That's not fair!" Barkus yelled. "You can't do that! Asking me all the questions at once!"

"Sure I can," Max said. "You didn't make any rules saying I couldn't. You are the one who must answer all those questions within a minute. But your time's up for my first question. What's the answer?"

"What was the question again?"

"When glass breaks, how fast do the cracks move?"

"A hundred miles per hour," Barkus said. He looked sure of himself.

"Wrong," Max replied. "It's three thousand miles per hour."

"Poppycock!"

"It's true, look it up," Max told him.

The sun girls watched in amazement as the boy from Earth outwitted the foreman of Triespion. The pig man's nostrils flared, his face turning fiery red.

"Quit laughing at me!" he shouted at the sun girls. "This is a ridiculous game!"

"You needn't be so mean all the time," Max said. "Making the clouds work so hard." The living chair let loose of the boy. Max stood up and rubbed his wrists. "I don't want to kill you, Mr. Snout. Maybe we can make another deal."

"What kind of a deal?"

"You leave Triespion forever and let the clouds take care of the work on their own. That way you won't have to die, and I can go back to my dad, where I belong."

Barkus Snout grunted. "I was only making sure things got done properly. Doing my job."

Max patted him on the back. "I don't want you to die, Mr. Snout. You can find somewhere else to be a boss. But don't be so wicked next time."

The ex-foreman of Triespion lowered his head. "So what were the answers to your other questions?"

Last summer Max's father had given him a book about strange facts of the world. "*Honey* is the only food in the world that never spoils," Max replied. "Forest fires move faster uphill than down. And lightning bolts are five times hotter than the surface of the sun."

"Ah! I almost had that one," Barkus Snout exclaimed.

"You almost had two questions right then, because the longest word in the English language in alphabetical order is . . . *almost*. Oh, and I know this isn't one of the questions, but bears can't run straight downhill."

"Really?"

Max nodded. "Cross my heart. I even found that out for myself."

"I suppose you think you've outwitted me with your tricks and cunning. But I'm not going to let a little Earth boy get the better of me!" He grabbed Max and shoved him off the porch, toward the edge of the hill. "It is you who is going to be pushed!"

Max dug his heels into the mud but the pig man was too strong. "Please!" he shouted. "Don't kill me, Mr. Snout! We made a deal! Neither of us have to die!"

The foreman pushed with all his strength. "I've changed my mind," he growled through his megaphone mouth. "I . . . have . . . a job . . . to do." He pushed and shoved Max closer to the edge. Before he could send the boy over, something grabbed hold of his arms and legs. He looked over his shoulder to see the sun girls and the living chair behind him. The sun girls pulled the foreman into the chair. "What are you fools doing? Let go of me!" The chair clamped its crooked, wooden hands around Barkus Snout's wrists. "Let go of me this instant!"

The living chair held on tightly to the foreman as it ran down the hill. Max fell into the mud, looking up to see the chair flipping over and rolling to the grinding cogwheels. In the chair's grasp was the wide-eyed pig man, squealing and snorting to get out. It was too late to be let loose.

Max turned his head and covered his ears from the screams and sounds of wood and bones breaking. All the clouds of Triespion stopped what they were doing and gathered to watch the wicked foreman's demise.

The celestial warehouse quickly erupted with cheers.

Max stood up and wiped the mud from his knees. The sun girls stood next to him giggling uncontrollably.

Skygirl came from around two large grease tanks near the base of the hill. She had a proud smile on her puffy face. "I knew you could do it, Max Meadows!" she beamed. She fluffed her dress and walked toward the hill. "We are free now, thanks to you."

All the clouds applauded Max. Especially the cat cloud.

***

Max's father opened his eyes. His son was looking down at him.

"You're missing the sunset, Dad."

His father sat up and stretched his arms. "I have a feeling there's going to be a lot more of them, son. But then anything can happen between today and tomorrow."

Max pointed at a group of clouds clinging to the hem of pink light on the horizon. One of the clouds looked like a girl in a white fluffy dress. She seemed to be waving.

Geoff reached and put his hand on the back of his son's neck. He squeezed it gently. "You really are my little hero, you know that?"

Max and his dad sat on Grandpa's Face, watching the last sliver of the sun disappear, going to wherever it goes at night when it's the moon's turn to own the sky. The man and his son would come back next Thursday to watch it happen all over again—the rotation of day to night. They'd bring orange soda with them and a bucket of popcorn. They'd discuss strange facts of the world— why bears can't run straight downhill—and talk about Max's mother wearing sunglasses in Heaven. They'd also bring a dream or two. It was to become tradition.

SOMETHING & NOTHING

Something can be better than nothing. Nothing is often not very desirable; something is usually much better. Sometimes, however, something you get is worse than getting nothing, making nothing better than something.

Something and nothing can be good or bad, making something and nothing the same.

Doing nothing is sometimes better than doing something. Doing something can be tiresome; whereas doing nothing can be relaxing. Always doing nothing is not as good as doing something, making something and nothing the same.

Something can be changed, where as nothing cannot. Nothing is not possible of turning into something for it would no longer be nothing. Something can turn to nothing, but something could never be nothing, and nothing ever something, making something and nothing the same.

You can't get nothing for nothing, because nothing is nothing. But you can get something for something, because something is something. You can get something for nothing, and you can also get nothing for something, making something and nothing the same.

THE COSMIC SOIL

Fireballs and rain, earthquakes and dust
The Earth is born from dirt and rust
Pools of lava and volcanic delight
Chaos in the daytime, but so pretty at night
Swarms of currents whip through the air
Roiling in mystery of what goes on up there
God looks down and likes what He sees
A planet is forming just below His knees
It started as nothing, but grew up fast
I hope He still likes it, 'cause I want it to last
Continents drift and crash into the sea
Forming new lands that will support you and me
The Earth makes friends with the moon and sun
From this day forward, a partnership's begun
The moon has her tricks, and the sun does, too
Everybody is working to prepare for you
They bellow and roar, shifting tectonic plates
This is what happens when God creates

VIOLET FONDANT

Somewhere between midnight and dawn, I hear the battle raging. Tracer lights zigzag across the thick, smoky night air. The loud piercing screams from the enemies machine gun fire and constant shelling jar me from my unguarded position. Oddly, I can translate the machine gun sounds to melody. Seems I had a tune in my head since childhood.

I am beginning to wonder why I am here—trapped in this shit-hole of a place, pinned down by sniper fire on a desolate ridge called, 'Pork Chop Hill'.

By the strafing lights, I see shadows of my trench-mate, whom rarely sleeps. His name is Ricardo Salvatore. We call him Sal. A good-natured kid for the most part, but has a bad habit of getting into insignificant fights; his quicksilver temper from his Irish-Italian father, I presume. Rumor has it his boxing career was cut short because of some trouble he got into back home.

With only a few weapons amongst us, looks like we're going to get our asses kicked. All we have are our individual Ka-Bar knives, six M-1 Rifles (all but two are inoperable), and a single M-1911. During the night, we received orders from HQ to move up the hill to relieve the beleaguered Fox Company. We were trying to find our way in the dark, but we became lost. Getting separated from the rest of our battalion was bad enough, but most perturbing was the fact we had to abandon our bandoliers and extra boxes of ammo. We took all we could and ditched the rest. As far as the enemy knows— we are loaded with Browning Automatics; flame-throwers, heavy rocket launchers, and honest-to-god hand grenades.

We are pathetic soldiers embarking on a hopeless mission. In this god-forsaken bunker, we defend this heap of dirt from the Chicoms, who seem to be replenishing by the hour. Wearing thin steel helmets strapped to our chins, we wait. Wait for the next barrage.

Staying down keeps our bells from being rung by a bullet—or being annihilated by the incessant shelling. We hear the distant machine gun fire ricocheting, maiming and killing indiscriminately. Rats scramble for cover. I stomp one with the heel of my boot. Fucking rats.

"Care for a Belgian, Sal?" I ask him.

I watch as his facial expression changes from excitement to confusion. I glance down at his right hand and notice his fingers were shot off, blood pouring onto the ground.

"My God, Sal! Your hand!"

He looks down at his bleeding hand and shrugs, as if no big deal. "I got thirsty, we're outta' water."

He raises his trench-knife in his other hand as though preparing for hand-to-hand combat.

"What do you mean, Belgian?" he asks.

My mouth opens, but no words come out. All I can do is stare at this poor, fingerless bastard while he bleeds to death.

"Stop staring at me as if you saw some fuckin' monster!" he shouts.

We say nothing for quarter of an hour.

"Chocolates." I say, finally. "My girl sent them to me. She's from England."

Another long pause.

"Ya gonna' give me one, or what?" he blurts out. "I gotta' go home soon." He glances at his bleeding hand. "Ma'll take care of this."

"Sure, just keep your bloody nub away from me." Reaching in my mess kit, I pull out a small box of assorted chocolates. I pop off the cover. Sal, thinking it was an incoming, falls to the ground.

"It's just the box-lid . . . relax," I tell him.

"Oh." He grins at me. "I knew that."

I give him an English Rose wrapped in brown fluted tissue. "Take your pick. They're all delicious." I watch as he rummages through the box, demonstrating a keen interest in the Violet Fondant creams. "Good grief, man! Don't pick them out like that! Use your other hand, for crying out loud!"

"Sorry, sorry!" He pulls his bleeding stump to his chest. "I only eat the ones second to the bottom. Guess you'll have to dig them out for me."

I sigh heavily, rolling my eyes. I was reluctant to ask, but did anyway. "Why the ones second to the bottom?"

"Because the top ones could have your finger-stink on 'em. I know how you Texas boys are . . . lyin' around, scratching your asses—picking your noses and God knows what else. I don't wanna' eat ass-stained chocolates."

"Then what's wrong with the bottom ones in the stack?" I foolishly inquire.

"I can't eat those, either. Those are the rejected ones, always at the bottom. And you know how people are—someone at the candy shop drops a few on the floor, they'll hide 'em on bottom."

It is becoming unbearably hot. Leaning against the dirt wall of the trench, I take off my helmet to cool my head, wiping my forehead with the back of my hand. I breathe deeply. Sal is becoming very strange. His reasoning—unreasonable.

Exasperated, I dump the layers of chocolates into the second tray. I give him the remaining pralines. "There, stump away in there all you want. They're yours."

"But I don't want the bottom ones! I already told you!"

"Damn it, Sal! Then don't eat those! There's nothing complicated about picking off the top ones and leaving the bottom ones for the rats."

"But I don't eat the top ones, either. Only the—"

"Second from the bottom, I know." I toss him the second tray, and take back the first. "Do what you want with those," I say, impatiently. "I'll eat the top ones in this tray and all the little niggers at the bottom."

His eyes widen. "Wha'd ya' say?"

I felt a sudden thunderbolt of pain on my left jaw. Startled, I realize he had just slugged me with his fist. Stumbling backward, I hold my face. "Have you lost your fucking mind?" I shout at him uncontrollably. "You're a raving lunatic!"

He stands silently for a moment, glaring at me. The blood from his mangled hand is soaking the side of his pants and oozing onto his boot. Sucking in air, he stoops over and slowly begins to pick up the tray of scattered chocolates.

"Bandage that disgusting hand, will ya'? You're getting blood all over the goddamn Belgians!"

He bolts upright, and yells back, "I can't! I left the first aid kit on the truck!"

I grit my teeth and rub my jaw. "Well, just keep your bloody mitts to yourself then. Don't get near me!"

"What if I want more creams?" he asks.

"Then I guess you'll just have to eat the ones you have and stop belly-achin' about ass-bottom chocolates!" I shove past him and stride over to the opposite end of the trench.

Sal makes his way over to me. Apologetically, he offers me his wallet, and says he wants me to hold on to it for safe-keeping. "Ma's picture is in there. Don't want nothing happening to her," his voice trailing.

Hundreds of bright flares begin to light up the heavens. A cacophony of thunder, explosions, smoke and fire. I quickly crouch and cover my head with my arms, bracing myself.

Seconds later, dirt clouds, rocks, and metal fragments fly all around us and rain into our trench. Waiting a few moments, I raise my head slowly. Realizing I am okay, I give a quick look over at Sal. Through the dust and haze, I see his head, a ghastly mass of blood and flesh pocked with dirt and shards of metal. Gritting teeth, I grab my rifle and rise up from the trench. I begin to shoot wildly. "No goddamn Commies!" In a rage, I continue shooting until my rifle jams. I am left breathless and sweating profusely.

Sal touches my arm. "Think I'm going to lie down now and eat my Belgians," he slurs through broken teeth.

He spits blood and moves to the other side of the trench. Slowly, he sinks to the ground and falls over to his side.

His empty eyes gaze at the box of Belgian chocolates.

I go over and kneel beside him. I push him upright and lean him against the wall of the trench. I pull off my shirt and undershirt. With the white undershirt, I begin to carefully remove the larger pieces of metal from his head. Gently, I wipe the blood and dirt from what remained of his face and mouth. "You're a fine soldier, Sal," I whisper proudly. I pat his shoulder. "Don't worry, I'll tell your Ma."

I lay the box of chocolates on his lap, tucking his bloody, fingerless hand into it. Putting the lid back in my mess kit, I think—I've had enough of death and chocolate.

LOST IT IN A HOLE

Somewhere down deep I lost it
Somewhere way down deep
There, can you hear it?
Can you hear it softly weep?
It called my name out loud
But I did not answer back
I lost it a long, long time ago
Knowing I'll never get it back
I lost it before I knew I had it
I lost it in a hole
I tried to get it out one day
With a sticky, long thin pole
I walked away in sadness
Trying to forget its name
Now I am alone without it
I will never be the same
Remember that it lived inside me
It nestled in my heart
A hole in a hole in a hole
I sit alone now in the dark
Somewhere down deep I lost it
Somewhere way down deep
It is there, can you hear it?
Can you hear it softly weep?

SMALL LIFE IN THE BIG FORGOTTEN

The couch is man's best friend. A cradle of lazy lust, the couch is also a tomb for the small life—a dark, forgotten abyss for the little things that get crammed between the cushions. They are the disregards, the unimportant throwaways that once had purpose. The crevasses are left to a pen with no cap, a bit of old string, and loose change with hardly a hope of ever being spent. And what would a couch be without left-over food, last year's TV guide, and Aunt Martha's eyeglasses? An ex-sweetheart's silver earring resides in the abyss, but nobody knows how it got there . . .

What goes on underneath the soft foam and cloth might sound a little insane. Maybe it is, but it goes something like this:

"So sick of being down here," cried Pen. Her white, plastic body is stained blue from tears of ink. "Just wish I could be back between warm fingers again." She looked to her saddened friend, Nickel. "To think I was so important. Look at me now. Have cat hair matted around my tip, and my pocket clip's broken."

"You're still beautiful, Pen," Nickel said, trying to cheer her up. "At least you served Stanley well in your day."

Pen sobbed even more. "I tried to write that girl's number down for Stanley, really I did. I never meant to leak on him. I'll never forget that awful day. Stanley really needed me, too. He thrashed about his office to find me, and the whole time I was right under his nose. Under a piece of paper by the phone, crying out for him . . . Stanley, I'm down here! Down here, I yelled as loud as I could. He finally found me, and I was so happy. I felt at home in his big hand, but when he tried to write down that girl's phone number, well, that's when I messed everything up. My ink wasn't flowing yet, but I was pushing as much as I could. So much that I . . . well, I got excited and that's when I leaked all over him. He cursed me and hurled me across the room into the couch. I let him down, Nickel, and now I'm scared I'll never have a chance to be on his desk, or by his phone, or in that wonderful shirt pocket of his. I didn't mean to leak on him, honest. Oh, Nickel, you'll never understand. At least you're solid."

"Yeah, but it don't matter much," Nickel replied. "I'm still only worth five measly cents. Nickels just don't have the value they used to . . . back in the good old days. My great-grandfather, on the other hand, was an Indian Head 1916 Double Die—he would be worth over a thousand dollars! That is, if anyone could find him . . . .

As for me, I can remember a time when I was important. Back when people worked hard for me. Especially the little ones. The kids would do chores just to get me in their sweet, little hands to run me down to the grocery to trade me in for a comic book, or an ice cream soda. Didn't take long for everything to appreciate to quarters, then dollars. Who wants an old, worthless nickel? I'm not even worth a flip in a wishing well, I tell ya'."

"These are sad days," Pen said, "but I know I'm worth something. One day, I know Stanley will need me again. One day he'll find a new girl, with a new number, and he'll come down here to rescue me."

"Don't count on it," Nickel said. "He hasn't come down here for any of us. Face it, Pen, we're doomed forever in the Big Forgotten. And why would he want you, anyway? Like you said, you hardly have any ink left. It's gone dried all over you. You look like an old floozy—on a worn out mattress."

"How dare you, Nickel! I still have some ink in me. You can't see it, but it's in there. He'll get me out one day! You wait and see."

"Well, sweetheart, I gave up hope a long time ago. The only thing he ever claws around down here for is that damn remote control that he wedges in with his big ass."

"Nickel, don't you dare talk about Stanley! He can't help his size."

"His size . . ." Nickel sighed. "Good grief, Pen. He's a jerk. Besides, I'm sick and tired of being smashed by his fat ass, and you know how String feels about it all."

"String is hopeless," said Pen. "If there's anything down here that Stanley won't ever need is String."

"Hey! I heard that!" String shouted.

"I intended you to," Pen told him. "You're only three inches away."

String was not amused. "Yeah, well, Nickel and I are going to bust out of here. We're going to kill that fat jerk, aren't we, Nickel?"

Pen looked to Nickel. "Is that true?"

"It's true," Nickel told her. "I was going to tell you our plan. Face it, Pen, he ain't never coming down here for us, and why should we be stuck down here forever?"

"Nickel," Pen said, "I thought you'd have more sense than that. You can't kill him, anyway. Like you said, he's too big; how would you do it?"

"We'll wait for him to lie down on the couch. When he drifts off to sleep that's when I'll sneak up between the cushions and get him right between the eyes!"

"I'm ready to revolt!" String bellowed. "Down with the traitor! Crush he who forgets the little things!"

"Right on, String!" Nickel agreed.

"The both of you are crazy! It won't work, plus I don't want Stanley dead. I just want him to come get us. Put us back where we belong. I want our lives back—get back in circulation."

"I'm going to cut off *his* circulation," String promised. "Put that big rear of his right in the grave. He put us in this tomb; don't you understand that? He doesn't love us. He only wants the big stuff, the big expense items that can't get crammed down the cushions. He can't forget them because it cost him too much money."

"Nickel?" Pen asked. "You're money. Don't you think he'll eventually need you for something?"

"Five pennies is hardly money anymore," Nickel replied, sadly. "Besides, I'm old. Been down here a long, long time. I have no shine left."

"You would if you were polished-up," Pen said. "Stanley will clean you. I know he would. He could put us all to use!"

"Oh, yeah?" String said. "Then how come he doesn't? I vote to hang him and throw his carcass inside the couch and see how he likes it!"

"I won't allow it," Pen declared. "I love Stanley, and I won't let either of you hurt him!"

"When he lays down, I'm going to strangle him," promised String. "And Nickel is going to put in his five cents inside Stanley's fat head, going to wedge himself in his ear hole and plug-up his brain. Make him go crazy. And, Pen, you could jab yourself into his eye."

"I wouldn't dream of it," retorted Pen. She turned from her friends and scowled. "I told you, I won't let you harm him. I still love him."

"Shh! Both of you!" Nickel said. "Be quiet. I think he's coming in."

The small things in the couch fell silent as Stanley opened the squeaky door to his apartment. The light came on, and footsteps could be heard behind the couch. He was getting near. He went to the kitchen, rummaged in the cabinets and walked over to the living room. When he sat down, the cushion flattened and sprinkles of dust fell into the crevice. Stanley said something, but the throwaways couldn't make out the words. There was another muffled voice. A girl's soft voice.

"Who's that with him?" Nickel whispered.

String didn't know.

"It's a girl!" Pen shouted. "A new girl for Stanley!"

"Pen, stay quiet," String rebuked. "You want him to sweep us out with the vacuum and put us in the trash?"

"He wouldn't!" declared Pen. "He needs me! He needs me to write down the new number! He needs me!"

The girl sat down next to Stanley and Pen was squeezed between the two cushions. She rolled onto the floor, clattering at Stanley's feet.

He needs me, she thought to herself. The remaining ink inside her began to flow.

Stanley picked her up, blew off the cat hair from her tip, and put her between his fingers. Pen felt warm.

245

She was thrilled to be in his hands again. Stanley handed her to the new girl with the new number.

"Oh, no need for that," said the girl. "I have my own pen right here."

Stanley rolled Pen around his hand for a minute before stuffing her back into the couch. Her friends were surprised to see her.

"Pen! We thought you were gone forever!" Nickel exclaimed.

She was stunned; Stanley's rejection had crushed her.

"Told you he doesn't want us," String said. "I say we kill him tonight! Soon as he lays down and goes to sleep, I'm going to tie myself around his throat until his fat face turns blue!"

Nickel agreed. "It's the only way, Pen. Maybe someone will eventually come take the couch and find us. Someone who cares about the little things."

Pen's ink leaked from her tip. She couldn't stop crying. "I love Stanley, but I suppose you guys are right. He doesn't want us anymore. But I can't help you kill him. I love him too much. You guys do what you have to. I'll stay here and write his suicide note."

Q

Mr. Roundhead was a lonesome O that so happened to be a square. His boring, round circumference was much more than he could bear. He rolled along dishearteningly, stopping only to briefly see, a lovely letter called a W resting by a tree. But the W wouldn't budge and so the O sadly left. His bulging, boring circumference hindered by a slightly bulging cleft. He bumped and bounced down a hill, complaining of his back . . . a spine that went round and round; the alignment out of whack. At the bottom of the hill he saw a letter immediately surprising. Her name was Wanda Y, and she was quite enticing! She batted her eyes flirtatiously, calling him by his name. Mr. Roundhead was now very happy, he'd found himself a dame. She grabbed him by the bulgy circumference and rolled him inside her house where she began to tease him unmercifully by unbuttoning her blouse. Her arousing fingers made him giddy, and something inside him grew. Mr. Roundhead was no longer an O . . . now he was a Q!

Q

THE POLK CITY GOODTIMES
BLOODTHIRSTY THEATER

It's Friday night and there's nothing like going to a good movie. All the young punks of Polk City congregate at the front of Bernie Kickshaw's theater in hopes of seeing the movie; the same movie that plays every Friday of every month. With tickets in hand, the leather n' stud clad punks mingle and talk, discussing the brutality of last week's showing, and how they plan to beat it.

Bern Kickshaw had come up with the idea to give the punks their very own playground, so-to-speak; an alternative to the streets. The theater was a battleground, and Bernie charged for it. Six bucks a ticket. Not that this idea was popular with the adults of Polk City, but like Bern once told the local paper: "*Look at it this way, it keeps the gangs off the streets once a week. Gives 'em a place to do their thing.*"

And their thing was called shredding. Despite the naysayers claiming it a "*demented marketing ploy concocted by a crazy, ole schemer*", the Polk City Goodtimes Bloodthirsty Theater was a nose-smashing success!

Bernie's plan was simple: Play one movie (didn't really matter what), and if at least one member of any gang could watch the entire movie without dying, passing out, or just plain giving up . . . well, nobody was sure what would happen. But the idea caught on quick with the punks, and they came in droves to gain the coveted title.

Eight and a half months into the same movie and nobody has yet made it through. Not even close, but the challenge is exciting enough to keep the young punks begging for more. Ole Bern's cash till was running hot.

The remainder of the week was spent cleaning up the mess. The Kickshaw Gasser, Bern's nickname given by the townsfolk (due to his fondness for drinking), employed several pre-punk prepubescent kids to scrub the blood out of the seat cushions, sweep up the hair and teeth from the floor, and wipe the stains off the silver screen, though several permanent blemishes remained. No matter how rough the shredding was the Friday before, by the next weekend the theater always sparkled like a freshly buffed diamond. Ole Bern might be a drunken, old kook, but he really knows how to provide a good time. And the young, spike-haired punks thanked him sincerely for it.

Friday evening and Polk City's punks are preparing for tonight's big show. They gather in the parking lot outside the theater, some parading around shirtless with their chests pumped while others show off their spikes and chains to the tattooed girls who are too busy arranging their breasts behind metal plates. Some of the punks stand in semi-circles, facing each other as they take turns chugging bottles of hot sauce to inflame their fiery angst. One punk dribbles burning plastic on his friend's armpits; another finds perverse enjoyment chipping his teeth on raw coffee beans.

Jax Sliver doesn't do any of these things. His pre-show ritual consists of meditating on the trunk of his car with his scarred, Neanderthal-like arms crossed over his chest. His spiky, red mohawk rests like some kind of wild animal on his head, matched by thick, dark muttonchops; all he can think about is the violence. He ponders the punches and the hard head kicks. He thinks about all the broken noses and cockeyed jawbones. He relishes the thought of bruises, scrapes, cuts, and jabs. He dreams about the blood. Lots of it. But what he thinks about most are The Whippy Whippy Wild Women, his rival gang.

He bears his teeth.

Jax Sliver is the leader of his own gang, The Discombobulated Snaggle Tits. Second in command is Bump Froddy, a thick-jawed lunatic who carries a bloodstained tube sock full of nails. Then there's Lil Necro Ninny, a head stomping maniac with enough rings in his face to hang a shower curtain. Lilly Liver is a fat, loudmouthed drag queen with a spiked iron glove and a pink bodysuit. Hackle Snaps, a lanky black kid with bright green hair, usually makes a mess of things by slinging snot out of his ringed nostrils whenever he punches someone. Together they make up The Snaggle Tits, and tonight Jax is determined to make it through the movie.

Bernie Kickshaw was busy warming up the projector when the doors were opened and the young punks rushed in to take their seats. Bernie had one rule for the punks: No violence until the movie begins. The last thing he wanted was a massacre in the parking lot. Who'd buy tickets then? He hummed to himself as he fed the film through the projector, already contemplating his profits for this week's blood fest.

He pulled a microphone close to his lips. "Your attention, please." Bern Kickshaw tapped the microphone, trying to hush the audience. "Fine punks of Polk City, listen up. As we do every week, we're gathered here to watch a good movie. If there are any newcomers to the show, please stand up."

The audience looked around. No one was standing.

"OK, good," said Bernie Kickshaw from the projector room high above the rowdy punks. The tips of his mustache brushed against the microphone. "We'll skip the disclaimers and warnings tonight and assume that everyone here knows what they're in for."

The audience cheered. Some launched cans of beer at the lavender curtain protecting the screen.

Bernie Kickshaw continued his weekly, pre-movie ramble that prepped the listeners: "As you know, the goal of this event is to watch the entire movie. The first one who makes it through wins. All the others . . ." Bernie reached for his liquor bottle and took a long, deliberate swig. "All others get pain."

And that sent the audience into an uproar. Popcorn went flying into the air.

"Remember, you are the architects of havoc," Bernie told the young punks. "The entrepreneurs of mayhem. The world outside these walls is afraid of you, but here . . . here in the ring of the bloodthirsty, you are free to unleash your rage. Free to crush the weaker around you. You represent pride. You represent anger. You, my fine punks, are the future of America. You are truly the brave!"

Everyone stood up and clapped. The Kickshaw Gasser was a crazy ole drunk, but how the punks did love his prep rallies! His deep, gruff voice sounded as though it came from Heaven, telling them that it was alright to fight. That it was A-OK to seek and destroy thy neighbor. And that it was quite alright to be a young punk in Polk City, USA.

The shredding didn't begin until Kickshaw started the movie and the curtain began to rise. It always started with loud cussing, cans hurled around the room, and a sneaky punch thrown here or there. By the time the movie title hit the screen, total pandemonium ensued.

There were always a handful of hopeful watchers, slumped down in their seats as they attempted to remain unnoticed. But they were usually the first to go. The more wily punks despised this tactic. They saw it as being weak-willed and let loose unparalleled ferocity upon those who tried.

Jax Sliver and the other Snaggle Tits waited patiently. Though Bump Froddy couldn't resist smacking his nail-filled sock upside the bald head of the punk sitting in front of him, the Snaggle Tits gang mostly remained in wait. Jax had worked on his plan all week: Stay unhurt for as long as possible and let as many of the other gangs wipe each other out. Then send in the infantry.

A member of the Animal House gang came crashing over the seats and landed at the feet of Bump Froddy. He instantly reared back with his sock, but Jax grabbed his arm.

Bump Froddy snarled. "This ain't no fun at all, Jax. We're here to kill."

"Not til I say so." Jax let go of the muscular punk's arm. "All part of my plan."

Baseball bats were swinging, and heads were rattled. The scene was as beautiful as it was horrific. Some unlucky punks were sitting wide-eyed in their seats, staring blankly with retarded expressions as blood trickled from their ears and mouths. Each gang had their own strategy. Some went all-out violent, while others opted for the don't-mess-with-me-and-I-won't-rearrange-your-face attitude. All in all, they were all having a pretty swell time.

The Discombobulated Snaggle Tits had always been one of the more aggressive gangs. But tonight was different. Jax Sliver was twenty five now, a geezer in the shredding game, and he was wanting out. He hadn't told the others in his gang about this newfound desire for retirement—they would surely beat the life outta' him for merely mentioning it. "Once a Tit, always a Tit" they'd always proclaimed. The only way out is death. Or a note from Mom. But nobody wanted the embarrassment of showing up to the Sunday night gang meeting with a note from their mother.

Jax had thought of a clever way out. If he could be the first to finish the movie then that oughta' earn him the right to do anything he damn well wanted without retribution. No member of any gang would stand against him. He would be king of Polk City. Un-fucking-touchable.

If . . . he could make it all the way through.

There was already big trouble heading his way. Jax noticed The Whippy Whippy Wild Women beating a path through the crowd. The ferocious girls, clad in black leather, and with blue and red painted faces, looked like rabid mandrills on the prowl. Dinging their wooden bats off the heads of rival gang members, The Wild Women carved notches in their heavily scarred breasts, tally marks for every man they dropped.

Jax was aware they were looking for him. Last Friday night he and his gang had clashed in the back row with an allied gang of The Whippy Whippy Wild Women. Bump Froddy and Lilly Liver had busted out the teeth of the leader, and The Wild Women swore revenge.

Jax rallied his troops. "Stand around me. Don't let anybody near."

Lilly Liver smiled and lifted her iron glove. "You just watch the movie, love. Let me take care of these bitches."

Lil Necro Ninny and Hackle Snaps grasped their bats. Bump Froddy, raring to get his sock a' swingin', stayed close to his leader. Jax was well protected but the violence was getting close. Lilly Liver found a beer bottle under a nearby seat. She reared it over her shoulder and threw it at the back of the head of a member of the BooBoo Angel Disciples. The man with red and yellow hair spun around to see who had attacked him. He reached back with one hand, felt the trickle of warm blood on his fingers, and then looked straight at Lilly Liver. She smiled and waved. The man gnashed his silver teeth and charged at the fat queen.

He jumped over the rows of seats, punching Lilly Liver in the chin.

"Oh, no you just didn't!" Lilly Liver barked, shaking the stars from her head. "Boy, I'm going to whoop that ass!" And she began beating the Disciple up and down the aisle with her iron glove.

The other BooBoo Angel Disciples had caught sight of their own being smacked down by the heavy-handed queen. They ran to rescue their friend.

Lil Necro Ninny pulled a slingshot from out of his back pocket and loaded it with a golf ball. Waiting for the whites of their eyes, Lil Necro stretched the band and let loose, thumping the ball off the forehead of a man called Wart. His yelp could be heard above all the screams in the theater, and he fell cross-eyed over the row of seats.

The other two Angel Disciples charged onward. Hackle Snaps reared back with his bat and swung. Though he missed his target, his back swing caught the rib of his opponent. The Disciple cried out, clutching his side as Lil Necro Ninny kneed him in the nose.

Jax sat in his seat, disturbingly undisturbed by all the fighting going on around him. He could hear Lilly Liver

255

cursing the man who'd punched her; Necro Ninny and Hackle Snaps were busy with others; and somewhere in this melee were The Whippy Whippy Wild Women busting balls and beating brains to get at Jax.

He watched the movie.

The light of the projector beamed across the darkened room, spotlighting the ensuing chaos. Bernie Kickshaw sat, looking out the little square window. He rubbed his hands together. He liked watching the blood. He really liked watching the girls.

"You doin' OK?" Bump Froddy asked Jax. "Keepin' an eye on the screen, aren't you?"

Jax didn't reply. Twenty-two minutes into the movie. Forty had been the record.

Bump Froddy pushed a punk from falling onto Jax. "We're going to make it this time, Jax! I can feel it!"

Jax still didn't respond. The movie was actually pretty good. He was surprised.

"Jax? Jax?" It was Hackle Snaps. "What's it about? What's the movie 'bout?"

"Bank robbers. Cowboys. Cowboy bank robbers. So far." A beer bottle whizzed by Jax's head. He ducked without realizing it.

"Them Wild Women," Bump Froddy growled, "they're gettin' closer, Jax!"

No reply. Jax kept watching the movie. He had made it twenty-five minutes.

Bern Kickshaw kept watching, too. Entertainment. Pain and blood.

Pain n' blood.

***

Jax looked into the mirror. His face was longer than it used to be, a little more face than it was six years ago. Where did all of it come from? Ol' Long Face. He was getting old.

Twenty-five.

When he was nineteen he had planned to be dead by now. Or at least accomplished. Which might be the same thing. He wasn't sure. All he knew was that he had a lot of fight in him, and he wasn't about to waste it all on schooling, or working, or living some exemplary life. He scoffed at the thought of walking around the world with a diploma. A stupid piece of paper to show the world he wasn't really stupid. He could show the world that with his fists. Knuckles seemed to sink in a little deeper than academics did. He had found a way to get his thoughts across to all the others; he mashed it in with his fists. Made them think. Think hard on this, motherfuckers.

He punched the mirror, the glass cracking in all directions.

"Looks like a road map," he muttered, staring at the broken mirror and ignoring the small beads of blood coming up from his cut knuckles. "Where do I go from here?"

He dabbed a spot of blood on the end of one of the cracks in the mirror.

"That's where I'm heading. To Blood Town."

He punched the mirror again, this time shattering it.

***

Micko McDitto of the Ballyhoo Brainbreakers was almost upon Jax before Bump Froddy took the punk out with an elbow to the throat.

"How long you into it now, Jax?" Bump Froddy asked as he stepped on Micko's bleeding head.

Jax looked at his watch. "Thirty-seven minutes."

"Only three more to break the record!" Bump Froddy yelled. He pumped his fist in the air as though claiming victory.

"Shhh!" Jax replied with a finger to his lips. "They're about to kiss."

Bump Froddy looked to the screen. Through the blood stains and dripping beer were two actors ready to press their faces together. A cowboy and a cowboy woman. Or would that be cowgirl? Oh, who the fuck cares . . .

Jax did! He was watching the movie.

The Whippy Whippy Wild Women were covered in fresh tally marks. Their baseball bats were painted crimson, and bits of hair dangled from the ends—matted, bloody punk hair dyed pink, red, blue, and green.

"Forty one minutes!" Bump Froddy shouted. He turned to congratulate Jax, but when he did his vision flashed white. It felt as if his brains had turned into a wave machine, the batter and juices sloshing back and forth in his skull. He fell into Jax's lap, spitting and huffing, and kicking his legs in seizures.

Jax didn't bother to look down. He simply put his hand over Bump's face and pushed him off. The big punk fell to the floor, red saliva bubbling from his quivering lips.

"Wild Women got Bump!" Lil Necro Ninny screamed, and he grabbed his sling shot and started firing marbles, gravel, and golf balls—anything he had stuffed in his pockets.

Lilly Liver and Hackle Snaps came to protect Jax.

"You bitch, back off!" Lilly demanded, swinging her iron glove at one of the Wild Women. "Hoe's going down!"

"What are you going to do, sissy-boy, stab me in the eye with your mascara?" asked the Wild Woman. Her mandrill-painted face looked alien in the theater's flashing light and darkness.

"I'm going to rip off your ugly face then spit in your eye sockets!" Lilly yelled. She grabbed the Wild Woman who had thumped Froddy's melon, and started ripping out hair. "I'll teach you, bitch, to go messin' 'round with us."

With all the commotion around him, Jax had to tilt his head to see the movie screen. He didn't want to miss a thing. The cowboy robbers were now on the run from the cow-police. Pigs on horseback, he thought. Kinda' funny.

On my way to Blood Town. At the end of the crack. Busted-up mirror. Long face. Twenty-five years old. Still fighting. It's all coming down to the credits.

The Wild Women and the remaining Snaggle Tits kept fighting. Fifty-six minutes into the movie and Jax was on the home stretch. He wondered for a moment who directed the movie, who were the actors, and would the bank robbers get away with the loot? In fact, he was so caught up in the make-believe action on screen that the real conflict around him almost seemed imitation.

"Cowboy punks," he said to himself. And in a quick glimpse within his mind he saw all the gangs wearing spurs and boots, vests, and ten-gallon hats. "S'cuse me, pardners. Yuns best get outta' my way a'fore I beat yer dadgum heads in with my boot."

He'd made it an hour. Twenty-one miles to Blood Town.

***

What would he do as ruler of Blood Town? Maybe he could get a cowboy hat that would distract from the longness of his face. Longness. Was that a real word? Maybe not to the uppity diploma people, but to a real man who carried his fists rolled up like pistols by his sides, any word would do. Jax Sliver was a modern day gunfighter, and his balls were his horse—big and tough.

"S'cuse me, pardner," he said to his broken reflection in the mirror. "Have I seen you 'round these here parts a'fore?"

Jax nodded.

"You look awfully familiar. Didn't I see you at the tavern? Playin' poker with a color'd?"

Jax nodded.

"Yeah, you brought that negro in to town with ya, didn't you?"

Jax nodded.

"And didn't I warn you to get him out a'fore I got myself some rope to hang 'em with?"

Jax nodded.

"Why'd you bring a smelly moon cricket to Blood Town, anyways?"

"To pick a fight."

Both Jax's nodded; the gunslinger in the mirror and the long-faced punk looking in to it.

***

One hour and twelve minutes. Only nine minutes to go. The cowboy robbers were corralled in a rocky ravine, cornered by the cow-police. Maybe police wasn't the right word, either. Sheriffs? Posse? Ah, forget it. The cow-police had their rifles trained on the robbers, but the cowboys weren't going down without a fight. Neither was Jax Sliver.

A Whippy Wild Woman was about to swing her bat on him. Jax had a decision to make: I'm either Jax in the mirror (the one who rides the plains on big, tough balls), or I'm Jax out of the mirror (the one who wants to retire from the violence). Which is it, cowboy punk?

The cowboy robbers were also faced with certain death, but Jax could see in their eyes that they weren't willing to give up their stolen loot. And he wasn't going to give up the winning title. Downed by a bullet or brained by a bat, the long faces all whipped out their weapons in unison and fired. As the bullets ripped through the cow-police, Jax's fists spread hurt across the Whippy Wild Woman coming down on him.

The Wild Woman crashed, her painted face now layered in a fresh coat of red. Lilly Liver brought her iron gauntlet down on another Wild Woman as Lil Necro Ninny and Hackle Snaps chased off the last two.

The theater was awash in moans and groans, blood and tears, and certainly beer and popcorn. A seemingly typical Friday night at Bernie Kickshaw's

Goodtimes Bloodthirsty Theater, but tonight wasn't typical. Far from it. The credits to the movie were rolling, and sitting in the back row was one young punk still watching.

Well . . . semi-young. He was, after all, twenty-five years old.

CHARLIE MANSON EYES

She gouged a spork and a knife in a head
Two gnarled fingers hanging above her soft bed
The face of Jeffrey Dahmer is tattooed on her toes
My best friend loves horror, that's just the way it goes

Alcapone is her first name, and her last is Timesquare
With a dog that barks backwards, she lives unaware
She sits unemotionally and listens to white noise
However, yesterday she went out to stab all the boys

From corner to corner, she checked out the scene
The elders were cursing as the little ones screamed
Her obsession is getting worse, killing both girls and guys
My best friend Alcapone has a problem I surmise

She carries a hammer and murders quite simple
Grabbed little Shirley and gave her a bloody temple
She disposes of the bones in a bucket of lye
Lets the skin rot off, but she kept the right eye

With it she gambled for the souls of many more
Killing twenty people including her neighbors next door
Alcapone often bathes in her victims' cold blood
Slinging the red fluid, she froths in the flood

Charlie Manson Eyes

Her fridge is full of skulls and brittle white bones
Though no one truly knows how many she owns
Today she called to invite me to her place
I look in the mirror and saw my worried face

Alcapone Timesquare is a swell friend of mine
But I have a serious problem, I feel in a bind
Do I call the police? Tell them what I know?
That Alcapone has killed forty people in a row

I decide to go over and knock on her door
She answers in a hurry; there is blood on the floor
I follow red streams to her dark living room
Which really isn't living, but adorned like a tomb

There's a lamp with human skin; a rug made of hair
Soft shriveled things give me a scare
Leaning on the wall, a corpse full of holes
A head without eyes and missing a nose

I glance at my friend Al, as she is saying to me . . .
"Care for some cookies, or a hot cup of tea?"
I tremble, I scream, "Girl, this cannot be right!
Killing forty people, and inviting me here tonight!"

"But I like you," she purrs softly, attempting to touch
Her fingers are icy, and her heart just as much
I shove her away and run for the door
Her hammer strikes me hard and I fall to the floor

Exactly at midnight I'm struck in the head
Pulled back to the kitchen and left for dead
But in my last gasp I see quite a surprise
She not only killed me, she has Charlie Manson eyes!

THOSE PECULIAR HANDS OF JOHNNY LIGHTENBOX

"Got hands like black holes. Everything I touch becomes nothing. Nothing, Dr. Basler."

"What about yourself?"

"Doesn't affect me. My skin is different, acceptable somehow to this curse I have. But everything else . . . Whoosh! Gone! Just like that."

"Just like that, huh? Well, it could be delusions. Are you afraid of germs, Mr. Lightenbox? Getting your hands dirty?"

"I can't get them dirty, Dr. Basler. I just make things cleaner. It would be easier if it were as simple as you say. I've been like this for three weeks now, trying not to touch anything. Making sure I don't trip when I walk by someone on the street. I can't shake hands with anyone. Can't eat with a fork or spoon. Can't do nothin'. I can't go on this way. Much longer, and I'm going to lose my freaking mind. Might start grabbing peoples' throats just for the hell of it, know what I mean? A man can only take so much."

"Mr. Lightenbox, I have found in my line of work that there is a solution to every problem. Whatever is going on with you, it may take some time, but eventually things do work out. I understand you're troubled, but believe me, I have dealt with much worse."

"I doubt you've ever had a case like mine. You have normal hands, Doc. You can touch things, hold things, pick up a book if you want. I can't wash myself. Water, towels, soap . . . It all disappears. Walls, doorknobs, clothing, whatever. It all evaporates in my hands. I can't hold a drink, brush my hair, or make love with my girl. Everything disappears!"

"Mr. Lightenbox, please don't take offense, but it sounds like Delusional Hysteria. It's a syndrome. Some people are so deeply intimidated of germs that they convince themselves that a single one might kill them. It's actually more common than you may realize. I had a patient once tell me he was afraid to look at strangers' faces. He thought he could get diseases from glancing at them."

"Delusional Hysteria . . . Sure. I wish it were that. Save the psychobabble, Doc. What I need is some serious fucking help here. I know what reality is, but I haven't been living in it for the last three weeks."

"Just where is it that you have been living, Mr. Lightenbox?"

"Feels like Hell."

"Hell is an infinite place. I doubt you would, or could, for that matter, come to me for help if you were completely hopeless."

"I'm certainly am with these cursed hands!"

"Alright, tell me how the problem started."

"Started with Margo."

"Margo?"

"Margo Cross. She's my girlfriend."

"I see. So you think your girlfriend caused your hands to . . . make things disappear?"

"I know she caused it. It might've been my fault to begin with, but I don't deserve this. We've been going steady for about three and a half years. We were pretty close, you could say. A few weeks ago, I picked up another woman at a club. Margo found out. Caught us fucking in my car. Margo was supposed to be asleep, but she woke up. Told me later that she watched us for awhile, going at it in the car like we didn't give a damn if the whole world were watching. She cried. Margo, I mean. Said she wished it was her in there. In there with my hands on her instead of that disgusting woman."

"Are you going to be alright, Mr. Lightenbox? Do you need a tissue?"

"I'm fine. It's just . . . Well, anyway, Margo watched us until I looked up and saw her. I saw her standing there, outside the driver's side window looking at us. She had her hands up to her mouth. Crying. I got out and tried to talk to her, but she ran off. Left me standing there like a jackass with my underwear around my ankles. Anyway, the woman I was with, the one in the car, she got out and laughed at Margo. Called her some nasty names. That's when I did something bad, Doc. Really bad. I punched her in the face. Hard. I mean, she fell on the sidewalk. I cried, but I wasn't sad. It was like I didn't understand. In some sick way, I blamed her for the whole incident. Her laughing at Margo, that's what got me. I didn't like the names she called her. She screwed things up for me."

"Where did Margo go?"

"I don't know. She left, and came back later in the night drunker than I've ever seen. She got into bed with me, and told me she wanted to fuck. Said it would be the last one. One to wipe the memory away."

"Memory?"

"The memory of the other woman."

"I see. So what did you do?"

"I obliged her. What was I supposed to do?"

"Was she still angry with you afterwards?"

"That's the strange thing, Doc. She didn't seem angry. Not like yelling and screaming kinda' angry. She just laid back and said she wanted me to know what I was going to be missing for the rest of my life."

"What would that be, Mr. Lightenbox?"

"The ability to touch or hold."

"The other woman . . . What happened to her, the one you punched?"

"Never saw her again."

"Was she hurt bad?"

"Hell, I don't know. Like I said, I never saw her again. Cops never questioned me or anything. Figured she must've crawled back to whatever sewer-hole she came from."

"Mr. Lightenbox, if you loved Margo so much why did you cheat on her?"

"I guess it would sound kind of bad to say the opportunity came up. I'm not sure why I did it. I just did."

"I'm trying to help you, Mr. Lightenbox, but I need solid answers here. There was a reason you cheated. Were you unhappy in some way? Did you have an argument with Margo a few days before, perhaps?"

"Not that I recall. We hardly ever argued about anything. Nothing significant, anyway. Guess I'm just a louse. Maybe Mr. Mean Head wanted a little something strange."

"Mr. Mean Head. Is that your name for your penis? You're saying Mr. Mean Head is to blame for your troubles?"

"I don't have any troubles other than my hands. Troubles I got, Doc, I erase them. Clean 'em out."

"Is that what you do, Mr. Lightenbox? You clean things out? Show me. I want to see what you can do with those peculiar hands of yours."

"Why should I?"

"Because I think you're imagining it. As I said before, Delusional Hysteria. The mind can believe just about anything you program it to."

"You don't understand, Doc. Trust me on this. My hands are wicked things. They're real, and what they can do is real."

"They look normal enough. You'll have to show me, Mr. Lightenbox."

"OK. Hand me that coffee cup of pencils on your desk, but don't touch me."

". . . Here you go."

"Don't touch me!"

"Sorry, didn't mean . . . Judas, it's gone!"

"Yeah, and so is the rest of my life."

"How . . . How do you eat? How do you put on your clothes?"

"I don't."

"But, but you have clothes on now."

"Margo dresses me."

"I thought Margo left."

"No, no. She's still around, but I can't touch her. And what good is a woman you can't touch?"

"To feed and clothe you?"

"Evil little twat she's turned out to be."

"What does she do that's so evil, Mr. Lightenbox?"

"Teases me. Dances and parades around nude in front of me. Laughs about it, too. Touching herself. Making me want her. She's the one that did this to me."

"How? How did she do it? Give me details."

"I don't know how exactly. All I know is when she ran away that night she claimed she made it with a gypsy. Said this gypsy gave her some sort of power called the darklight that will make me never able to love a woman again."

"She had sex with this gypsy?"

"That's the insinuation."

"And this gypsy gave her this, uh, darklight-power to make your hands erase things?"

"Yes."

"You haven't touched Margo in what . . . ?"

"Three weeks."

"Yes, I see. What about Mr. Mean Head?"

"What about him?"

"Does he ever, you know, tempt you to do things?"

"I'm not following, Doc."

"Mr. Lightenbox, I'm going to play Devil's advocate. Why haven't you just touched Margo anyway? Make her pay for what she has done to you? Seems to me that living with such a curse might bring on a furious or desperate mindset. Most would tend to lean toward revenge."

"I can't, Dr. Basler. Who'd dress me? Who'd clean and feed me? I'm nothing without Margo's help."

"Hmm . . . Nothing, huh?"

"Dr. Basler, the reason I came to talk to you is because I've just about reached the point of killing myself. How much longer can I go on like this?"

"I don't know. You tell me."

"Sometimes I do want revenge, but mainly on the gypsy. This wretched curse! Maybe the gypsy could take it off. Get rid of it."

"How would you find the gypsy, Mr. Lightenbox?"

"Nothing short of torture would get Margo to say."

"That might work, but aren't you forgetting one vital thing? Margo could punish you further by letting you starve. Mr. Lightenbox, have you ever thought about working?"

"Working?"

"With those hands of yours, you could be quite valuable to someone in need."

"Yeah? Like who?"

"Oh, I don't know. There are certain people who could benefit from hands like yours."

"Nobody wants this. Except you?"

"Possibly. You may benefit from it as well."

***

"How did it go, Mr. Lightenbox?"

"Fine."

"Just fine?"

"It was terrific, Dr. Basler. I enjoyed myself."

"What did she say?"

"Said if I had kids, she hoped they died while I'm watching."

"How flattering. Sounds like her."

"That's not all. She also said she'd be waiting for me when my time comes. But then she started crying. Started screaming and hissing. Making weird noises like a cat getting its nuts yanked off. But then she whispered for you, Dr. Basler. Wanted you to save her."

"Me? Probably the first time she needed me in years. So, what happened next?"

"Nothing happened."

"Nothing?"

"Absolutely nothing."

"So it's all done? Nothing left of it?"

"Like I said, Doc, absolutely nothing."

"I hated her. She was always in the way. Mucking things up for me. Mr. Lightenbox, where did you—"

"—Johnny."

"Say again?"

"Call me Johnny. I think we're a bit passed the doctor-patient relationship, don't you think?"

"Sure, Johnny. Under the circumstances, I suppose we are. But tell me, where did you do it?"

"In bed. And as I laid next to her warm impression, I started thinking about things."

"What sort of things, Johnny?"

"I held off for far too long, Dr. Basler. Far too long."

"With opening up and letting go?"

"Exactly."

"Do you regret it, Johnny?"

"Not in the least. In fact, I did just fine."

"Tell me, Johnny. What happened? Give me the details."

"She struggled a bit, trying to get away. I reached down and slowly poked holes into her belly with my finger. Sorta' like jabbing a pin in a sandwich bag full of tomato juice. Blood squirted everywhere, but I got it all wiped up, no worries. Then her eyes got real big, like she just shit herself, and that's when the screaming started. You should've seen the look on her face when her lips came off. Teeth hangin' out like busted piano keys. One by one I touched them away.

Then went her nose, her right eye. Never seen such an ugly face in all my life. Arms and legs. Her tits. Then her ears and hair. But, I kept her alive long enough to see that nobody would be finding her. I wanted her to know that. Not even a blood spot."

"Johnny, you've done me a tremendous favor. It's worth every thousand, I assure you."

"Dr. Basler, tell me something now, why did you want your wife killed, anyway?"

"Because, Johnny. Mr. Mean Head needs the strange. You know how he gets."

"It's a funny thing, isn't it, Dr. Basler?"

"What's that?"

"That I came to you for help, and as it turned out, it's me helping you. I should charge you double for the talk."

"That would be fraud, Mr. Lightenbox. Johnny, look . . . I have something to ask you."

"Yeah? Shoot."

"Would you be interested in another job?"

***

"What did he say, Johnny?"

"He called you a dirty pig-fuck, and said something about you sliding down a razor into a bucket of alcohol."

"What does that supposed to mean?"

"Means he won't be bothering you again."

"Wonderful news, Johnny. Guess I'll be having his lady for supper every night."

"She's all yours now, Dr. Basler. Mr. Mean Head gets the strange."

"Let me see those hands, Johnny. I want to look at them."

"Don't touch."

"They don't look at all different than other hands, do they?"

"Just regular-looking. They could be on anybody's arms, I reckon'."

"Completely normal in appearance. What makes them do that, I wonder? Maybe this gypsy has more . . ."

"More what?"

"More of whatever it is that makes your hands do that, Johnny. If so, we could do anything."

"I don't know where to find this gypsy."

"What about Margo?"

"Already tried. She won't tell me a thing."

"She might tell me. What if you brought her here and threatened her?"

"Threatened her? With what?"

"Your hands, Johnny. Those fabulous hands."

"Won't do any good. She knows I need her."

"But you're forgetting something. I know about your hands now. I can take care of any needs you might have."

"No offense, but I don't want your hands on me, Doc."

"Johnny, Johnny, Johnny. You shortsighted man. I have women that work for me. I'll keep you clothed and fed. You can keep working for me. Put those marvelously, cursed hands to good use."

"Well, you might have something there, Doc."

"Does Margo know you come to see me?"

"Yeah, she drops me off every day. Getting her up here wouldn't be a problem, but getting her to talk about the gypsy . . . She ain't going to say nothing."

"Don't worry about that. She'll talk. I can get anybody to talk. That's my job. So, is it agreed?"

"Sure. Yeah, it's agreed. I'll bring her in tomorrow."

"Terrific, Johnny. Don't you worry about a thing. This is going to work out just fine."

***

"Hello, Dr. Basler. I'm Margaret Cross. Nice to meet you."

"Thank you, and please, have a seat. Mr. Lightenbox has told me a little about you."

"Oh?"

"Good things, I assure you. Care for anything to drink? Soda? Cup of coffee?"

"No thanks. I'm glad to hear I haven't been slandered. But why I'm here, I still don't—"

"—Ms. Cross, sometimes in order to delve deeper into the psyche of a troubled person it requires the assistance of someone a little more familiar to the patient. Helps open doors, so to speak."

"Sure, I understand."

"I'm aware that Johnny, Mr. Lightenbox, has acted in such a way as to disrupt your relationship with him. Possibly in a way that cannot be repaired?"

"Disrupt? Ha! It was a little more serious than a disruption, Doctor."

"But do you think it is something irreparable?"

"That's difficult to say at this point. I don't think anything is passed trying."

"Are you then at peace with your relationship with Mr. Lightenbox? Say, forgiving of him?"

"I don't understand where you're taking this. If I'm here to help open his doors, why am I being analyzed?"

"I'm not trying to analyze you, Ms. Cross. I simply need to understand exactly where we are with this thing. Mr. Lightenbox feels you still harbor awkward feelings toward him. Possibly a deep-seated resentment. For what he did."

"I resented it very much. Wouldn't you feel the same way if it happened to you?"

"Infidelity seems like an impossible hurdle to overcome, but with proper counseling two people can learn to trust again. I've helped with several seemingly wrecked marriages and relationships. First, we need to understand what caused the breakdown of trust. Why Johnny felt the need to turn to another woman."

"Johnny lost control. Couldn't keep his libido in check."

"You blame wanderlust?"

"I blame him! He may have convinced you otherwise, but he knew damn well what he was doing."

"Are you sure?"

"You saying it's my fault he picked up some ugly, overweight hooker, and had sex with her in our car?"

"There is a possibility you might have indirectly led him to want to stray."

"Now *that* I do resent, Doctor! What right do you have to—?"

"And could it be that maybe you put him under such duress with your gypsy magic that he felt compelled to run away to the arms of another woman? And that you aggravated his temper to such degrees as to inflict a mental meltdown, causing him to do something that he'd never normally do?"

"Johnny, you told him about the gypsy?"

"Honey, Dr. Basler needs you to tell us where the gypsy is."

"You told him?"

"I had to. How else was he to help me?"

"Johnny, you idiot. You can't be talking about this. I told you. You want the government to come take you away as a lab rat?"

"Ms. Cross, what is said within these walls is purely confidential. Besides, imagine how ludicrous it would sound for me to tell someone about Mr. Lightenbox's unique problem. I'd be the one having to see a professional."

"I hardly find you professional, Dr. Basler, and talking about gypsies isn't why Johnny came here. He needs help with his real problem. The man lives in a perpetual porno, for crying out loud! Constantly staring at other women. He never stops talking about them. Won't quit with his perverted connotations. Hey, honey, doesn't the sun look like a nice, big golden vagina this morning? He has actually said crap like that to me. It's not normal. Not even for a man. Has he told you about Mr. Mean Head?"

"He's mentioned him, yes."

"Mentioned him, huh? Mr. Mean Head runs his life. More like ruins it."

"His affinity with his manhood is the least of his problems, Ms. Cross. I need you to tell me where this gypsy is so that Johnny here can get on with his life. There will be time to get his other problems worked out, but the poor man can't even put on his own clothes. Hasn't the punishment gone on long enough?"

"Johnny, you really shouldn't have told him."

"Margo, I can't keep living like this. Someone was bound to find out sooner or later anyway. I had to tell him. I have to get better. Please, tell the doctor where the gypsy is so we, I mean, so I can get better."

"Johnny, you'll just have to live with it. You dug your own grave."

"He could hurt you, Margo. Accidently, of course. In Johnny's own words, a man can only take so much. I don't think you want to push him over the edge, do you? Johnny, please tell me something."

"Yes, Doc?"

"Where do you sleep at night?"

"In my bed, why?"

"With Margo?"

"Yeah, I sleep on my back, though. I keep my hands away from her or the covers. Keep the palms down to my belly."

"What if you were to, say, accidentally roll over one night? What if you had a bad dream. No, a sexual dream . . . and you rolled over and accidentally put your arms around her? What if you accidentally brushed a finger over her skin, across her face, or reached down between her thighs?"

"Dr. Basler, Johnny needs me. Your threats are not going to work. And you better believe I'm going to report your hideous ways of practice."

"Oh? What if you couldn't talk at all, Ms. Cross? What if your mouth was cleaned out?"

"Johnny, you just going to sit there and listen to this arrogant bastard threaten me? Johnny? Johnny, what are you doing? Sit down, Johnny . . . Johnny . . . Get away from me!"

"I can manage myself, honey. Really, I can."

"You can, huh? Who has been holding a spoon to your lips for the last three weeks? Who's been bathing you and wiping your ass every day?"

"I can manage all that, honey. I have a friend now. One that has money and work for me."

"What kind of work can you do with those hands?"

"I can clean."

"What are you, Johnny, a freaking comedian now or something?"

"Dr. Basler can take care of me."

"And I will, Margo, you can rest assured. I know about his hands; what they do. I want them. But even more, I want to know where the gypsy is."

"You can just rest un-assured, Doctor, because I'm not telling. You can go to Hell."

"That's where Johnny's been living in his relationship with you. In Hell. Now that he has been working for me, he is feeling much better about himself. I think he will turn out fine, don't you, Johnny Boy?"

"What've you done, Johnny? What have you been doing for this scum?"

"Nothing. I haven't done a thing."

"What is he talking about then?"

"Johnny, I'm the doctor. You listen to me now, not her. I know what is best for you. Don't you want beautiful women taking care of you? I have power, money, everything you desire. How about your life back? I can give you that! A life with beautiful women and plenty of sex."

"That's what I want, Doc, but if I can't touch them what good is it?"

"They can touch you. Lay back and let my women do for you what your own, jealous girl will not. Think of Mr. Mean Head, Johnny. He would sure be happy! Happy for the rest of your life. Isn't that what you want? What you've always wanted?"

"Yes. Exactly what I want."

"Good then. Margo, if you please, tell me where the gypsy is."

"Go fuck yourself! And you, too, Johnny!"

"Johnny, I'm the doctor. Listen to me now. You need sex. You need it badly and that is what I'm going to prescribe for you. Touch her, Johnny. Touch her ass. And those breasts . . . They're just waiting for your attention. Touch them, Johnny. They are yours, after all. You have three and a half years invested in them. She's been keeping them from you."

"Margo, listen to me, please! Tell the doctor. Don't make me do this. Please, tell the doctor where the gypsy is!"

"Johnny, don't . . . Johnny, look what you're doing!"

"Margo, I love you . . . Please, honey, I need my life back. I don't want to hurt you. Please, Margo, tell the doctor."

"Don't touch me! Good god, Johnny, get away! Don't. Stop, Johnny! Johnny . . . Johnny, stop!"

"She's all yours, John. Don't let her push your ego around. She shouldn't have done what she did to you, Johnny. Listen to her beg. How pathetic. She sure hasn't shown you any consideration or remorse. It'll go on until you die, Johnny. That rancorous slut. Dancing around in front of you. She hurt you bad, Johnny, and I think you owe it to yourself to get what she has been shutting out. And the doctor always knows what's best, don't I, Johnny?"

"Margo, tell Dr. Basler where the gypsy is. Tell him where to get the darklight."

"I can't. I can't tell."

"Margo!"

"I can't, Johnny."

"Tell him, you bitch! I need my life back!"

"That's the way, Johnny. Stand up for yourself! Boost the good ole self-esteem! Free Mr. Mean Head! Come on, Johnny, you can do it! Show her you aren't going to take her shit anymore."

"My wrist! My hand! JOHNNY!"

"You better tell me where the gypsy is, Margo. Much longer and there won't be anything left of you. Johnny . . . he's out of control."

"No . . . I won't tell you . . . You sick . . . sick son of a bitch."

"Johnny Boy, looks like you were right. She's not going to listen to reason."

"Margo, tell the doc. Tell him. Tell him, Margo!"

"Fuck you, Johnny! You brought this misery on yourself!"

"Johnny, that's not true. She instigated everything. Trust me, I know. I'm the doctor."

"No, Johnny, don't listen to him. Johnny. Please! I love you, John. Please . . ."

"She had such beautiful eyes. A pretty smile."

"Johnny . . . Look what you've done. I'm bleeding. Bleeding all over . . . I got no hands, Johnny. Please . . . Johnny, I can't see . . . I can't see!"

"Tell the doctor, Margo. Tell him and he'll make me stop."

"Johnny . . ."

"Yes, honey?"

"I'm getting cold."

"You're getting cold, Margo, because you're dying. Losing a lot of blood. Best tell me so I can call for an ambulance. I have a phone right here on my desk. I can have paramedics here in a couple minutes."

"OK . . . just . . . just get him away. Keep Johnny away from me."

"Tell me where the gypsy is."

"Rot in Hell."

"Honey, tell us. Tell us before it's too late."

"Johnny?"

"Yes, honey?"

"I hope you get what you deserve."

"I will, honey, don't you worry."

"Johnny . . . I hate you . . . I hate . . . you . . . for . . . this . . ."

"Well. Not quite what I had expected, Johnny my boy. I thought she would have caved long before it came to this. Pity, too. Such a waste of a pretty woman, but could you please do me a favor and kick her over to the other side? Her face is leaking all over my carpet, and frankly, it's making me sick."

"Yeah. She's all messed up, Doc. All messed up."

"You have to go now, John."

"Go? Where to?"

"To the Fringe. You have to go to the Fringe."

"How far is it?"

"I'm already there. But for you it's right over the line."

"I don't understand."

"Johnny Boy, we're lunatics, you and me."

"We are?"

"Yes, Johnny, we are."

"I feel different."

"Because you're free. You've set yourself free, and now Mr. Mean Head can do whatever he likes. That's the beauty about the Fringe. It makes the world a better place for people like us. We can do whatever we want. There are no boundaries, Johnny, because everything about our world is hunky-dory when you're a goddamned lunatic."

COLD BLUE

I am Death. Cold and blue. Frigid as arctic waters, an entity without a face. I neither breathe, eat, nor sleep. I live not in time, nor with a conscious. I emerge from the darklight, often edging quietly upon those unaware.

SYLVIA'S LAST DANCE

It's humiliating having to stand here on this platform, staring forward while he's peeking under my skirt. His mother doesn't care. She's too busy taking clothes from the rack and asking the saleslady how much everything costs. My eyes are focused on the escalator. I see people riding down from the second floor with shiny shopping bags in hand; they don't pay any attention to me. I'm a lifeless mannequin to them. One man glances over at the boy with his head stuck under my skirt. The man laughs and nudges his wife. She shakes her head disapprovingly as they both continue on their way. Everybody's always on their way, up or down the escalators. Day after day.

"Charles Clarke Gilbey! Stop that, this instant!" the mother finally orders, snapping her fingers at the boy. "Get over here. Now!"

I feel the little brat's head slide out from under my skirt. Before he can get away, I give him a swift kick in the rear. He spins round and stares at me with mouth agape, eyes widened. "Mom!" he cries. He runs toward her, rubbing his backside with his hand.

Not my first time dealing with snooping boys.

The day goes by as usual. I stand on my little white box, watching people glide down the escalator, and eavesdropping on snippets of their conversations. I hear it all. The good, the bad, and the ridiculous. It's funny the things people say when they don't think anybody is listening.

***

Nine o' clock the mall closes, and the shopping day is finally over. My feet are killing me. You'd think I'd be used to it, but try maintaining a pose for eleven hours straight while wearing these stilettos. Inertness wears on you after a while. Nobody's looking. Good. I shift my weight to the left foot, bending my knee slightly. What's the harm? A girl's gotta' do what a girl's gotta' do.

Oh god, here comes Rich Watson pushing his buffer down the aisle. Like every night, he walks by me, pretending I don't exist. He buffs the floor while the salesladies straighten the clothes on the racks. Bill the manager collects checks and money from the registers. He's got a cigarette dangling from his mouth (his way of being a rebel, I presume) then turns off the overheads, leaving only a few lights remaining. It's getting to be like clockwork around here. Way too predictable. After Bill locks the doors, he heads out to his car and goes wherever he goes . . . that's when Rich the night janitor gets weird.

He waits ten minutes and I hear the buffer machine cut off. I know he's coming. He always does. My eyes are still fixed on the escalator, but there's nobody on it, only shadows playing along the handrails.

"Hey, beautiful. Miss me?" It's Rich, standing in front of me with his big chopper cheeks, and those lustful, beady eyes gleaming behind those smudgy glasses. His breath reeks of alcohol. "I missed you, baby doll. Thought 'bout you on my days off, though. I got real excited. I wish you'd been with me. I'd make you happy, like I always do, baby doll."

I want to slap his fat, ugly face, but I retain self control. Maintain my pose. Keep a steady gaze. Doing what mannequins do best.

He steps onto my white stand. His whiskey-soured breath overwhelms me. "I wanna' kiss your sweet, lovely lips," he tells me, his fingers tracing along the line of my chin. He whispers in my ear: "You got the prettiest face of 'em all."

Sure. Bet you say that to all the dolls.

He slips his arm around my waist . . . don't even want to think about it. Instead, I think about Dillon, the handsome, chiseled-faced mannequin over in men's wear. As the creep snuggles closer, I pretend to be in Dillon's arms. I can't see him from where I'm positioned. I want to turn my head, but can't—but I know the man of my dreams is there behind me. He's on his stand, wearing a dark, wool suit, blue tie, and highly polished shoes. Something about a man in a nice suit makes me sparkle.

The creep gives me a quick pat on the backside and jumps down, "Thanks, baby doll. See ya' tomorrow night." Guess I should be thankful he only goes so far. I put up with him. I have to.

He leaves me standing here. Typical man. Typical night.

But one man who *isn't* typical is Dillon. With the creep out of the way until tomorrow, I can safely turn and look at my fair-haired prince. I adore his stance. He has one hand tucked in his suit pocket; the other held out as if gesturing for me to come to him. And I do.

I wait until I hear the buffering machine fade to other places in the mall. Too bad for the other "baby dolls" in other stores, but I can't help them. I have a date with Dillon.

Stepping from my pedestal, I walk silently across the carpet. My steps quicken as I cross over the aisle to men's wear—my heels striking the glossy, buffed tiles. The overhead security light flickers and I move eagerly toward Dillon. His face brightens, and he winks at me, smiling broadly. Stepping down from the dais, he breathes a sigh of relief— "I didn't think this day would ever end." I rush to his arms and he closes them around me, holding me tight against him. His chin rests on the top of my head and we hold each other in silence for a long moment.

"I'm going to do something about that creep slobbering all over you," Dillon declares.

"Please, don't," I beg him, muffled against his chest. "Not tonight. Let's just enjoy each other while we have our time."

Dillon leads me by the hand to a location in the store that we call the dance floor, a spacious tiled area between the perfume and cosmetic counters. We've been dancing here every night. Dillon moves a small stereo behind the counter and places it on top of the glass. We have a favorite radio station we always dance to.

"The nights go by so fast," I complain to Dillon. He smiles at me and reaches to turn up the music. "I wish we could always be together. Like how the real people are."

Dillon walks back to me. His eyes make me want to crawl inside them and curl up. "And they're the ones who don't even appreciate it," he says. "I hear them arguing all the time."

I put my head against Dillon's chest. He smoothes my hair tenderly. Perplexed, I ask, "If we were like them, do you think we'd be arguing with each other instead of being happy as we are?"

"I don't know, Sylvia." Dillon lifts my face; lightly kisses me on the mouth. "All I know is there's no reason to wish we were any different. Look at what we do have."

"Each other," I say, staring into his eyes.

"And about six hours before anyone interrupts us."

"I wish it could be longer. I wish it could be all night, and all day, for the rest of our lives."

He looks down at me with his smiling blue eyes and brushes a soft kiss across my forehead. "It will be," he promises.

"Forever and ever?"

"Yes. And ever. We can dance through the night although we have to be in our places before daybreak."

The radio is playing a romantic song. A man croons with a soft, melodic voice. I like to think he's enchanted with his princess, maybe dancing with her, like Dillon and me. The lighting in the store is low, allowing the few remaining spotlights overhead to illuminate our movements. I picture us leaving glowing prints on the floor with our feet. Love prints that never fade.

The man on the radio sings something about hearts on ice, how the love inside them cannot freeze. I wonder if that is true or not. Do the people I see every day riding the escalator keep their hearts padded warmly, or does love inevitably frost over in time? Is there such a thing as too much of each other? It just doesn't seem possible.

Dillon leads me across the dance floor. My body is pressed against his; I can't stop wondering if we are the only two in the whole world who are in love. I've never had any real desire to be human—satisfied more or less being what I am—but I admit to having some envy of their ability to do what they want, when they want. I suppose I should be grateful, like Dillon says. Content with the time we do have together. He promised me we'd dance forever. I believe him.

***

I hear them behind me. Moving men. Moving Dillon. Putting him somewhere different. Rearranging his pose that I adore so much. I can't turn and look. So I stand here on my white box and pray they don't move him too far.

"No, the arms come off like this," I hear a man say.

They're taking my Dillon apart! Why would they do that? Can't they move him the way he is? I want so badly to turn and look at what they're doing to him. I just stare forward at the escalator and all the people with shiny shopping bags.

"Now do the legs, but don't bend 'em too much, Joe. You'll snap the pins."

I am feeling sick. What are they doing to my prince? Why are they taking off his arms and legs?

"The truck'll be here shortly. Just finish disassembling that thing and box it up. Got to make room for the new ones."

The new ones? What new ones? Where are they taking Dillon?

I move. Barely. My eyes . . . brim with tears. I want to jump off my stand and run to Dillon. Save him from being taken away. I have to stand still. My eyes. I can't see. Dillon? Please don't leave me here! We have to dance tonight. You promised. Dillon. Dillon. Dillon—?

***

It's been seven months and I haven't moved an inch. During that time, several boys have peered up my dresses and skirts, but I don't react. I don't care when the creep touches me. I just let everything happen . . . I stare blankly ahead.

I don't pay attention to the shoppers anymore. Tune out their conversations. Guess I'm doing what I should've been doing all along; standing here and being inanimate. An object.

I don't know where they took my Dillon. All I know is he's no longer near me; no longer in the store; no longer standing there with one hand in his pocket and the other held out to me. I haven't looked to see who replaced him. It doesn't matter. It's not Dillon, and now that he's gone, I'll stand here day and night—never moving again. The tears still come though, especially in the early morning hours when Dillon and I used to spend our nights on the dance floor. I wonder sometimes if it's still there, the open area, with our footprints aglow. Probably not, but I don't go looking. I had my last dance.

BLOOD ON HER WINGS

Surrender to seclusion
Look at what has become
To an angel barred from flying
Will you ever rise again?
Or have your wings become a burden
Too heavy for the sky
Should you ever cut them off
Would you consider throwing them away?

Blood on her wings
She's fallen to the ground
Blood on her wings
Scarlet roots keep her bound

To an angel that lost her heaven
I offer you my golden sword
To cut the burden from your shoulders
Would you look at me with shame?
Are your arms strong enough to carry
Or will you drag your wings behind
Stumbling within a broken body
Will your sacrifice be enough?

Blood on her wings
She lies down to die
Blood on her wings
Does she now dare try?

REDNECKIN', HELL TRUCKIN' (A LOVE STORY)

The Grim Reaper is dead. Murdered with its own sickle.

The Devil wasn't too happy about this.

He stooped to wipe the blood from his hooves, and in an act of pure outrage, kicked the Reaper's corpse in the face. "That's what you get for dying on the job!" Death's head came off its foundation and rolled across the ground, leaving behind a trail of slick black blood.

The Devil scowled at a wide-eyed demon trembling in the corner of the room. "Take this garbage and throw it in the furnace. Get it out of my sight," the Devil commanded, pointing a long, gnarled finger at the headless Reaper. "How am I going to get a new one? As if I could ask God for favors. . . What a mess we're in now!"

The frightened demon did as the Devil demanded, grabbing the Reaper by its long, dark robe and dragging the corpse to a nearby furnace. The demon struggled to double over the corpse to fit it into the opening, then lifted it and shoved it into the blaze. The smell was putrid.

The Devil retired to his throne, pondering his predicament. Without a Reaper, there'd be no new souls delivered to torment. No fresh sinners to punish. No additional screams filling the endless corridors, shrieking at the taste of boiling acid being poured down their extended gullets while fiery-eyed, demonic livestock

297

perform acts of genitorture and necrophilia. What good is Hell without all that?

"Boring!" the Devil yelled at the top of his brimstone-coated lungs. "Something must be done about this!"

The Devil ordered his right-hand gargoyle, Rancus Romar, to gather Hell's finest and bring them to the throne—eighty-eight demons of the highest order, the greater echelon that dwelled haughtily upon the upper rings of Hades. These snooty fiends with golden horns and silver claws were among the most superb tormentors of Hell. They were known collectively as The Regal Court of Prestige Demonkind.

"My delightful scoundrels of pain and suffering," the Devil said, standing before them. "I am faced with a dilemma, an eniginama, if you will."

"Is he trying to say enigma?" whispered one of the demons to another. They both shrugged.

The Devil continued, "The Grim Reaper has been murdered, and I can't have the Gates of Hell turning into a traffic jam of bewildered souls not knowing where to go." The Devil raised his hand, shaking his finger in the air. "Moreover, I don't want them forced back to the living world where their repentance could really fuck things up for us."

The demons of the Regal Court stood rigid as the Devil paced back and forth, inflicting grooves in the ground with his sharp, piercing hooves.

"But first, I want to know who killed the Grim Reaper!" The Devil's long red tail swooshed back and forth as he walked. His black, arcing brows furrowed. "I'm ordering The Regal Court of Prestiginious—"

"Prestige!" the demons shouted aloud.

"Yeah, yeah, whatever," the Devil groaned, flipping his hand. "I want you assholes to find out who the murderer is! Fail me, and I'll have you cast into the Unholy Reservoir of Chunk n' Dung!"

The eighty-eight demons shuddered.

"You have twenty-four hours to find the culprit."

The Regal Court of Prestige Demonkind looked at each other in doubt. One dared to step forward. "One measly Earth day, my lorditude?" asked a muscular-built demon by the name of Zxin-Ziboc.

The Devil approached the demon, rubbing his red scaly hands together. "Do you need more time?"

"Yes, my immoral lorditude. More time would be nice." Zxin-Ziboc stared forward as the Devil circled him.

"How dare you use that despicadable word in my presence!" the Devil shouted. He stepped around to face the shivering demon.

"It's despicable . . . Sir," the demon rectified.

"Whatever," the Devil said, grabbing the demon by the foundations of his golden horns. He pressed his face close, and then called to his right-hand gargoyle, Rancus Romar. "Take Mr. Zxin-Ziboc here to the far corner of Hades and pitch him into the Unholy Reservoir of Chunk n' Dung. Oh . . . , and, Rancus? Be *nice* about it, for heaven's sake!"

Zxin-Ziboc's eyes darted from Rancus Romar back to the Devil. "But, but, Sir? The Unholy Reservoir—?"

"—Yes," the Devil said, his hot, foul breath filling the demon's face. "And leave him there for the remainder of Eternity. That should give him enough time to contempilate."

The demon bowed his head in shame. "It's contemplate, my most worthy lord of sin and depravity."

Sweat rolled down the wrinkled foreheads of all the other demons. No one dared say a word as the Devil lit up a cigar and sat on his throne of flesh and bone, peering over his demonic chapel. A grin crept across his face as a devilish idea came to mind. He snapped his fingers just before Rancus Romar walked out of the room with Zwin-Ziboc in tow. "Rancus! On your return, bring me the Primal Truckin' Boys!"

The gargoyle's nostrils flared in revulsion. "Sir? My dishonorable lordhood, please reconsider! Don't involve those rambunctious redneck hicks! We certainly have enough trouble as it is."

The Devil slid his hands together. "Ah, yes! Trouble is just what I need."

Rancus Romar threw up his arms in disgust and then hauled poor Zwin-Ziboc to his doom. He had half a mind to join him.

***

"Yee-Haw! Forty tons of rattlin steel and bone a'rollin' down the highway! Ain't no Earth smokie going to pull over this bad boy, I tell you that much!"

"Hey, there, big guy. This here's the deal of the centuries! Nobody pays like the Main Man, himself. All we got to do is round up a few hundred-thousand lost souls. Them stragglers that returned to Earth a'cause of the backup at them Eternity Gates. Hell, if not for that Reaper fella dyin'-off like he did; we wouldn't have gotten ourselves this here sweet deal. Why, if I could, I'd just be inclined to give 'em a peck on the cheekbone."

"I hear ya, Red Man. We've been truckin since the Creation, and there ain't never been a deal like this a'fore. Way I see it, it ain't likely to happen again."

"Ah, shit, Half Elvis, don't you remember the good old days? Back when we'd down that yak piss Schlitz in a can and pick up living Earth girls at truck stops? Now, *them* were the days!"

"Yeah, I remember! I also recall you catching yourself a case of fire-itch from off one of them lot lizards."

"Ain't no sense in bringing that up, Half Elvis."

"Breaker breaker, good buddies, this here's your eighteen wheeler-dealer, Mr. Rotten. Me and Leech Daddy are tailing your backsides."

"Welcome to Earth, pardners! We'll need all the help we can get for the soul roundup. Where's that other no-good buddy of ours?"

"Quart Low? He's a'comin. Pullin up the rear."

"Sounds 'bout like him. Well, hot-damn! Wooo-Wee! We're gonna be a powder keg to be reckoned with! Nobody's going to mess around with these five wreckin machines. We're a bunch of achin', breakin', hellbent sumbitches . . . rollin down this here concrete pathway to deee-fuckin'-struction! So what are you in for, Mr. Rot?"

"Ten."

"Ten thou?"

"No, jackass. Ten. As in Mister Rot-ten. Get my dern name right!"

"Gotcha', good buddy. Just a slip o' the tongue is all. I forgot how particular you get."

"Well, I'm signed up for twenty five and a smidgen. Yourself?"

"Thirty two even."

"Shit on a stick, Half Elvis! And here I thought I had a good deal cooked up. How'd you pull that off? Ol' Scratchpot never pays me over twenty five."

"1692. Hauled a heap o' them witches out of Salem. Devil was grinnin like a hound dog in a chicken coop. Just got to find a way to his heart, Mr. Rotten."

"Ah, the good old days."

"Days are still good far as I see it. I mean, the sinnin' is worse than ever. And long as bad folks keep dyin', we'll be in business til doomsday."

"Half Elvis, you always were an idealist."

"Hey, there, yappin good buddies. This here's the real deal behind the wheels. I can slice 'n dice with the best of 'em and get where I'm heading to boot. In time, I might add. Whatcha' varmints got to say for yourselves?"

"Quart Low? 'Bout time you showed up. Glad to have you on the roundup with us."

Half Elvis, Red Man, Mr. Rotten, Leech Daddy, and Quart Low came barreling up out of the ass of Texas. Perched in the cabs of their trucks, the five gear-jamming demons kept their rubber burning the Texas blood slick highway, plowing innocent cars and miniaturized Earth semi's to crushed oblivion. They left nothing but death and exhaust behind.

"Listen up, good truckin buddies. Half Elvis here. Hate to break up the gibber-jabber, but I spy a waterin' hole coming up."

"I could sure use a drink or three!" Quart Low announced.

"I'll second that," Red Man added. "We got time for a quick stop?"

"We'll make time," Half Elvis said. He yanked the chain dangling near his head, the horn producing one of the most horrendous, blasphemous noises ever heard on Earth. A warning of things to come.

The Primal Truckin' Boys wheeled into Big Tate's Truck-A-Palooza. The buildings rattled, heads turned, and jaws dropped as the five titan-sized semi's came roaring off the sun-scorched highway and into the lot with the words "MADE IN HELL" displayed boastfully in large letters across the upper windshields. The trucks were three times the size of Earth rigs, colossal giants not meant for the likes of this world. The trailers were wide enough to house whales, and the tires big as carousels. The mud flaps were like theater curtains with silhouettes of voluptuous, naked demon girls exposing shapely legs and breasts with silver flames whisking up from between their thighs.

The demon truckers climbed down the ladders, looking like pig-faced trolls standing next to their massive iron horses. Several Earth truckers scurried out of the way as the flannel-wearing, blue jean clad rednecks from Hell strode by; Big Tate's Tavern their destination.

***

The tavern was packed full with ruffians. A brawny, tattooed tough guy in a sleeveless leather jacket was shooting 8-ball with his equally tattooed, dangerous-looking woman; a cigarette dangling from both their lips. Smoke filled the room, creating a silver haze hovering over the longhaired and bald heads of those sitting at the booths and tables. Tight-jeaned waitresses pranced with trays of beer, shaking their hips to the Southern fried rock music blaring from the jukebox. The bartender kept serving drinks, never straying too far from the 12-gauge pump shotgun hidden under the counter—insurance in case the flannels and leathers got out of hand.

"Mother of all demons, would you look at that!" declared a toothless, tattooed man sipping beer at one of the many round tables in the room. He jabbed his friend in the ribs. "Check out those clowns coming in."

His buddy turned to see the Primal Truckin' Boys shoving their way through the bikers and truckers. Everybody who saw them made way. All others got tossed.

Half Elvis was first to reach the bar. In front of him was a bald, heavy knuckled biker. "Outta' the way, Princess. I'm next!" He grabbed the biker by the scruff of his jacket and pitched him aside. The red-eyed demon leaned against the bar and shouted for the bartender. "Hey, barkeep! Need five beers over here, pronto!" He jabbed his thumb over his shoulder to his fellow trucking demons. "Then take their orders."

The bartender literally dropped what he was doing and immediately started pouring beer for Half Elvis. The man's hands were shaky, fumbling over the tap. Very uncharacteristic. In his day he'd fought off many a robber, busted up fistfights between rival biker gangs, manhandled anybody dumb enough to grab one of the waitresses, and once even clubbed a drunken sheriff's deputy over the head with a sack of frozen Brussels sprouts . . . but the demons standing at his bar didn't look like anything he wanted to tangle with. Their mashed-up pig noses, snarling lips, twisted teeth, and red eyes sort of put a damper on his legendary "bad-assery".

Mr. Rotten and Leech Daddy took a seat on two stools and then started banging their fists on the bar, rattling the liquor bottles on the shelves. The entire room fell silent as all eyes were on this most unbelieving sight.

"Barkeep! Got shit in your ears or somethin, buddy?" Half Elvis looked to his demonic companions and snickered, waving the bartender over. "Said I need five beers in a hurry. Not after the Second Coming, for cryin out loud."

"I'm right on it, Mister!" the bartender said, topping off the five mugs and sliding them across the bar to the thirsty demon. "All on the house, no charge."

Half Elvis took the first mug and downed the beer in one swift gulp. "Well," he said, pounding the empty glass on the bar; he burped loudly, and then wiped his mouth with the back of his hand, "that's mighty Christian of ya." He took the second mug and guzzled it, and then picked up the third.

Quart Low nestled in between Half Elvis and Mr. Rotten. He pointed to the liquor bottles on the wall behind the bar. "That one there with the white sticker."

The bartender turned to look. "Southern Comfort?"

Quart Low nodded, gesturing with his hand for that particular bottle. "Yeah, gimmie a couple shots of that Comfortin' stuff."

The bartender handed him the bottle. "Take as much as you want."

"Thanks, Mr. Keep."

He then looked to Mr. Rotten and Leech Daddy. "And—and what will it be for you guys? Everything's on the house."

"I wanna try the second shelf," Mr. Rotten said, looking at all the bottles.

305

The bartender's mouth fell agape. "The whole shelf?"

Mr. Rotten reached across the bar and grabbed the bartender by the collar of his shirt. "You got a problem with that?" Mr. Rotten pulled the man off the floor.

"No problem! Not at all! I mean, you-you-you can have it. Both shelves if you want."

"Naw," Mr. Rotten said, letting go of the shaken man. "Just the second one."

Red Man put his hand on Mr. Rotten's shoulder. "Don't go gettin all schnuckered up again. You remember the Eighties when the last time you drank a whole shelf of whiskey. You started dancin' to Debbie Gibson songs all night. Talk about embarrassin!"

Mr. Rotten smacked the palm of his hand against the bar, causing the bartender to about jump out of his skin. "Scratch that order! Just fetch me a bottle of sumthin'nother."

The bartender nervously handed him an unopened bottle of tequila then took Red Man and Leech Daddy's requests. He glanced to the door, contemplating running for it as the hulking demon boys sat drinking their beer and liquor. Most of the other patrons had already snuck out; the tavern windows vibrated from truck engines as the Earthlings fled the parking lot.

"How 'bout a game of darts, puss boots?" Half Elvis said to Red Man, poking him in the chest with his finger. "I beat you every time, and you dern well know it."

"Oh yeah? Then let's have at it. I'll have every number and my bull's eyes closed out a'fore you can whistle—Oh, Glorious Satan."

"I'd like to see that," Half Elvis said. "You'd be doin' good to hit the dartboard instead of your dadgum foot like you usually do."

Red Man shoved Half Elvis.

Quart Low quickly stepped between them. "You boys simmer down! We ain't got time for you two bickerin' at each other."

"He started it," Red Man declared, jabbing a thumb at Half Elvis.

Half Elvis snarled and waved him off. "Your Momma started it when she shagged that mangy goat."

"That does it!" Red Man shouted, taking a swing at Half Elvis.

Mr. Rotten was knocked off his stool as Half Elvis and Red Man became entangled in a whirlwind of fists.

Quart Low stepped back, shaking his head disapprovingly before looking over his shoulder at the bewildered bartender. "They do this time ta' time. They're actually best friends, if you can image that." He put the bottle of Comfort to his scaly lips and finished it, slamming the empty soldier down on the counter. "Fetch me a fresh bottle of Jack while they tickle each other on the floor like a couple girls. This might take a minute."

The bartender raced to fill the demon's order. "Wh-where are you all from?" he asked, setting the bottle on the bar. "I mean, not meaning to pry or—or anything." With a shaky hand, the bartender twisted off the bottle's cap, but accidently knocked it over as he stepped back. He watched in horror as the bourbon spilled on Quart Low's arm. "Fuck me—I'm sorry, Mister! Here, let me clean it off—"

"Simmer down there, pardner. Ain't no reason to get your panties all in a wad. I can absorb booze in all the right places." Quart Low's ragged smirk looked wicked on his lumpy, piggish face. He nodded at the bartender, and then to his arm on the counter. "Lookey there, if that don't beat all."

A small hole appeared on his forearm, and a slender black tongue snaked out. The tongue lapped the spilt booze then slithered back into the closing hole. The bartender's stomach churned, and he doubled over to throw up.

Quart Low smiled proudly. "You Earthies always were a bunch of wussus."

Half Elvis and Red Man grappled on the floor, smashing pool cues and beer bottles over each other's heads. Mr. Rotten was tempted to join in (after having been knocked off his stool), but instead calmly dusted himself off, sat back down, and demanded a cold brew. He watched the brutality, hoping the two demons might knock out each other's teeth.

"You two sissies quit pulling each other's hair and let's get back out on the road," Quart Low said. "We still got souls to round up."

The fighting was beginning to make Mr. Rotten edgy. He balled his fists and started striking the bar. Violence excited him. Even his internal organs often battled each other.

Having had enough of sitting on the sideline, Mr. Rotten stood up and grabbed an empty beer bottle. He bent a finger for the bartender. "Open your mouth," Mr. Rotten demanded. The bartender—his eyes bigger than Dallas—did as he was told. "Wider," Mr. Rotten said. And when the bartender had his mouth stretched as far as he could, Mr. Rotten crammed the entire bottle into the man's mouth, breaking his teeth at the gum line.

"Why'd you go and do that for?" Quart Low asked. He sighed as Mr. Rotten laughed hysterically at the paralyzed Earth man. "I actually liked him!"

Mr. Rotten reached across the counter and punched the back of the beer bottle protruding from the man's mouth, smashing brown glass daggers deep into the bartender's face. "Signed, sealed, and delivered," Mr. Rotten said, winking at Quart Low, and then sitting back down on his stool with a cockeyed grin.

The bartender fell to the floor, his body flopping in convulsions.

The smell of blood caused Half Elvis and Red Man to stop in mid-swing.

"Hey, Elvis?" Red Man said, heaving for breath.

"What?"

"What say we call a truce? I've got a sudden hankerin' for some Texas chili."

Half Elvis crawled to his knees and rubbed his chin. "Yeah, I could go for a bowl myself. All this fightin . . . Whew! Worked up an appetite."

"There's a diner just 'cross the parking lot. I saw it coming in," Red Man said, breathing heavy. "Texas chili. Now that's some sweet ass, spicy manna from Heaven!"

"Norm'ly," Half Elvis said, slowly getting to his feet; he helped up his friend, "that word makes my skin crawl. But under the circumstances, I say a bowl of spicy chili does sound a bit Heavenly." He looked to the others sitting at the bar with drinks in hand. "You fellas comin' with us to get some vittles?"

Mr. Rotten looked to Quart Low and Leech Daddy. "Naw. We're going to stay and drink. Kick around the bartender a while a'fore we gotta split."

"Suit yourselves," Red Man said, heading for the door with Half Elvis behind him. "But I'm going to get me a belly-full of hot fart fuel before we head out on the roundup."

Quart Low nudged Mr. Rotten. "Wouldn't want to be a dust mite stuck in his driver's seat.

***

Half Elvis and Red Man nearly shattered the diner's front glass door. The sounds of utensils clanking against the floor filled the room as every face turned to gawk at the two demons strutting toward a booth. Half Elvis smelled the fragrance of spices on his forked tongue, which kept darting in and out of his lips.

"Service!" Red Man yelled, pounding the table with a fist. "We're hungry!"

A freckle faced woman with strawberry blonde hair came to the table with a pencil and tablet in hand. She had round hazel eyes and rosy cheeks; she was chewing a wad of gum. "Keep yellin out like that and I'll squirt your gizzards full of pepper spray. I don't put up with uncouth rednecks."

Red Man looked to Half Elvis. Both demons shrugged.

"Alrighty," the rosy cheeked waitress said, "what's it going to be for you guys today?"

"We want some Texas fire chili," Red Man said. "Extra, extra spicy!"

The waitress smacked her lips as she chewed her gum. "You're a couple of them types, huh? Think you can handle anything. Alrighty, it's your stomachs. Don't blame me, though. You want the Atomic Fire Bomb or go all the way to Hell with What-In-Blazes-Was-That?"

"The hottest stuff you got in the house," Red Man said, rubbing his hands together.

Half Elvis looked to the waitress's name tag. He winked at her. "Wendy's the hottest stuff in the house, Red."

She winked back at him and smiled. "Why thank you, sweetie. You get half price."

"See there," Half Elvis said, kicking Red Man under the table, "a bit of politeness goes a long way with a purdy lady."

"With me it's the only way," Wendy said, matter-of-factly. "But I ain't a prude or nothing. A man worth his onions has got to know when to play cool or turn up the heat, know what I mean?" She turned to leave. "Two bowls of butt burners coming right up."

"Cute little thang, ain't she, Red?"

"Hotter than a two dollar pistol."

Half Elvis leaned back and put his arms behind his head. "Think I got a chance?"

"Not a prayer's chance. She's just workin you to get a good tip is all," Red Man said, now gnawing on the corner of a menu, trying to stave his hunger. "What she needs is a real man. Red Man!"

"Shit. More like a speckled toad pecker is what you are."

"You're one to talk," replied Red Man. "Look at that scrotum you call a face. I bet your daddy tried pulling your chin up over your forehead when you were born to hide that ugliness from your momma."

"I'm getting 'bout sick n tired of you cuttin' bad," Half Elvis said, but his anger subsided as a big brown bowl of steaming chili was placed under his nose (crackers on the side). Wendy the waitress winked at him. She'd been keen enough to bring along two bottles of cold beer.

"That was fast," Half Elvis told her, unrolling his utensils from the napkin.

"I don't mess around," Wendy spouted. "Five years dealing with roughnecks like you, a girl gets pretty quick on her feet. And on her wits." She licked her lips then popped a bubble with her gum.

"This crap better play pandemonium on the backside," Red Man said, wasting no time digging into his chili with a spoon in one hand and a fork in the other. "That's when you know it's especially good. If it blasts out your seat cushion when you're drivin down the road."

Wendy snubbed her nose and walked away.

Half Elvis exhaled. "Red Man . . . ?"

He didn't bother looking up, but kept digging in his chili as though he'd lost something valuable in it. "Yeah, what izzit?"

"You sure know how to turn on a woman. A romanatic is what you are."

"A wha—?"

"A romanatic. You know, like when a man is real good at making women feel all squishy on the inside. I saw it on her face. You squished her up alright, just in the wrong kinda way."

"You mean a romantic?" Red Man said, glancing up through his thick eyebrows. He kept blowing on his chili.

"That's what I said, a romanatic."

***

The Devil's think tank was called to attention. "Have you imbeciles found who killed the Grim Reaper?"

"We have strong suspicions, our lord," stated Halethorpe Ovendale, the Chief Speaker of The Regal Court of Prestige Demonkind.

"What is his name?" demanded the Devil, coming down off his throne.

"Your lordship, I dare say it's not male."

The Devil stamped the heel of his cloven hoof into the ground. "Give me a name!"

"Betty."

The Devil lowered his face to the Speaker. "Did I hear you correctly?"

The speaker closed his eyes, and mumbled softly, "Betty Crinkle."

The Devil held his breath for several seconds. At last, he exhaled. "You mean to tell me that a demoness named Betty Crinkle murdered the all-immortal Grim Reaper?"

"Not a demoness, your superior wickedship." Halethorpe cringed. "Betty Crinkle from Turtle River, Minnesota."

The Devil gnashed his teeth. "If I was forgiving I'd throw you into the Unholy Reservoir of Chunk n' Dung for your incompetenancy. But I'm not forgiving. I'm the Devil." He walked around the demon, breathing on his neck. "Instead, I'm going to have you strung up by your vocal chords and your insides pulled out your arse an inch a year." He stopped in front of Halethorpe and bared his sharp white teeth.

The rest of The Court began to chatter, trying to come up with another potential killer. They also debated who would be the next speaker of The Regal Court. There were no volunteers.

"Rancus Romar!" the Devil yelled. "Where in Hell are you?"

"My lord. I am here!" He scrambled to his hooves.

"I'm sending you on a mission."

"A mission, Sir? Where to?"

"Earth."

"Earth, Sir?"

"I want you to report on the Primal Truckin' Boys. See how the roundup is going."

"My most vile Excellency, I'll get right to it!"

***

Half Elvis and Red Man had scraped every morsel out the bowls and were now in a state of intense abdominal pain. The chili had done them in just as Wendy the waitress had said. They sat with their hands on their bellies, staring dishearteningly at remnants of beans and meat splattered on the table.

Two Earth truckers stared at them.

"What do you suppose they are?" asked one of the men to the other.

"If I had to guess, I'd say they escaped from prison."

Half Elvis rubbed his glazed eyes with the backs of his hands. "Feels like a volcano erupting in my tummy."

Red Man moaned; his head lolled back against the booth.

Wendy came to the table. "You boys ready for another round?"

Half Elvis groaned, waving her off.

"Six bowls apiece," Wendy said, shaking her head. "Never seen anybody make it through two. You boys are something else, I tell ya." She placed two glasses of water on the table. "You going to be alright? Want me to call an ambulance?" She snickered at the two demons slumped with chili smeared on their faces. "You both look a mess." She went to retrieve a bus tray and came back, chewing her gum as loud and deliberately as possible. "You can help me clean up. Don't be shy."

Half Elvis wiped the sweat from his forehead, took a sip of water, and then hesitantly helped Wendy collect the dishes. "What time you get off work?" he asked, staring at the freckles on her face. He thought they were . . . (what was the word?) . . . cute.

"Why, you asking me out for a date?"

"Would you go if I did?"

Wendy smacked her lips. "I might," she said, wiping the table with a damp cloth. "Might not. Dependin'."

"Dependin' on what?" Half Elvis asked.

"On what you're expecting."

Half Elvis looked to Red Man. "We might look mean, but we got hearts of gold."

Wendy stopped and put her hands on her hips. "Well, ain't no way I'm going out with the both of ya. I'm a one man kinda gal."

Half Elvis reached for her arm. "I mean just me. Forget him."

"Where're you two from, anyways?"

Half Elvis licked his lips. "Ohio."

"Ohio? I doubt that."

"Why's that?"

"I dunno. Something different about you two. The way you smell."

Half Elvis sniffed his armpit. "What's wrong with how I smell?"

"Nothin'. Just different is all."

"Brimstone."

Wendy shrugged. "That some kind of deodorant I don't know about?"

"It's the spice of life where we come from."

"Smells like hell to me," Wendy said, playfully holding her nose.

Half Elvis smiled. "Come with me. Get out of this dump and hit the road awhile. I'll bring you back when we're done."

"Done doing what?" Wendy asked, smacking her gum.

"Done with the roundup. We had a massive backup at the Eternity Gates. The Devil sent us to gather the lost souls before they can repent."

Wendy spat her gum into the bus tray and pulled a new piece from her apron. "I spent years repenting, and look where it's got me. Stuck in Big Tate's Truck-A-Palooza, serving rat burgers and chili all day to rednecks and demons. Think I might ought to be going to church instead of with you."

Half Elvis snarled his upper lip. "Church is overrated."

"You're kidding me about this, aren't you? This bit about coming from Hell. Got to admit though, that's probably the most unique pickup line I've ever gotten." She unwrapped the gum and popped it in her mouth, chewing it as hard as she could. "Sure. Why not. Need to spice up my life a little anyway."

"Spice," Red Man moaned, barely lifting his head from the table, ". . . don't say that word."

Half Elvis kicked him in the shin. "Go get the others. Me and Wendy want to talk alone a few minutes. Don't we, turtle dumplins'?" He pulled her to his lap, glaring at Red Man. "I'll pay for the grub. Just get the others. We need to be hittin the road."

Red Man slid out of the booth, leaving Half Elvis and the waitress in a tangle of arms and kisses. The unabashed, gooey affection upset the demon's stomach worse than the six bowls of chili.

As he walked out of the diner to the parking lot, Red Man considered his feelings. He always felt shunned by Earth women. These broads were supposed to be easy, according to the other Truckin' Boys. He reached up and felt the stubby, rigid horns on his head as he walked toward the tavern. "I wasn't meant to be a lady's man," he grumbled, grinding his twisted teeth. "I was made for truckin!" He stopped short of entering the tavern and turned to his truck. He then looked back at the tavern door. "Ah, fuck 'em. Let them eat my dust." He turned from the tavern and walked briskly to his truck.

***

"Wendy Winters."

"That's a funny name," Half Elvis said, toying with the black bra strap on her shoulder. "Least your parents didn't name you Summer."

"Yeah. Or Johnnie."

Half Elvis scratched his head. He didn't get it.

"So, tell me what Hell's like," she said, leaning back into the demon's arms. "Is there really fire? Does the Devil have a forked tail and pitchfork and all that?"

Half Elvis patted her leg. "He lost the fork during the Christian Crusades. Got so mad he threw it into the Reservoir of Chunk n' Dung. Afterward, he sent countless souls to find it, but they never came back. Wasn't their fault, but the Devil . . . he's got a temper somethin' nasty."

"Sounds like my boss," Wendy said. She looked to the other patrons in the diner. None of them dared look back. "Good thing he's off today or he'd be out here skinning my hide."

"I doubt that," Half Elvis said, showing her the size of his hand. His skin was thick and hard as granite. "He so much as looked at'cha crooked, I'd fold his teeth back in his face."

Wendy rested her head against Half Elvis' chest. She reached down, rubbing her fingers over the demon's soft flannel sleeve. "It's hard to find true love . . . and one never knows when it'll get lost again."

An hour later, the front door to the diner opened and three drunken demons staggered in. Most of the patrons had already gone; tips left on the tables. Half Elvis and Wendy Winters were cuddled in the booth, wrapped in each other's arms, asleep with love stricken grins on their faces.

"Hey, Half Brain!" yelled Quart Low, shaking the sleeping demon. "Wake up!"

"Huh? Wha—?" mumbled Half Elvis.

"Who you got there on your lap?" Quart Low hovered over the sleeping, freckle faced waitress.

"Wendy. Wendy Winters. She's my gal."

"Well, where's Red Man? His truck's gone."

Half Elvis rubbed his eyes then woke Wendy who had passed out with her head against him. "Time to get up, muffin bumps. We need to hit the road."

Mr. Rotten pulled the woman off Half Elvis. "Where's Red Man?" he asked, shaking a fist at his fellow demon trucker.

Half Elvis jumped to his hooves and pulled Wendy out of Mr. Rotten's grasp. "How am I s'posed to know? We chowed down some vittles and rested a bit. He was supposed to have gotten yuns rounded up."

"Yeah, well, he didn't," Mr. Rotten said. "He's done gone. Split on us. I bet he figures to hornswoggle us by gettin back to Hell with the first load."

"You think he'd do that?" Half Elvis put his arm around Wendy's waist. He held her close, resting his scaly cheek on the top of her head.

"His truck's gone. What do you think, lover boy?"

Half Elvis bit down on his lip, considering the possibility that Red Man had deserted them. "Well, let's get. Maybe we can catch up to him out on the road."

"You better believe we will," Quart Low stated. "And when we do . . ." He punched his hand with his other fist.

Leech Daddy and Mr. Rotten did likewise.

***

The asphalt cracked and sulfur spewed into the air. Rancus Romar, sitting atop a ferocious, horned beast with nine eyes and six powerful legs, burst through the crumpled road. The six-legged beast raised its head and roared at Heaven above; its opened mouth exposed misshapen teeth and a tongue made of fire. The rider on its back pulled the reigns tight, controlling the wild brute, and guiding it (snorting and fuming) through the

319

wreckage of cars and trucks—casualties of the Primal Truckin' Boys.

The two demons took to the desert, exceeding speeds of eighty miles an hour. It wasn't long until Rancus Romar spotted Big Tate's in the distance. He recognized the lingering stench of brimstone in the air, and he knew that the Primal Truckin' Boys couldn't be far.

***

"Hey, good buddies." It was Half Elvis on the horn, leading the convoy. "I don't see a sign of Red Man anywheres."

"Forget him," Quart Low replied on the CB. "Let's get to fetchin' souls."

"I'm with ya there, pardner," said Mr. Rotten. "We'll catch up to that scoundrel soon 'nuff. Let's get on with the roundup!"

Half Elvis put his left hand on Wendy's leg; kept his other on the black, leathery steering wheel. "There's a map in the glove box," he told her. "Reach in and grab it, if ya don't mind."

Wendy pulled it out, looked it over. "We heading to New Mexico?"

"To start with. We'll work our way up to California. S'pect we'll probably find a heap of damned souls in L.A."

Wendy looked out the side window. "Sign says there's a little town up ahead called Valentine."

Half Elvis took his hand off her leg and grabbed the CB. "What say we stop at the next town? See if we can get us a little somethin to toss in the back."

"Sounds good to me," Quart Low said. "Nothin worse than haulin empty trailers."

There wasn't much to Valentine; a few hundred folks, a few stores, and a whole lotta nothing to do. Vandalism or an occasional fist fight made for front page news. Once, in the summer of '87, Jose Ramos, hyped on peyote, backed over his wife with his dirt brown El Camino. He dragged her body under the back bumper until she popped out the front with a bloody, cockeyed grin on her face, flopping a mangled hand as if to wave goodbye to her tripping, delinquent husband. The Sheriff called the whole thing a terrible incident. Jose was never arrested.

He re-married a month later, and even twice after that. Jose loved his women, but sooner than later they always developed a bad habit of getting in the way of his damned car bumper.

Tomorrow's paper, however, would read like nothing this little West Texas town had ever experienced before: GOD LOOKS OTHER WAY, AS HELL COMES TO VALENTINE!

Pastor T.J. Duncan would blame the whole thing on adultery and rock music.

Parents ran out to their yards to grab their children. Doors slammed shut, deadbolts locked, and guns were cocked and loaded. Almost every window had eyes peering from behind curtains at the massive trucks deterring off Highway 90 and into their nothing to do town.

Douglas Hurst—Lt. Douglas Hurst—stood defiantly on his front porch, shotgun in hand, while his wife tugged at his arm to get inside.

"Let go of me, woman!" he yelled, jerking his arm from her. "I can't aim straight with you tugging my flippin arm off!"

"Doug, you can't see a blasted thing without your glasses!" his wife shouted at him. "Get inside before you shoot yourself in the leg with that thing."

The Primal Truckin' Boys parked their beastly rigs in front of Douglas' house. The sun twinkled off the chrome bumpers and exhaust pipes. The demons cut the rumbling motors. Crawling down the ladders from their cabs, the truckers gathered in the road to discuss what to do next.

Wendy Winters held on faithfully to Half Elvis's forearm, listening as the demons talked.

"What do yuns say 'bout that waterin hole?" Quart Low said, nodding to a small tavern across the street from where they were standing. "Could go for another drink. Maybe we'll run across a few thirsty souls."

"I'm for that," Mr. Rotten said. "Need to kick my buzz up a couple notches." He turned to Half Elvis and Leech Daddy.

"Alright," Half Elvis said, "but let's keep it brief. I want to get to Cali before Red Man. Don't want him gettin too much a lead on us."

The four demons and Wendy hurried across the street to the tavern. Douglas Hurst scurried around their trucks and followed them, his shotgun clutched tightly in his hands.

There was nary a soul in the tavern, only kicked over chairs and an abandoned pool table with the balls set for the next shot. Mr. Rotten grabbed a cue and started sinking them.

Half Elvis, Wendy, and the others strolled to the bar.

"I'll be bartender," Wendy said, crawling over the counter to the other side.

Half Elvis turned to Quart Low. "She sure is a purdy little peach."

Wendy smiled at the Boys. "So, what'll it be?"

Half Elvis pointed to beer bottles lined up behind the bar. "A couple o' those."

"They're warm," Wendy said, touching them and making a soured face.

"Everything's warm where I come from."

"Suit yourself." She handed him two beers and looked to Quart Low and Leech Daddy. "Same for you?"

They glanced at each other then nodded.

Wendy handed them their warm beer, and two extra for Mr. Rotten. She then tugged at Half Elvis' arm. "Think when we're all done with the roundup, you might maybe take me back to Hell with you? I mean, just for a visit. Not like I'd want to stay forever or anything. But I'm curious to see."

Half Elvis swallowed hard. He hadn't thought about that possibility; but she couldn't go to Hell (not least while she's still alive), and he couldn't stay here on Earth with her. Not forever. He decided to lie. There was still time to play. "Sure, turtle dumplins', I'd love you to go back with me."

"Should I bring a fire extinguisher?"

He laughed. "It ain't really like that. I mean, there's fire but it ain't like it's all over the place. Mostly a lot of torture. A bunch of screamin', stuff like that."

"Why would God really send people to Hell?" she asked, going to a cooler and getting a cold beer. She popped the cap and swigged. "Like, if I was God, I just wouldn't make bad people in the first place. That would sort of save all the trouble, don't you think?"

"Got me." Half Elvis shrugged. "But I don't think God makes bad people. They sort of make themselves."

"Like homos do? Or are you one of those that believe they're born that way?"

Again, Half Elvis shrugged. "I don't know much about homos. I guess they're that way because of . . . Shit, I don't know."

"I thought all homos go to Hell?"

Half Elvis finished his beer. "Hell ain't for homos, babe. Hell's for nonbelievers."

"So Jesus really is God's son?" Wendy asked. She handed Half Elvis another beer.

"That depends if you're a believer or not."

"So if not, I'll be going to Hell with you?"

"This is makin' me nervous talkin 'bout it," Half Elvis said. He opened his beer and guzzled. He set the empty on the counter. "I'm just here to do the Devil's work."

"God makes you nervous?" Wendy crawled up on the counter and started poking him in the side. "Or is it me?"

"Stop it," he snapped, twisting to get away.

"It's me, isn't it? You're scared of me!"

"Neither one. I'm just the way I am."

She kept prodding him with her forefinger. "Big bad demon from Hell all scared of little ole me. Imagine that."

"I ain't scared of ya, just don't like bein poked on is all."

She jumped off the counter and chased him. "Poke, poke, poke! Little tickle angel here to torture you!"

Quart Low and Leech Daddy stood dumbfounded. They weren't sure what to make of it: An Earth girl chasing a demon around the room with her finger? Just didn't seem right.

The front door of the tavern suddenly swung open. Light gleamed like a halo around a dark silhouette of a man with a long gun in hand. The demons squint their reddened eyes.

"Hell ain't welcome in Valentine," said Douglas Hurst, stepping from the sunlight and into the bar. He pumped his shotgun. "I'm going to send you back where you came from. Piece by bloody piece."

Quart Low turned to Leech Daddy. "Is this fucker kiddin'?"

Half Elvis and Wendy stopped their play. She looked to her demon and then back at the man standing at the front door with his gun aimed at them.

"Elvis," she said.

"Shh," he told her, pushing her behind him. "Stay put. We'll take care of this."

Douglas held the gun steady, barrel pointed at Half Elvis. "Come at me and I'll blast you right through Heaven's Gates."

"Thou shalt not commit murder," Half Elvis told him.

Mr. Rotten put down his cue and came to stand next to Half Elvis.

"That rule don't apply to your kind, devil. I've been prepared for this day a long time." Douglas snarled his upper lip. "Pastor T.J. Duncan is on his way over. He's bringing the Bible with him. We'll see what hot lead and a bit of the Good Word does for you."

Leech Daddy put down his beer and started toward the emboldened man. Quart Low watched from the bar.

"You're even uglier than I thought you'd be," Douglas said, swinging the barrel of his gun to Leech Daddy. "I've seen road kill I'd rather snuggle up to."

Leech Daddy edged closer.

"Bible talks about a day when the Devil will walk to and fro, devouring the weak. But you came to the wrong place. You don't mess with Texas!"

Wendy nudged Half Elvis. "Can guns hurt you, honey? He can't really kill you, can he? I mean, you being from Hell and all."

Half Elvis glared intently at the man. "Don't go worrying your sweet little head 'bout me," he told Wendy, who was peeking from around him. "It'll take more than what he's got to put a damper on my day."

Douglas swung the barrel back at Half Elvis. "The shells I got in this gun . . . They're special. They've been blessed. The Lord's my gunpowder today."

Half Elvis reached behind him and patted Wendy. "This do-gooder's 'bout to learn better."

Douglas saw something move in the corner of his eye. He swung the gun to shoot but Leech Daddy reached out and grabbed the barrel. The gun went off, a deafening explosion. A neon bar light over the bar burst to pieces, the shattered, plastic frame dangling against the wall by its cord.

"Release me, you filthy demon-hound!" Douglas demanded, struggling to get the gun free from Leech Daddy's grasp. "I'll blast your godda—"

The demon placed his free hand over Douglas' mouth and yanked the gun away. He threw it to the floor then took hold of the man's nose.

"Here it comes," Half Elvis said. "Smoochie. Smoochie."

Leech Daddy removed his hand from Douglas' mouth. The man's eyes grew wide and full of fear. The demon lifted him into the air, putting his lips against the man's and releasing a long worm from his mouth.

Wendy's fingernails dug into Half Elvis' side as she watched. "Whoa . . . ! Did'ja see that?"

Douglas Hurst's legs kicked desperately as the long worm emitting from Leech Daddy's mouth entered his own—the bitterness of each segment boring grooves into his lips as the razor sharp worm scraped over his teeth and down to his throat.

Leech Daddy gnashed his teeth together, snipping off the worm. The blunt end of it squiggled through Douglas' lips, disappearing into his mouth, and down his gullet into the soft, delicate workings of his body.

The demon released Douglas. The man staggered around for a moment, trying to catch his breath—trying to regain his equilibrium, and clutching his stomach. There was something foul rolling and expanding inside him. He raised his arm to wipe his lips. "Filthy, perverted devils." He fell to the floor, scratching at his belly, and raising his shirt to see a thick lump wriggling under his skin. "Get it out of me, Lord!" he screamed, pinching at his belly, trying to mash the thing inside. "Get it out of me!"

Wendy stepped from around Half Elvis, wanting a better view of the thrashing man on the floor.

Douglas' insides were boiling. Smoke erupted from his mouth and nostrils; a grey-white plume seeping through the backside of his pants. The stench of brimstone filled the room and all the demons inhaled deeply. Wendy held her nose, repulsed by the stench, but

327

she was intrigued by the man's misery; his internal organs being turned to hot-peppered soup.

He let out a terrible scream as every pore on his body expanded and tiny worms began to sprout, bending their red bodies in loops and circles, like elongated, colored maggots feasting on raw chicken. The worms lifted the body and carried it out the front door of the tavern. There was no top or bottom to Douglas Hurst, only a smoldering cluster of flesh, smoke, blood and worms rolling out to the street in one agonizing heap, rolling out to shrivel and die in the hot Texas sun.

"Wasn't that a sight?" Half Elvis said, coming to stand next to Wendy. He grabbed hold of her hand.

She smiled like the Devil himself. "Awesome. Let's go do it again."

***

Wendy and the Primal Truckin' Boys went house to house, kicking in doors and ransacking homes for lost souls. They found two playing blackjack on a storage trunk in the attic of lady Foggs' house; another was hiding under Wayne Denton's bed. The raid turned up many others, as the town of Valentine unexpectedly seemed to accommodate more afterlife stowaways than a sunken cruise ship.

A lot of the houses possessed other secrets as well. Quart Low found what he believed was a voodoo doll. What it was doing this far from Barbados, he couldn't guess. The hollow-eyed doll wore a handcrafted grass skirt, painted-on shoes, and a pouch on its side that contained nine 3-inch long needles.

Bibles were plentiful as guns, and the truckers lost count of how many private stashes of "girly mags" they had run across—often the ladies of the houses were just as surprised; one woman actually thanked the demons for exposing her husband's infidelity. Quart Low stood up for the man. "It's only soft porn," he said, handing her the rolled-up magazine. "No big deal."

She glanced inside then threw it at her quivering husband, scolding him: "You like looking at these dirty tramps so much, try sleeping with them under the stars!"

Pastor T.J. Duncan's house was a treasure trove of debauchery; of course, he called it "relinquished items soon meant for the Good Lord's landfill". He obviously wasn't too keen on letting demons rummage through his four-bedroom, two bath, clandestine den of sin, but when confronted with what they found in his "special black picture book" . . . the preacher quickly fell silent and sat down on the sofa. He stared shamefully at the floor.

"Looks like we might be gettin back to you one day," Half Elvis told him, tossing the picture book to the disgraced preacher's feet.

Some of the men folk formed a lynch mob, marching down the street with guns, rakes, hammers, and baseball bats. The trucker demons were busy raiding the Alonso household when the mob caught up to them. Half Elvis and Wendy were out front, kissing on the porch, demon love permitting.

"What in damnation are they?" asked someone in the mob.

"Beats me. But let's show 'em we mean business!"

Half Elvis broke his lip lock with Wendy. "Guys!" he yelled, pounding his fist against the front of the house. "Think you better come out and take a look. We got ourselves a welcomin' committee out here!"

Mr. Rotten peeked out a window. "He's right. There's trouble a'brewin out front."

The three demons came out on the porch to confront the mob.

"Whatever evil you are, you ain't welcome here!" declared a man toward the front of the crowd. He cocked his gun to prove he was serious.

"Outta' my way," Mr. Rotten grunted, pushing Quart Low to the side. "I'll take care of this shindig, myself." The crowd retreated, running from the demon. "What'cha scared of?" Mr. Rotten yelled, balling a fist and shaking it at them. "Didn't you come to fight?"

Mr. Rotten turned back to his buddies on the porch. "Thought they called this the home of the brave?" He looked back at the cowards running for their lives. "Well . . . shit fire."

Rancus Romar watched astutely from the roof of a nearby house. The Primal Truckin' Boys were out of control just as he had expected. They appeared to be more interested in fighting than doing their jobs. They were on Earth causing mass havoc wherever they went. That's what you get, he thought, sending a bunch of rednecks.

He was delighted to report of their negligence. But he also knew what that meant.

***

"So what news have you brought of the roundup?" the Devil asked, not bothering to look at

Rancus. The Devil was busy using a crucifix to dig out crud from under his long fingernail.

"Well, your heinousness, they . . . Uh, well, you see . . . They're not exactly doing what you told them to do."

The Devil slowly looked up. "What *are* they doing?"

Rancus Romar cleared his throat. "Well, Sir, they're rednecking everything. Causing us more trouble than good."

"Rednecking?" repeated the Devil. "How does one go about doing that?"

"It means—"

"—I don't care what it means!" the Devil interrupted. "I want to know why they aren't doing what I told them! Why aren't they back here with a load of those—those—oh, whatever you call 'em . . ."

"Dead people?"

"Yes! Dead people! All those centuries of violence and discord I've sewn into the world and not even a new soul to show for it! Damn those troubled-some rednecks to Hell!"

"Sir?

"What is it?" the Devil said, gritting his teeth.

"It's troublesome, and they're already damned to Hell . . . The rednecks, I mean."

"Come here, Rancus. Get over here!"

Rancus Romar approached the Devil's throne. The Devil clasped his fingers around the crucifix, glaring down at the demon below. "Do you know the story of Pumpernickel Pete?"

Rancus shook his head. "I don't believe so, my wicked King."

"Sit down a second."

"Right here on the ground?"

"Yes, you fucking dimwit! Where else would you sit? In my lap?"

Rancus dropped to his butt, staring wide-eyed at the Devil.

"It all started when Pumpernickel Pete died and came to Hell. He lived his life on Earth as a lawyer. He was one bastard of a lawyer, too."

"Like most, Sir."

"No, Pete was an even bigger bastard than most. Even by lawyer standards." The Devil took in a deep breath. "But that's irrelevenant to the story."

"You mean, irrelevant, Sir."

"Yes, but anyway, Pete eventually died and came to Hell. You know why he came to Hell?"

"Because he was a bastard?"

The Devil stood up and stomped his left hoof. "That's partly why, but more because he was an aggravating, pestiferous little asshole, like you!"

Rancus lowered his head. "Yes, Sir."

"Now shut up and quit correcting my speech. I'm telling a story." The Devil sat back on his throne. "Pete wanted fame. He had already acquired a decent fortune for himself as a . . . ambulanance chaser? I think that's what they call them. But he wanted to be the most renowned New York lawyer in the world."

"There's only one New York in the world, Sir."

"I know that, you contemptible fathead! What I meant was, he wanted to practice in New York, but be the most famous . . . Damn it, Rancus! Quit sidetracking me!"

"I apologize, Sir."

The Devil put a hand to his horns and sighed deeply. "Seeing how desperate Pete was, I offered him a deal. Gave him the magic knack it takes to win in life. In exchange, of course, I got his soul. But what made him unique was that he was so very good at being bad. I knew he was something special. All he needed was a dose of glory."

"I'm not sure what this has to do with—"

"—Stay quiet, I'm still talking." The Devil pounded his fist against the bony armrest of his throne. "Now, where was I?"

"He needed a dose of glory, Sir."

"Yes, thank you. Well, Pete happily signed his soul to me. But he had this notion that he could get what he needed from me and beat me at my own game to boot. Thought if he could kill the Reaper he'd never be brought to Hell. Planned on cheating his way out of our contract. What do they call them, reneggers?"

"No, Sir. I don't think that's what they're called. I believe you mean Indian-givers."

The Devil cocked his head. "This story has nothing to do with Indians, you imbecile. Stay quiet. Quit being an idiot."

"Yes, Sir."

"So Pete thought he could cheat me. But what Pete didn't know was that even if he could escape Hell, which he didn't, he would never be accepted in Heaven. He'd become an everlasting dwingling."

"A dwingling, Sir?"

"Yes. A dwingling soul, roaming Earth forever as a derelict. A roaming, homeless asshole."

"Wouldn't that be dwindling?"

"No," the Devil said, snapping his fingers. "This time *you are* wrong! Dwindling means decreasing."

"Well, what does dwingling mean, then?"

"Shut up, Rancus."

"Yes, Sir."

"Pete was such an asshole-bastard that he was perfectly alright with being an aimless wanderer. He figured he could swindle peoples' money as a ghost. Now, tell me, Rancus, what good is money to a ghost?"

"I'm not sure, Sir. No good at all?"

"Exactly. But Pete didn't care. Swindling and scamming came as natural to him as eating, breathing, and farting. He didn't really need the money, but that's the beauty of it. He just didn't want anybody else to have any." The Devil scratched himself between his legs. "You see, Rancus, he followed his nature. He was a lawyer, a complete grub. I bet it was him who killed my Reaper. It was most definitely him."

Rancus Romar sat before his vile lord, too scared to say much of anything; too scared to move.

After a long, uncomfortable silence, the Devil stood up. "I bet you want to know why his name was Pumpernickel Pete, don't you?"

"It crossed my mind, Sir," Rancus said.

The Devil, snorting and pointing at Rancus, began to laugh uncontrollably. "You fool, his name wasn't Pumpernickel at all. I just made that up!" The Devil made a gesture with his hand and two demons came forth and snatched Rancus Romar from off the ground. "Pitch him into the Unholy Reservoir of Chunk n' Dung," the Devil directed.

"But . . . But, my diabolical lord!" Rancus pleaded. "My most blasphemous, foul monarch of all that is evil and corrupt! Have mercy on me!"

The Devil watched gleefully as Rancus was dragged away by his horns to the place where even flies and maggots dared not go.

A figure appeared in the shadows of the Devil's door. The Devil cocked an eye. "Who might you be?"

"Red Man, form'ly one of the Primal Truckin' Boys," the figure said, stepping from the shadows and into the light of hellfire.

"Formerly?" asked the Devil. "Come closer so I can see you properly."

Red Man approached the throne, dragging an olive green duffel bag behind him. "I brought you somethin'."

The Devil looked down at the bag. "Tell me it's not the Pope?"

"Almost as good," Red Man said, proudly. "It's a down payment. The soul of a son of a preacher man. Got a bunch more, too, kickin back in muh truck." Red Man reached into his shirt pocket and took out a cigar. He stuck the end in his mouth and chewed on it. "I left the other truckers on Earth. They're too busy fiddlin' around with Earth girls."

"Of the flesh?"

"Yeah. Muckin' things up."

"Revolting," said the Devil.

"And that ain't all. They're killing instead of collectin'. Raisin' almighty hell."

"So I was told," the Devil said, drumming his finger against his lips. "Maybe I should bring them back. Put you in charge of the roundup. What do you say to that?"

"Sounds downright en'couragin'," replied Red Man, taking the cigar from his mouth and biting off the end. He spit the nub to the floor. "Only problem is how to get 'em back. Don't rightly think they're going to come willin'ly. They're havin a heap of fun up there."

The Devil leaned back in his throne and grinned. "I'll leave that to you."

"They ain't going to listen to me, I can gar'entee you that."

The Devil grinned. "Oh, they will listen. Tell them if they don't come back immediately, I'll have them strung up by their hooves and dunked headfirst into the Trench of the Infernal Sphincter."

Red Man nodded as he fired up his cigar. "That might do the trick."

"Of course it will," the Devil said. "I'm Prince Charming when it comes to trickery."

The Devil sent Red Man back to Earth and then called upon The Regal Court of Prestige Demonkind. He wanted to sentence some unfortunate demon to a horrendous punishment . . . just for the hell of it.

***

Half Elvis was in love. Wendy Winters was pretty sure she was, too. As the other demons wrecked what little was left of the town of Valentine, Half Elvis decided to propose to his freckle faced waitress. He got down on one knee, took her tiny soft hand in his, and looked into her eyes. "I know we just met an all, but I feel like somehow we've known each other all along. Like we was meant to be. Do you think that? That we was meant to be?"

Wendy giggled; her cheeks turned red. "Seems that way, Halfy. It really does."

Half Elvis kissed her hand. "Would you murry me?"

She giggled again and smiled. "Of course. I'd marry you today and stay with you forever."

He looked at her sincerely. "Even if that meant going to Hell forever?"

She lost her smile; her big, hazel doe-eyes turned suddenly serious. "Halfy, I'd go anywhere with you. To Heaven . . . to Hell, or anywhere between."

Her hand was warm. Yes, he was in love with her. He also loved Earth. He wanted to travel the highways with Wendy, see all the wonderful sights from the windows of his truck. And there always at his side, Wendy the waitress, holding hands and kissing until . . . well, damn . . . until she grew old and died. He wasn't sure what would happen then. The Devil would probably have a new Grim Reaper instated or even worse—what if . . . what if Wendy was taken to the other place? What if she went up instead of down? He couldn't go there. He'd be cut off forever from his little love muffin. He didn't want to think about that.

Instead, he pondered the two of them rolling across the country, spending romantic nights on the California coast. They could drink cold beer on the Golden Gate Bridge, climb the cables, cut them, and watch helpless Earthies fall to their deaths in the water below. They could travel back East, make love on the White House lawn. Spend a weekend tearing down the Capitol. They could drive west and deface Mount Rushmore, head up to skinny dip in the Great Lakes. They could even go back to Texas to piss on the Alamo! Just him and Wendy, demon and dame, redneckin' and Hell-truckin' through a love story across America.

Valentine was dead. Really. The truckers now had a few hundred souls to haul. They started their trucks and hit the road, raiding every home and store along the way to California. The demons were tanked up on booze and adrenaline, so consumed in their fiendish frivolity that nobody was thinking about Red Man—except, of course, Red Man.

He was trailing them, trying to catch up, and picking through the scrap they left behind. He'd reap what they sowed. Souls were souls, after all. But the Primal Truckin' Boys were running out of party time. Red Man hit the gas pedal.

"Hey, good buddies, Quart Low here. Hate to bust your bubbles, but we've picked up a tail of smokies."

Half Elvis looked in his side mirror. Blue light special. "Now the real fun begins!"

Wendy nestled close to him. "What do we do now, Halfy?"

He kept his hands on the wheel. "Nothin', turtle dumplins'. Just keep drivin to California."

Quart Low got back on the radio. "I'm going to take these doughnuts for the ride of their lives!"

Bringing up the rear of the convoy, Quart Low slammed his brakes and the truck skid sideways, tearing a large hole in the highway. He mashed the gas, forcing the cab to lift off the asphalt. The trailer almost tipped over, but Quart Low cut the wheel and the cab leveled. The truck was now running head-on with the smokies.

It was state trooper soup: The monster machine from Hell came at them head-on, the driver behind the windshield a scaly-faced demon grinning ear to ear.

The truck smashed through the helpless cars, sending glass, hoods, blue lights, and tires airborne. Quart Low stomped the brakes and the truck skid to a halt. White smoke filled the air. The trucker demon shifted into reverse, hit the gas, and sent the trailer hopping. He stomped the brakes again, turned the wheel, mashed in the clutch, and shifted into first. The truck spun around. He mashed the gas pedal hard. The cab jumped slightly then took off like a pole cat backed into a porcupine. The truck rammed through the smashed police cars. Flattened cop hats and car parts littered the highway. Dead doughnuts—Red Man was grateful of every one.

"Quite a nifty mess you made there, pardner," said Red Man into his CB.

"Red, that you?" Quart Low asked.

"Sure 'nuff. Tailin yer backside."

"Whare'd you run off to, Red? We thought you done left us for good."

"Naw. Just took a load to Hell. But I'm back."

"Why didn't you wait on us?"

"'Cause I got a sudden idea to pull a good one on Ole Scratchpot. I found a way to keep us on Earth a good long while. Undisturbed."

"How's that, Red?"

"I stole the key. The key to Hades."

"You stole the . . . key? *The* key? How'd you pull *that* off?"

"Snagged it off ole forked tail himself when he wasn't payin attention. Reached right out and snagged it off the throne."

"Red, you're either loaded with brass balls or total stupidity. So you're a' tellin' me we got possession of the key to Hell? We can come n' go as we please?"

"That's what I'm tellin ya."

***

"Where's my key?" the Devil screamed, stomping back and forth.

"You had it around your neck, Sir; the last time I saw it."

"Come here!" yelled the Devil at the demon speaker. "Do you see the key around my neck?"

"No, my lord. But that's usually where you have it . . . Lord, Sir."

"It was that damn redneck trucker!" proclaimed a fat demon by the name of Smeetchstitch. "The redneck trucker stole your key!"

"What makes you so certain?" the Devil asked.

"Because you said he was the only one around when you lost it."

The Devil bent his finger for Smeetchstitch to come to him. The pudgy demon walked slowly, trembling in fear.

The Devil bopped him on the head with his knuckles. "You imbecile. I didn't lose the key. It was stolen!"

"Of course, my unrighteous wickedness. I meant only that he stole it—"

The Devil waved him off. "Forget about the Grim Reaper's killer. Right now I want you to focus on getting my key back!"

The Court cowered from his rage.

"I'm going to send all of you to Earth. Whoever doesn't bring it to me will live Eternity in the Hairy Pit of Stench-Maximus."

"But, Sir," Smeetchstitch said, "only one of us can bring it back."

"My point, exactly! So you dimwits better get finding fast!"

Smeetchstitch stepped forward. "My lord? I have more bad news to declare."

The Devil cringed.

"If the key is gone, we won't be able to get out."

The Devil's eyebrows tightened; his teeth clenched. He stomped his feet. "Well, shit on crackers. That burns me up!"

It was a bad day in Hell.

***

The Primal Truckin' Boys had pulled over to the side of the road, waiting for their buddy Quart Low. They saw Red Man's truck following behind.

"Well, well, look who showed up," said Mr. Rotten.

Wendy and the three demons watched as Quart Low and Red Man got out of their trucks. They had parked across the street.

"What brought'cha back, Red?" Mr. Rotten yelled, watching as Quart Low and Red Man crossed the street. Wendy held on to Half Elvis's arm.

"Didn't wanna miss the party," Red Man said, coming to stand face to face with Mr. Rotten. He held up the key to Hell. "And to bring a gift."

"What-izzit?" Mr. Rotten asked, swiping to steal the key.

Red Man withdrew. "The key to Hades. I stole it from the Devil."

Mr. Rotten snarled his lip. "Is that so? Well what made you run off in the first place?"

"I wanted to get us more time on Earth before we had to go back. Figured if I could get the key, we might never gotta go back."

Half Elvis closed his eyes. Could it be true? Was it possible he might be able to stay here on Earth with Wendy? Forever? Well, not forever, but until she . . . No. She couldn't die. He'd protect her.

But what about the other team? What if . . . What if archangels came down for her? And even if it were possible to fend off Seraphim, sooner or later the Devil would find a way out and bring the truckers back to Hell. They would be tortured for their defection, and Half Elvis couldn't stand the thought of Wendy being thrown into the Reservoir of Chunk n' Dung, or exiled to any other of Hell's many revolting desolations.

He opened his eyes and admired her freckles, her shiny, strawberry-blonde hair, and her perky red lips.

There was only one thing to do, he decided. He took her by the hand and pulled her back to his truck.

"What's going on, Halfy? You mad at me?" she asked, alarmed by the intensity of his expression and how hard he was grasping her; his leathery forehead wrinkled, his red eyes became almost fire-like.

"We gotta go," he told her, glaring at his trucking buddies who were still admiring the Devil's stolen key. "Got to get far away from them."

"But you heard what Red Man said, you guys might not ever have to go back to Hell. We can get married. You n' me, Halfy."

"What Red did was stupid. He's provoked the angels. They'll be coming down for us, and for that key." He looked up at the sky as though expecting to see war chariots appearing from the clouds. "I doubt we've got long. Me and you . . . we gotta go, now."

"But . . . but where we going, sweetie?"

Half Elvis closed his eyes again and inhaled deeply. He hated to say it. "To church."

***

"Half Elvis flipped his doggone lid," Quart Low said on his CB.

"Hey, each his own," Mr. Rotten replied. "Besides, I don't think his lid was ever really screwed on that tightly to begin with."

Quart Low growled on his radio. "Maybe so. But he ought not've split on us. 'Specially for some Earthie woman."

"He's horns over hooves in love with her," Red Man interrupted. "You should've seen him at the diner. Had mushy love spewin outta his mouth like lumpy gravy."

"You don't think they're runnin' off to get hitched, do ya?"

"Nothin' surprises me anymore."

"Well, guess it's like Mr. Rotten said; each his own. Me, though? I say we truck on to Cali. Get drunk and pick us up some women of our own. Have fun then maybe head over to Vegas to shoot some craps."

"Sounds like a plan to me, Quart Low. What 'bout you Leech and Ten?"

"Rot.

"Say again?"

"It's Rot-ten."

"I get'cha', pardner. You guys up for some funnin' around?"

All four demon truckers blew their horns and even the angels in Heaven dreaded having to come down for them.

***

Pastor Yarberry wasn't sure what to make of Half Elvis or the beastly truck parked in the church's gravel lot. The demon refused to step foot into the church; but opted to wait on the front step, insisting Wendy go in and get saved.

"It's for the best," he told her.

She thought they were here to get married. Why else would he have brought her to a church?

Pastor Yarberry—white-haired, white-lipped and grumbly—took Wendy inside. Half Elvis sat on the front step, sighing deeply, and then he did something he'd never done before.

He prayed.

"Look, I know I ain't one to be askin much from ya, but I really do love her. I hope you see that. And this here prayer ain't for me. It's for her. I don't want her going to Hell on my account. So maybe if you can see it through to help her believe in you, things might turn out alright. She's an angel, but you probably already know that, seein' as how you made her and everything. She needs to be in Heaven with you some day, not with me in Hell. It hurts me to give her away like this, and I understand I ain't never going to get to see her again once she's up there, but it's for the best. For her best, I mean. So if you

344

would please put it in her to understand, and maybe give that there preacher fella a little extra push in his ministerin', I'd sure appreciate it. I know I ain't your favorite or anything, but just for the record, between me and you . . . I think you're alright."

Half Elvis waited on the front step of the church. He watched the darkening sky, waiting for the Lord's reply. He didn't receive a booming command from Heaven as he had hoped. No bush caught fire and started talking to him. No angel came forth with scroll in hand to deliver the good news of Wendy Winters' name having been written in the Book of Life. But a little brown and white bird did swoop down from the sky. It looped in the air about ten feet above Half Elvis, chirped a couple times, raised its rear and squirted on the demon's head.

He looked up toward Heaven. "Appreciate ya!"

THE TRANS-MENTAL SUPER SPEEDWAY OF
NICHOLAS WELCH

For Nicholas Welch, life has been a car wreck ready to happen. The little, lunatic driver inside his head wasn't ready to hit the brakes just yet. With his foot pressed on the accelerator, the lunatic disregarded the caution flags and was intently driving Nicholas into a wall of insanity.

Nicholas was beginning to detest his creative mind. Originally, his dreams had proven essential in helping to develop his artistic concepts, but with his deteriorating saneness skidding off the imaginative highway, he dreaded closing his eyes at night. Hundreds of skeletal faces with bony hands reached out to him in dream: palms full of nasal bones, palatines, inferior nasal conchaes, maxillaes, zygomatics, vomers, lacrimals, and rattling mandibles. How scientific, creative, yet frighteningly haunting his art had become.

Nineteen years ago, Nicholas was a rising star in the art world with a critically acclaimed piece entitled *Sin of the Skin*. The following years his career began to plateau, but his creations of late have turned to a more provocative approach, garnering him recognition from all over the world.

The casual observer certainly could question the validity of his talent, but the lunatic driver in Nicholas' head became fixated on promoting his peculiar style of creativity from the underground galleries to the most prestigious venues. Sultio, the lunatic, convinced Nicholas that it would only take a bit more time to show the critics there is more to art than conventional portraits and uninspiring bowls of fruit.

Nicholas had many devotees over the years, those whom offered themselves to hopefully become his next masterpiece. He never offered to pay them (what good is money to a dissected corpse?), but the people weren't interested in payment. The world had plenty of attention-seekers, teenagers trying to prove a point, or lonely souls desiring to be a star, if only for a fleeting moment. It wasn't uncommon for Nicholas' talent to be denounced in the newspapers; his critics often labeled him a hack. What they didn't know, however, was how accurate they were in their descriptions.

With steady hands and a sparkling scalpel, the artisan carefully peeled the faces off his superstars. Most of them requested no anesthetics, preferring the purity of the experience. Nicholas was unlikely to give it to them regardless; the art was much more fierce when it screamed!

***

The sun had been up for nearly fifteen minutes, the dawning sky lit with swirls of pink and blue light. Nicholas stood on the top step of his Chicago studio. The tail of his trench coat blew open from a sudden gust of wind. He walked down the steps onto the sidewalk, absorbed in his thoughts. Footwork was now hindered by a limp.

The artist checked his reflection in the driver's side window of a parked car. His hair was flecked gray from age, his goatee long and ashen.

"What have you become?" he said to his reflection in the car window. He swallowed hard, not wanting to accept how his body has aged, how he constantly talks to himself, and how he had allowed his once stable mind to succumb to the authority of an obsessive lunatic. He pulled at the loose skin around his neck, refusing to believe he was responsible for his insanity.

Sultio had started as a voice but quickly turned into something much more sinister. Had this demon always existed within me, he wondered? Nicholas, staring at his reflection in the car window, questioned things he had done as a child, like when he decided to douse his gerbil cage with gasoline and set it on fire. Or when he secretly urinated into the milk just to see the expressions of his family at the breakfast table. Had those been the first influences of Sultio?

Nicholas looked down at his shoes then turned and walked. "Scuffed and stained, just like me," he mumbled to himself. He came to a curb, stopped for a moment, and with eyes half closed, he stepped into the street. Nicholas knew his luck all too well; he could walk blindly into traffic and no one would hit him. If he could rename the demonic driver in his head, he'd call it Crueltus.

As expected, Nicolas made it safely across to the other side. Two, teenage boys with backpacks whizzed by him on skateboards, weaving in and out of the crowd as if being pulled by an invisible rope. Nicholas tugged at the black, leather collar of his trench coat, took in a deep breath of the industrial morning air, and jammed his fists deeply in the pockets of his coat. He mixed into the crowd in search of the perfect face.

There were many people on the sidewalk this morning, all with unique features: big noses, pug noses, strong chins, chiseled cheeks, and large, colorful eyes. They were all wonderful, possibly, but not one of them suitable for Nicholas' art. It takes that extremely special face, that rarity with an angel winking from behind the eyes. The skin doesn't have to be young, but certainly free of scar, and easy to stretch. The hair must be clean, silky, and fine. The lips must be full, moist, and ready to utter the words—make me your masterpiece! Everything must be perfect, but it seemed this side of Heaven was running low on ethereal beauty. Sidewalks were aplenty with self-righteous superstars, every one of them believing they were something special. Not one of them was worth a second glance.

All Nicholas could think about was Sultio's words from the night before: "The perfect face is out there, Nick. All you have to do is find it."

The demon, in all its unequivocal assurance, seemingly had forgotten its rightful place. Hell wasn't inside Nicholas' head . . . or was it? The lunatic's demands never ceased, nor did the speed in which Nicholas was forced to maintain. Nicholas was an old vehicle now with a tail pipe dragging the road. He was barely able to take the curves any longer.

"I'll get you out of my head one day," Nicholas said to himself. He was shoved aside by a tall blonde woman carrying groceries.

"You let her get away!" It was Sultio, hovering six feet from the ground. The little lunatic appeared like a ghost in the wrinkles and folds of all who passed through him; head topped with a red helmet, and body dressed in a blue patch-clad, racing jumpsuit.

If the passers-by could see the floating lunatic, they showed no sign. Has everyone grown accustomed to my madness? Or, worse, Nicholas wondered; maybe they're tired of me. It had been several days, after all, since the last devotee offered himself to the art. A month ago, Nicholas' studio door had been nearly beaten down with desperate hands to get inside, but these last couple of weeks seemed strangely vacant.

"She didn't have the perfect face," Nicholas said, batting the hovering lunatic away with his hand. The artist walked through the ghost, trying to find space for himself in the crowd of rushing work-goers.

"Nick, you wouldn't know the face if it came up and hit you on the head. You should have snagged her when you had the chance."

"Leave me be, Sultio. I can handle it."

"You keep saying you can but you let a good one get away. Who is to say you might screw up again? We need the art, Nick. The cupboards are getting low. Things are getting ratty again. We need more exposure. Got to prove the critics wrong. Find the perfect face, Nick. The one that will propel us to the top!"

"I'm already over the top, Sultio. Can't you see that? You've been pushing me so long that I can't think straight anymore. I can't hunt for the perfect face forever. I'm tired and old, Sultio. I'm too damn old."

The lunatic punched Nicholas in the gut. The artist doubled over. "Not old, Nick, you're just giving up!" Sultio shouted. "But I'm not going to allow it! Those hands of yours . . . they create masterpieces. You'll find the perfect face. Just keep looking."

Nicholas couldn't see Sultio's eyes through the little, dark visor on his helmet. The hovering demon floated beside the artist, driving him faster. "Win that checkered flag before the race is over, Nick. You only have a few more laps to go."

Nicholas rubbed his stomach where Sultio had punched him. "I'll find the face. Told you I would. Just go away and let me be. You're racing me again. I can't deal with the race right now."

Sultio's crooked-toothed smirk reminded Nicholas of barbed wire, sharp and stretched tight. "You're a good man, Nick," the lunatic said. "Remember that. I'm rooting for you. You can't give up now; we're too close to the finish line. But you will have to hurry, but don't overheat your engine."

Nicholas nodded and carried on in search of the streets for the perfect face—that special one that might make the demon driver finally shut up and leave him alone. Nicholas wasn't sure when the race began in his head. All he knew was that he had to win it.

Between the egos of the suit and tie people on the sidewalk, Nicholas saw the humble and the meek, the strong and determined, and the younger generation of familial wealth. He wondered if these people were as determined to win their own races. Did they wake up in the mornings, strap a helmet to their heads, and rush out to the track to beat their opponents? What drove them to become better?

"I envy the winos," Nicholas mumbled to himself as he walked. He pulled his fists from his coat pockets. "Drunken and lazy. Spectators of the race. Sitting in the stands and watching us crazy people trying to outrun each other. Which is worse? Crashing or sitting back and watching it happen?"

Sultio was more like a pit boss—the motherfucker on the radio always demanding the car go faster.

The speedway was full of racers today. Everyone had on their helmets, hands on their personal steering wheels, trying to run everyone else off the road. Nicholas refused to be intimidated by them. With his foot on the gas pedal, he maneuvered through the crowd with ease, checking every face as he passed them by. It didn't take long for him to wear out. He needed a pit stop. His sanity was running a quart low and Nicholas could hear the valves rattling.

He lowered his head and ignored the other cars. What if there wasn't such a thing as the perfect face? "Who cares about the critics," Nicholas whispered to himself, looking down at his stained, brown shoes. "They just go to the galleries to rubberneck. I've done nothing but build the world a speedway of crashed out race cars."

Nicholas could barely feel his fingers. Everything was going numb.

"Sultio," he called out. "I can't finish the race. I've had it. I'm beat." When he lifted his head the lunatic was staring at him.

"You pathetic loser, get back out there!"

"No. Let me rest. Don't drive me this way. I can't keep up with them any longer."

Sultio reached out and put his hands around Nicholas' neck. "I'll kill you if you don't win this race! It's the only thing that matters."

Nicholas gnashed his teeth and pushed the lunatic away. "I'm beginning to welcome death," he said, reaching down into his coat pockets. He then turned to get back out on the speedway.

***

Later that afternoon, Nicholas came back to the studio with a struggling young woman. He had hold of her hair, forcing her into his apartment.

He kicked over a chair in the middle of the room, then sat the girl on the floor. The single light bulb on the ceiling flickered as if repulsed by such violence underneath it. Nicholas collapsed beside the sobbing blonde.

"That's not the face," Sultio said in disapproval. The demon was across the room from Nicholas and the woman. He was hidden in shadow, crouched in the air as if readying to pounce.

"I can see that!" Nicholas yelled. He balled a fist and shook it at Sultio. "I know what the face is, and I'm never going to find it. Hers will have to do."

Sultio floated from out of the darkness. His mouth was open and there seemed to be fire catching between his teeth. The lunatic moved closer, head slightly tilted on his neck, and his eyes became illuminated blood drops behind the tinted shield of his helmet. His fingers raked at the patches on his jumpsuit. Physically, he was small and unthreatening, but his presence always made Nicholas tremble. "Nick, you're making me upset. You shouldn't make me upset like this. You ought to know better by now."

Nicholas cowered from the hovering demon. "Take another look at her. She'll do fine, Sultio. She's pretty and young. Look and see for yourself. The critics will love her."

The lunatic lowered himself to the frightened girl. He reached out, took her by the chin, and studied her for a moment. "It's junk, Nick. She has the haggard eyes of a harlot. The nose is too long. The lips too thin. Peroxide's frazzled her hair." Sultio shoved the girl away. "Go get something real, Nicholas. Don't bring me junk."

Nicholas stood up and walked to the door. "Get up," he said to the girl. "I'll take you back where I found you."

The girl didn't move. She couldn't take her eyes off a silver scalpel blade on the floor. There was a fine crusting of blood dried on its edge.

"Leave her with me," Sultio insisted. "You go get the face. I'll take care of her."

Nicholas paused before leaving. "You're going to hurt her just for the fun of it? Not for the art, just for the pleasure . . . ?"

Sultio lifted his head and smiled. "She needs a little body work is all. Tap a few pings out. Nothing serious."

***

Nicholas wandered the busy city sidewalks, visually checking the tired faces now going home from work. After an hour, he gave up and found a quiet alley to hide.

"Curse you, Sultio," he said, leaning against a graffiti-covered wall. He barely had any feeling in his legs and collapsed to the ground with knees pressed to his chest. "I want to be a spectator. I want out of the race."

A small hand fell on his shoulder. He looked up.

"What's wrong, Mister?"

A young boy, no older than ten, was standing before him.

Nicholas frowned. "Everything."

The boy pouted, mocking Nicholas. "You look terrible. Old and worn out."

Nicholas reached and touched the boy's hand. "I wish I could be like you, young and full of energy. You have a full tank of gas, ready to run over the world."

"Mr. Welch, you're the fastest car there is. You can't give up. You got to win the race, just gotta!"

Nicholas crawled away from the boy. "How—how do you know about the race?"

"Everybody knows you, Mr. Welch. You're famous. Going to be, anyway. I made a bet with my girlfriend that you'd win the race. You aren't going to make me lose the bet are you, Mr. Welch?"

Nicholas leaned his head against the wall and moaned loudly.

"If you win, I get to kiss my girlfriend," the boy said. "Her name is Delphia. That's because she's from Philadelphia. It's what her mom named her. She's kind of skinny, though, and her chin isn't much, but that's okay with me. I still want to kiss her."

"How do you know about me? What's your name, kid?" Nicholas asked, lifting his head. He sat up and began to crack his knuckles, something he hadn't done since he was a child.

"Better not do that, Mr. Welch. Remember what your mom said. You don't wanna break off your fingers." The boy shook his head disapprovingly. "You're a sight, Mr. Welch. Not looking so good these days."

Nicholas stared at the boy. "Who are you? What's your name?"

The boy's pupils widened. "We're all basking in the darklight together. Burning our engines."

"Wait," Nicholas said, shaking a finger at the boy. "I know you, don't I? Yes, I know who you are!" He crawled to the boy and shoved him. "You came back!"

The boy's eyes rolled up into his head and his throat began to twitch. He sounded like a cat. No, not a cat, but a motor—a car motor.

"Get away from me!" Nicholas yelled. "You're not real. You can't be! I left you behind years ago!"

"You wanted to be a race car driver, so don't blame me. Couldn't make up your mind, could you, Mr. Welch? Mom, Dad, you told them: I'm going to be a race car driver when I grow up. Then you changed your mind. Mom, Dad, look, I painted a picture. I'm going to be a famous artist one day. They said you could do it all if you wanted. Little Nicholas Welch can do anything he puts his mind to . . . Well, that's what they said." The boy jabbed his finger at Nicholas. "You don't fool me, though. I might be young, but I know when to hit the gas or get out of the fucking race!"

Nicholas was trembling. "I was just being a kid. Dreaming of my future. It was a long, long time ago. Why are you doing this to me? Why are you haunting me? It's you who's haunting me, isn't it? Not Sultio, it's been you all along."

"No," whispered the boy. "It's you." The boy turned his back to Nicholas and folded his arms across his chest. "It's always been you, Nick. You've never forgiven yourself for not becoming all the things you said you wanted to be. Now you're old, on your final lap, and you can't live with yourself. All past failures. You think getting across the finish line will end the race. But it won't. Not even death's good enough for Mr. Big Shot, Nicholas

357

Welch. But if you do get that checkered flag, I'll be there waiting for you in the darklight, and after you wave it around awhile for all the fans, we'll hang it on the wall and talk about how you wanted to be an author, a rock star, an astronaut, an oceanographer, an architect, a comedian. The list goes on and on, doesn't it, Mr. Welch?"

"No!" Nicholas screamed, cupping his ears and thrashing his head from side to side. "You're all wrong about everything! Death isn't the finish line. Success is! All those people out there are beating me to it. Whoever gets there first gets the flag, and they're all winning! But I'm fast, damn it! I'm real fast. Look at me. I have big, fast wheels. Big fast motor. *Vroom! Vroom!* I'm loud. Loud and fast. I'm a real speedy son of a bitch!"

"Is that man crazy, Momma?"

"Don't point. It's not nice. Stand back, he's getting up."

Reality revealed itself. A crowd had gathered around him; some were pointing, others watching with their hands to their mouths. The whole city seemed to be enjoying his most hideous moment. There was nowhere to hide from all the spectators watching the tragedy of this twisted wreck of a man. They desired blood and broken bones. They wanted to see his brains running out across the ground, and glass debris jutting from his crispy, fried flesh. And fire . . . Lots of fire!

Was there some demoralized need to see Nicholas Welch razed by flames and injury? How could the world snicker and laugh as his life was spinning out of control? Because it meant one less car on the track—one less speed machine to reach the checkered flag of success. Nicholas hated them. Winos. Children. Their parents. All lazy spectators.

Nicholas shoved his way through the onlookers. "Look at me!" he yelled, standing with his arms held out. "Everybody get a good look at Nicholas Welch because I'm the winner!"

At first, the people looked at each other in stunned silence, then someone charged the mad artist, cornering him against the alley wall. Adults and children joined in the melee, every face becoming distorted until there was nothing left of their human features. Nicholas saw them as a monkey. A laughing, excited primate.

"That's what you are!" Nicholas yelled. "You people are a monkey!"

But the monkey was bigger than Nicholas! It grabbed him by the coat collar, tossed him over its shoulder, and carried him to his studio. Behind him, Sultio and the taunting young boy followed, harassing Nicholas as the monkey carried him down the street. The artist had defied himself too many times, and with that burden must come punishment.

Nicholas lifted his head to better see his reflection as the monkey carried him passed a store window. Someone had put a helmet on his head, a blue and red helmet, like the kind worn by Richard Petty. The world was mocking him—the world was always mocking him! The monkey pushed Nicholas' head back down to its shoulder.

The monkey's laughter rattled the windows of the nearby buildings. More and more people rushed out to join the monkey; everyone wanting to get their hands on the artist. Nicholas had finally found his fame, though he wanted no part of it. He clawed at the helmet on his head, but the strap wouldn't loosen.

He looked up and saw a massive human head in the street. The monkey threw him off its shoulder toward the head. Nicholas spread his arms wide to stable himself in the air. His vision remained clear, but everything around him folded in on itself, as if the world had been forced inside a translucent wedge.

Nicholas suddenly froze in midair. His body was horizontal, ten feet off the ground. He stared at the head in front of him. It was wearing a huge, black cowboy hat.

Its face turned to Nicholas and he was able to see who it was—Mr. Petty, laughing and chewing up the world.

Nicholas felt everything behind him being sucked into the vacuum of Petty's gaping mouth. The monkey howled and protested being consumed; its huge feet pounding the pavement.

Nicholas tried to say something but when the words came out of his mouth, Mr. Petty had already eaten them. Everything was racing forward to feed Mr. Petty. Everything except Nicholas Welch.

There was no sound. There was no laughter, no monkey, and no more race. There was absolutely nothing but Nicholas Welch frozen in midair before the gigantic, head of Richard Petty.

"Pardon me, Mister," Mr. Petty said in a surprisingly calm, Southern-twanged voice, "but you're wearin' my helmet."

Nicholas reached for the strap. "Please, take it," he said. "I don't want the damn thing."

Petty's mustache came alive, the two ends extending from his face. They wrapped around Nicholas' body and up to his head. Like fingers, the tips of the mustache unsnapped the helmet and pulled it off. They played with the helmet, tossing it up and catching it. The mustache then snapped back like rubber bands to Mr. Petty's face, taking the helmet with it.

"Feels good to retire," Mr. Petty said. "You ought to slow down a little, Mr. Welch. Slow down and enjoy things while you still have time. Take a sip of life every now and again. It's pretty good."

"I want to slow down," Nicholas admitted. "For some reason I can't allow myself. It's like I'm torturing myself to always keep going. I don't know how to stop."

There was only one way to stop the race. "I have to win," he said, and his body was set down to the ground. The monkey was behind him, reaching to pick him up. "Yes," Nicholas muttered to himself. "I'll stop once I win the race." He turned around and yelled at the primate. "Take me to my studio! I won't run from you!" He looked down at his stained, brown shoes then kicked them off his feet. "I'll never run again."

The monkey's hands came around his throat. Nicholas was yanked up from the ground and belted back onto the monkey's hairy shoulder. The primate wasn't laughing anymore. Instead, it revealed its large teeth; a proposition that it might kill Nicholas if he didn't accept its face.

"Take me home," Nicholas said. "I'm feeling good, now."

***

When the monkey reached the studio door, it paused and listened as a woman on the other side coughed and gurgled then whimpered to a concluding silence.

"Go on in," Nicholas said; his face pressed against the monkey's shoulder. "Open the door. Go inside."

With little effort, the monkey pushed through the door. Sultio jumped up with a demented smirk on his face. He had a finger dipped into a small, round hole in the young woman's abdomen.

"I was just checking her oil," Sultio explained as he pulled his finger from the wound and hid his hands behind his back. "Air filter was a tad dirty, too, Nick. She needed a new one." A slop of bloody ichors trickled to the floor from between Sultio's legs.

The monkey and Nicholas watched as Sultio kept making hand gestures toward the woman as if in search of some explanation of her death and nudity. The little lunatic finally shrugged his shoulders and smiled. "What can I say? I had to get under the hood to see what was wrong."

The monkey shoved Sultio aside. With a hand the size of a bed mattress, the primate lifted Nicholas from its shoulder and stood him upright on the floor. The monkey fell to its back, grunting and hissing for Nicholas to scoop off its face.

"I've never done so many at once," Nicholas complained as he scanned the room for his tools.

Sultio smiled and handed him the scalpel.

***

It was late into the night and Nicholas still hadn't cut through every tendon. The work was tedious and messy, and the artisan was getting tired. Getting any rest this night was futile, as every complaint was conquered abruptly by the monkey's constant whining to get the job done.

By early morning light, the primate's forehead was flayed back over the side of its skull, carefully sliced in three segments. Clamps were used to keep the skin taut so that wrinkles wouldn't set in and the valuable expression lost. Miraculously, through five hours of surgery, the primate remained alive and conscious. There was no anesthesia, of course, only the precision of Nicholas' blades that left the monkey anxious to become his masterpiece.

Finally, during the ninth hour, Nicholas sliced through the final strand of muscle, and the monkey's face slipped freely from the skull. The eye sockets were stringy with sinew, teeth splotched red with blood, cheekbones wormy with slivers of veins and muscle, but at least the oozing had stopped. Nicholas used a wet rag to dab the hard, primate bone clean until everything was smooth as baby seal fur.

Then the restructuring began.

Nicholas fought with the facial skin to piece it back together, stapling segments in place, and coating the foul mask with formaldehyde. He molded the nose into shape with plaster, a jaw line constructed of wire, and marbled eyes were fitted into the sockets to keep the face lively.

As usual, during such dissections, flies made their way into the studio. Sultio stayed busy with the swatter, but the primate's corpse became a dish far too compelling to turn down. The corpse had to be thrown out soon. Nothing was going to stop the worms from coming.

"I'm just about done, Sultio," Nicholas said, threading the lips into place. "I'm on the final lap now."

Sultio floated over to the corpse and stared down at it. "You haven't even started, my friend."

"What are you talking about?" Nicholas shouted. His face contorted. "There's the face! What else is there to do?"

Sultio shook his head. "None of them have the face. You've been wasting your time, Nick. Just ordinary people with average bones from average Joes. Nothing special about them."

Nicholas stepped between the corpses and Sultio. His fist was cocked back as if to hammer the lunatic to the floor. "By themselves they were ordinary," Nicholas said, "but look at them now! Together they are the perfect face! I never knew it would take so many, but that is my masterpiece!"

"No, Nick, you are wrong." Sultio's voice wasn't gruff and demanding as usual. Strangely, the little, floating lunatic sounded melancholy.

"If that's not the perfect face," Nicholas said, gulping hard, "then there isn't one. I won't go looking again. I'm going to listen to Mr. Petty and take a break from the race. Every time I go out looking, I find something I don't want to know about myself. I see my reflection in the eyes of those people out there, see myself looking back at me, and I don't want to see it ever again. No more racing, Sultio. I'm quitting for good. You might as well take off your helmet now."

"Then cut the face and grab the checkered flag while you still can. You have known all along where the perfect face was, how it smiles at you in every window. The artist always denies himself the most, doesn't he, Nick, ole boy? Scared that after he does his best work, whatever comes after won't measure up. And it doesn't, usually. So he always substitutes, puts off the masterpiece until it can't be put off any longer. Just cut it, Nick. Cut the perfect face and be done with it."

Nicholas nodded like every other time the demon driver turned his wheels. He reached down next to the primate's corpse and took hold of the scalpel. "You really want me to do it?"

"No," Sultio whispered. "If I had my way, I would keep it on. Keep in the race. But I can't. I'm just the pit boss, Nick. You're the driver."

Nicholas grabbed the lunatic by the throat. "It's been a long, hard run, hasn't it, Sultio?"

"That it has, Nick, ole boy. That it has."

With one swift stroke, Nicholas cut the perfect face from his head, reached out the window and took the checkered flag in his hand. He waved it around to all the admiring fans, and then fell into the monkey's cold blood. The race for one man's dreams had been won, finally, and forever the trans-mental super speedway of Nicholas Welch would be open for any contender to challenge him.

"Drivers . . . start your engines!"

THE FOLLY OF POLLY PINTONOLLY

Frinkleberry stew is made with bright purple goo, and it tastes its best around noon. That's the magic hour when the stew has its power to turn you into a cartoon. But Polly Pintonolly got hungry and jolly; she ate a bowl way too late. She developed warts of different sizes and sorts, and the bumps quickly affected her gait. Now she walks really funny, like a one-legged bunny, and her friends they all point, laugh, and snicker. Polly Pintonolly made a very big folly by not watching the town's timely ticker. The clock was very tall so it could be seen from the mall, but Polly wasn't paying close attention. She ate the forbidden stew made with bright purple goo, and now she's been placed in detention.

"Look at her walk, and listen to her talk," mocked the guards while Polly tried to beg.

"Wazzle warts consume me," she said rather gloomy, "and they're growing right up my other leg."

She turned around and hobbled as her rear end wobbled, trying to find a way out of jail. However, the walls were built tight and painted off-white; she had no money for bail. Her crime was rather serious in a town quite delirious—the stew a sacred meal in Frinkle Town.

The people accused her strongly that she ate very wrongly, and passed her over to a judge named Brown.

The court was jammed tight with onlookers' delight, waiting for the judge's final decision. A crowd so immense that the bailiff had to dispense, taking most out to watch on television. Polly pled innocence to the misfortunate incidence, but Judge Brown was determined she was guilty. He ordered her back to jail, where it felt like hell; she was given one pillow that was filthy.

"I lay here and quiver, praying to God, will you deliver?" said Polly aloud to the walls. She saw a bug in a crack with blue wings on its back, crawling 'cross the mortar toward the stalls. She reached out her hand, felt the little bug expand, growing to the size of a moose. "Please, please, Mr. Bug, they treat me like a thug, but I gave them my very best excuse."

The bug had spiny thighs, antennas with black eyes; it wanted far from Frinkle County Jail. "Climb upon my wing and we'll fly off to Beijing," said the moose bug with a very prickly tail.

"But are you able to break us free without the guards noticing me?" asked Polly in a voice apprehensive.

"With these pincers on my face, I'll dig us out of this place!" promised the bug positioned for the offensive.

It put its weight against the wall; the moose bug broke through it all, causing a siren to wail loud overhead. The bug looked at Polly, who exclaimed, "Oh, my golly!" and ran quickly into the hole by her bed. The guards were immediately alerted to an escapee who deserted; they quickly grabbed their helmets, sticks, and mace. Leaving their doughnuts on a table, the fat jailers were barely able, their legs having trouble keeping pace. They huffed like sweaty hogs, but determined as hunting dogs to catch whomever dared to break free. Polly and the bug had already pulled the plug, and were now soaring higher than any tree.

She leaned and looked down at the sight of Frinkle Town, hoping it would be the last time. "Good riddance forever! I'm on a personal endeavor!" she shouted, wondering if it would truly ever rhyme.

The flight across the ocean was turbulent with commotion, but Polly hung on with both hands. Moose bug's flapping blue wings drowned out everything, as he headed for unfamiliar lands. The Orient was the goal for these two wandering souls, but moose bug was beginning to have a doubt.

"Do they eat bugs in China, or is that in North Carolina?" asked the bug with a slightly worried pout.

"N-n-neither one I think," replied Polly quite in sync, "but m-m-maybe we should stop and get warm." Her face was getting colder because the wind up here was bolder; and on the horizon, there appeared to be a storm.

"I see an island down below, so that's exactly where we'll go," replied moose bug to the girl on his back. With wings fully extended, the island sounded splendid, but the ride down was full of bounce and flak.

Polly held on tightly but lost her grip just slightly, and unfortunately that was all it really took. The next thing she knew she was staring at her shoe, up close in her face like a book. The world had spun around; which way was the ground—she wondered as she swung her arms and kicked. Not that it mattered where her body particularly splattered, but some things she liked to predict. But that wasn't going to happen with her arms up and flappin', at least not while moose bug's around. He doubled back to get her, his wings a spinning blur, and he delivered her safely to the ground.

"Thank you, Mr. Bug." And she gave him a hug while standing on the beach of paradise. "Just look at all these trees, coconuts and seeds, isn't it all so very nice?"

"Except for the storm," said moose bug forlorn. "I think we better find shelter soon. We'll sleep through the night, wait til mornin' light, then get up and get going by noon."

"Ah, can't we just relax?" asked Polly for the facts: "Why do we have to hurry off and go? Can't we stay for awhile and enjoy this little isle—it's not like anybody'll know."

"Well, I suppose we probably could, but first we'll need some wood. Let's go build us a shanty from the weather." Moose bug took her by the hand and led her from the sand to where the trees all grew tall and together. "Grab that offshoot over there; we have no time to spare. The storm will be upon us pretty quick." Moose bug cleared the ground as Polly walked around. She collected twelve branches and a stick.

She had laid out a wide foundation when she felt a wet sensation. "Hey, bug, I think it's starting to rain." She looked up to the sky, got a raindrop in her eye, as the thunder began to rumble like a train. Polly anxiously helped secure a safe shelter to assure that the rain wouldn't be falling on their heads. With bug's forethought and ingenuity, his amazing instinctual congruity, they used palm leaves to make their cushy beds.

When day turned to night there came an awful fright that maybe they should have carried on. Instead of stopping on a notion, they could be well across the ocean, but now that opportunity was gone. They waited several hours for the storm to lose its powers, but the thunder and the lightening never stopped. Polly was getting frightened, and moose bug's instincts heightened, as the sky overhead flashed and popped.

Then suddenly they heard a shout, glanced down and all about were totems rising up from the soil. The posts were painted green with wooden faces or so it seemed—to the largest of these totems they were loyal. King of the totem tribe began desperately to describe that he was the chief of Jāka Jāka. He lifted a spear and aimed, and not so quietly proclaimed, his voice rattling loud as a maraca.

The totems started to lean, their expressions growing mean, the posts sprouting teeth, horns, and claws. Their eyes began to glow as the wind continued to blow; spiders crawling out their parted jaws.

Polly was very scared but moose bug merely stared as the totems uprooted from the ground. They lurked around like demons, shipwrecked spirits of former seamen, raised from their earthly burial mound. The rain kept on falling, as the totems were appalling, leaving moose bug and Polly in suspense.

"Invading you have intended, and my tribe's been quite offended," said the chief with a scowl so intense. "Since I drank a magic potion, I've ruled the Indian Ocean; now pray that I don't decide to kill." The chief's painted face looked like something from outer space; wooden expressions that displayed his ruthless will.

"We're not here to overtake. It was simply a small mistake," said Polly to the chief of the tribe. "And to be quite specific, we're actually in the Pacific." She hoped to spare her life with a bribe: "If we send you back a boat, something to keep you all afloat, will you allow me and my friend to depart? We didn't mean to upset, so please accept our deep regret; we just didn't have a map or a chart."

The chief totem scowled, his wooden throat deeply growled: "Tell me, why should I trust in your words? We're pirates from the grave, so I doubt you'd truly save; your promise is as flighty as the birds."

"That ain't true at all," replied Polly with a drawl. "I'll send back a boat to this land. You can sail the seven seas—do exactly as you please; I'll even confirm this by shaking your hand."

The totems discussed their choices, speaking in angry voices, but the chief finally decided to take a chance. They needed a sturdy boat, so he put the motion to vote; the sea was their only true romance. The waves had dragged them under, had torn their ships asunder, but the pirates were eager to go back. Being imprisoned within the earth was like the days before their birth—the future seemed very, very black. So this tribe of desperate souls desiring new life beyond the shoals, allowed Polly and the bug to stay and rest. The storm was passing through, hopefully tomorrow's skies are blue, and so the chief wouldn't be so highly stressed.

As the hours drew on and on, the night broke to dawn; the storm had moved away to other lands. Moose bug was fast asleep with Polly near his feet, the pirates groping wildly with their hands. Prodding at Polly's legs, they gulped beer from ghostly kegs; they eventually woke up their sleeping guests. Polly was surrounded—she was startled and dumbfounded—the pirates began grabbing at her breasts. She slapped away their hands, and blinded them with sand. "You brutes think you're so sly and clever. But now the deal is off," she said with a cough. "You can stay here on this island forever!"

Moose bug punched them in the guts, swiftly kicking their butts, projecting them onto the soil. Polly jumped upon his back, persisted in the attack; moose bug's fury was heated to a boil. He stomped madly at the ground, cursing the island that he'd found then took to the sky like a Mynah. They flew high above the clouds, passing jets with engines loud; and headed to the Eastern coast of China.

When they arrived at a port, they met a very friendly sort, a man by the name of Cheng Fú. He offered them advice and a warm bowl of rice, telling them what they should probably do. "Go to place called The Pail where they serve special ale," he said as they stood on the quay. "A waiter will bring you the drink, the most unique kind, I should think. A taste distinctive, in every kind of way."

Polly blinked her eyes at this man so very wise. "Thank you for sharing your food and wit."

Mr. Fú then simply bowed, but he looked very proud. "You're welcome, yes, but I hope you don't forget."

Moose bug finished with his food, and was in a much better mood when Polly reached out for his hand. They walked on the pier, everyone seemed of good cheer; inside the bar was a very noisy band.

Polly took a seat as moose bug rubbed his feet; both were exhausted from their trip. A waiter brought them beer, it was called Internal Fear, and moose bug was first to take a sip. He spat it back out, releasing a piercing shout: "Uh! This stuff tastes like utter crap!" Polly immediately sniffed her drink, and it truly did stink, looking down to see the beer spray on her lap. She jumped up from the table, but moose bug was not able, the beer dripping across his buggy legs. He shrunk down in size, disappeared from Polly's eyes, falling through a narrow grate of bamboo pegs.

The waiter came out running; his expression perplexed and stunning: "In China, green tea is best, not beer!" He declared Polly was illegal, and screeched like an eagle, "You, lady, best get out of here!"

Exiting the noisy bar, Polly didn't make it far. She was stopped by a tall, bearded man. He was wearing black sunglasses, tinted darker than molasses; and had a paper rolled tightly in his hand.

"I'm Frank from the CIA, and I'm taking you away," he said, holding up his warrant paper. "I was sent to hunt you down, take you back to Frinkle Town to put an end to this little story's caper. You have the right to remain silent, so don't get smart or violent, and I won't have to cuff you on the plane. We're flying back home normally, quietly and formally, because flying on a bug is insane."

On the way across the ocean, Polly made no erratic motion; she sat silently by the window in deep thought. She smiled pleasantly to herself while pondering her mental health; in her head, she was hatching a devious plot. She'd escape once they landed; do something sneaky and underhanded by kicking Agent Frank in his shin. She'd run away forever; keep the police on an endeavor, making them wonder where she's been. But for now she played it cool, sitting next to this arrogant fool; she pondered as deeply as she could. Polly Pintonolly might have made a blundering folly, but this time she finally understood.

In China don't sniff your drink, or they'll throw you in the clink, leaving you until you're rotten-blue. Tiny islands are best to avoid, or lecherous pirates will get annoyed . . . and never ever eat Frinkleberry stew!

YOU AND THE BIG BRIGHT WORLD

You are in a dark tunnel. There is a light at the end and you are thrust into the big bright world. Immediately you want to explore, but the two, fleshy limbs at the end of your body won't work. Frustrated, you scream and cry, but after some time passes, the limbs begin to strengthen; you are now capable of walking around. You stop crying so much and develop a curiosity about the big bright world.

Standing over you are two tall beings who both agree that you are too little and dumb to go out on your own. Your curiosity turns to mischievousness—you break things and constantly get into trouble with the two taller yous. They finally have enough of it and send you to this place with other beings your size.

There are desks and books about the big bright world. After a very long time, you get tired of the desks and books, and you leave the place and start your expedition into the big bright world. Before you can get too far, however, there comes a hurt in your middle expanse. You go back to the two taller yous and they fix the hurt, but you are stuck with them all over again.

After a while, they get sick of always fixing the hurt and they shove you back out into the big bright world, but it doesn't appear to be all that bright anymore.

In fact, it looks dark and grim, much like the tunnel from which you first came. You wind up in another place with other desperate yous—and more desks, and more books about the big bright world. Except these books are harder to understand than the first ones, and you start to realize what you are being told about the big bright world is a lie. A big one!

You get anxious and leave the place of books and desks for another place that consumes all your time. This place treats you badly, making you do hard things for green paper. You hate it, but it keeps your middle from hurting. A depressing amount of time passes before you find that you have saved a few pieces of green paper. You trade them for a place much like your original taller yous had—only much, much smaller.

You keep a metal box by the road so the other yous can send you white oblong paper in exchange for your hard-earned green ones. This makes you bitter and angry; you stay up late drinking bubbly stuff, trying to forget. It doesn't work for long, and you find yourself back at that place where they treat you bad and make you do hard things.

The white oblong paper always keeps coming. The green ones get harder to earn. You drink more and more bubbly stuff, telling yourself one day it'll all change . . . one day . . .

You dream, hoping that a better life is right around the corner. But it isn't. When you open your eyes, you are right back in that hard place again; this time with an ache in your head. This prolonged period of misery happens repeatedly until you realize one day that your skin has become wrinkly and your limbs not working again. Now your hair is gray and thin just like your insides.

You seem to forget all the stuff you had learned when you sat in the desks.

Finally, you see the darklight. It comes unexpected one day. You ask yourself why, what did you accomplish? You want to go explore but the big bright world doesn't want you anymore. It spits you out and you wither away, confused but excited, dying to get a glimpse of that huge glorious afterlife.

UNDER A SLEEPING MOON

Wandering lust through a long winter stare
Spying through windows at frivolous fare
Peeking on All-Stars telling stories all told
Where silver shines green instead of translucent gold

Twinkling cusps and black bowtie grins
A punch well taken on the brunt of the chin
'Round comes tomorrow, bring lack of dessert
No money to spend, alas, not even a spurt

Throes of empty pockets offer no joy
Counting many others to writhe and woe
While many rejoice on a baker's warm bread
Leaving tonight's coldness to the hungry instead

Lifting the window as the chatter spills out
Forty young dancers and a woman about
Flakes drifting in to delude cups of wine
A lunatic preaching about the wealth of his crimes

Sleeping moon freezes, but a lamp still shines
Upon a murderous weapon that lays by my side
Glinting in shadows cast from an eye
Heads turn quickly as preparing to die

Spilt wine dribbles as patrons take flight
Dashing from perches to escape the darklight
In from the window a flurry of dust
Snow-white carpet now lay in red rust

CITY OF ELEVEN NIGHTS

The road was narrow; full of twists and turns, but that didn't stop the bus driver from keeping a heavy foot on the gas pedal. If anything, the danger of crashing seemed to invigorate the mad woman with four squiggly arms and a star-shaped head. The passengers behind her stared wide-eyed out the side windows; they were too afraid to say anything. Most held onto their seats with white knuckles.

Galerrie Flynn held on tightly to one of the four chrome poles in the aisle. Unable to find a seat, the tall, slender woman with bright pink skin, solid white eyes, and a round, oblong head opted to stand rather than wait for the next bus. She'd waited long enough—twenty six years, in fact—to get this opportunity to go to Big Dash City. She had only seen sketches of it in her childhood picture books; buildings suspended midair from kites the size of football fields. Galerrie's parents had promised to take her there someday, but that day never came.

Until today.

She felt a tug on the left side of her black skirt. She looked down and saw a man with brown and tan skin with an overlarge skull for a head sitting beside her. There was a child next to him; probably his son, she presumed, seeing that the boy's fleshless cranium resembled his father's, only smaller.

"Can you help me with a question?" the man asked. His eye sockets were deep, empty chasms; and his small grey teeth, square and slightly out of alignment. "I'll offer you my seat if you would kindly help me with these directions." He held up a map. "My son and I need to get off at Angle Street. But this darn map is confusing."

Galerrie took the offered map and studied it for a moment. Her white eyes scanned the blue and red lines. "Looks like it's right after Searchlight Corner. Fourth stop, but don't hold me to it." She looked to the bus driver. The four-armed speed demon did not appear to be the helpful type.

The bus careened around another sharp curve and Galerrie nearly fell into the skull man's lap. He held up his arm to keep her from falling.

"Thanks," she told him, holding onto the pole with one hand, and slowly pulling herself back to her feet. "This ride's getting a bit treacherous, huh?"

The man with a skull for a head whispered to his son. He then looked up at Galerrie. "Here. Take my seat. My son can sit on my lap."

He moved over and Galerrie looked behind her at other standing passengers eyeing the opportunity to sit down before she could. She wasted no time and moved in next to the man and his son. "Again, thank you." She smiled at him, revealing her own perfect set of white teeth. "So what's taking you two to Dash City?"

The man with a skull for a head gestured to his son. "His name is Viberace. We call him Vib. He was born with Spiral Spinyngitis. He can't stand up for long before his brain gets dizzy and he falls over. Got it from his mother's side."

"That's so sad," Galerrie said with a slight frown. She patted the boy on the knee. "He's adorable."

"I want to take him to see the sights. Figure it might do him some good since his mother's fatal fall. I'm hoping the trip might lift his spirits a little. Mine, too." The man extended his hand. "Oh, the name's Nochtimus. Nochtimus Bloose. I'm happy to meet you."

She shook his hand. "Galerrie Flynn. I'm going to be a contestant on *Pick a Monster*."

"The TV game show?" The man seemed impressed.

"I won a scratch ticket back home. I've wanted to go to Big Dash City since I was a little girl, so finding the winning ticket is a dream come true for me." She stared forward into a void, thinking of her picture books. "Not sure how I'll do on the show, though."

Nochtimus attempted a smile but he had no lips. "I watch it every chance I get. I'm sure you'll do great." He pointed to the bus driver. "If she can get us there in one piece that is." He glanced out the window to a steep ravine. The star-filled sky illuminated the ground below. This was no place for a speeding bus.

Galerrie stared at the back of the driver's pointed head. Three of her wiggling arms were wrapped over and around the steering wheel, the fourth arm on the knob of the gear shift. "Shame to think I've waited all these years for this opportunity just to go spilling over the side of a cliff."

Nochtimus reached down between his legs and came up with a red and black backpack. He unzipped it and dug around for a minute then came out with three candy bars. He offered one to his son who was sitting on his lap, staring out the window. "Care for a treat?" he asked Galerrie.

She gladly accepted.

"Vib's mother used to eat these all the time. Whenever she started getting brain dizzy, she'd sit down and eat two or three bars. Maybe it's the sugar, not sure, but they seem to help Vib, too."

"Is it something he'll grow out of, or . . . ?"

Nochtimus dropped the backpack to the floor. "Afraid not." He leaned in close to Galerrie and whispered: "It'll eventually kill him. That's why I want to take him now to see the city while there's still time."

Galerrie looked down at the candy bar in her hand. The dim lights from the bus's ceiling reflected off the shiny, silver wrapper. Galerrie felt guilty eating the candy. Wouldn't it be better if Nochtimus kept it for his ill son? She handed it back. "I think you better keep this. He needs it more than I do."

Though Nochtimus' bony face prevented any real expressions, Galerrie could sense his despair over his son's condition. She looked at the small boy sitting on his lap, his skull face reflecting in the window.

Another abrupt curve and everyone leaned steeply in their seats.

"Twelve minutes to arrival," the bus driver said over the speakers. "First stop will be Valiance & Martyr Boulevard."

Galerrie looked over her shoulder. The passengers behind her appeared relieved the trip was nearing its end. She turned back to Nochtimus. "Mind if I ask where you two will be staying during your visit?"

Nochtimus fumbled with the backpack at his feet. "We'll find a place, I'm sure. The main thing is getting to see all the sights. I figure to start right away. No sense wasting valuable time, right?"

He was hiding the truth, Galerrie suspected; he didn't have the money for a hotel. He probably had been doing all he could to save for food and the bus ticket. Rarely did people get the opportunity to come to the Big City. Money was hard to come by since the Deep Depression, and with only one company shuttling folks to and from the city, prices were outrageous.

Galerrie opened her purse and rummaged inside until she found her wallet. She unsnapped it. "I've got enough to cover a couple nights for you both. I mean, if that's okay with you?"

She could see him trying to smile. "You'd do that for us? Total strangers?"

"Not totally," Galerrie said. "I mean, I know your names."

The man with a skull for a head leaned back in his seat. He kept an arm around his son. "That's the nicest thing anyone's ever done for us."

***

Galerrie became lost in reverie, her mind drifting back to when she was was a child. She saw herself sitting on the floor, looking through her picture books. The sketches were black and white, simple ink drawings capturing the grandeur of Big Dash City. Through this hazy hallucination, Galerrie could still see reality and the speed-crazed bus driver. She could hear the stirring passengers behind her gathering their belongings. In the corner of her eye she saw Nochtimus and Vib sitting quietly beside her; the little boy was staring out the side window, looking to be contemplating his bony reflection.

The picture book in Galerrie's mind turned its own pages. She saw images of giant kites of all colors that filled the night sky. Below them, attached to long ropes, were swaying buildings of different sizes. Some of the buildings' windows were opened with light spilling out. Galerrie could see the workers in their offices, diligent in their duties. One lady was typing furiously. She had bright red fingernails matching the color of her stiffly, spiked hair.

The next page turned over and Galerrie saw something terrible approaching on the horizon. It was a tornado! The black funnel twisted into knots, charging the city at a ferocious speed. Mouths formed on the sides of the twister, revealing angular, ugly teeth that chewed through the kites' magical ropes. The kites were flung one by one into the atmosphere, dropping the buildings as brilliant eagles abandoning their prey.

Buildings crashed to the ground, scattering glass, dust, concrete, and steel. Galerrie winced as the tornado neared the building where she had seen the woman with red fingernails and spiky hair. The woman continued her rapid typing, and with one hand on the keyboard, she casually reached over with her other, shutting the window as if that would keep away the approaching danger.

The bus came to a sudden halt, jarring Galerrie from her trance. "Valiance & Martyr Boulevard," the bus driver shouted; the speakers crackled like frying bacon.

The bus door opened and two pink and purple serpentine passengers slithered by Galerrie's right leg. One of the serpents was a man with a long yellow beak, the other was female; her head was alive with many tiny serpents—babies attached to her scalp by their tails. Their long, spindly bodies intertwined with each other, coiling in knots as their parents exited the bus and went on their way. The bus door closed quickly; the driver announced loudly the next stop: "Omega Street and Henceforth. Three minutes!"

Galerrie carefully closed the picture book for the final time. She didn't need it anymore. She could see the city with her own eyes. The colorful kites in the sky were spectacular compared to her picture book and its modest black and white images. She had not expected the city to be glowing with such lively luminance—vibrant candy lights that looked edible if only Galerrie could climb up to reach them.

"Omega Street and Henceforth Boulevard!"

The bus screeched to a jerking stop, and several passengers rose to their feet, forming a line to make a quick exit. "Imagine that," Nochtimus said, nudging Galerrie with his elbow. He hadn't meant to do it so hard. His knee was shaking, causing his son's reflection to shudder, as though it were made of vintage film skipping frames. "We made it! Alive, I might add!"

Galerrie clasped her hands together in excitement. "It's even more beautiful than I imagined!" She leaned forward and stole a glance out the window next to Nochtimus and his son. The buildings swayed gently by their magical ropes attached to the sky-kites high above. Tons of concrete and steel were swinging in the wind, the dazzling lights shining on the streets and houses below.

Vib made a grunting noise.

"He likes the lights," his father translated. "They make him happy."

"They make me happy, too," Galerrie said to the boy. She could feel her heart quickening; a tingling

sensation radiating from her fingers to her toes—
WELCOME. WELCOME. WELCOME.

"Searchlight Corner," the bus driver announced
over the crackly speakers. Several passengers exited the
bus. The driver announced the next stop: "Angle Street.
Two minutes."

Galerrie fidgeted in her seat. She attempted to
compose herself by smoothing her skirt, and brushing
strands of hair from her forehead. She adjusted her
posture. Many passengers took this stop, the bus was
now half-empty. There was plenty of room for her to get
a seat somewhere else, but she remained seated next to
the man with a skull for a head, and his bony-faced son.
Their presence comforted her. At least until the next stop.

***

"I want to thank you for the money for our
lodgings." Nochtimus smiled the best he could, a tight,
lipless attempt. "Maybe we'll get lucky and see each
other around this grand city."

"I certainly hope so!" Galerrie exclaimed, standing
up to allow the two skull heads to get off the bus. "Please
take care of Vib. Don't let him get dizzy." She watched as
they exited the bus, Nochtimus carefully helping his son
down the steps. Giving a quick wave from the window,
Galerrie turned and moved toward her seat.

There were other passengers on the bus, but after
Nochtimus and his son got off and the door closed, the
vehicle felt strangely empty. Galerrie moved to the seat
closest to the window, the one where Nochtimus had

been sitting. It was warm. She closed her eyes and leaned her head on the aluminum frame, imagining Vib's face in the window staring back at her with those black hole eyes and toothy grin. She raised her hand and pressed her fingers to the glass; the reflection disappeared.

"Next stop, Dawn Street."

She thought of her friends back in her hometown of Kooplah Kloopah. They were probably at work, complaining about their new boss. How they despised the factory. Galerrie loathed it, too, but she was grateful of her loyal friends. She often thought of moving, possibly finding employment, and a place in the suburbs of Klaffetville or Nobs. Leaving her friends behind would be tough, but making new ones of their caliber would prove more difficult, if not impossible. They were once-in-a-lifetime type of friends who felt amusement and admiration for Galerrie's obsession of going to the Big City; and here she finally was. They would surely be delighted for her now.

It was nice having met Nochtimus along the way, someone to share the same experience. It was one thing her friends couldn't do—share that special enthusiasm with her. Sure, they hated the nowhere-life of Kooplah Kloopah, the mediocrity seemingly to coat every inhabitant like molasses. "It'll do" was the town's unspoken motto. Everything was always just good enough in Kooplah Kloopah; the jobs, the pay, the roads, and every boring thing connected with the town.

Good enough was *not* good enough for Galerrie. Somewhere in life she'd caught a bug. A wandering bug that sometimes liked to spread its wings. The wind would rush and sweep her off her feet, carrying her by the roots of her imagination to some far off place, then dropping her back into reality. The worst part was realizing that she hadn't actually gone anywhere but a short-lived daydream, a wishful fantasy that always left her feeling defeated. She would look down at her feet standing on the cold, hard factory floor, listening to her friends complaining about how they detested working there.

"Dawn Street," the bus driver announced.

Galerrie stood up and lifted her bag from the overhead compartment. It was heavy, full of clothes and all things a young woman might need on a trip, but probably would not. The small, dim walk lights aided her down the aisle. The shadows near her feet appeared to take swipes at her ankles as she stepped off the bus.

It was late. At least it felt late. Galerrie stood on the corner of Dawn Street and Bliss. She watched as the bus continued without her, several remaining faces staring out the side windows as the tailpipe coughed out black, oily smoke into the warm night air.

Galerrie had been the single passenger to get off at this stop. Her heavy bag in hand, purse strapped over her shoulder, she turned to look at her surroundings. She could see the outlines of the buildings in the sky, and parts of the giant kites above them shielding the city from invading starlight.

She wasn't sure about the direction to her hotel. Hotel Delirium. It was an odd name, but the brochure promised small, comforting rooms. And a pool. On the map it seemed to be a couple blocks south from the Dawn/Bliss intersection. Remembering what Nochtimus had said, "this darn map is confusing", Galerrie wished he was here to help her.

She chose a direction and went with it, listening to dogs barking from the neighborhood. A man yelled for them to shut up, but Galerrie didn't see anyone walking the sidewalks. She wondered if Nochtimus had found a room for himself and Vib. She didn't want to think they were wandering about while his son was getting brain dizzy. At least they had the candy bars, Galerrie remembered, and she was relieved she hadn't eaten the last one.

The row houses on both sides of the street were tall and looming, the façade and roofs aglow by the buildings' lights in the sky and from tall lamps on the sidewalks. Circular porch lights burned amber, attracting multitudes of flying insects. "Come one, come all," Galerrie said, giggling to herself as she watched the bugs swarming the lights. "All you can eat." She felt silly talking to herself though no one was around to hear. But what was the harm? "You can be a little ridiculous," she told herself. "It's alright. Do whatever you want. You're on vacation for twelve days and eleven whole nights!"

The cars parked on the road looked like sleeping mechanical animals waiting for their masters to awaken. Shadows lay still under the tires, hiding from the streetlights that seemed eager to devour them. The cars made Galerrie think of her friends back home; how they waited for the weekends to dally and socialize. The cars— they would wait all night for the chance of a joyride.

Galerrie heard voices from up ahead. Sounded like teenagers giggling and talking in raised voices. Galerrie stopped and rearranged the purse on her shoulder.

"He kissed me! Can you believe Rakky Limpoo kissed me? Ahhh! He finally did it!" shouted a delirious girl with telescoping eyes and a triangular, blue mouth. She hurried down the sidewalk with three of her friends. "I thought I was going to die right there!"

Galerrie smiled at the girls as they approached her. "Excuse me, but do you know where I can find Hotel Delirium? Am I going the right direction?"

The teens stopped and the girl with telescoping eyes (who seemed quite intoxicated with her recent excitement) scratched the side of her head. "Isn't that the dinky place next to Zeppy's Lounge?" she asked one of her friends who had a translucent head full of orange liquid. It sloshed back in forth behind her face.

"I think so," said the orange girl. She pointed in direction that Galerrie was going. "It's 'bout three more blocks that'a way. On the other side of the street, though. It's right next to Zeppy's Lounge."

"Zeppy's," Galerrie repeated. "Got it. Thank you very much for your help."

The girls waved goodbye then flitted away, one of them chattering about Rakky Limpoo's shrimp-like kissing lips.

***

Dinky, was a good description of the place. Smaller than the houses around it, Hotel Delirium was a three story row house in relatively run-down condition. The yellow paint flaked from the face boards, and the redbrick, front porch was in desperate need of repair; the steps were crooked, and the handrails covered in rust. Nevertheless, the place did have a peculiar charm about it, and if the rooms were clean (and bug-free), Galerrie figured the size of the building didn't much matter.

Certainly, the rates were right; the game show was reimbursing her for her food and lodging.

When she crossed the street, she saw three men coming out of Zeppy's Lounge—one of them was in a wheelchair. The bar next door to the hotel seemed to be a happening establishment. Galerrie heard the patrons inside shouting and howling, and girls' loud laughter. She hoped she wouldn't be disturbed once in her room. Though she didn't have to be at the game show studios for another day, tomorrow she planned to do some sightseeing and wanted to be well rested.

The tallest of the three men noticed her crossing the street. He whistled.

Ignore them, Galerrie thought to herself. Don't need trouble the first night in town.

"Hot legs!" the man yelled out. "I got a place for you to sit!" He pointed to his face; not so much an ugly mug as it was a surprisingly young one. His eyes were big ovals, bright green, and his chin strong. He had a thin, dark mustache whisking up at the ends; his cheeks layered with slits. "Let me help you with that bag," he insisted. Despite his drunken state, he moved quickly, approaching Galerrie in several long steps.

She kept her distance. "Thank you, but I can manage."

The man's friends quickly surrounded her.

The redeye man in the wheelchair had more than enough upper body strength, but his skinny legs were nearly the size of Galerrie's arms. "Hey, hot legs. Name's Wheelbilly," he said, jabbing his thumb at his own chest. "If you're tired of men pushing you around"—He pounded his chest with his fist—"come on over, here's one you can push."

Galerrie smiled politely. "Sorry, just got in to town and I'm very tired. I want to get checked in to the hotel." She didn't want to appear too helpless or scared. "I get out of sorts when I'm tired. You'll have to excuse me." She attempted to walk passed them toward to the hotel.

Wheelbilly rolled in front of her, blocking her from going any farther. "What are you doing tomorrow?"

"Sightseeing." She glared at him with her solid white eyes.

"All day long?"

"Most of it, yes."

"You need company?"

Galerrie looked at the other two men standing around her, especially the taller one with the oval eyes and the sharp, witless smile. Wheelbilly backed off, allowing her passage to the hotel. "You'll have to excuse Deet. He's a desperate case."

"I'll excuse him," Galerrie replied, trying to shoulder her way around the good-looking man with the turned-up mustache.

"And me?" Wheelbilly asked, rolling alongside of her. "Am I excused, too, darling?"

Galerrie didn't reply. She headed to the front door of the hotel, struggling to keep the purse on her shoulder as she toted the heavy carry bag up the front steps.

Wheelbilly waited on the sidewalk. "Hope we get the chance to talk again. I love your legs!"

She let the door slam behind her and approached a frail, elderly man behind the front desk. The nametag on his chest: Gert Bentles.

***

The lobby reeked of must, cigarettes, and old wood—odors accumulated over the decades. The two

394

gold-shaded lamps on the front counter were dim, giving the small room an antiquated feel. Galerrie dropped the carry bag to the hardwood floor as she leaned against the counter. Gert Bentles was too old and slow on his feet. He lumbered toward Galerrie like an aged robot with bad batteries. His hunched back looked as if another year to his spine would likely complete a circle. Galerrie drummed her fingers on the counter, trying not to smirk at the man and his condition, or how long it was taking him to walk to her.

"I have a reservation for—"

Gert raised his hand. "Let me come closer so I can hear." He hobbled forward. "Alright," he mumbled, barely able to lift his head up high enough to look at her. Cupping his ear, "You need a room?"

Galerrie pulled out the brochure from her purse. "Actually, I already have a reservation. I was told the Makkison Production Company had set up the—"

—The phone rang.

Gert held up a shaky hand. "Dag-nabbit. Dern old thing always waits til I get clear 'cross the room before it rings."

Galerrie thought that was hilarious; *clear 'cross the room*. The phone was only four feet away. "Please, allow me . . ." She walked over and grabbed the phone, carefully lifting the cord over the two lamps. She handed it to the old man.

"Happens ev'ry time, I tell ya." He picked up the receiver. "Hotel Delirium, Gert Bentles here. How may I help you?"

Galerrie put her back to the counter and listened to the old man give directions to the hotel. She watched the front door, wondering if Wheelbilly and his entourage of drunken delinquents were outside. She glanced down at her legs. Long, slender, and pink. "Hot legs," she muttered to herself, appreciating the compliment.

She had always been proud of her legs. Even as a young girl, the boys seemed impressed with them. They were always longer than the other girls' and that got her lots of attention. It was her nose that was the problem— long and pointy. She had been called needle-nose more than once.

"Sorry 'bout that," the old man said, hanging up the phone. "So you got a reservation, miss 'us?"

Galerrie turned to face him. "Yes. Though I'm not sure if it's under my name or the company that booked the room for me. I'm going to be on the *Pick a Monster TV* show day after tomorrow. They are paying for my room."

"Yes, I remember the call." Gert looked up at her through his bushy-white brows. "They said something 'bout you staying eleven nights in the city?"

"That's correct."

"Well, I'll need a deposit, regardless who is paying."

"I can handle that," Galerrie said. She placed her purse on the counter and rummaged for her wallet.

"Only one bathroom for each floor," Gert told her. "So don't lollygag too long. Others'll need to get in there."

Galerrie nodded. "No lollygagging in the bathroom. Check."

"And if'n you want to watch the television box, it'll cost a dollar an hour. And we don't get dirty channels."

"No dirty channels. Gotcha."

"And no room service anymore. They quit on me a while back, and I'm too old to be runnin food up and down them stairs and hallways. So you'll have to go out for your grub. They got san'wiches and stuff next door."

Galerrie didn't bother telling the old man about Wheelbilly and that maybe going next door wouldn't be such a good idea. There must be other places to eat, but tonight she could get by without. She was more tired than hungry.

After receiving the deposit, Gert gave her a tarnished, brass room key #37, and pointed to the squeaking, wrought iron caged elevator . . . "Third floor. The room is direct'ly 'cross the elevator."

Galerrie thanked him and placed the purse-strap back on her shoulder, and picked up her carry bag. "Goodnight," she said to the old man who shuffled back to his chair and a turned-down television box. Though the screen was only slightly visible from her perspective, she could swear she saw a skin flick. Dirty channels.

***

The door to room #37 creaked when it opened. The lights were off. Galerrie moved cautiously inside; she jumped nervously when she heard tires squealing from street below.

"Probably Wheelbilly and crew going home," Galerrie muttered as she fumbled for the light switch. She found it and flipped it. The room was bigger than she expected; however, she was reluctant to share a bathroom with other guests. The brochure had mentioned that minor inconvenience and she came prepared with disinfectants and aerosols.

She flung the heavy carry bag on the bed and sat her purse on the night table. On the far side of the room was a single window. The white, stained curtains were beginning to fray, the frills on the ends needing to be trimmed. After a struggle to lift the sticking sash, the window finally opened. A sudden rush of hot air filtered through the room. The hotel was obviously old, but that was fine with Galerrie. The place had real character.

Galerrie rummaged through the carry bag. She pulled out a pair of purple and black striped pajama bottoms and a solid black tank top. After dressing, she searched the bag for her toothbrush and paste. She came across her worn leather journal, putting it on the other night table next to the headboard, and went back for the hygiene products.

The bathroom was cattycorner across the hall next to the elevator. She looked both ways, up and down the hallway, counting six doors besides hers. She hoped there wouldn't be complaints to contend with in the morning. Fact was, she liked lollygagging in the bathroom. What normal girl wouldn't?

The aged, white paint in the bathroom was chipping, and the floor had rust stains from years of water leaking from the tub. A clear, plastic curtain hung from metal hooks on a bar above the tub; hardly a sufficient veil should someone come busting in on her. She checked the door lock. Flimsy, but it worked.

The mirror had a crack at the bottom, and there were flakes stuck to the glass. Galerrie immediately sprayed it with a can of disinfectant, wiping it clean with a bit of toilet paper. She looked at herself in the mirror, turning her head slightly, considering her long, pointed nose, her solid white eyes, vibrant pink skin, and her perfectly rounded cheeks.

One of her goals while in the city was to purchase a wig. She had never seen herself with hair, and thought it would be a kick to wear it on the TV show. What would her fellow townsfolk back in Kooplah Kloopah say about it? The entire town will be watching! Would her friends, whom she adored dearly, poke fun at her for wearing something as ludicrous as a wig? Probably, but only in fun. And that's one of the main reasons Galerrie came to Big Dash City—to get away from the same-ole-same and have fun. She wanted to try all the things in life that she couldn't do back home. At least wouldn't dare do in front of others she knew.

She brushed her teeth and giggled at the thought of how unlikely her trip to Big Dash had originated. The godsend came in the form of a scratch ticket she had purchased on a whim at the local grocery while standing in line. Her best friend, Carella Junkett, had been with her at the time. "Go ahead and buy one, Gal," she had insisted, but Galerrie wasn't the type to waste a dollar on chance. She relented only after her friend's optimism wouldn't let up. "Money comes and goes," Carella told her, "and so will your dreams if you don't pursue them."

It was worth a buck.

Back in her room, she heard the sounds of laughter from the street. She went to the window to investigate. Two cars had been woken from slumber, their headlights burning brightly in the night. She saw Mr. Green Eyes getting into the passenger side of one of the cars, followed by two scantily clad women with long, blonde hair. Galerrie wondered if they were wigs. She couldn't wait to see what it was like to wear one; everybody in the city wore them; and she checked that off on her mental to-do list as being one of the first things to accomplish. Who knows, she thought, running her hand over her smooth, pink head; I might just take a brand new me back home.

She turned from the window and went over to the night table beside the bed. She clicked the switch on a small reading lamp and turned off the overhead. After pulling back the covers, checking the mattress for any creepy-crawlies, she then lay down, reached over for her journal, her mind flooding with thoughts of the city. She wanted to write them down, starting with the bus ride, and then the nightmare of the tornado and the typing woman in the building with bright red fingernails.

She also wanted to log any preconceived ideas of what she might experience before actually experiencing them. Part of the enjoyment was comparing the two afterwards to see how close her expectations were to the truth. She pulled a pen from the journal, popped off the cap, and pressed the tip to the paper. But before she could produce a single word, her eyes closed and she was off to sleep, dreaming about tomorrow.

***

A car horn awoke Galerrie from her slumber. At first, she couldn't remember where she was; the room was unfamiliar, her eyes were having a difficult time adjusting to the daylight spilling in from the open window. Galerrie threw back the covers and jumped out of bed. She rushed to look outside. Below, on the street, was a black box truck with a white hood. Whoever was inside the vehicle was laying on the horn. Galerrie shut the window and pulled the ragged curtains.

"Too early," she grumbled, wiping the sleep from her eyes. Her stomach growled. "And no room service."

She went to her carry bag to retrieve her robe. She found it under a red makeup kit. Wigs, she reminded herself as she stared at the red box. That made her smile. I'll take a shower, get dressed, find someplace for breakfast, and go out on the town. Buy myself the prettiest wig I can find.

The bathroom floor was cold to her feet. She searched for a towel to lie down. She found one folded on a shelf above the toilet and reached for it. As she opened it, something fell out and to the floor. She looked down.

"Dear god!"

***

Gert Bentles thought he had seen it all in his forty-six years running the Hotel Delirium, but this was about the most revolting thing he'd come across. He stood at the bathroom door with a broom and dustpan, shaking his head. "Folks leave behind the strangest things, but this 'bout tops it."

Galerrie stood in the hallway, hand held to her mouth. She refused to look into the room. "I can't go back in there until that thing's gone." Her usual pink face was flushed almost white. She looked as though she might get sick.

The old man slowly shuffled into the bathroom. He grunted and moaned until he finally reemerged, holding the dustpan out in his shaky hand.

Galerrie turned her head and raised a hand in protest. "Please . . . get it away from me."

"I'll drop it in the dumpster 'round back," Gert said. He started toward the elevator but stopped short of it. With his back to Galerrie, and the dustpan still held out in front of him, he said, "I'll fetch you some clean towels." Then continued on his way.

Galerrie had lost her appetite. All she could think about was that horrible thing on the bathroom floor as she hesitantly re-entered the room. She closed the door behind her. "Wash it from my mind," she told herself as she dropped the robe from around her and took off her pajamas. The knob in the shower was difficult to turn. She used both hands, but almost slipped when the knob suddenly twisted and the water came out forcefully. "Think about something else. Something pleasant." She stepped into the shower, pulled the clear curtain. "Wigs. First on the agenda. I can eat later. Hopefully."

Gert left a stack of brown towels by the door. He listened for a moment as Galerrie showered. There was nobody else on the third floor; he'd seen to it. He put his hand on the wooden door—felt the crackly white paint. "They said you'd be pretty," he whispered. "But I never believe 'em until I see for myself." He turned from the door and stared at room #37. He had the other key.

The small hotel soap had a faint smell of lavender. Galerrie took it out of the wrapper and used it to clean herself. She wondered about Nochtimus and his son; hoped they were doing well, and having fun seeing the sights. Nevertheless, something he had said kept replaying in her mind. When she offered money for a motel, Nochtimus sounded surprised: "You'd do that for us? Total strangers?"

"Not totally," Galerrie had told them. "I mean, I know your names."

She knew their names even before he had told her. But how? Where had she seen him before? Lathering her hands with soap, she washed her face under the showerhead, thinking of where she could have met the two skull heads prior to the bus ride.

"It was at the grocery. They were standing in line behind me and Carella when I bought the winning ticket!"

Did they follow me to Big Dash City? If so, why?

She washed the soap from her face then turned off the water. Coincidence, she told herself, reaching for a towel but not finding one. That's all it was, coincidence; the little boy is sick, and his father decided to take him to see the big city. I must have overheard their names. She wiped the water from her eyes with the heel of her hand, stepped out of the shower, and to the cold, stained floor.

The floor sagged and creaked from constant moisture. Galerrie walked to the door.

"Mr. Bentles?" she called. There was no reply. Slowly, she opened the door and peeked out. At her feet were the towels. She picked them up and closed the door, locking it.

She dried off and put on her robe, collected her pajama bottoms and shirt, and went back to her room. She had brought a small mirror in her carry bag. She retrieved it and set it on the dresser. The red makeup box was packed full of lipstick, mascara, powder puffs, and fingernail polish. She considered getting dolled up, but decided against it. Leave it for later and do-it-up right, she determined, wanting instead to hurry out to find a store that sold wigs.

While staring at her reflection in the mirror, she noticed something behind her. She turned to see that a chair had been placed in her room. On it was a black body suit.

"How'd that get here?" she said, getting up to check it out. She held up the body suit. It was one piece and had the feel of Kevlar. "Body armor?" She was at a loss for how or why there was body armor left in her room on a chair that wasn't there before she—

—There came a knock at the door. "I need to talk. It's important," said a voice from the other side.

"Mr. Bentles?" she muttered.

Galerrie dropped the body suit to the chair and went to the door. She was hesitant to open it. "Mr. Bentles, is that you?" He did not answer. "Mr. Bentles?" Slowly, with one foot near the bottom to hinder anybody shoving his or her way in, she opened the door.

"I have to talk to you." It was Nochtimus Bloose. His son was not with him.

***

"He saw to it that you'd get the winning ticket," Nochtimus told her, sitting on the bed. His empty eye sockets looked deeper than any hole. "He sent me to make sure you got to the city."

Galerrie sat beside him. "Who did? Who are you talking about? Why would anybody go out of their way to make sure I'd win a ticket for a game show?"

Nochtimus looked distressed. He kept glancing to the window as if expecting somebody to come crashing through. "I don't have a lot of time to explain. I wanted to let you know they are watching you. They've been following you since the bus ride to the city."

"Who, Nochtimus? Who is watching me?"

"They call themselves Readers. They watch us from the netherworld known as the DarkLight Delirium. The game show . . . it's not real." He stood and went to the window, looking out to see if anybody was around the hotel. He then turned back to Galerrie. "The Author tricked you, Galerrie. *Pick a Monster* was his way to get you to the city; bring you into his story. You never had a choice. Your whole damned life has been planned out from the day you were born. I know this because the Author did the same thing to me. I found out years ago."

Galerrie stood up and laughed. "Nochtimus, are you kidding with me? I mean, seriously?"

He approached her; held out his small brown-skinned hands. "My dream was to cure my wife and child. Find a way to somehow rid their disease, or at least slow it down. Give them a chance to live normally. But I never stood a chance. The Author didn't allow it. He wants the Readers to pity me. Me and my family are nothing but a pathetic attempt to capture the Readers' mercy.

He won't let any of us live, Galerrie. Not even you. He controls every aspect of our existence, and once the Readers get into your head, they'll rip your life apart, drive you crazy until you either kill yourself . . . or . . ."

"Or what?" Galerrie asked, her eyebrows raised.

"Or the Author finds some heartbreaking ending to your life's story. It's his choice how you end, Galerrie, not yours."

Galerrie exhaled and sat back on the bed. She looked up to the ceiling, closed her eyes. "*Pick a Monster.* The game show host asks the contestants different questions about geography, history, famous people. Stuff like that. While the contestants are thinking, they are circled and harassed by people wearing scary costumes. Monster costumes. Whoever first answers correctly gets to pick a monster. After several rounds, the one with the most monsters gets to enter the last phase of the game. That's where he or she watches the other contestant's monsters kill each other—pretending, of course—and all the fake blood and stuff . . . The viewers love it. The show gets great ratings." She looked to Nochtimus who was now standing with his hands clasped in front of him. He wasn't trying to smile as he seemed to often do; his expression was one of real concern. Galerrie continued: "That's all it is, a kooky TV game show. The last phase consists of the final contestant getting one card each night for eleven nights. Glowing cards with pictures of different settings on them, such as haunted houses or graveyards or something. The contestant has to guess which monster belongs to which card. On the eleventh and final night, if he or she guesses wrong, that particular monster kills the contestant. Pretending though, like I said. It only looks real on TV."

Nochtimus picked up the black body suit. He held it up. "That's the fictional TV show you were made to believe. The real game is being played in your head. In your mind where the Readers see everything you think and do." He offered the body suit to Galerrie. "Here. Put this on. You've got to take control."

Galerrie took the suit and looked it over. "And how is this supposed to change my life?"

"Become a villain. Or a super hero. Good or bad, that doesn't matter, but whatever you choose, you must wear the suit. It's the only chance you have to escape whatever fate the Author has planned for you. You've got to become something different."

Galerrie laughed. Had Nochtimus lost his mind? "You're basically saying by wearing this thing, I can take control of my own life from this . . . this story I'm supposedly living?"

"That's *exactly* what I'm saying."

Galerrie laid the body suit next to her on the bed. "Where is Vib?"

Nochtimus looked down at the floor. "He had a spell. It wasn't good."

Galerrie stood up and walked over to the grieving father. "Is he okay? Did you take him to a hospital?"

Nochtimus shook his head. "Didn't have the chance."

Galerrie put a hand to her forehead. "I'm so sorry, Nochtimus. Wha—when did it happen? Last night?"

"Not long after we got off the bus," he said. "We were looking up at all the buildings in the sky. I let him stand too long. I got caught up in the sights. We stood looking, and I was pointing out the kites above the buildings, how the wind keeps them aloft. That's when I heard Vib making those sounds he makes when the sickness comes over him. But this time the candy bars didn't help. He started wobbling back and forth on his feet, and then collapsed. I tried talking to him, rubbing the side of his head, but he wouldn't snap out of it. He just lay there on the street corner, kicking his legs and slamming the back of his head against the concrete. He was dead within a minute."

Galerrie was speechless. She looked at the black body suit. It lay on the bed much like she imagined Vib's body on the street. Still. Empty of life.

Nochtimus wasn't crying, or maybe he couldn't. Since he had no normal eyes, Galerrie assumed the tears were falling on the inside. She could almost hear them trickling around in a puddle inside the man's head. She put her arms around him. "I am so sorry."

She was taller than Nochtimus by a couple inches. His gray skull lay hard against her chest. If he couldn't produce tears of his own, she did a good job crying for them both.

"The Author was responsible," Nochtimus said faintly with his face next to her. "He could have stopped it from happening."

Galerrie waited several seconds before saying anything. It was unbelievable that Vib had died so suddenly after getting off the bus, but even more difficult to believe an omnipotent, unseen Author was to blame. "I'll wear the suit," she finally said.

Nochtimus stepped back from her and looked to it. "It's your only hope to save yourself."

***

The morning light glinted off the buildings in the sky, laser lights reflecting from the tiny windows where office workers performed their duties. On the ground, huge shadows crept along the streets and across rooftops of the row houses, triangular shades of darkness cast by the kites. Galerrie and Nochtimus walked together on the sidewalk. They passed Zeppy's Lounge. The bar looked all but abandoned in the daylight. No neon signs, no drunken patrons falling out the door. No sign of Green Eyes or Wheelbilly.

"I saw something this morning," Galerrie told Nochtimus as they walked. "It was in the bathroom. I unfolded a towel and it fell out."

"What was it?"

"I'm not sure. But it was the most hideous-looking thing I've ever seen," she said. "It was about a foot long. A black, shapeless blob with eyes all over it."

Nochtimus remained quiet.

"It appeared to be wet even though it had been in a towel. It didn't move, but I could see it breathing, and all its eyes were looking at me. They had some kind of film over them, like slime or something."

"Did it say anything to you?"

Galerrie looked at Nochtimus. "How do you know it could talk?"

"They don't usually," he said, staring forward as they walked. "They sometimes slither out from the Delirium. I used to find them all around my house back before I knew not to look into their eyes."

"It didn't say anything. It just stared at me for a second until I ran out of the room."

"Is it still there?"

"No. The hotel manager came up and took it out to the dumpster."

"How did he know to come up? Did you call for him?"

Galerrie shrugged. "Well, not exactly. I mean . . . honestly, I don't know how he knew to come up. I was so freaked out about that thing. I just know he was there with a broom and dust pan."

Nochtimus put his hand on Galerrie's arm. He stopped her. "The Author did it. He made him come up."

Galerrie pursed her lips. "As a part of my story?"

"We all are, Galerrie," Nochtimus said, clutching onto her arm. He looked down again, saddened by his revelation. "The Readers see everything . . ." He pointed to the row houses around them. To the buildings in the sky. To the shadows creeping at their feet. "It's all created for them, for their enjoyment. Everything. Even me."

Galerrie touched his hand. "You are real, Nochtimus. I'm real, too."

"For now, yes," he said, letting go of her. "At least until the story is over."

"And you're scared the Author will kill you at the end?"

Nochtimus exhaled deeply and nodded. "I'm scared to death."

"If that's what you believe then maybe you should get away from me. Get far, far away. Before the Author has a chance."

"It wouldn't matter," Nochtimus told her. "I was away when Vib died." He covered his face with his hands. "When he was taken from me."

Galerrie's face contorted to a scowl. "This is crazy talk. I just came to the city to be on a game show. I'm not a super hero, or a villain." She gestured to the black body suit that she was wearing. "I'm just a boring girl from Kooplah Kloopah getting to see the big city."

"A city that doesn't exist except in a story," Nochtimus corrected her.

"Enough." Galerrie put up a hand. "Please, just stop it. I don't want my trip turning out badly, and hearing about your son dying . . . That is awful. And I am truly sorry, but I think maybe . . . Maybe we should go our own ways."

Nochtimus turned from her and started walking. "My ways are your ways," he muttered under his breath. He walked away with his head bowed and his hands in his front pockets. "Not like I have anywhere else to go."

***

Galerrie wasn't sure why she put on the black body suit. Had she done it to calm Nochtimus, or did she actually believe that there were monsters watching her from some unseen place called the Darklight Delirium? She stood on the sidewalk, observing the city folk heading out to their sleeping cars to wake them for work.

The thing on the bathroom floor. How did Mr. Bentles know to come up to get it? He had even been perceptive enough to bring the broom and dust pan.

Another coincidence, perhaps? Just like Nochtimus and his son being behind her in line when she bought the winning ticket? And for that matter, she'd never won anything in her life; however, the one time she gambled on chance, her dumb luck granted a wish she had had for years—to go to the city of her . . . dreams?

She recalled once again what her best friend Carella had told her: "Go ahead and buy one, Gal. Money comes and goes, and so will your dreams if you don't pursue them."

Chance. It didn't make sense. Or did it? Was she forced to reveal her thoughts to the Readers? Was this the monster she picked; or was it her *chance* to defy them?

"Forget it. Go buy a wig," she said to herself. "The entire thing is irrational."

She began walking, trying to put the thoughts of monsters out of her mind. Vib's death, the thing on the bathroom floor, and Nochtimus' crazy talk of the Author—she had to forget it. She never liked people being upset with her. It bothered her enormously that

411

Nochtimus walked out of her life the way he did, but he had to go for his own good, she thought. I've got to enjoy my time here. I can't spend my entire trip worrying.

She came upon a corner store and decided to go in and ask for directions to a place that sold wigs. She also needed sunglasses. The store reeked of cleaning chemicals. A young, velvet-skinned girl with silver loops growing from her shoulders was busy with her fingers picking in a plastic bucket of bubblegum; her mother was standing behind her, yanking at the girl's shoulders to get her to leave. The clerk behind the counter looked annoyed. Galerrie approached him.

"Excuse me. Do you sell sunglasses?"

The clerk pointed to a tall, revolving display.

Galerrie waved. "Thank you."

There were all kinds of styles of glasses ranging from the typical to the outrageous. Some had blinking lights on the rims, others had multiple lenses. Galerrie picked a modest black pair, tried them on, and looked at herself in a small, square mirror attached to the display. She decided against them and opted for a pair of blue mirrored.

She paid for the glasses and asked the clerk where she might find a store that sold wigs.

"Two blocks down the road, thatta' way," he said, thumbing over his shoulder. "Take a left at the next intersection, and keep going straight until you come upon Lost Wanderer Boulevard. There's a liquor store and right across the street from it there's a ladies boutique. They have every kind of woman-stuff you can think of. Sorry, I don't remember the name of the place."

Galerrie thanked him and left; the little velvet-skinned girl was still digging for the perfect piece of bubblegum.

***

Jerõ was the name of the store.

Galerrie pushed open the tinted, glass door and was greeted with a pleasant smell of incense. Three women with olive green gas masks on their faces stood talking to each other. Galerrie walked passed them, her purse swinging from her shoulder.

One of the women turned to her. "May I help you?"

Galerrie removed her sunglasses and nodded. "I'm looking for a wig. Looking for a selection, actually."

"Right this way." The woman mumbled something to her friends, then led Galerrie toward the back of the store. "We have an extensive collection to choose from. Long, short, curly. Natural hair or monofilament. Just about every style, color, and texture."

"I'll say," Galerrie replied, gawking at all the pieces. She dropped her sunglasses into her purse. "May I try them on?"

The saleslady tugged at the nozzle of her gas mask. "Uh, you mean every one?"

Galerrie cracked a smile. "No, no. Just a few. How about that one up there?" She pointed to a light brown, longhaired wig. "I've never worn one before. I'm very curious."

Thick, tinted goggles hid the sales clerk's eyes. The mask reminded Galerrie of a character from one of her childhood books—Frax the miner who happened upon an underground race of little, fuzzy purple people. "With your pink complexion," the lady said, pointing to a different wig, "you might consider a darker shade."

Galerrie thought about it. "Sure. How about that one there? The black one next to the blonde."

The sales clerk reached for it.

"Wait," Galerrie said. "I'm sorry, but I think I like this one over here better."

The clerk stood with hands on hips.

"Yes. That one," Galerrie told her. "May I try it?"

The woman handed it to her. "With your pointed nose and round cheeks, I'd go with something straighter, if I were you."

Galerrie held the wig in her hand. The outside of it felt soft, but the inside liner was like burlap. "Sure. I'll try that one over there." She pointed to a black, straight, longhaired wig.

"Good choice," the clerk replied curtly, replacing the wavy wig and retrieving the selected one. She handed it to Galerrie. "It's definitely you."

"But I haven't even tried it on yet."

"Trust me, I know faces. I've been doing this for years. That one is perfectly you."

Galerrie looked the wig over in her hand. It felt soft. The hair was thick, black, and straight. She tried it on.

"Like this," said the sales clerk, taking the wig off and reapplying it. "Pull it over your head this way, and then down."

Galerrie looked at herself in a long mirror. Wow. She looked . . . "Different, for sure." She turned to the clerk. "Never seen myself with hair before. Where I come from, nobody wears these."

"A country girl, are you?"

"Slightly."

"Thought so, by the accent."

Galerrie put a hand to her mouth as if to stop her accent from falling out. She was embarrassed by it. She didn't like that strangers could automatically assume things about her because of the way she spoke. Not that she had a particularly bad accent—most in Kooplah Kloopah made her sound "big city-ish"—but here in the real deal, she was sure to stand out. She turned back to the mirror, struck a pose. Puckered her lips.

"You're right, it does suit me," she told the sales woman.

"Like I said, been doing this for years."

"I'll take it." Galerrie spun on her heel and looked at the clerk. "How much is it?"

"Sorry, it's not for sale."

Galerrie cocked her head and smiled wryly. "Seriously. How much?"

The woman didn't flinch. "Not for sale. Not to you, anyway."

Galerrie's tone of voice became sharp. "And why not? What did I do?"

"That particular wig is reserved for someone else."

Galerrie pulled it off. "Then why did you show it to me?"

"Because it suits you, but it's not for sale."

"Do you have any others like it?"

"All on order, I'm afraid."

"How long until they arrive?"

"Could be a week."

Galerrie had plenty of time to wait, but she wanted a wig for tomorrow's filming of the show. "Do you have anything close in style to this one? Maybe in the back?"

The sales clerk stepped to the side and gestured to all the wigs on display. "What you see is what we have."

Galerrie's mouth quivered at the corners. "Well, then. May I try the wavy one again?"

The woman reached for it. "It doesn't fit your face."

"I'd still like to try it, please."

"Very well."

The woman reluctantly handed her the wig. Galerrie tried it on; putting it on the way the clerk had shown her. She looked in the mirror but did not see herself.

"What's wrong?" the sales clerk asked.

"I—I don't know." Galerrie put her hand to her temples. "I don't look like me. It's like I've turned into someone else."

"A new look should do that."

"No. It's not the wig," Galerrie sounded anxious. Her hands began to tremble. "I feel different inside."

"Do you want to sit down?"

"Yes, I believe I will," she moaned.

The front door of the store opened and in walked two men dressed in black.

"Guns," Galerrie whispered. She saw the them in her mind. "Those men have guns. Under their coats. They're going to use them."

The sales clerk looked to the front of the store and saw the men approaching her co-workers.

Galerrie felt dizzy. All she could think about was the thing on the bathroom floor. It was staring up at her. All those eyes. "The men . . . They're going to shoot! They're going to kill everybody in the store . . . ."

The sales clerk didn't know how to react. She took a step forward, as if considering going to talk to the two men.

"Don't," Galerrie ordered, grabbing the woman's arm. "It won't do any good."

"I should—should call the police."

"Is there a rear exit?"

The woman pointed to two swinging doors. "Back there. In the stockroom."

"Go. Get out of the store and call the police."

The sales woman took a last look at her coworkers. The men held pistols to the women's heads. She looked to Galerrie. "Aren't you coming with me?"

"No," Galerrie said sharply. "Get out of here. Now!"

The clerk froze. "I'm scared. What if they—?"

Two gunshots rang out, followed by the sounds of two bodies hitting the floor.

"Get out!" Galerrie yelled, shoving the woman to the double doors.

The gunmen looked to the back of the store where Galerrie was standing. One of them pointed to her, and they both came running with guns drawn.

Galerrie stood in front of the stockroom door, blocking it so the sales clerk had time to get out of the building. She looked down at the black body suit she was wearing. "Am I a super hero or a villain?" She wasn't afraid of the gunmen, and couldn't understand why. All she knew was she felt an overwhelming will to stand and fight.

The assassins aimed their pistols at her face. "You're coming with us," declared one of the gunmen. He was wearing a long, dark coat, as was his partner. Both had on ski masks and sunglasses. "Don't try anything stupid and you won't get hurt."

Galerrie didn't flinch. She stood unfazed by the gunman's threat and the guns pointed at her. "You followed me from the hotel, didn't you?" she said.

"Didn't have to," the gunman replied. "We know where you are. Where you go." He took off his sunglasses and then pulled off his ski mask, revealing those familiar translucent green eyes. "Can't say I care much for the new 'do. I prefer you the way you were." He reached and pulled off the wig, exposing Galerrie's head. "I can see your face better. See those pretty white eyes."

Galerrie smelled alcohol on his breath. "Where's your other pal?" she asked. "The one in the wheelchair?"

Green Eyes thumbed over his shoulder to the front door. "Outside. Waiting."

The thing on the bathroom floor blinked its eyes and Galerrie could see Wheelbilly sitting in the back of a truck. A black box truck with a white hood. He was naked. Slobbering.

"Forget the wig," Green Eyes said, throwing it to the floor and stepping on it. "But you're coming with us."

"Can't do that," Galerrie said. "I'm not going anywhere with you."

Green Eyes snapped. "You don't have a choice, hot legs. You either go with us alive, or you leave in a body bag." He blew a kiss at her then smiled. "But I think you might just end up liking me." He reached with his left hand (the gun was in his right) and touched Galerrie's arm.

The thing on the bathroom floor blinked again— eyes all over its black and shiny body. Galerrie gasped. She looked down at the gunman's hand on her arm. His fingers came off much easier than expected. Galerrie hardly heard the bones break. Looking at them in her hand, she dropped the crushed digits one by one to the floor.

The bullet was gray and had very small indentions on the sides caused by the poor rifling in the pistol's barrel. Spiraling in incredibly slow rotations toward Galerrie's face, she stepped out of the way and watched the bullet sink into one of the double doors behind her. She felt a prodding sensation near her right collarbone. She looked and saw another bullet had struck her. It had bounced off the body suit and was now spinning through the air toward the wigs.

Galerrie glanced to her would-be killers. Judging by their faces, their brains obviously hadn't yet realized what had happened, and that Galerrie was perfectly unharmed by their bullets. Green Eyes, in shock from his mutilated left hand, appeared to be coming to his senses. His eyes enlarged as a tidal wave of pain cascaded on him. The perverted smirk was gone, replaced by an almost childish expression of fear. Both assassins' guns were also in slow motion, ejecting the shells. Galerrie watched as the two pieces of brass flipped end over end through the air; the slides on both pistols sliding back into position.

The thing on the bathroom floor rolled over to its back. There were more eyes on its underside, and a round suctorial mouth with sharp, raspy teeth. "We are Miish, eyes of Readers."

Galerrie wanted to get out of the bathroom. Get away from this awful-looking thing on the floor. But she had to know what it was, why it was appearing in her mind. "Why are you here?" she asked it, keeping her hand on the bathroom doorknob. She was ready to run out to the hallway and yell for Gert the hotel manager to come take her nightmare away.

"We watch from Delirium. We see all you do."

"It's not possible. You—you can't be real!" Galerrie proclaimed. Her voice was panic-stricken. "Why do you want to torment me?"

"We are Readers. We do not interfere. We watch, we read."

Much like the daydream Galerrie had had on the bus, there was a haze overlaying a reality—she could see the two gunmen (Green Eyes was nearly in tears, staring at his bloody, fingerless hand; his partner was re-aiming his weapon at her). In the foreground, however, she was standing in the bathroom with Miish.

"Our eyes feast on imagination. We devour what the Author feeds us."

"Leave me alone. You disgust me."

"The Author made you for us. We must keep reading."

"Tell the Author I want no part. I just want to be left alone."

"Imagination . . . we must have more and more."

Green Eyes was now looking at her. He raised his gun. There was a scowl on his face.

"The gunmen want to kill me," Galerrie said to Miish, staring at the two assassins through the layered haze. "Can the Author help me?"

"The Author creates. We watch."

Green Eyes pulled the trigger, but the bullet had not ejected. Galerrie had time to deliberate.

"What happens if I die?" she asked Miish. "Will that be the end of me? There's nothing else?"

"There is always another story for us to read," said the thing on the floor. "Yours will be like all others. It will come to end."

"I don't want to end!" Galerrie snapped. "You can't watch me forever!"

"Until the Author has finished with you, we read."

Galerrie opened the bathroom door and stepped out, reentering to reality with the gunmen.

Two bullets were spiraling toward her heart. She watched as the slow motion projectiles were reflected by the body armor. Green Eyes pulled his trigger again, releasing another bullet.

The body armor protected her, and all she had to do to avoid a head shot was simply step out of the way. Everything was running in a fraction of normal time, everything except Wheelbilly who was rolling toward her in his chair. He had something in his lap. It appeared to be a book.

"Your mind's made up, is it?" he asked. "You don't want to participate?"

Galerrie didn't reply. She was afraid of the Reader's in her mind.

Wheelbilly looked down at the four fingers on the floor. "I should've known Nochtimus would have gotten to you before I could. Did you know his son died?"

"He told me," Galerrie replied, brusquely.

"A pity. But did he bother telling you who we are? Where we come from? And what we want?"

Galerrie stepped to the side as another bullet glided by her head. "You are from the Darklight."

Wheelbilly raised his arms. "We are from a greater mind than our own. And seeing as you have the ability to sidestep bullets and rip off fingers, I assume you have been blessed with these abilities by the Author."

Galerrie sneered.

Wheelbilly rolled his chair closer to her. The top of his head was just under the barrel of Green Eyes' gun. He snapped his fingers and both assassins put away their weapons. "But what isn't true is the truth. Miish, I assume, didn't tell you that it is the embodiment of forgetfulness. Had you allowed it to bite into you, your existence would have never been. You'd have been wiped clean of the writer's memory, and your own."

Galerrie believed neither him, nor the ugly thing on the bathroom floor. She wasn't convinced she was living a story, and was beginning to regret ever purchasing that damned winning ticket. The trip had started out fine. She wasn't too thrilled when she'd first got on the bus to find it full, but standing a few hours to get to come to Big Dash City was a minor inconvenience. She had expected this to be the trip of her life. She was partially right; her dream had come true.

But what a tangled nightmare it had quickly become.

"The story is all you have," Wheelbilly told her. "And since I am a part of it, I'm on your side. I want it to continue." Wheelbilly held up the thing in his lap. Indeed, it was a book; a book titled, DarkLight Delirium. On the cover was a painting of two white creatures sitting in chairs at a table. The chairs were floating on a purple river, flowing over a brown landscape while other creatures held feathered rods under their chins, and stared at the night sky. At the bottom was a pair of eyes. Deep blue and glowing. "The eyes are of the Author of this book. I fear he is drawing us to a close, but Miish will continue reading if the Author keeps writing. But it's up to you, Galerrie. How interesting do you want this story to be?"

Galerrie's steady gaze relaxed a little. "I just came to the city to be on a game show, and to sightsee. I'm not a crime fighter or any kind of special person." She looked down at the black body suit. "I'm a simple person from the small town of Kooplah Kloopah. That's all I know. I have a lot of friends there. We work hard and hang out when we can. There's nothing really all that unique about us. Certainly not me. I don't know why anyone would want to watch what I do, or read my thoughts. My mind isn't original or anything special. I'm just me. Plain, mostly."

"You're not plain." Wheelbilly put the book back on his lap. "Nothing plain about a tall, pink woman with no hair, a pointed nose, and solid white eyes." He pointed to Green Eyes behind him. "Nothing plain about any of us. Just look at the backdrop the Author provided us; buildings floating in the sky from giant kites? If anything, the Author is somewhat deranged. Probably a bit of a lunatic. But sometimes it takes a different outlook to create a glimpse of originality." He tapped the book on his lap. "You won't find vampires and werewolves in these pages. Too ordinary. But what you will find are troubled examples of love and desperation. Some of the stories border on the absurd, others are melancholy testaments to the Author's . . . Well, his tortured mind. But they're all beautiful in their own way. Me and you? We're a part of it. Part of the book." Again he tapped it with his forefinger. "Right now, Galerrie, if you reconsider, and allow us a longer story, those of the Delirium will keep reading."

"Who are they?" Galerrie asked. "Who'd be interested in reading about me?"

Wheelbilly pointed to you. "Look. Look closely behind the print. See those eyes?"

Galerrie lifted her head.

"You have to open your mind, Galerrie. Look hard, you'll see. There are eyes reading. Do you see them?"

"I—I think so . . ." Galerrie said, squinting, contorting her face, trying hard to see you, the Reader. "I think I do."

"Now look away," he directed. "We don't want to distract too much. The Reader is absorbed. Let's get back to the story." Wheelbilly reached down and grabbed Green Eyes' fingers off the floor. He handed them back to his friend. "Galerrie, what I'm proposing is the chance to become something that will never truly die. You'll be in print forever, always alive in the eyes of a Reader. If you allow fear to talk you out of this opportunity, our story will end. We'll never be remembered, and those interesting eyes you saw reading you will never have the chance to really know you, or what you could become. Now is your chance, Galerrie. Right now is your chance to exist forever."

Galerrie didn't want to disrupt the story, but she took another quick glance at you, the Reader. She had to be sure you exist forever, too. She was scared of the idea of having you watching her forever. Can you blame her? It isn't a normal thing. Not even for a fictional character like Galerrie, but I'm not sure I believe she's fictional. She has feelings, so she must be real. She bleeds. She hurts. Sometimes she cries. But then, I'm not a normal author and I sort of enjoy torturing my characters. I'm not really a lunatic; I just need the darklight to operate.

I need Galerrie to make a decision; though I could force her to become an offbeat crime fighter of Big Dash City. That was my initial idea, but through the pages I've come to love her too much to do that. Consequently, I'm going to do what my Creator has done for me—I'm going to give her the choice.

Wheelbilly rolled closer to her, took her pink hand in his. "Let's go. We'll turn you into something very special. You'll be immortalized forever. You will be written about over and over, never to—"

"—I don't want that," Galerrie interrupted. She pulled her hand away. "I just want to go home. I want to get away from this city and back to Kooplah Kloopah where I am safe. I'm not a super hero. I'm not special enough to keep reading. But most importantly, I want to go home where my friends are."

Wheelbilly stared at her for several seconds in disbelief. He lowered his head. "Okay . . . Okay . . . If you're sure."

Galerrie put her hands to her face and began to cry. "Yes. I'm sure."

"Then what is wrong? Why are you crying? You don't have to do anything you don't want. You can go home. It's all your choice now, Galerrie. You can end the story."

"I know. But I probably will disappoint the Reader. I'm sorry. I just don't like people being mad at me."

***

The bus ride home wasn't nearly exciting as the trip to the city. Galerrie sat alone by the window, staring at the back of the man's head sitting in front of her. He had thin, flexible horns jutting from his blue scalp. There were veins extended from the tip of one horn to the next, clear, hose-like conduits carrying his deoxygenated blood back to his heart. She wondered if the man had a difficult time getting to sleep. How did he put his head down? How did he keep the veins on his head from being tangled?

Galerrie thought of Nochtimus Bloose and his son. Spiral Spinyngitis. It had killed him. Galerrie closed her eyes. She was getting dizzy. She thought of her friends. She thought of you, too, the Reader. Wondered what you thought of her for running away? She sunk down into her seat and covered her face. She doesn't want to think about you anymore. She doesn't want you looking at her.

A PLACE BEYOND HAPPINESS AND PAIN

I thought somehow I would be able to keep her. Thought maybe if I bought her a block of chocolate, it would make her love me. All it did was turn her into a diabetic. I thought buying her a bouquet of flowers would put a glitter in her eye. All they did was turn them red— she's allergic. Thought I could write a song for her on guitar, but she's tone deaf. Nothing left to do but wrap a washcloth full of ice around my heart and hope the bruising doesn't swell too much.

I called her last week to tell her I loved her, yet somehow I was let down. Maybe I thought I'd never let that barrier down again, maybe thought I couldn't; she sliced through my feelings like a steak knife carving the guts out of a warm, baked potato. I could feel all the hot butter sliding out of me when she hung up.

Try to get her out of my mind at night when nobody is looking, but all I do is wake up with matted eyes from all the dried tears. Midnight love. Imposter. Charlatan dreams. They'll strangle the best of me, yet all I do is try and push them away until I shove so hard they get pushed all the way round the world and come back the next morning to slap me hard in the face. Dreams always come back around—everything does . . . clouds, the sun, love, and her face in my memory. There's no frost to freeze it, no heat to burn it away.

My heart is weak, my mind strong, but it wavers as if thoughts were the wind and my body a loose shoestring snagged on a twig. I try to perform. I move about the day in ways adverbs and adjectives push on a sentence. I don't just walk. I walk lethargically. I sleep energetically. But that was before she occupied the desolation spot of my passenger seat; before I became mental road kill in the only head I could understand—my own.

Once, months ago, she told me she would consider going out with me . . .

Yeah, okay. Find me a plumber that never gets shit on his hands and I'll find you a filthy liar. Every good intention cowers behind the back of an unfair reason. Everything follows order, it seems, except my fuse burns from the middle out. If I were an explosion, the smoke would clear before the fire started. Nothing makes sense. Welcome to my life.

I've never been a good kisser, but I made one heck of an attempt to find a nice set of lips to land upon. Her face was the runway, and I wanted to glide right in for the crash. I'd have settled for an explosion if she would've at least turned on the landing lights.

Always had an emergency for my lips.

I guess the white picket fence is still a long ways off for me. No dog named Rover. No cat at the foot of the bed. Not yet, anyway, but I am saving up cash for the animal shelter soon; maybe get me a forty year old, cancer-ridden parrot for starters. Gotta' find something alive, no matter how close to death it may be.

I see her as my home. Not the parrot! I'm talking about her. *The her.* I see her in my dreams as a beautiful home. My beautiful misery. She has more than two rooms—more than four—uncountable hallways leading to many unopened chambers. She's complicated, you know. I'd move into her and explore, but damn it, I don't have enough furniture to decorate every room. I'd be leaving her half empty, deplete of all what she deserves. No lamp in the corner, no table to keep a drink by the bed, and that is what scares me most. I could never measure up to the inevitable "Cliffs and Biffs" she surely goes out with. They have the fancy cars and the Big-Daddy doughnuts to keep her blind from the sunlight and day-to-day mendacities. Must be nice living a 24-karat diamond life, but all I have is cardboard attempts at love and reality. I don't own a vacuum cleaner to suck up the dirt that I'd track on her carpet. All I can do right now is dream. One day, maybe, I will be good company and I can at least come over for a visit.

She's a beautiful home. Built right there in the cul-de-sac of my heart. Though I know her address all too well: 501 Fuck Off Street.

But I can dream, can't I? I still want to take her stepping out across the dance floor of my big imagination. Because I love her. Because it feels like she has been with me a lifetime and I don't want to find another home. I want to sleep lethargically next to the true love that I've always known. Forever is a long time, but after a while you get used to it. I can live on in dreams, and move into her one way or the other. Except this time, I have something to live for. I have hope.

And in my last dream I kiss her soul, and somewhere along the way, with nerves astray, I've caused sparks to flash in her eyes—right where hope usually runs out.

This time it's different. No dead ends. She will kiss me back, and my heart will find a place beyond happiness and pain. I have finally found love. I finally found someone to keep me thinking. Someone warm to wrap my arms around, move into, and know as home.

COMING 2011

From Sleeping Moon Publications

THE CELESTIAL GREEN

A novel by K. Voi Veck